To win the game, they'll have to risk losing their hearts…

When a bizarre child custody stipulation pits popular sports blogger Gracie Gable against football superstar Jake Malone, losing the battle for her twin nieces isn't the only thing Gracie has to worry about. Forced to live for three months under the same roof as the sexy tight end, will she fall prey to his flirtatious pursuit? Or worse, will the skeletons in her closet destroy her chance for the love and family she so desperately wants?

Neglected by his parents as a boy, Jake doesn't believe in happily ever after. Yet living with Gracie and the twins might be enough to change his mind—and his womanizing ways. But when the press unearths a scandal from Gracie's past, will he lose the one woman he was ready to open his heart to?

Visit us at www.kensingtonbooks.com

I0665228

Books by Mackenzie Crowne

The Players Series
To Win Her Love

Published by Kensington Publishing Corporation

To Win Her Love

A Players Series Novel

Mackenzie Crowne

LYRICAL PRESS
Kensington Publishing Corp.
www.kensingtonbooks.com

First Electronic Edition: August 2015
eISBN-13: 978-1-61650-737-4
eISBN-10: 1-61650-737-3

First Print Edition: August 2015
ISBN-13: 978-1-61650-738-1
ISBN-10: 1-61650-738-1

Printed in the United States of America

For Tim

Smile of a rascal. Spirit of a lamb. Heart of a lion.

Miss you, brother.

Chapter 1

Like pure, walking sin, Jake Malone closed the distance in a deceptively lazy saunter. Gracie Gable fought the nearly overwhelming urge to take off running. Clenching her jaw, she lifted her chin. Without knowing her true identity, the various press publications flooding her blog's inbox with requests for interviews had been stymied in their attempts to track her down physically. How the hell had Jake?

And oh, God, why now?

A horrified groan rumbled deep in her chest. Having no idea what was in Pete's will, she couldn't afford to do anything to jeopardize her guardianship of the girls—like going toe-to-toe with the Manhattan Marauders' *Outlaw Tight End* right here on her brother-in-law's front lawn. She shot a worried glance down the historic farmhouse's long driveway, relieved to find it empty. With a little luck, Pete's attorney would be delayed long enough for her to deal with the famous all-pro's justified, but still overblown ego. She'd promise him anything—apologize profusely for insulting his integrity, offer him a bribe, whatever would get rid of him before Anthony Spinoza arrived.

Six foot five, with a fallen angel's face and the body of a god, Jake continued to approach. Gravel crunched beneath the heels of his boots, marking his long-legged swagger, as his thigh muscles flexed and stretched under faded blue jeans. A worn and battered leather bomber jacket rode his yard-wide shoulders. His trademark black Stetson and snakeskin boots completed the image of the Outlaw who held his own against opposing defensive lines and cast him in countless feminine fantasies. Hers included. She'd enjoyed more than her share of secret imaginings concerning the Marauders' number one tight end.

Though his nasty insults during their disastrous exchange on her blog the other day should've dealt a death blow to her foolish infatuation, the two-dimensional image she'd admired on her TV screen couldn't have prepared her for the flesh and bone temptation that was Jake Malone. Dismay crowded panic as every double X chromosome in her body quivered with giddy, XXX delight.

The X girls danced with anticipation, and the erratic thump of her heart increased with every fall of his size fifteen feet. *Down, girls. He may look like every woman's deepest sexual fantasy, but those boots are more likely to stomp us into the ground than end up under our bed.*

As angry as he must be to have taken the trouble to discover her true identity *and* find her, she could clearly imagine him grabbing her with those meat hooks he called hands and shaking her until her bones rattled. *Try it, buster. If you think the press is in a frenzy now, wait till I'm done with you.*

The silent threat boosted her flagging confidence. She angled her chin a bit more defiantly. At five ten, she was used to looking most men in the eye, but despite the added height from her three-inch heels, her gaze fell even with the sharp blade of his nose. Dark stubble shadowed the solid line of his jaw and upper lip, the same blue-black as the silky locks falling below the brim of his hat to brush his collar in the shaggy hairstyle popular among the ranks of pro football these days.

Disturbed at how badly her fingers itched to shove the hat from his head and stroke the glossy strands, she curled her hands into fists, and met his gaze. Blatant curiosity sparkled in eyes as verdant green as the needles of the pine trees lining the drive at his back. A slow smile curved his cleanly cut lips.

Huh? A sneer or even a dismissive smirk she could understand, but a smile? Where was his anger? She blinked when, instead of snatching her up, and shaking her like a dirty rag, he spoke in an easy, Texas drawl.

"You don't look like any Anthony I've ever met."

"Excuse me?"

"Anthony Spinoza. I'm supposed to meet him here."

Meet Anthony Spinoza? Why would Jake be meeting with Pete's lawyer, and why pretend ignorance of her identity? Why the pretense? Her temper simmered as logic provided a nasty explanation. Jake Malone had powerful connections and was famous for his ability to strategize. How many times had she applauded his knack for finding his opponents' weaknesses and using them to his advantage? Somehow, he must have found out, not only who she was, but her reason for being here today. She wouldn't put it past the seasoned predator to play her, acting as if he didn't know who she was, then pouncing when she relaxed her guard. *Like hell!*

She bared her teeth in a tight smile. "Do you have business with Mr. Spinoza?"

"Of a sort." He didn't expand on the cryptic comment, crossing his arms, and raising an inquisitive brow. "Are you his assistant?"

Oh, he was good. The question contained the perfect amount of curiosity to make it believable. "No, I'm not. I'm supposed to meet him as well."

"Oh, yeah?"

Speculation replaced curiosity in his dark green eyes. Starting at the top of her head and moving down with a slow thoroughness, his gaze traveled her body, pausing momentarily at her chest. Her nipples immediately pouted in response. She fought the urge to slap her palms over them and prayed her fitted winter coat provided the necessary camouflage. Biting her bottom lip, she attempted to calm the girls by picturing him a good foot shorter with scrawny arms and nerdy glasses perched on a bulbous nose.

The vision refused to form.

His steady inspection continued down over her slim skirt. Winged eyebrows lifted at her leather half boots, and his smile slid toward a smirk. He examined her calves beneath the sheer protection her panty hose provided before his gaze made the return trip to her face.

"I should have known."

She bristled at both the disdain in his eyes and his snide drawl. "What, exactly, should you have known?"

"Sorry, sweetheart. You're a looker, but you're a little young, even for an old hound dog like Pete Thompson."

Hound dog? The derogatory description made no sense when attached to the loving older man her sister, Sarah, had adored, but then the rest of his comment registered. The insinuation quieted the remnant whispers of feminine awareness. Indignation strangled thoughts of crushes, walking sin, *and* expediting his departure.

She matched his stance, crossing her arms. Over the years, Sarah had done her best to break Gracie of her quick temper. When her sister's efforts had failed, she'd predicted one day, the personality flaw would get Gracie into more trouble than she could handle. Today was shaping up as that day, but the possibility didn't stop her from reacting to the insult his speculation represented.

She pinned him with a narrow-eyed stare. "Pete Thompson happens to have been my sister's husband."

His dark brows shot up. "No shit?"

She cleared her throat. "No shit."

He startled as though having his words tossed back surprised him. After studying her in silence for a long moment, the legendary charm for which he was famous made an appearance. Matching dimples popped in his cheeks with his unrepentant smile. "My apologies."

Whether the apology was for his implied insult or her familial connection to Pete, she couldn't tell. Before she could ask, he stuck out a hand and doubled down on his ruse of having no clue of her identity.

"Why don't we start over? Hello, I'm Jake Malone."

She should call him out, of course, demand he tell her what he was up to, but she couldn't resist the opportunity for a little tit for tat. She unfolded her arms to place her hand in his. "Gracie Gable."

"Nice to meet you, Gracie."

Despite her supple leather gloves, the tingling warmth of his large, bare fingers reached hers. She tugged back her hand, relieved when he let go. Equilibrium shaky, she sucked in a stealthy breath, crossed her arms once more, and cocked her head to study him. She tapped a fingertip to her bottom lip in mock concentration.

"Jake Malone? Isn't there a semi-famous…um, *soccer player* or something with the same name?"

His wry grin said he clearly recognized her slight for what it was. "Famous football player, actually. I play for the Marauders."

She repaid his slow inspection with one of her own, sliding her gaze from his dark hat to the tips of his booted feet. At two hundred forty-seven hard-muscled pounds, there was a lot of territory to cover. All of it radiated the superbly conditioned perfection of a pro athlete. Her pulse picked up a notch as her gaze roamed over powerful thighs, past trim hips, and over a flat stomach to a broad chest and impossibly wide shoulders. By the time she reached the chiseled line of his jaw, she'd forgotten how to breathe. She needed every bit of concentration to offer him a smirk instead of licking her lips.

"I should have known."

As paybacks went, repeating his insult was lame, but it was the best she could manage. He surprised her by laughing a full-throated, head thrown back, rumble of male approval. His eyes twinkled with appreciation when he lowered his head and winked. Despite the disturbing fluttering in her belly, she didn't try to disguise her satisfied smile.

"Touché, Gracie Gable." Hip cocked in a seemingly relaxed pose, he glanced away to look up at the house for the first time. "So, the old man was married?"

"Pete?"

Rolling his shoulders, he tucked the fingers of both hands into the front pockets of his jeans and nodded. She frowned at the unmistakable tension in the tight line of his mouth. What was that about? Her future was at stake here, not his.

She followed his gaze. Steady and welcoming, the familiar weathered shingles and pitched roofs of Thompson Farm brought a pang of grief to her heart. As always, whenever she visited the Long Island home Sarah and Pete had shared, Gracie was reminded of the promise she'd given her sister before she died. A promise neither had expected to come due this soon.

"To my sister. She died three years ago." Even after three long years, the words left the foul bite of burnt ash on her tongue.

"I'm sorry." He turned, his eyes full of sober intensity.

The erratic whip of emotions, from panic at why he was here, to helpless feminine interest, and back to suspicion made her dizzy. Enough already. If he was going to cause a scene, she wanted their confrontation over and done with while they were still alone. "Why are you here?"

Thick lashes lowered at her bald demand, shuttering the green of his eyes. He shrugged. "Damned if I know."

Confused, she opened her mouth to demand a better answer when the distant crunch of gravel announced the arrival of two vehicles bumping down the drive. She stifled a self-disgusted groan. He'd managed to sidetrack her, and she was out of time.

Outmaneuvered by a pro...with killer dimples.

A dark sedan stopped behind Jake's SUV. A sleek yellow sports car rolled to a halt several yards away. The door swung open and a petite, redheaded woman rose from the small high-performance machine. The bold, red-woolen power suit covering her curvy frame should've clashed with her mane of rusty curls, but somehow didn't. Bright and vibrant, her steady blue gaze roamed the face of the house and surrounding property before landing on Jake. She lifted a slim hand in a flirty, fingertip wave and beamed a smile.

Gracie disliked her on sight.

A thin, older man emerged from the second vehicle. Only the pale oval of his face beneath a classic fedora relieved the steady black of his heavy overcoat, conservative business suit, and wingtips. He clutched a briefcase in one gloved hand. Crossing to the woman, he greeted her in a short exchange. They turned together and headed up the walkway.

"Lawyers." Jake grumbled at Gracie's side. "They usually have a slick, plastic look. Figures this one resembles an angel of doom."

Her head whipped around at his odd comment, but his gaze was locked on the approaching couple.

She turned and eyed the woman. "The redhead doesn't resemble any lawyer *I've* ever seen."

He chuckled and cast her a slight smile. "I'm sure she'll be happy to hear that. Her name is Victoria Price, and she isn't a lawyer. V is my publicist."

His publicist? Am I about to be double-teamed?

She braced for disaster as Anthony Spinoza and the vivacious "V" arrived.

"Mr. Malone." The black-clad lawyer greeted Jake then smiled at Gracie. "Miss Gable, I'm Anthony Spinoza. Thank you for coming."

Gracie nodded and shook his offered hand.

"I see you've met Mr. Malone. Miss Price is acting as his representative this morning."

Okay, what the hell is going on?

Obviously Jake was here for some reason other than to have it out with her over their blog spat, but what the reason was, she couldn't imagine.

"Call me V, please. Everyone does. Nice to meet you, Miss Gable."

Gracie shook the publicist's hand, noting the Texas accent similar to Jake's. "Likewise."

"It appears we're all here." Anthony lifted a hand toward the front door. "Shall we proceed?"

Gracie's gaze flew from face to face, desperate to discover why Jake Malone and his publicist would be sitting in on the reading of Pete's will. No plausible explanation presented itself.

Well, crap. I've slipped down a rabbit hole.

Chapter 2

Relief washed through Gracie when Mary Clark opened the farmhouse door. Mary's familiar gray curls, soft Irish brogue, and sympathetic, moss green eyes were a lifeline in the midst of lunacy. Tall and thin, almost to the point of frail, Pete's long-time housekeeper and cook greeted her with an enveloping hug and an encouraging smile. Anthony introduced Jake and V, then Mary led them into the formal living room. The lawyer shed his hat and heavy coat to take a seat on the long couch. Setting his briefcase on the coffee table, he pulled a thick file from inside and began shuffling papers.

Mary held out a hand toward the love seat and two wingback chairs facing the couch. V slid onto the love seat, as Mary made herself comfortable in one of the chairs. Jake refused a seat, choosing to stand behind the love seat at V's back. He shoved both hands into the front pockets of his jeans, only to yank them out again. One wide palm scraped over his jaw before he dropped his arms to his sides.

Why, he's as nervous as me. The rabbit hole deepened beneath Gracie's feet.

"Would you like to sit?" Anthony peered at Gracie from behind wire-rimmed glasses.

On shaking knees, she dipped to perch on the edge of a chair.

For the next ten minutes, she fidgeted impatiently, ready to come out of her skin. Pete's lawyer listed and explained what she considered generous but unimportant details. Several paintings in Pete's impressive collection would be donated to a local museum, a stretch of marshland adjoining the estate would be turned over to the wetland society, and several acres and the small guest cottage at the back of the property were deeded to Mary. Along with the cottage came a generous pension and the request she remain on as the farm's housekeeper, contingent upon a satisfactory guardianship agreement, of course.

At the mention of the guardianship, Gracie's heart pounded in a thundering gallop. She twisted her hands in her lap. To her right, V whipped her head around to stare up at a silent Jake. Gracie paid them little heed. She leaned forward in her chair, willing Anthony to say the words that would fulfill the promise she'd given Sarah and make the twins hers.

"I would like to say Mr. Thompson's remaining wishes are a cut and dry disbursement of his assets." Anthony picked up a new sheaf of papers. "Unfortunately, that is not the case. Because of their young age, the guardianship arrangement for his minor children was Mr. Thompson's main concern."

"Minor children?" V's breathless demand drew Gracie's attention. Turned, as V was, to stare up at her famous client, Gracie couldn't read the expression in the publicist's eyes.

Jake, on the other hand, had gone stiff, his jaw clenched as if chiseled from stone. Beneath the tight skin of his thickly muscled neck, a bulging vein stood out in stark relief. When he swallowed, the slow drag of his Adam's apple contracting appeared painful.

"As their closest relative, *you* are the logical choice as guardian."

Gracie forgot about Jake's odd tension. She jerked her head back around and was dismayed to find Anthony hadn't addressed *her*. His dark-eyed gaze held fast to Jake's. The room began to tilt. Her breath came out in a whoosh with the lawyer's next words.

"However, your father wasn't at all confident you would be interested in taking on the task of seeing to your young sisters' welfare."

"My sisters?" Jake choked.

"His father?" Gracie leapt to her feet, her manic heartbeat echoing in her ears.

Anthony slipped the glasses from his nose. His dark brows crashed together in a frown, and his confused gaze bounced between her and Jake. "I'm sorry, I assumed everyone knew the players."

She spun on Jake. "Pete Thompson was your *father?*"

Deep grooves bracketed his thinned lips. He jerked one shoulder in a taut shrug. "Technically, though sperm donor is a more appropriate title."

The breath clogged in her lungs. Jake Malone was Pete's son? Her bid for guardianship of the twins included tangling with a professional football star? Holy shit. This couldn't be happening. A chill washed over her, making her shudder. So much for fearing Jake was here to pick a fight in front of Pete's lawyer. That scenario was infinitely preferable to reality.

She slapped a hand to her forehead. "I don't believe this."

Jake snorted. "How do you think I feel? I just found out I have…?" He turned to Anthony.

The lawyer's lips tightened in a cautious frown. "Angela and Charlotte are your six-year-old, twin half sisters."

"Jesus." Jake's eyes slid shut, and he pinched the bridge of his nose.

V spun on the love seat and slipped her fingers into his free hand. He opened his eyes. The pained smile on the publicist's full lips matched the sympathy in her eyes. Gracie's brows rose at the poignant glance and gesture, evidence their relationship went beyond that of publicist and client.

Focus, Gracie. Maybe things aren't as bad as they seem. What did Anthony say? Pete didn't expect Jake to want the twins?

"If Pete wasn't sure his," she flicked a stabbing glance at Jake before turning back to Anthony, "*son* would want the responsibility of caring for the girls, he'd have made other arrangements. Before she died, my sister expressed her desire I raise the girls in the event something happened to Pete. I assure you, I *do* want the responsibility."

Anthony held up a hand. "We're getting ahead of ourselves. Your brother-in-law knew of your sister's wishes and took them into account, partially."

"What does that mean?"

"The custody arrangements laid out in Pete's will are a bit unconventional but, under the circumstances, he felt unconventional would be in the best interest of the twins."

"What, exactly, are these custody arrangements?" Jake's low growl was barely audible. "Don't keep us in suspense, Spinoza."

"Then let me explain." Anthony cleared his throat. "According to Pete's wishes, guardianship of the twins will be decided ninety days from tomorrow. Until that time, the two of you are to share custody of the girls. Here. On the farm."

The blood froze in Gracie's veins, even as her heart sank. The potentially catastrophic consequences of being thrown together with a league superstar were nothing compared to the possibility of losing the girls. They loved her as much as she loved them, but… Had Sarah known the twins had a big brother, and a famous one at that? Did *they* know about him?

Stupid question. Even if they didn't, they would soon. For six year olds, the idea of a big brother, especially one like Jake Malone, would be huge. Fear clawed at her with razor-sharp talons. How could she compete with that, and what was up with the three-month time period? What happened at the end of the ninety days?

A guttural growl made Jake's opinion of the bizarre stipulation clear.

V squeezed the hand she still held. "Hear him out before you fly off the handle, Jake."

He scowled at her and pulled his hand free but kept his mouth shut.

Anthony sifted through the sheaf of papers. "You'll have three months to get to know the girls and their routines. Mrs. Clark will assist you."

Mary bobbed her head in a silent nod.

"You'll be expected to live here and, excepting incidences where the girls are in your presence elsewhere, be back in residence no later than eight p.m. each night or forfeit your claim. If one of you decides the arrangement is not to your liking, you need only walk away. The other will automatically gain sole custody, along with the remainder of the estate and all its holdings, with the exception of the twins' trusts, of course."

A sneer twisted Jake's lips. "Why bother with the ridiculous ruse? Dear old dad had to know his rules would take me out of the running before the race even began. Football season is in full swing. I travel to eight different cities over the next twelve weeks."

"Your professional schedules have been taken into account, of course." Anthony offered Jake a strained smile. "On those occasions you travel with the Marauders, your presence at the farm will be excused."

"Well, damn. That's a relief." Sarcasm dripped from Jake's drawled reply. He rolled his eyes at V as if to say *do you believe this?*

"The same professional courtesy will be extended to you, Miss Gable, though I assume much of your business can be done from here at the farm."

"Thank you." She hoped to cut off any expansion of what her business included. This situation was alarming enough without having to introduce herself as Gridiron Girl. She held her breath but didn't hold out a lot of hope. Evil gremlins were running this show, and they didn't seem to have an ounce of sympathy.

"Still, if the facilitation of your web design service or Gridiron Girl website requires an absence, you need only let me know."

She squeezed her eyes shut on a wince as Anthony aided the gremlins in their mischief.

The silence was deafening. Heart pounding, she peeked through scrunched eyelids, sneaking a sidelong glance at Jake from beneath her lashes. Twin emerald laser beams locked her in place. V stared at her in bug-eyed disbelief.

Jake's low voice purred with deceptive calm. "Gridiron Girl website?" For a moment, she considered playing dumb or maybe breaking into a verse of "It's a Small World." Screwed, no matter how she answered, she fought back a hysterical giggle and settled on brazen sarcasm. Straightening her shoulders, she lifted her chin and met his angry gaze. "Funny, when you pulled up out front, I figured you'd come to apologize for being an arrogant ass the other day."

A muscle twitched along the sharp line of his jaw. "*You're* the Gridiron Girl?"

She pumped up one shoulder in a negligent shrug. "What can I say? We homely cowards need to make a living somehow."

A satisfying glint of guilt flared in his eyes. Or maybe it was wishful thinking on her part. The flash of emotion was gone before she could properly categorize it, replaced by glaring heat.

He propped his hands on his hips and shook his head. "Oh, this keeps getting better and better."

She bared her teeth in an ice-cold smile. "You can say that again."

"Well, this is awkward." The smile pulling at V's perfectly painted lips appeared forced. "I suggest we deal with one issue at a time, beginning with the custody situation."

Gracie couldn't agree more. Heart in her throat, she addressed Anthony. "All I have to do is move in for three months and at the end I'll gain full custody?"

"Claiming victory already?" Jake's narrowed gaze locked on hers, one dark brow lifted in challenge.

"Are you saying you *want* to take on the responsibility of six-year-old twins?"

"Fuck no." Blind panic rounded his eyes. "What the hell would I know about raising little girls?"

The band of tension squeezing her chest snapped loose. She curled her toes against the rush of relief threatening to buckle her knees. "Well, then." She swung out a hand. "There you go. You may not want them, but I do."

His brows beetled in a scowl. The uncertainty in his eyes said he wasn't sure if he should argue her point or give in gracefully.

V cleared her throat. "My client needs a bit of time to consider the situation. When does he have to give you his answer?"

"I don't need—"

"Jake!" V's sharp command cut him off.

He spun around and paced to the window. Shoulders bunched, he thumped the brim of his Stetson against his thigh and stared out at the winter afternoon.

Anthony offered V a weak smile. "Mrs. Clark made arrangements for the twins to spend tonight with a friend from school. They will return home after the funeral tomorrow morning." His gaze encompassed both Gracie and Jake. "You are required to be in residence by eight tomorrow evening and, with the exception of pre-approved professional absences, every night thereafter for ninety days."

Jake spun around to snarl at his publicist. "Not a chance, V. I refused to jump through hoops for the asshole when he was alive. I won't follow his demands now he's dead, especially for a couple of rugrats I've never met."

Gracie winced at the loathing in his voice for Pete and opened her mouth to protest the insult to her nieces.

V beat her to it. "Shut up, Jake." She turned to Anthony with a forced smile. "Other than the curfew requirement, are there any other conditions?"

"Ah, no." He speared long fingers through his thinning hair. "However, I should explain one small caveat to the arrangement."

Another disdainful snort sounded from the back of the room. V shot a stern-eyed warning over one shoulder.

Anthony's dark eyes softened as they settled on Gracie. "I realize you are ready to take immediate custody of the girls, Miss Gable, and, in my opinion, a speedy decision on guardianship would be best. However, while your brother-in-law foresaw Mr. Malone's reluctance to accept the requirements of the will, he insisted his son be given the opportunity to get to know his half sisters."

Gracie nodded. From Jake's reaction, there didn't seem much chance of him complying. Just in case, she needed a few things clarified. "I understand, but what if we both manage to meet the requirements? What happens then?"

"That's where the caveat comes in. If, at the end of the allotted time, you are both still here, the girls will choose between the two of you. Ultimately, they have the final say on which of you will be their guardian."

Gracie was too shaken to react. Jake wasn't. He spun from the window and closed the distance to glare down at V. Gracie could only watch wide-eyed as he seemed to expand, growing even larger than normal in his hot-eyed fury.

"Are you satisfied?" His voice rose with each word. "What kind of asshole leaves this kind of decision to a couple of six year olds?" He pinned Anthony with a heated sneer. "And what's with you? Aren't attorneys supposed to *advise* their clients, steering them away from asinine stipulations?"

"Jake!"

Anthony held up a hand, quieting V. Gracie couldn't help applauding his composure, if only in her head, even if his serene appearance appeared forced.

Though his face paled, he met Jake's glare and spoke in a steady voice. "I did exactly that, Mr. Malone, but in truth, I was nothing more than an employee of your father." He paused briefly, as if considering his words. "I would never share a confidence of a client but, as the man is dead, and the situation complicated, I can tell you, Pete Thompson felt this arrangement allowed him to make amends for past wrongs. Specifically, the way he treated your mother and you. In his opinion, offering you the opportunity to gain his estate, while seeing to the welfare of his daughters, was the perfect solution."

Scoffing disbelief flared in Jake's darkening glare, proving him unwilling to attribute any altruistic characteristics to the man who sired him.

V rose from her chair. Anthony followed suit.

"We appreciate your candor." She shook his hand. "We'll be in touch."

He nodded and handed her his card. "By all means, contact me at my office."

Like a grumpy child, Jake stomped from the room without further word. With an apologetic smile, V hurried after him.

Anthony collapsed back onto the couch. A green tinge colored his face, pale against the austere black of his suit. He began shoving papers into his briefcase with shaking hands.

Gracie could empathize.

She jumped when Mary laid a gentle hand on her shoulder.

"Take heart, child. All will work out. You'll see."

She swallowed. Hard.

Chapter 3

"I need a scotch, Henry. Make it a double."

The waiter nodded and turned for the bar. Jake jammed his coat on the hook beside his usual booth at the back of The Tap Room. Considering his mood, he should've cancelled his weekly lunch with Tom, but thanks to this morning's multiple hits, he was running on autopilot. He'd found himself in the pub's private Manhattan parking garage without any recall of having gotten there.

Sliding into the booth, he checked his watch. Too late now. Tom would be here any minute and, knowing V, she'd already filled him in on this latest disaster. Not that Jake could blame her. Even before this morning's unbelievable revelations, the shit had hit the proverbial fan, and he had no one to blame but himself. He'd screwed up royally with his asinine behavior on the Gridiron Girl's blog.

Fuck. Gracie Gable's blog. What were the odds, and what was the world coming to when an obscure, online exchange could threaten to derail an all-pro, record-breaking season?

He shot an impatient glare at Henry behind the bar.

How could he have made such a rookie mistake? What the hell was he thinking, letting Tuck goad him into logging on to see what his teammates were snickering about? This was his tenth season, for Christ's sake. He knew better than to involve himself in the ramblings of rabid fans. Especially female ones. Unlike men, who offered verbal shoulder thumps of camaraderie for a win or voiced their displeasure at a loss by questioning a player's athletic skills, women dragged personal attributes into the conversation, going straight for the jugular—when they weren't zeroed in on an even more vulnerable body part.

Women, V always claimed, were much cruder than men when discussing the opposite sex. The commentary on the surprisingly popular blog verified her claim's validity, in his opinion, and, like a voyeur with a key to the women's locker room, he'd read every word. He snorted, recalling some of the more outrageous observations.

To her credit, while clearly entertained by the suggestive discourse of her followers, or minions, as she called them, Gracie Gable refrained from adding to the down and dirty dialogue. Before things got too raunchy, she steered the various conversations back to the subject at hand—football.

He had to admit she knew her topic. Interspersed amongst the speculation of various players' stamina and body parts, her posts contained insightful debates on statistical possibilities, bemoaning the confusion caused by the rash of new rules imposed by the league, and predictions for the following week's match-ups. Impressed by the Gridiron Girl's comprehension of the game, everything was fine until he stumbled upon the post labeled *Now, That's A "Tight End."*

Unease had tickled his spine as Tuck's laughter echoed in his mind. He'd sat forward at his desk and clicked the mouse, hoping to find an exposé on one of his many peers across the league who held the same position as he. The hope died a quick death. Unease became disquiet when his image filled the screen. The full color photo showed him stretched out in midair, capturing the moment before his fingers gripped the ball in what *should* have been his most recent touchdown catch—if not for the ref's bullshit call of offensive pass interference.

He'd ground his teeth at the reminder. He might have a reputation as a man who lived to flaunt the rules in his personal life. In fact, he cultivated the rebel status, but when it came to the game he loved, he didn't screw around. He took pride in being a clean competitor. The whispers of "dirty play," since the controversial call had left him steaming in a slow burn. The furor over whether or not he should've been slapped with an unnecessary roughness penalty as well pissed him off until he wanted to howl out his rage. The slow burn flared to a raging inferno as he read the Gridiron Girl's take on the play:

Jake Malone's exploits on the field are normally a thing of beauty, but I'm afraid the pressure to break the touchdown record may have gotten to the Outlaw Tight End. Though I want to accept his claim the contact in this week's disastrous collision with Brian Tuttle was incidental, the replay clearly shows Jake dropping his shoulder a moment before impact.

"Son of a *bitch*."

No one felt worse than he about the concussion Brian suffered from the hit, but football was a full contact sport, damn it. Brian understood that and had accepted Jake's condolences with a philosophical shrug when they spoke after the game.

Despite her obvious knowledge of the sport, like his other self-appointed critics, the Gridiron Girl had never come up against a two-hundred-sixty-pound defender, jockeying for position while moving at top speed. Dropped his shoulder a moment before impact? Shit. Attempting to avoid a helmet-to-helmet collision was more like it. The woman didn't have a clue what she was talking about.

The cacophony of critical voices questioning his integrity from the safety of their various publications had reached critical mass. In his mind, a picture formed of a mousy woman with buckteeth and a flat chest, exacting revenge against a male population that continuously overlooked her. Her keyboard offered an opportunity for retribution and, through her anonymous blog, she repaid the slight to her pitiful existence by slashing at her male victims' pride.

Not this time, sweetheart.

His fingers flew across the keys.

That hit had nothing to do with breaking the record. Pro players understand this league isn't for pussies. Brutal hits are part of the game.

His comment should've been one more cyber blip, lost in the billions of others popping up throughout cyberspace on a daily basis but, as his luck was running lately, she responded immediately.

Dirty hits may be part of the game, but they're beneath a player with the athletic abilities of Jake Malone.

The compliment did nothing to ease the haze of his anger.

Putting up with the asinine opinions of armchair quarterbacks is also part of the game. The hit wasn't dirty. It was incidental.

She saw things differently.

I call 'em as I see 'em. Anyone who follows the game knows Jake is a master of contortion. His ability to twist his body for optimum benefit is a big part of the reason he's in the running for the touchdown record in the first place. It's impossible he didn't know exactly what he was doing when he dropped his shoulder last Sunday and I, for one, consider it a shame he resorted to such a dirty tactic.

Fury boiled in his blood.

A woman who does her insulting from the anonymous safety of cyberspace is either a coward or so homely she'd choke a dog. I'll wager it's the latter in your case, lady, and, as such, you wouldn't know incidental contact if it bit you on the ass.

He hit enter. His fingers hovered over the keyboard, and he winced at the harshness of his reply. Despite the red haze of his fury, it wasn't like him to be cruel, and never to a woman. He loved the female of the species, enjoyed everything about them. Their softness, the way they smelled and tasted, even the contrary way their minds worked delighted him. He'd been blessed with the ability to charm even the most contrary among them, but he'd never had a woman attack his professional ethics before.

He flattened his lips in a guilty grimace, until her smartass comeback replaced his guilt with disbelief.

Attacking a person's looks when you don't have an argument based on facts is a juvenile tactic. Does your mommy know you're using her computer?

He ignored her insult to his maturity, his fingers flying across the keyboard.

My argument is *based on fact. You've never played the game or you'd understand the physics involved in avoiding contact when tangling for position. The hit was clean and incidental.*

She kept right on taunting.

You're right. I've never played the game, but anyone—who doesn't need glasses—can see Jake twisting his upper body as Tuttle closes in. Maybe you should have your eyes checked.

The woman was a piece of work. A goddamned piece of work.

My eyes are fine, and I was twisting my upper body to avoid helmet-to-helmet contact!

He hit send then cursed and held his breath. Would she notice the first person reference?

She rushed him in a full-out blitz.

You're upper body? *Well, well. Ladies, it appears we have none other than the Outlaw Tight End himself visiting our little football clutch. Nice of you to stop by, Jake.*

"Shit." He scrubbed his hand over his face as Henry approached the booth.

The waiter delivered Jake's drink and handed him a menu. "Will Mr. Walden be joining you today?"

"I'm expecting him."

Henry nodded, slipped a second menu onto the other side of the table, and left Jake alone.

Picking up the glass, he downed a healthy swallow.

Having gotten an eyeful of Gracie Gable, he knew how far off the mark his assumption about her looks had been, but there was no mistaking the voracity of her blog followers. He'd watched in horrified wonder as the exchange lit a firestorm of feminine outrage. The minions, previously content to let their unspoken leader clash with an unruly visitor, went wild.

Dozens came out of the woodwork to flay him alive. Forty-eight hours later, the exchange had gone viral, generating enough traffic the popular web page now resided in the cyber world's version of the stratosphere.

And the firestorm continued to spread…with costly consequences.

Still, as frustrating as he found being fined by the league and called on the carpet by the Marauders' front office, having two little girls dropped in his lap made his professional troubles look like a day in the park. Jesus, six-year-old twins. What the hell was he supposed to do with them?

"Get to know them," V had insisted as she paced the gravel driveway of Thompson Farm after the reading of the will. "They're your half sisters. Aren't you the least bit curious about them?"

"No."

His stubbornness only pissed her off further. She'd gone from suggesting, to cajoling, to demanding in three minutes flat before slamming into her shiny sports car with a growled warning. "Be at the farm by eight tomorrow night, or else."

He swallowed the remainder of his glass. Though he knew V's soft heart was concerned over the idea of two little girls left alone in a world that could be cruel, her motives weren't purely altruistic. As always, his career came first and, from what V had said, Carolyn Wainwright, the Marauders' new owner, wasn't the only one grumbling. Thanks to the furor over his blog performance several of his endorsement contracts were in jeopardy as well.

In full damage-control mode, V considered Pete's custody fiasco an unexpected gift. Those girls need a stable home, she'd argued, and who wouldn't be charmed by reports of the Outlaw Tight End trading in his Manhattan babe lair for a historic farmhouse and dates with supermodels for carpooling and teacher conferences?

"Carpooling, for Christ's sake," he growled low in his throat.

"Talking to yourself, Jake? That's not a good sign."

Chapter 4

Jake frowned at Tom Walden. A deep chuckle accompanied the humor dancing in his friend and mentor's clear blue eyes as he shrugged out of his coat. Despite nine years of retirement, he maintained the athletic form that had helped make him one of the top quarterbacks of the previous decade. Big and blond, he could pass for much younger than fifty. Only the light sprinkling of gray at his temples marked the passage of time since he'd thrown his last official touchdown pass. As the league's players' liaison, he rode a comfortable desk these days, but he'd look right at home trotting from the tunnel of any of the league's stadiums.

He tossed his coat over the back of the booth and sat. Eyeing the drink in Jake's hand, he leaned his elbows on the table. "Are you planning to fight the fine?"

"I should. It's bullshit."

"Maybe."

Jake scowled. "What do you mean, maybe? That blog shit happened on my personal time and has nothing to do with the league. Costa passed down the fine because he still has a hard-on for me over Bridgette."

Dating the general manager's nearly jailbait niece in his first pro season had been a mistake, but how was he to know Doug Costa would go on to become the league commissioner, or he'd still be gunning for Jake a decade later?

"What's his fucking problem? It's been ten years."

Tom shrugged one shoulder. "Some guys have long memories when it comes to a guy screwing with a family member. Especially a young, *female* one."

"Screwing her isn't the same as screwing *with* her. She came on to me, remember? You were there. Tell me she didn't look twenty-five. I didn't have a clue she was only eighteen, and if I'd known she was Stick-up-his-ass Costa's niece, I never would've touched her."

Tom sprawled back. "I'll go to bat for you if that's what you decide."

"But?"

"But, do you want my advice?"

"Do I have a choice?

Tom grinned at his disgruntled tone. "Pay the fine. V's right. With everything else you've got going on right now, you don't need the hassle of a legal battle with the league."

Jake lifted his glass, remembered it was empty, and shot a scowl at Henry behind the bar. "Since you've obviously spoken to V, I won't waste my time filling you in on the details of the old man's will."

"If she wasn't pulling my leg. What she told me sounded farfetched."

Jake held up his glass, grunting when Henry nodded from the bar. "Even with her imagination, I doubt V could come up with twin half sisters and a three month lockdown in the middle of the sticks to determine custody."

"Damn. She was telling the truth?"

"Unfortunately."

Henry approached the table, delivering a second scotch to Jake. "What can I get you, Mr. Walden?"

Tom arched a brow at Jake's glass. "Why don't you bring me one of those?"

"Yes, sir."

Tom waited until the waiter walked away. "Congratulations, big brother. When are you moving to the farm?"

"Who says I am? What business does a rabid dog like Pete Thompson have fathering kids at sixty anyway? Fathering kids at all?"

Jake shredded the corner of the cocktail napkin beneath his glass. Money and prestige were all the fucker cared about. Raised sipping from the Thompson sterling silver spoon, Pete spent his life rubbing elbows with politicians and business magnates, looking down his nose at anyone not holding a million dollar portfolio. Unless, of course, that someone wore a skirt.

The heir to the Thompson Empire divided his time between chasing after million dollar business deals and sniffing for his next lay. In both circumstances, once the transaction was completed, he moved on, unconcerned over any lingering consequences. Family connections protected men like Pete from both financial failures and pregnant waitresses from the wrong side of the tracks. He certainly hadn't been concerned about Elaine Malone *or* her illegitimate son...not until her son's name was tossed around in connection with the pro draft.

He sighed. "I don't owe Pete Thompson a damn thing."

Henry delivered Tom's drink then hesitated, glancing at the untouched menus. He beat a hasty retreat when Jake snatched up his fresh drink and tossed back a healthy swallow.

Tom picked up his glass. "No, you don't, but the press is going to eat this up. Face it, buddy, your free pass has expired." He grinned as he toasted Jake across the table before sipping.

"I'm glad you find this amusing."

Tom rolled his shoulders in a lazy shrug. "Just facing reality. You've had a good run, thumbing your nose at society's rules. The press let you get away with your no-holds-barred lifestyle because of your photogenic looks and ability to charm."

Jake bared his teeth in a sneering smile. "They let me get away with my lifestyle because of my talent on the field."

Tom grinned. "That, too, but if you think they hounded you over the blogosphere mess, wait until they find out about six-year-old orphaned sisters. And they *will* find out. If you don't show up at the farm, they'll crucify you."

"You think I don't know that?"

"I think your feelings for Pete are clouding your judgment, but there are two innocent little girls who need you to do the right thing."

"What's the right thing? Show up at the farm or not, either way I'm screwed. I know what it's like to be abandoned by your blood. I can't walk away now that I know about them. I'd never be able to look myself in the eye again, but taking custody?" He shook his head in vehement denial. "No fucking way. I don't know shit about kids."

"My sons would disagree."

He snorted dismissively. "They're teenage boys, not six-year-old girls."

"They weren't born teenagers, and it's not like you'll be dealing with diapers and two a.m. feedings."

Horror bloomed in Jake's gut. He gulped at the contents of his glass.

Tom chuckled. "You're not getting any younger, buddy. It's time to grow up."

He curled his lip in a jeer. "Gee, Dad. All I want is to borrow the car."

As they had countless times since they met during Jake's rookie season, and Tom's last, Tom's lips tilted in a knowing smile. Claiming Jake had more talent than sense, the all-pro quarterback had appointed himself Jake's guide through the rough and tumble world of pro sports. With few exceptions, his council had proven right on the money. Unfortunately, his advice often leaked over to the personal side of things. For the most part, he'd met with failure there, and yet that hadn't stopped the happily married man from trying.

The perfect husband and father, Tom believed family grounded a man, especially one who lived in the supercharged world of a pro athlete. For years, he'd been encouraging Jake to find a good woman and settle down. No doubt he'd see this situation with the twins as a step in the right direction, but damn it, this mess held no resemblance to Tom and Sharon Walden's storybook existence. Having six-year-old strangers dropped into his lap wasn't the same as deciding to raise babies with the perfect woman. Besides, the wild child son of a bastard father and a drunken mother could never fit in the perfect family mold.

Tom sighed. "You're in the middle of a career-making season, but you're thirty-three. Football won't last forever."

"I still have a few more years."

"Maybe, if you remain healthy. Then what?"

"Then whatever I want. I've made enough money to live comfortably for several lifetimes and I've invested well."

"Alone?" Tom sat forward. "Or will you still be chasing after the playboy bachelor life like your father, running from woman to woman when other men your age are collecting social security?"

"Apparently, my *father* cast off the lifestyle and got himself a family." *Married.*

Jake swallowed the remainder of the scotch. After a lifetime spent casting aside acceptable-for-screwing-but-not-for-marriage swimsuit models and waitresses, had the confirmed bachelor had a change of heart regarding the institution? He snorted. More likely, the fucker had sniffed around the wrong *type* of woman and gotten caught.

He knew nothing about Pete's deceased wife, but one look at her sister told the story. Thanks to V, Jake knew more about women's designer fashions than any man should. The price tag for Gracie Gable's chic boots would've covered half a year's rent on the forty-year-old trailer he called home as a kid.

He'd bet his right nut the Gable girls came from money. Pete wouldn't have shared his name with a woman who didn't. An unwanted pregnancy with a woman from a background he couldn't simply blow off must have stuck in the old man's craw. Which might explain Jake's inclusion in Pete's convoluted custody ruse. What better way to pay back a scheming debutant for trapping him into marriage than to deny her family what Pete would consider the ultimate prize?

The fortune he'd left behind with the twins.

Jake didn't buy for a minute his inclusion in the will had anything to do with regrets. If so, a simple, *these are your half sisters, they're all yours* would've sufficed. *Make up for past sins, my ass.*

He couldn't prevent the bitterness seeping into his tone. "A family he's left *me* to raise."

Tom swilled his drink, his gaze contemplative. "The only good thing he's ever done for you, as far as I can see."

"How do you figure? I'm not cut out to be a father."

"I think you're wrong there, but what about this aunt V mentioned? Gracie is it? From what V tells me, she's willing to take custody, leaving you to play the role of big brother. Sounds like a workable solution."

"That's because you haven't met her."

"What's wrong with her?"

"First, there's *who* she is. Did V mention she runs a blog? A popular *football* blog for women?"

Tom's blond brows shot to his hairline. "She's the Gridiron Girl?"

"Right the first time."

His friend choked on a laugh. "Well, damn."

"You think that's funny?"

"Hilarious. Holy shit, when the press gets hold of this…" Tom sobered, but humor still twinkled in his eyes. "I can see how *who* she is might be something of a problem, but you said first. What else is wrong with her?"

Jake's lips pulled tight on a frown and he shifted uncomfortably. "There's nothing wrong with her, precisely, it's just that…shit. The woman could be the poster child for trust fund bimbos."

He winced at his derogatory description as a vision of the sexy blonde formed in his head. In truth, while the trust fund part was dead on, bimbo might be a stretch. She certainly hadn't dressed the part of the typical bimbo, but her sophisticated wardrobe disguised neither the sultry interest in her gem bright eyes during her payback once-over, nor her hoochie-baby body above miles of killer legs.

Nearing five ten, by his estimate, her legs made up most of her above average height. His mind conjured up several raunchy scenarios involving those legs, and he ran his tongue around his teeth and sucked. Her stunning face and shoulder-length, honey blond curls were more than a match for her luscious curves and just as alluring. Below exotic, violet blue eyes that cut straight to a man's libido, her flawless skin, marred only by a small, sexy mole at the corner of her wide mouth, covered world class cheekbones that screamed patrician lineage.

Hell, she even smelled expensive.

The memory of her subtle perfume, tickling his senses like a beckoning finger tipped in glossy red, sent a rush of blood to pool in his lap. He shifted, uncomfortable, and cursed the stray dog gene he'd inherited from Pete. Christ, his life had taken a sharp right turn toward fucked-up-ville and here he was fantasizing about Pete Thompson's sister-in-law.

He cleared his throat and banished the image from his mind. "She claims to want custody, but how well is a trust fund party girl going to handle sudden motherhood?"

Tom cast a glance at the empty glass in front of Jake. "As well as you're handling discovering you're not an only child?"

"Fuck you."

White teeth flashed when Tom laughed.

Jake shook his head. "My point is, the value of Pete's estate is a heady incentive to meet his demands, but I imagine she'll be singing a different tune when faced with the reality of day-to-day parenting. Women like her are used to a steady stream of admirers. Three months trapped on a rural farm in the middle of nowhere isn't exactly a fertile dating field."

The idea made him frown. Three months. Ninety days in the sticks would be hell on a person's sex life. He shifted his shoulders against the sudden itch crawling up his spine. Yet another reason to stay the hell away from that farm.

"Are you worried about her or yourself?"

He scowled at the direct hit. "Both." He shoved a hand through his hair. "Hell, even if she isn't the ideal guardian, at least the twins know her. But what if she bolts before the deadline? Then I *am* screwed."

"What if she doesn't? Don't underestimate the maternal instinct. It's a powerful thing. Ask Sharon. This woman, this Gracie, may surprise you. For that matter, you may surprise yourself."

"What the hell is that supposed to mean?"

"Kids have a way of growing on you."

Jake's scornful laugh of dismissal brought the return of Tom's annoying, knowing smile.

"Go to the farm, Jake. Give the press a nice human-interest story, and they'll forgive you almost anything. As for the twins and Gracie Gable…" He shrugged. "You have ninety days to figure things out."

* * * *

Jake sprawled on the soft leather couch, his bare feet propped beside his laptop on the granite coffee table. Elbows winged out with his hands cradling his head, he stared at the view of Central Park beyond the glass wall of his Upper West Side condo. Fashioning an apology to the Gridiron

Girl that didn't come off as groveling hadn't been pleasant, but at least it had kept his mind off the cluster fuck his life had become.

He winced and crossed his feet at the ankles.

Tom was right…not that Jake would admit it out loud. He wasn't getting any younger, but he'd rather not contemplate retirement until he had to, and he refused to do so in the middle of a record-breaking season. Despite his off the field reputation, he gave everything he had to the game. His resulting stats from ten years in the league were nothing to laugh at, but he was the first to admit, he'd gotten lucky when the Marauders picked up his contract. Two years later, they'd fielded what many considered the best offensive line in decades. Thanks to the talent surrounding him, the touchdown record was within his grasp and he was on track for the hall of fame. No way was he going to blow it.

Unfortunately, with the season at the halfway mark, anything could happen. In the blink of an eye, an injury, another controversial call, or a streak of bad luck like the one currently dogging him could snatch away everything he'd worked for. Taking his eye off the prize and uprooting his life to play nursemaid to a couple of orphaned six year olds was an added pressure he didn't need or want.

Career concerns aside, he wouldn't condemn two innocent kids to life with a man who didn't have the first clue how to go about building a happy family. No kid deserved that. Shit, he wasn't even sure he believed in the concept. The girls deserved someone whose experience wasn't limited to a missing father and a mother who drowned her disappointments at the bottom of a vodka bottle.

Screw Pete and his from-the-grave manipulations. Fine. The twins were his half sisters. Occasional visits and gifts for birthdays and holidays he could handle, but considering his career and its grueling schedule, no one in their right mind would expect him to drop everything to raise a couple of kids.

Gracie Gable claimed she wanted the twins. As far as he was concerned, she was welcome to the job. V would be pissed, but she'd have to find some other way to repair his image because he wasn't stepping foot on Pete's farm anytime soon, much less spending the next twelve weeks there.

His gaze focused on the laptop screen. Wasn't repairing his image what his public apology to the Gridiron Girl was all about? Sitting forward, he reread the words he'd typed earlier before tapping a fingertip to the keyboard and posting them. A new comment appeared below his almost immediately.

I appreciate the apology, Jake. Let me add mine. We get a bit rambunctious here from time to time, and I admit to having enjoyed baiting you. Sorry about that.

A smiley face icon accompanied her half-assed apology. Well, hell, what did he expect? Gracie Gable hadn't achieved a slot on the top one hundred sports blogs list by taking anyone's crap. Including his. Reluctant respect hummed in his throat, interrupted by a soft ding when a message box appeared at the bottom corner of his screen.

The Gridiron Girl has invited you to a private chat.

Shit. Not a good idea. Look what happened last time. He stared at the screen. The chat box taunted him.

"What the fuck? You face down three hundred fifty pound defensive linemen for a living. Don't be such a pussy." He flicked a finger over the mouse and clicked. A new window popped up immediately.

Jake?

In the flesh.

Like you, I was shocked this afternoon, or I would've taken the opportunity to say I'm truly sorry for any trouble I caused you. Creating a firestorm with the press wasn't my intention.

He raised his brows in surprise. Considering his insults the other day, not to mention his inclusion in Pete's will threatening her hopes for custody of the girls, her apology was completely unexpected. Then again, from the way he reacted at the reading of the will, she probably figured there was no chance he'd take Pete up on his posthumous offer. Why shouldn't she be magnanimous?

Did she know she'd already won? Would she ask him what he intended to do? And would he tell her? Not a chance, but giving up the game before he'd even taken the field went against his competitive nature. A consolation prize was in order. He tapped at the keyboard.

I appreciate that. Are the press hounding you, too?

Like rabid wolves.

He grinned. *Welcome to my world, darlin'.*

He imagined her incredible eyes going wary as she blinked at his endearment on her computer screen. The picture brought a wide smile.

Ugh. I don't know how you stand it.

He grunted. Typical trust fund babe. Did she think she could ignore what didn't meet her approval? His lips curved as he muttered, "Ignoring me won't be easy, princess. Not when you're raising two little girls who share my DNA."

Comes with the territory, although my interaction with you and your minions caused a marked spike in the rabid wolves' normal interest.

The screen remained blank and quiet for a long moment. He could practically hear the bristle in her tone when she finally replied.

You weren't faultless in the exchange, pal.

His quiet chuckle echoed in the silent condo. Oh, yeah. The little blogger with the hoochie-baby body had some spark. His groin tightened as he imagined fanning that spark until it burst into a full-fledged wildfire and he shifted in his chair. *You're right. I wasn't.*

Another pause.

I said I was sorry.

As did I.

His hand hovered over the keyboard. He'd done what he set out to do, made his apology, just as the Marauders' owner insisted. Considering where Gracie would be residing starting tomorrow, he'd be wise to end the conversation and sign out, but he found himself willing her to continue, to see where things led. He smiled when another comment popped up on his screen.

They're giving you a hard time?

A derisive scoff flared his nostrils.

Who? The press, the league, or the Marauders front office?

You're not making me feel any better.

Was I supposed to?

Well, shoot. I heard about the fine. I'm sorry.

A wry snort blew from his nose. *Yeah, well, don't worry about it. I'm not exactly popular with league management, and that's strictly my fault.*

The screen remained black and silent long enough he thought she'd gone.

I never thought this would get you in trouble with the team. What happened?

He settled the laptop on his lap and slouched back on the couch. *They threatened to bench me.*

Bench you? Are they crazy? You're the most talented player in the league. What could they be thinking?

All things considered, her artless compliment surprised the hell out of him. Yet, other than her doubt over his assertion the hit on Tuttle was clean, until he'd insulted her, the rest of her comments had been more than fair the other day. Complimentary in fact. Apparently, the little darlin' was a fan. He'd simply been too pissed off to notice. The least he could do was put her at ease.

They won't be, since I've apologized.
They insisted you apologize?
Publicly.
Ah, I see.

Shit. He'd made it sound as if he'd been forced, which, in a way he had. Still, once he'd calmed down, he'd realized an apology was warranted. The team had made their demand before he'd had the chance to do so on his own.

I'd planned to contact you before they made the threat.
Is that so?

He frowned at her obvious doubt. *You don't believe me?*
Hmm. Did they really threaten to bench you?

He narrowed his gaze, noting she hadn't answered either way. *The team's owner made her millions online. She's cyber sensitive.*

A long hesitation.
Good!

A reluctant chuckled escaped. *That's mean. Has anyone ever accused you of being a bloodthirsty blogger?*
You're the first, but I like it. Maybe I'll put it in my bio.

He laughed. Fan or not, she didn't pull any punches. *Funny. Are we good? And before you answer, my apology comes with two sideline tickets to the next home game.*

The smiley face made another appearance.
Careful, Jake. You don't want anyone accusing you of offering a bribe.
I'll take my chances. The tickets will be at the will-call booth.

Several seconds passed.
Thanks, and about the touchdown record, I'll be celebrating right alongside everyone else when you achieve it.

He laughed aloud at her not-so-subtle good-bye and snapped the laptop closed. Celebrating, huh? Sounded good to him. Especially if the celebration was a private one. He dropped his head to the back of the couch, shut his eyes, and smiled.

Those occasional visits to spend time with the twins presented some undeniably inviting possibilities.

Chapter 5

Silvery light from the full moon brightened the early evening landscape of Thompson Farm. The unseasonably early storm left sparkling icicles hanging from the eves of the house. Like a life-sized snow globe waiting for childish hands to shake the world and disperse the pristine image, the surrounding evergreens sagged beneath the weight of six inches of newly fallen snow. Gracie turned in a full circle, nearly falling when her ankles tangled with Murphy's leash. The two-year-old border collie-Jack Russell mix danced in circles as she hopped on one foot and attempted to free herself.

"Murphy! Settle down before you knock me on my ass."

Big, dark chocolate eyes gleamed at her above his doggy grin. She rolled her eyes and shrugged a shoulder to readjust the slipping strap of her laptop case. Lifting her gaze in time to catch the taillights of the cab disappearing at the end of the drive, she eyed the two sets of fresh tracks leading up to the house, then off again. Her lower lip stung beneath her chewing teeth. Jake's SUV was nowhere in sight, but with three hours left to go until the terms of the will went into effect, she couldn't relax.

He'd made it clear he wanted nothing to do with the farm or the girls yesterday, but what about the money? Jake might never have to worry about where his next meal came from, but Pete's estate was worth millions. Would a man walk away from that kind of money simply for spite? Or would V convince him to change his mind?

Why had he made no mention of the will and its bizarre stipulations during their online conversation following his surprising apology? The omission concerned her as much as his flirtatious tone. What was up with all those *darlin's* he tossed around, and what the hell had happened to the angry giant who stomped out of the room yesterday, his hair standing on end? What did it mean?

God, if he showed up at the farm tonight...Ugh! The implications were terrifying to consider. Maintaining the secret of her paternity had never been a problem before, but then, she'd never been around anyone who might make the connection. A pro football star, for heaven's sake. One lit by the glare of interest from the league's front office. How the hell had this happened? Evil forces had converged to spin a chilling version of her worst nightmare. If the situation wasn't so worrying, she'd have to laugh at the irony but, as things stood, laughing was the last thing she felt like doing.

God, what a mess! She dragged her suitcase up the walk, her shoulders sagging as if the weight of the world pressed down on them. With her other hand, she juggled a small duffle bag and Murphy's leash. Her laptop banged against her hip as the dog danced at the end of the strap, tugging her up the porch steps.

The front door opened and the leash ripped from her fingers with his excited lunge. Her grip loosened on the duffle. She dropped the suitcase handle in a scramble to save her laptop, catching the leather satchel before it thudded to the porch's wooden planks.

"Auntie Gracie!"

She grinned at the shrieked greeting and braced for impact as dark-headed munchkins charged into the cold night air. Two small bodies slammed into her legs. Four skinny arms wrapped around her thighs. Dual peals of excitement pierced the quiet night. Evil gremlins and nightmare scenarios temporarily flew from her mind as her sister's eyes twinkled at her over her nieces' identical smiles.

She squatted to squeeze the twins close in a group hug. Murphy squirmed close to lick every inch of exposed skin. Over giggles and a slurping tongue, Gracie's heart settled into the joyful cadence of love.

Angel was the first to pull back from the hug. She peered at Gracie's mouth in the low light. "That's pretty lipstick."

"Isn't it great? It's called Pomegranate Passion."

Angel's head bobbed in agreement. Gracie pressed her mouth to her niece's cheek. She pulled back a moment later, leaving behind a perfectly shaped lipstick tattoo.

Angel dove for Gracie's purse, rummaging in the side pocket to pull out her compact. She popped the top open to study her reflection critically then looked up with a wide smile. "Can I put some on my lips? I promise not to make a mess."

Gracie laughed. A future diva, Angel already had an eye for fashion and a passion for makeup. "I don't see why not, as long as you wash it off before going to bed."

Angel squealed and danced from foot to foot.

Mary clucked her tongue. "It's cold enough to freeze Hades out here!"

Charlie craned her neck to look over her shoulder at the housekeeper, framed by the open door. "Who is Hades?"

"Never you mind, Charlie girl." Mary rolled her eyes at Gracie's chuckle. "Come inside now, the lot of you. Before you catch your death."

The twins raced inside with Murphy at their heels. Gracie hefted the duffle and rose to her feet. Mary bent to grab the handle of the suitcase.

Gracie followed her inside. "Have you heard anything?"

Mary shut the door, rolling the case to the foot of the stairs and turned. "Not a peep."

A shudder of cautious hope rippled through her. No news was good news in this case. The grandfather clock in the corner of the foyer showed five eighteen. Two hours and forty-two minutes. She swallowed her nerves and glanced into the den. On their knees in the center of the antique rug with a wriggling Murphy between them, the twins competed for his attention and argued over who should unclip his leash.

"Do they know?" She shed her winter coat without looking away from the trio.

"About Jake Malone, you mean?"

She nodded and met Mary's somber gaze.

"Aye. It was left to me to explain. They know nothing about the terms of the will concerning custody but, well, considering the circumstance, they needed to know about him."

She chewed her lip. "How'd they take it?"

"How do you think? What little girl wouldn't be excited to learn they have a big brother? I'm surprised they didn't pin you down first thing and tell you about him. He's all they've talked about since I told them."

Childish giggles drew her attention. Gracie's lungs constricted and she fought against a sudden rush of threatening tears. The warm arm slipping about her shoulders dragged her right up to the edge of losing the battle.

"You're worrying over a situation you can't control and, if you ask me, it's unnecessary. From what I saw, the man isn't interested. I'd bet a pound he doesn't show up on our doorstep. And if I'm wrong, well, the girls may be dazzled by the idea of a big brother, but they *love* you."

"I hope you're right."

"Of course I'm right." She gave Gracie's shoulder a quick squeeze before slipping the duffle from her fingers, along with her coat, and turning toward the staircase. "Shall I be leaving your things in the blue bedroom or would you rather the master suite?"

"The blue room is fine. It's closer to the nursery and the girls." She shot a glance in the den and lowered her voice. "He can have the master suite. If he shows up."

Mary nodded. "We've had dinner already. I left a plate for you in the kitchen if you're hungry." She winked and headed up the stairs.

In the den, Angel's eyes flicked to Charlie in silent communication. They looked up to meet Gracie's gaze across the distance. A shadow of uncertainty darkened Angel's bluebell eyes. Older by three minutes, she had instinctively taken on the position as her twin's protector from the time they could walk, boldly accepting responsibility for the many instances of mischief the pair created. Unfortunately, the current situation was beyond a six year old's understanding.

"Daddy went to heaven."

Grief tightened Gracie's chest at the quiet comment and squeezed a bit tighter when Charlie straightened from her romp with Murphy to slip her hand into her twin's. Gracie crossed the room to set her laptop on the coffee table before joining the girls on the floor. With an arm around each of them, she hugged them close. "Yes, he did."

"He went to see Mommy and Jesus." Charlie cocked her head, peeking up from beneath thick lashes. "Miss Mary said Mommy must be happy to see him. She missed him a lot. She misses us, too."

Gracie smiled even as her heart wept for Sarah's girls. "That's exactly right. She misses you both terribly, but she'll have to wait a long time to see you. It's nice your daddy is there to keep her company, don't you think?"

Identical heads of inky black curls bobbed in agreement against her chest.

"Timmy said we're orphans."

"What?" Gracie broke the hug to look down at Angel.

"Orphans are kids who don't have mommies and daddies because they went to heaven. Timmy said orphans live in," she scrunched her nose in concentration, "an orpha… an orphan jij."

Of all the…"Oh, baby. Who is Timmy?"

"We had a sleepover at Hanna's house," Charlie supplied. "Timmy is her big brother. He's nine."

"Well, don't listen to him. You have me and Miss Mary, and you'll live right here on the farm."

"With you?" they asked in tandem.

Oh, God. She didn't want to give them false hope when she didn't know what would happen in the next three hours, much less at the end of three months, but they needed reassurance.

"Would you like that?"

"Oh, yes!" A bright smile spread over Charlie's face.

Angel's smile came more slowly and was more wary than bright. "*We* have a big brother, too."

"His name is Jake," Charlie added, "and he's not little like Timmy. He's big."

Very big.

"Big brothers are supposed to live with their sisters. How come he doesn't live with us?" Angel's grumbled question came across as more of a complaint.

A tricky question Gracie would have a better idea how to answer in— she glanced at the clock—two hours and thirty-eight minutes. She pasted on a smile she didn't feel. "Well, he's a grownup. Grownup brothers don't always live with their sisters."

"Can we go visit him?" Charlie jumped to her feet to race to the coffee table in the center of the room. Murphy scrambled after her. Giggling at the dog's interference, she shoved his nose aside to pull a sheet of paper from the drawer. She returned to hold out a crayon drawing. Primary colors depicted two little girls with a larger boy between them. "I drew him a picture."

Gracie pretended to study the drawing with interest, a difficult task with tears threatening. The evidence of Charlie's fascination with the brother she'd yet to meet didn't bode well for Gracie's chances if Jake chose to meet Pete's demands. As for taking the girls to see him if he didn't... She wasn't sure that would be a good idea. Jake hadn't exactly been thrilled to learn of the existence of his "rugrat" half siblings.

"We'll see."

A frown wrinkled Charlie's brow. "We'll see means no."

"No, we'll see means maybe. He's a busy man, Charlie."

The frown morphed into a scowl and jolted Gracie. A facsimile of that scowl had been on the front page of *Sports Daily* on Monday morning and again in the formal living room across the hall yesterday. Other than their eyes, so like Sarah's, the twins were pure Pete, with jet-black hair and warm complexions. Their uncanny resemblance to Jake was unnerving.

"Maybe we can get him to come here to the farm for a visit sometime."

Charlie's scowl blinked out, replaced with excitement. She skipped from foot to foot. "We can show him our room, Angel, and he can see how fast I ride my bike. I want to take off my training wheels. Miss Mary says I'm ready. So, can I?"

"If Miss Mary thinks you're ready, sure."

Charlie immediately ran for the closet tucked beneath the staircase.

"Wait, baby. Not tonight. It's dark outside."

She skidded to a stop and turned. "I'm not afraid of the dark. I don't even have a night-light anymore."

Gracie smiled and rose to her feet. "You're getting so big, both of you. But your bike's in the barn and there's snow on the ground."

Charlie cocked her head and pursed her lips. Her eyes brightened. "Then we could go sledding. Miss Mary took us shopping for new snowsuits 'cause our old ones are too small. They're pink! Do you think he has a snowsuit?"

The incongruous vision of the Outlaw Tight End zipped into a shiny, pink snowsuit loosened the knot of tension and made her chuckle. "Oh, I sure hope so. In the meantime, why don't we go upstairs? I could use some help unpacking."

"I get to try your lipstick."

Gracie grinned down at Angel, still on her knees at her side. "Of course."

A happy smile met her reply. Angel hopped to her feet in a flash and raced for the stairs. Murphy bounded after her. Gracie laughed, her heart lighter than it had been since the reading of Pete's will. Charlie might be dazzled by the idea of a new big brother, but Angel's support was literally in the bag. The makeup bag.

Gracie would bet a million dollars Jake Malone didn't own a single tube of lipstick.

Chapter 6

Gracie leaned with her hips propped against the kitchen counter. The glass of wine Mary handed her ten minutes earlier rested forgotten by her elbow. The girls and Murphy were upstairs, hopefully settled for the night and blissfully unaware of the waiting game underway. She glared at the clock. Less than half an hour remained until the deadline.

"The clock hands won't spin any faster by watching them." Her back to Gracie, Mary set out the makings for her nightly cup of tea.

Gracie picked up her glass then set it aside again without drinking. "I can't stand it. He may have no interest in a ready-made family, but with the value of Pete's estate in the balance..." She shrugged. "Only a fool would turn down that kind of money."

Mary glanced over her shoulder. "Jake Malone didn't strike me a fool."

She groaned.

"Then again, he doesn't need the money."

There was that. Manhattan's fifty-five-million-dollar man had scored dozens of endorsement deals in addition to his multi-year contract. He might be twenty-five thousand dollars poorer, thanks to her and her blog, but the Marauders' number one tight end wasn't exactly hurting for cash. Still...

The teakettle sent out a shrill whistle. With a twist of her wrist, Mary shut off the burner. "If you want to go on up, I'll make myself comfortable in the den and wait."

Tempting. She shook her head. "I don't think I could—"

They both spun to stare down the hallway at the solid knock on the front door.

Oh, God.

After a long moment, Mary rested a gentle hand on her shoulder. "Go open the door, child."

She would if she could get her legs to move. They'd frozen in place.

Mary gave her a gentle nudge, shooing her toward the hallway. "Problems are more easily solved when faced head on."

She grimaced, wanting to argue *this* particular problem was more complicated than anyone knew and wouldn't be easily solved, but what was the point? No one else would be knocking on the farmhouse door at this time of night. Jake had arrived.

The outrageous requirements in Pete's will set in motion potential consequences he couldn't have foreseen, and she had no choice but to play out the resulting train wreck. With a fortifying breath, she stalked down the hallway and opened the door.

Sure enough, Jake's large frame filled the opening, typically gorgeous in faded jeans and a leather bomber jacket. The fingers of one gloved hand were wrapped around the strap of a large duffle bag slung over one wide shoulder. He held a briefcase in the other.

No expression showed on his face, but the lines of strain bracketing his mouth gave him away. So much for the flirtatious and friendly man from this afternoon. The angry giant was back. He was here but wasn't happy about it. Her dwindling hope sparked on a tiny ember. Ninety days was a long time to put up with an arrangement with which a person wanted no part.

"Hello, Jake."

"Gracie."

"I didn't think you were going to show."

His lips thinned in a sneer. "Don't you mean you *hoped* I wouldn't?"

She blinked. After their charmingly congenial conversation this morning, his coldly furious comment was a sharp slap of reality. She straightened her shoulders and braced herself against the snarling predator who'd managed a direct hit. "I made no secret about the fact I want the girls."

His eyes narrowed along with his sharp snort. "And Pete's estate doesn't exactly represent pocket change."

"Excuse me?" Her jaw wanted to drop. How dare he infer she wanted the girls because of Pete's money? Sure, she'd recently assigned that exact agenda to him, but she never would've made the accusation out loud. Not to him, anyway. Jake, it appeared, didn't suffer from the affliction of tact.

She snapped her mouth shut and met his challenging regard with a disdainful glare. With his hands full, she could knee him in the balls and slam the door in his face. Sorely tempted to follow through on the tempting fantasy, she didn't get the chance.

He shook his head and sighed. "Shit. I didn't mean that."

She crossed her arms.

Guilty frustration blazed in his eyes. "Sorry. I don't react well when I'm pissed."

"I imagine that must be quite a problem for you. From what I've seen, you're pissed more often than not."

His brows shot up.

She bared her teeth in a blatantly false smile. "Sorry. I don't react well when I'm insulted."

She blinked, thrown off balance when the angry giant suddenly disappeared.

He dipped his chin and the bad boy Outlaw, adept at charming the masses *off* the field, deployed one of his many secret weapons. The brackets of strain softened into dimples with his pained smile. "I can tell. You look like you're fantasizing about landing a fist to my nose."

She smirked, refusing to be charmed. "I wouldn't use my fist, and the fantasy places the landing about two feet *below* your nose."

He barked a laugh, half chuckle, half wince. "Ouch." Shuddering in a typical male reaction to a threat aimed at that most vulnerable area, he tucked the briefcase under his armpit and held up his right hand as though swearing an oath. "I promise never to insult you again." He stuck out his hand. "Truce?"

Considering the insults he'd tossed out with all but one of their conversations, she doubted he'd be able to keep his promise. She didn't return his crooked smile, reluctantly placing her hand in his for a quick pump before stepping back and swinging the door wider in silent invitation. He hesitated briefly before stepping over the threshold into the foyer. She shut the door against the winter chill, watching silently as his smile faded behind a steady inspection of his surroundings.

What did he see? A warm and welcoming home as she did? He glanced down the hall, eyeing the exquisite grandfather clock at one end. Sarah once explained the antique had belonged to Pete's grandmother. Did Jake know that? Did he feel a connection to his long ago ancestor and mourn the fact the piece would pass on to his half sisters instead of him? Did he feel cheated out of his rightful place in Pete's life, or did the bitterness over whatever transpired between them prevent any sense of familial connection?

When he finally spoke, he proved her silent questions far off the mark. "Where are they? I expected the ru...uh, the twins to greet me."

She smirked at the slip. "The rugrats are in bed."

Humor twinkled in his eyes even as confusion puckered his brow. "Bed? It's not even eight."

Clearly, he had no clue when it came to kids. "They have school in the morning. They'll be up at six. You can meet them then."

"Six? A.m.?"

The genuine horror in his drawl cooled the residual embers of insult, and she bit back a smile. "Do you have any idea how long it takes a six year old to choose the perfect outfit for the day? Times that by two. Then there's hair to be done." She cocked her head and studied him. "How are you with a curling iron?"

"Fuck."

She couldn't help herself. She laughed, and letting go of the tension of the last twenty-four hours was sweet. They were both here. Disappointing, but reality. She'd simply need to stay sharp and do her best to head off any potential disasters the situation provided, but she'd never been a glass-is-half-empty kind of girl. Life would work out for the girls *and* her. She'd see to it. She wound down to a chuckle.

"I'm not sure why, but I'm compelled to warn you. The girls will tear you to shreds over that type of language."

She grinned at his wince, which quickly became a scowl.

"I'm glad you're enjoying yourself. At least one of us is."

She rolled her eyes. "No one's forcing you to be here."

He tugged the glove from one hand, then the next. "Clearly, you don't know V."

The confirmation he'd been coerced sobered her. "No, I don't, but ultimately it doesn't matter *why* you chose to comply with the terms of the will. What matters are those girls upstairs."

He sighed and bent to set the duffle and briefcase at his feet. When he straightened and met her gaze, the brackets of tension were back. "Cut me some slack, will you? I'm as much a victim of this situation as you and contrary to what you obviously believe, I'm not a heartless bastard. I won't do anything to make an already tough situation worse for a couple of six year olds."

Fair enough, but his presence would make matters worse, for her most definitely, but more importantly, for the girls if he didn't intend to stay past the time stipulated in the will. By his own admission, he knew nothing about little girls and had no desire to, but he'd made an appearance. Did he understand the impact of losing yet another person from their young lives would have on the twins?

"You may not intend to."

The question in his arched black brows was eerily similar to many she'd fielded from his half sisters. "But?"

"But they're scared and confused and have already lost too much. Once they discover you're here, they're going to expect you to stay and be a part of their lives. That means hair bows, tea parties, and plenty of little girl drama, and not just for ninety days."

He stiffened but said nothing.

"However you feel about Pete, the girls are innocent and vulnerable to the exciting idea of a big brother. If you aren't planning on sticking around for the long haul, please, I beg you, turn around and walk away."

She held her breath when he didn't immediately respond then lost her last hope of gaining immediate custody when he shook his head.

"Look, I realize you care about the girls and my presence complicates things. I have no idea what will happen at the end of this..." He hesitated, rolling his shoulders in an uncomfortable gesture. "This exercise, but whatever happens, I promise, I won't up and disappear from their lives, okay?"

His promise didn't tell her why he'd accepted the demands of the will when he'd been adamantly against the idea yesterday, but then, she'd said it didn't matter. She couldn't demand an answer now. With nothing left to do but accept the situation and hope for the best, she nodded. Her face must have betrayed her disappointment, because he dipped his knees to make better eye contact.

Humor danced in his eyes. "Curling iron, huh?"

She cleared her throat against the helpless flutters erupting in her belly and lifted her chin. "If you're staying, we're sharing duties. Including those with the curling iron. I'll handle the hair wars tomorrow. You can start by helping with pancakes in the morning and work your way up to the fun stuff."

He chuckled and bent to retrieve the briefcase, swinging the strap of the duffle over one shoulder. His laughing green eyes pinned her in place. "Sharing, huh? Sounds interesting. So, Gracie." Animal white teeth flashed in his wicked smile. "Where am I bunking?"

Chapter 7

Busy trying to control her erratic breathing, Gracie struggled to answer. Before she could, his head jerked up and his eyes went wary. His dark brows rose and his Adam's apple bobbed on a heavy swallow. She followed his gaze to the top of the staircase.

Murphy bounded down the steps, a neon green bow unraveling at his throat. The frilly pink tutu wrapped around his sleek chest slipped toward his back legs. Giggles competed with the thump of tiny feet descending the stairs. In the lead, as usual, Angel was the first to spot Jake. Her eyes went wide, and she stumbled to a stop.

Gracie yelped out a warning, but it came out too late. Charlie promptly plowed into her twin. In a tangle of arms and legs, they tumbled down the remaining steps. Like human bowling balls, they swept the dog's legs out from beneath him and landed in a heap on the landing.

Gracie gasped. Beside her, Jake stepped forward, his hand outstretched. He needn't have bothered. The girls sat up immediately, their eyes wide with hesitant curiosity. Murphy scrambled to his feet and performed a full body shake. The tutu slipped farther. Then his head snapped up and his intent, dark eyes landed on the stranger at Gracie's side.

Stepping forward, she meant to throw herself in the path of the fur-covered missile launching off the landing. With canine dexterity, the forty-pound scrapper avoided her outstretched hands. He shot past her, the green bow flapping behind him like a neon silk contrail.

She spun.

Jake's big body stiffened as he braced against the impending collision. Murphy landed sure-footed, only to skid across the hardwood floor. Momentum carried him strait for Jake's long legs.

No stranger to dexterity, Jake danced to the side. He snagged the dog's collar and halted his progress. Murphy wriggled wildly, the claws of his scrambling paws clicking on the hardwood floor. He bucked, and Jake pivoted his upper body sideways.

The move would've worked, too, if Murphy was a normal dog, intent upon jumping up to plant his paws to Jake's chest. She knew from experience that wasn't the case.

"Murphy, no!"

Quick as a flash, he dropped his nose and whipped up his head. She cringed as his skull made solid contact with Jake's unprotected crotch.

A loud *oof* accompanied the unexpected head butt. Jake's briefcase clattered to the floor. Stunned pain etched his features.

"What the fu—" When he bent forward, the duffle slid from his shoulder to join the briefcase at his feet. He cupped one hand over his injured crotch and shoved the dog away with the other. Jaw clenched and long legs bent, he crossed one knee in front of the other. His eyes slid shut on a pained moan.

Gracie bit her lip at his vulnerable contortion, leaping forward to grab Murphy's collar before he could launch a new assault. Long, dark lashes lifted to reveal Jake's pain-hazed eyes. They pinned her to the spot.

"*Oh* crap." She leaned down to wrap her arm around Murphy's neck.

Jake's chest expanded on a ragged breath. He opened his mouth, as if to speak, then snapped his teeth shut on another low moan. If looks could kill, her dog's spotted hide would soon be bleeding from a dozen cuts. Unfazed by the daggers shooting from Jake's eyes, Murphy's wagging tail sliced the air as he strained against her hold.

Then the daggers changed targets.

Considering her admission of a similar fantasy moments earlier, she couldn't blame Jake for his accusing glare. But geez, what did he think? She'd used telepathy or something to get her dog to do what she couldn't? *If only.* Yet, the results were the same. Swallowing against the slightly hysterical giggle clawing its way up her throat, she straightened and patted Murphy on the head.

Charlie's quiet voice interrupted the angry flush flooding Jake's features. "Is that him?"

Standing shoulder-to-shoulder, the girls watched Jake with curious, identical blue eyes. Angel's black brows were beetled in a frown spookily similar to his. Gracie turned. Jake had straightened to his full height. Only a slight stoop telegraphed his remaining discomfort. He stood stiffly under the girls' intent regard.

Angel jutted her chin at a belligerent angle. "Are you our big brother?"

His gaze sliced to Gracie, and she was surprised to see the sharp edge of panic eclipsing the pain in his eyes.

Well, isn't this interesting? Is big, bad Jake Malone afraid of a couple of six year-old girls? Oh, the possibilities....

She twitched with the need to do a giddy, happy dance and settled for the silent celebration ripping through her head. The cranial victory party was short-lived however, once she glanced at the girls. Their tension matched his.

Damn it! As much as she'd enjoy seeing him fall flat on his face, she simply couldn't let it happen. Ninety days was a long time, and if Jake ultimately failed to win the girls over, she'd do plenty of celebrating when she gained custody. In the meantime, she'd do what she could to make the transition from strangers to strange siblings easier—for the girls. They'd just lost their remaining parent, after all. They were orphans.

The term made her flinch inwardly. Hanna's brother Timmy might be correct technically, but if she ever got her hands on the big-mouthed brat, she'd strangle him. She tightened her grip on Murphy and held out her free hand. "Come here, girls."

Suddenly shy, they shuffled off the landing and down the final two steps. As one, they moved close to her side. She wrapped her arm around their shoulders, encompassing both. "Angel, Charlie, this is Jake Malone. Your half brother."

Charlie tilted her head and studied his face. She spoke in a stage whisper. "He's really big, and he looks mean."

"Grownups always look mean when they don't know what to say," Angel retorted with surprising insight.

Gracie met Jake's unsure gaze and lifted a challenging brow. His eyes narrowed marginally when she shrugged and smiled.

Okay, big guy. Ball's in your court.

He finally looked away and, as if he'd forgotten his encounter with Murphy, his face relaxed. His green eyes cleared and softened as he dropped into a crouch. Eyes level with the twins', he glanced between them. "You're right. Sometimes when grownups don't know what to say, it makes them mad, and being mad can make a person look mean."

Charlie pressed closer to Angel's side. "Are you mad at us?"

"Why would I be mad at you?"

"Because sisters are supposed to live with their brother." She tossed a quizzical glance at Gracie before turning back. "But we didn't know where you were."

Angel turned a scowl on her twin. "He could have found *us*. Even if grownup brothers don't live with their sisters, he could've asked Daddy if he could come visit us."

Jake opened his mouth then shut it again without speaking. Was he unsure how to explain the estranged relationship between him and Pete? Sympathy tugged at Gracie's heart—for the twins, not him.

"Oh, baby." She brushed a hand over Angel's inky curls. "It's not Jake's fault. He didn't know about the two of you until yesterday."

"Why not?" Doubting blue eyes burned at her.

What to say? She knew nothing about the conflict between Jake and Pete. Her sigh was long and drawn out. "It's complicated, girls."

The flat line of Angel's lips said she wasn't satisfied with her answer.

"Jake only found out about you yesterday and here he is. I'd say that means he's happy about having little sisters."

She shot a warning glance at Jake. If he said anything to contradict her, she'd….

His eyes widened.

She was no less shocked at her defense of him and quickly turned away. What was she thinking, aiding the enemy? As uncomfortable as he appeared in dealing with the girls, he was bound to screw things up if left to his own devices. A possibility she'd do best to keep in mind.

When she met his gaze again, he lifted one dark brow in silent question. Was he waiting for her to explain the sudden change in living arrangements? She shrugged, letting him know any explanations for his presence at the farm were his deal, but if she hoped he'd falter at the awkward task, she was disappointed.

He cleared his throat. "I thought I might stay here at the farm, if that's okay with you girls."

Angel's back went as stiff as a poker.

Charlie squealed with delight. "Like a sleepover?"

A strained smile pulled at his lips. "Something like that."

"Oh, yes!" Unable to contain her excitement, Charlie clapped her hands. "A sleepover, Angel. Jake is going to stay for a sleepover." She stilled suddenly, wary eyes sliding his way. "We can call you Jake, right?"

He nodded and some of the strain left his smile.

"Are you going to stay for breakfast? We're having pancakes."

He glanced at Gracie. "I heard that somewhere. Actually, I thought I'd stay longer than one night." He turned back to the girls and surprised Gracie by repeating, "If it's okay with you and your sister."

Charlie bobbed her head in a pleased nod. Angel remained stoically silent on the subject. Gracie squeezed her shoulder in a hug.

"Okay, munchkins. It's way past bedtime. Upstairs you go."

Angel turned without a word and headed for the stairs. Charlie frowned, a sure sign of imminent mutiny.

Jake cocked his head. "I'm a little tired myself."

Mutiny averted, Charlie walked backward, following her twin. She offered Jake a shy smile. "I like having a big brother."

His Adam's apple bobbed on a swallow as he rose from his crouch. "I...." He nodded. "I think I'm going to like having little sisters, too."

Then he winked, and Gracie rolled her eyes at the blush spreading across Charlie's cheeks. Small white teeth flashed in her beaming smile before she turned to race upstairs after her sister.

Jake puffed out his cheeks on a harsh breath. Turning his head, his narrowed gaze paused on Murphy before lifting to tangle with hers. "Is he yours?"

"Yes." She tugged the dog back a step and patted his shoulder. "His name is Murphy."

The low grumble of his voice held a distinct warning. "His name will be mud if he ever head butts me again."

He was threatening her dog? So much for their truce.

She gave a defiant lift of her chin. Oblivious to her returning anger, Murphy barked happily, his wagging tail thumping her thigh. He lunged against her hold. Jake's brows dipped as his stare slid into a warning glare.

Oh, bullshit. If he's going to accuse me anyway...

She let go of the dog. He leapt forward. She had the satisfaction of seeing Jake spin to his side, lifting one leg over his crotch in protection, but then he deftly grabbed Murphy's collar, stopping him short with an outstretched arm.

Green eyes, as cold as sharply cut emeralds, sliced her way. A glaring Jake Malone was downright intimidating and gave her a new empathy for those opposing lines he faced every week.

Instinct demanded she take a step back. She scoffed mentally. This wasn't pro football and brains, not brawn, would win this particular competition. She crossed her arms, silently insisting the move wasn't one of self-protection. "Please. He's a dog. The head butt was an accident."

His fingers still gripping Murphy's collar, Jake moved with a speed she should've expected, considering his exploits on the field. He stepped forward, crowding her until she quivered with the need to step back or chance their bodies touching.

"Maybe the first time was an accident, but letting him go and hoping it happened again wasn't." He lowered his head until they were nose to nose. "Be careful, darlin'. Control your bloodthirsty fantasies *and* your dog. If you don't, you won't like the consequences."

His woodsy spice cologne must be short circuiting her brain because, instead of poking him in the chest and telling him to go to hell, here she stood, mesmerized by the light striations in his sparkling emerald eyes. Her nostrils flared at his clean, male scent, and she bit at her lower lip.

She blinked when he dropped his gaze to her mouth. Oh, dear Lord. She'd never actually witnessed a man's pupils dilating. With undisguised male awareness? Oh, hell. Her mouth instantly went desert dry, and her pulse shot into overdrive.

Snap out of it. Intimidation is his game, not seduction.

She swallowed with an audible click, and thankfully, he raised his head before she could do anything stupid—like lift her mouth the mere inch necessary to find out what it would be like to taste him.

To hell with brains. When dealing with an overload of brawn and sex appeal, retreat was self-preservation's best friend. She followed her initial instinct and took a wide step back.

Dimples formed along with his slow, satisfied smile. He held her gaze as he bent to scratch at Murphy's head with long fingers. "You're going to have to watch that head, buddy. We're outnumbered around here. We guys need to stick together."

Murphy quivered with pleasure, adoration shining from his dark eyes. Jake's soft chuckle skittered over her rattled nerve endings, leaving goose bumps. Apparently he wasn't averse to claiming a little tit for tat, either. The sneaky jock had been trying to intimidate her, all right, and he'd succeeded. Well, if he thought she'd let him get away with it again…

God, it was going to be a long three months.

Chapter 8

With the girls off to school the next morning, Jake returned upstairs to do…God knew what. Go back to sleep, probably. That worked for Gracie. Out of sight and all that.

Having apparently taken her demand they share duties to heart, he'd wandered into the kitchen at six oh five, his eyelids drooping with fatigue. She considered it a bad sign she found the cowlick causing his thick hair to stand up on one side adorable, and the rough shadow of beard darkening his strong chin incredibly attractive.

She tried not to stare as he offered Mary his assistance with the breakfast preparations, but geez. Who knew a glob of pancake batter smeared on a man's tattered T-shirt would only enhance his masculine appeal? A barefoot Jake, flipping pancakes in rumpled jeans and a T-shirt, gave a whole new meaning to the word sexy and was a domestic vision she wouldn't soon forget.

The following half hour had been an exercise in tension. Angel shifted anxiously in her chair and Jake's discomfort had been evident in the nerve jumping along his jaw. Charlie and Mary hadn't seemed to notice. The housekeeper held court over the meal as she always did, as if this morning was no different than any other at the farm. As if Pete's son hadn't taken up the position where Pete always sat.

Gracie had to give Jake credit. Having made the decision to adhere to the demands of Pete's will, he was making a concerted, if somewhat stilted, effort. Despite his obvious nerves, he was still Jake Malone, a man known for his ability to charm. Looking like he hadn't slept a wink, he set about using that charm, attempting to draw the girls into conversation by inquiring after their likes and habits. Charlie soaked up his attention like a sponge. Hanging on his every word, she jabbered like a magpie in response. Angel refused to cooperate, pushing bits of pancake around on her full plate in stubborn silence.

Gracie wasn't sure if his interest was real or if her warning last night had sunk in. Only time would tell, but witnessing the adoring animation in Charlie's eyes, and the occasion flashes of interest Angel couldn't quite hide behind her distrust, Gracie's mood went from sour to gloomy. As hard as the fact was to swallow, Jake was here and, considering his competitive nature, he'd play to win. Which meant he wouldn't be going anywhere.

He'd made it clear he had no interest in a ready-made family, and he certainly didn't need Pete's money. What was he after? If his seeming desire to get to know the twins was sincere, what happened when the three months were up? The girls choosing her wasn't a foregone conclusion. What would happen if he won the custody battle? He claimed he wouldn't walk away, but what did that mean? What if he handed the girls off to a stranger and went back to his famous life? Her heart would be broken, and his abandonment would be one too many blows in the girls' young lives.

Confused and disheartened, she spent the morning working, relieved he'd disappeared upstairs the moment the girls' school bus pulled away.

The beauty of her web design business was the ability to work from anywhere. All she needed was her laptop and some peace and quiet. The farm delivered the quiet. Peace was more difficult to achieve, however, since her mind kept supplying an image of the man upstairs, his muscled body sprawled across the sheets in masculine relaxation.

Out of sight, my ass!

Losing herself in the world of bits and bytes wasn't as easy as usual this morning, but she eventually pulled it off. Too soon, reality intruded in the form of several afternoon appointments. She wandered into the kitchen for an early lunch before heading for the city. Murphy trotted over to investigate his bowl. She set her laptop case on the corner of the table and piled her coat and purse on top.

Seated at the table eating her lunch, Mary frowned her displeasure when Gracie bypassed the hearty soup simmering on the stove to pull a cup of yogurt from the fridge. She grinned, tearing off the lid, and dug in with a spoon as she dropped into a kitchen chair. Digging her cell phone out of her purse one-handed, she punched in the number for the local taxi service. A woman dispatcher answered after a single ring.

"Good morning, I need a—" Gracie's mind went completely blank when she looked up and found Jake filling the doorway.

Gone was the sexily mussed sleepyhead from this morning. Dressed in fresh jeans and a dark, collarless sweater, he stood hip cocked with the bomber jacket he'd arrived in last night slung from a crooked finger over one shoulder. The adorable cowlick had been tamed, but his thick hair still sported a slightly wild appearance, brushing against his collar in a glossy, shaggy mane. This morning's stubble had been scraped away leaving a slight shadow on his cheeks and the cleft creasing his chin. Clear as a spring dawn, his green-eyed gaze started at her feet and slid slowly up her body before settling on her face.

The X girls bolted to their feet in a standing ovation.

"Cab. I need a cab." She squirmed in her seat and mumbled into the phone.

He spoke over the answering dispatcher. "Where to?"

Murphy abandoned his lunch to trot to Jake's side, pressing against his thigh in gleeful welcome. She shot her dog a disapproving scowl—which he ignored, the traitor. Jake grinned, bending to scrub at his head with a rough hand.

"Hold on a second." She held the phone away from her ear. "The train station. I have several appointments this afternoon."

He straightened. "I'll take you."

The station was only a mile and a half away but…trapped in a car with the Outlaw Tight End? Whistles and catcalls joined the ovation. *Abso-friggin-lutely not!* "Thanks, but that's not necessary."

"I don't mind."

"That's okay." She held up the phone. "I've already called for a ride."

"I'm headed that way."

She clenched her teeth and mentally grappled about for a valid excuse to send him on his way. Alone. Her gaze snagged on her uneaten yogurt. She held up the cup with her free hand. "I'm not quite ready. You go ahead."

He draped his coat over the back of a chair. "I'm in no rush. I'll wait."

Crap.

He sniffed at the air and spun his head in Mary's direction. "Do I smell homemade chicken noodle soup?"

Mary nodded. He rubbed his hands together and stalked to the cabinets to pull down a bowl then plucked a spoon from the dish strainer on the counter. He ladled up a healthy portion before returning to the table, an arched brow winged Gracie's way.

Embarrassed heat flushed her cheeks. God, she'd been sitting there like a dummy, yogurt in one hand and the phone in the other, as the dispatcher waited. She clenched her teeth. Setting aside the yogurt, she slapped the phone to her ear.

He took things into his own hands, literally, by snatching the phone from her fingers.

"Hey!"

Mischief twinkled in his eyes even as he tilted his lips in an innocent smile. "Cancel that order. She's got a ride." He pressed a thumb to the screen then held out the phone.

She snatched it back. "What happened to the truce you mentioned?"

"What?" In a wholly male move, he lifted a leg over the back of the chair beside hers and dropped to sit. He pointed toward the window with his spoon. "I'm doing you a favor. Have you looked outside? It's snowing."

She glanced out the window and found he was right. Heavy flakes floated past the pane.

He spooned up a mouthful of soup, groaning and dipping the spoon for another taste. "By the way, you might want to exchange your skirt for some slacks." He sat back, rocking the chair on two legs, and cocked his head to peer down at her feet. "And the hot footwear for something a little more practical."

"Hot footwear?"

He let the chair legs drop to the floor, winked, and dove the spoon back into his soup. "Slushy snow and sex on heels aren't a good combination."

She jerked straight and glanced down at her favorite Michael Kor knockoffs. Her gaze flew to Mary. The housekeeper's eyes were owl wide.

Sex on heels?

Was he flirting with her? The possibility increased her heart rate to manic. She shot him a sidelong glance. He slurped a spoonful of soup. No, he wasn't flirting. Not with her. He couldn't be. They didn't particularly like one another. Besides, Mary was sitting right there, listening intently, but his teasing sure felt that way.

Her panicked gaze flew to the window. "Maybe I should reschedule my appointments."

Silent laughter sparkled beneath thick lashes as he looked up from his bowl. "Nah. It's only flurries. You'll be fine." He scraped along the bottom of the bowl and slipped the spoon into his mouth. His eyelids drooped to half-mast and he moaned as if savoring the last bite he'd ever experience.

Goose bumps broke out and she swallowed.

He sat back with a satisfied sigh and graced the housekeeper with a dimpled smile. "That was incredible, Miss Mary. Marry me and I'll set you up in the world's finest kitchen."

Mary colored prettily but pinned him with knowing eyes. "You're a bold one to be sure, but I've lived too many years to be swept away by a charming smile and a set of brawny shoulders."

Deep and masculine, his laughter permeated the feminine confines of the housekeeper's domain. Mary stood. Shaking her head, her smile remained as she carried both his and her bowls to the sink.

He eyed the yogurt cup. "You going to eat that or are you finished?"

Gracie didn't think she could swallow another bite. Nodding wanly, she stood when he did. He grabbed his coat as she slipped into hers and gathered her laptop and purse.

"I should be back by five, Mary."

"Take your time, child. I promised the girls a chocolate tea party this afternoon. Hot cocoa for a snowy afternoon. I'm thinking a batch of cookies would go nicely."

Jake paused in shrugging into his jacket. "Chocolate chip?"

Mary rolled her eyes. "As if the girls would eat any other kind."

He jammed his arms into the sleeves. "Any chance you'll consider making that a double batch?"

She turned from the sink, a dishrag hanging from her fingers. Her eyes glittered with calculation. "I might. If you'll consider passing by the train station and delivering Gracie to her appointments in the city."

He dipped his chin in a curt nod. "Done."

"Mary!"

"I won't have you catching the sniffles and passing them on to the girls." She waved a dismissive hand. "Off with you now. I've things to do."

Double teamed and unsure how to regain control of her commuter plans, Gracie stalked out of the kitchen and down the hallway. Murphy trotted at her side. A chuckle sounded as she reached for the front doorknob.

"Are you sure you don't want to change your shoes?"

She spun around. "What's with you and my shoe—aah!" She jumped back.

A mere inch away, he dipped his head, bringing them even closer. "I can't help it. I'm a leg man. There's nothing sexier than a long-legged woman in a pair of three-inch heels." Like a predator on the scent, he stepped forward, crowding her up against the closed door.

Her shoulders thumped against wood.

His drawl smoothed into a seductive purr. "I'd sure hate to see them ruined when they get wet. The shoes, I mean." He paused for a long, suggestive beat and his lips tilted in a distinctly wicked smile. "Your legs would only look better wet."

She gasped. "Stop doing that!"

"Doing what?" The mischievous glint in his eyes ruined his attempt at looking innocent.

"Making suggestive comments like you're...like you're flirting or something. I'm the enemy, remember?"

He dropped his gaze to run his eyes over her body in a slow survey. "Oh, princess. You could never be the enemy."

She mentally stomped her heel down on the prickles of awareness his sexy tone and blatant once-over produced. Hah! Rattled by his not-so-subtle flirting, she'd forgotten who she was dealing with. Too bad for him he'd overplayed his hand.

Princess, my ass.

Royalty was rare amongst the residents of the New York City Housing Authority. The art of street fighting wasn't. If the all-pro superstar thought he could blitz her with a few well-placed innuendos, he deserved to learn what it was like to get sacked.

She widened her eyes, batting her lashes as if dazzled by his flirty compliment, and puckered her lips on a breathy "Oh." She nearly ruined the affect by smirking when her acting skills proved more adequate than she'd hoped. His gaze dropped to her mouth and stayed there.

Another step sandwiched her between his body and the door. Doing her best to ignore the giddy leap of her heart, she pressed her spread fingers against the soft sweater covering his chest, beneath his open jacket. His glittering green gaze lifted to tangle with hers and, though she longed to experience the kiss the sensual intent gleaming in his eyes promised, she was no more a fool than she was a princess.

Already at a disadvantage with her unwanted housemate, gaining firsthand knowledge of what it was like to lock lips with him would only make matters worse. No, if she was going to survive living with him for the next ninety days, it would be best to lay some ground rules right now. For *both* of them, but first, he was going to learn who *he* was dealing with.

Holding his gaze, she rode her hand up over the hard plains of his chest to his shoulder then twined her fingers into the silky hair falling to his collar. She had to cut off an appreciative moan. *So soft.* A fascinated shiver lifted the fine follicles of hair on the back of her neck and arms when his pupils dilated once again. He dipped his head another inch.

Heated spice tickled her senses, making her mouth water and her nostrils quiver in greedy delight.

Oh, holy hell. He smells better than Mary's chocolate chip cookies.

He lowered his head until no more than a breath separated his lips from hers, and she momentarily lost track of her agenda. Gleaming striations brightened the green of his eyes as they smoldered with the promise of lovely, decadent secrets.

A sigh shimmered from her lips when he closed the remaining distance between them. Her eyes slid shut as, warm and surprisingly tender, his lips brushed hers, nibbling in no particular pattern. Small brush fires flashed to life throughout her system. Heat flared when he deepened the contact, sliding his arms around her and demanding entrance to her mouth with a hot flick of his tongue. A nagging disquiet hovered at the edge of her awareness, but she was helpless against his seductive onslaught.

She obliged him, opening her mouth to curl her tongue with his. Spice and heat tempted and teased. What was a woman to do when faced with such an irresistible combination? She sucked at the silky tongue tangling with hers then moaned at the rich flavor exploding on her taste buds like a sumptuous treat.

Strong arms hauled her up against a muscled chest and thighs. Iron hard interest pressed against her belly.

Snap out of it! Swallowing Jake Malone's tongue is not *part of the plan.*

With an inward wince at her flagging willpower, she moved with more panic than grace. Fortunately, her lack of finesse didn't matter. A healthy shove to his chest with one hand accompanied a sharp tug on his hair with the other. A quick jerk of her high-heeled boot behind his knee finished the job and the Marauders' number one tight end toppled backward to sprawl at her feet.

Murphy barked excitedly and pranced around Jake's prone form.

She sucked in air. "Not your enemy, huh? Wanna bet?"

He shoved the dog aside and sat up. His astonished eyes never left hers. "I can't believe you did that."

She angled her chin defiantly. "Suit yourself, but never try and play me again or you'll get more of the same."

"Play you? Isn't that like the pot calling the kettle black?" He had the audacity to laugh at her glare and pushed to his feet. "I'm a professional athlete. I play for a living and excel at…." He raked his gaze down her body and grinned when his gaze met hers once more. "Contact sports.

Anytime you want a rematch, princess, I'm happy to oblige. But I have to warn you, I'm a quick learner. Best you remember that."

She bared her teeth and ignored the residual heat humming through her bloodstream, leaving her limbs weak. "I'm not a princess and I fight dirty. Best *you* remember *that!*"

Spinning around, she fled outside, giving Murphy the command to sit when he would've rushed out behind her. The door closed at her back, but she didn't bother checking to see if Jake followed. The crunch of his boots on the snowy steps told her he did. He keyed the remote, making his big SUV chirp. Furious, more with herself than him, she rushed across the distance and wrenched open the passenger door. She slid inside, closing the door and snapping on her seat belt with shaking fingers as he skirted the hood for the driver's side.

Crap. That certainly hadn't gone as planned. Sure, she'd managed to toss him on his ass, eventually, but what was she thinking, letting him kiss her? And what was she thinking, kissing him back? Damn it. Far from laying out some much needed ground rules, all she'd gained by getting close enough to perform the toss was a new appreciation of his spicy-sex scent.

Okay, lesson learned. Grappling with the seasoned pro…hell, getting within ten feet of him was a bad idea.

The vehicle started with a well-tuned purr. Eyes trained straight ahead, a pained wince drew her attention.

He rolled his hips, lifting them slightly, and rubbed a hand to the butt cheek on the side closest to her. "Damn. I'll probably have a bruise."

The man collided with three hundred pound behemoths for a living, and he was complaining about a little bruise on his butt? Right.

She rolled her eyes. "You deserved it."

One last rub to his ass and he settled in his seat. He shifted into drive. "No man deserves to get knocked on his ass for a bit of flirting."

"You kissed me!"

The challenge in his eyes brought guilt, even before he tossed down the gauntlet. "Do you really want to argue over who kissed whom, princess?"

Ugh. No. No, she didn't.

She thinned her lips in a flat line of displeasure. "I told you not to call me that."

"You did? Well, now, *princess*, I must have missed that." He laughed when she gave a frustrated huff and brought the car to a stop at the end of the driveway. "Where to?"

"The train station."

"No way in hell. There's a batch of chocolate chip cookies on the line. Besides, I promised Mary."

"She's not going to know."

"I will." He pulled onto the rural road, heading in the opposite direction from the station. "Where are we going?"

She huffed a breath. "Park and Twenty-third."

"There. You see. That wasn't so hard, was it?" He shot her a grin. "If the idea of sharing a commute with me is such a hardship, why didn't you drive yourself?"

"Huh?"

"I haven't had time to explore yet but, according to Mary, there are several vehicles in the garage. Why were you calling a cab?"

She shrugged a shoulder. "I don't drive."

His brows winged upward comically. "Ever, or only in principle."

"Ever. I don't have a license."

He turned to give her a blank stare. "You're kidding, right?"

"I live in Manhattan. Public transportation takes me wherever I want to go. Why go through the hassle of learning to drive when I'll probably never own or need my own vehicle?"

He shook his head and the horrified disbelief in his eyes suggested she was nuts. "For the sheer joy of driving?"

As if to back up his comment, he picked up speed, guiding the high-powered machine around a long curve as though they were gliding on glass. He tossed her a toothy grin and a waggled brow.

She rolled her eyes and faced forward again then gasped and dug her fingernails into the supple leather of the armrest. Her eyes went wide as he accelerated toward a slow moving combine hogging most of their lane.

"It's all fun and games until you plow head on *into a tractor*." The last few words came out on a squeak.

He whipped into the other lane at the last second without ever taking his foot off the gas pedal.

The man was either insane or one of those maniac adrenaline junkies. What was she thinking? Of course he got off on adrenaline surges. He played professional football for a living.

Lazy confidence filled his tone as he guided the big vehicle back into the correct lane. "It's a simple matter of picking your route and showing no fear."

She yanked her seat belt tighter. "Tell me that again when you're trying to navigate Time's Square in noontime traffic."

His low chuckle danced down her spine.

She sniffed. "You're insane and I'll stick to cabs, thank you."

"Cabs? And you're worried about a random piece of farm equipment?" He shook his head. "I've been in several city cabs that were little more than rolling death traps."

"From what I can see, you're an expert at rolling death traps."

His deep laughter filled the interior of the car. She remained silent for several long moments, but finally her jittering nerves got the better of her. She turned to study him.

"Where are you headed, anyway?"

"The Sports Complex."

"Isn't there a concert there tonight? The field can't be available for practice."

"No practice today, but there are game tapes to watch, and I'll get in a workout while I'm there."

Great. The last thing she needed was the mental picture forming of a hot and sweaty Jake, working those impossible-to-miss muscles. She shoved the image aside. "Did Mary mention Pete had a section of the barn converted into a gym?"

Crap. Why had she mentioned that? The less time he spent at the farm, the better. Either he was a mind reader or the instant heat in her cheeks gave her away.

Wicked intent curled his lips in a wide smile. "Well now, princess. I'll keep that in mind. If you volunteer as my spotter."

Oh, yeah. A very *long three months.*

Chapter 9

"Jake Malone?" Max Grayson's stride never faltered from the quick pace he'd set on the treadmill beside hers, but his dark brows shot up to his hairline. His forehead glimmered with healthy sweat. "The Outlaw? The other half of your ugly, viral spat? *That* Jake Malone?"

Gracie jacked up a shoulder to swipe at a bead of sweat sliding down her temple. She shot Max a grimace. "You mean there's more than one?"

Creases bracketed his stubbled cheeks when he grinned. "Not as far as you're concerned."

She rolled her eyes then glanced around the busy gym. The hum of a dozen treadmills couldn't drown out the thud of running feet or the grunts of exertion and clang of free weights. As usual, the physical proof of her friend's persistence and determination to realize his dream sent a thrill straight to her heart.

"Business looks good, Max."

Her attempt to shove the conversation in a different direction failed miserably.

"Oh, no. You're not dropping a bomb like that then changing the subject." Head cocked, he studied her. "*Jake Malone.*"

"Shh!" She glanced around at those close enough to hear. Most of the gym's occupants wore headphones. No one paid them any attention.

He punched at a button on the panel in front of him and stepped onto the side runners to straddle the slowing belt. Doubt shimmered in his slate gray eyes. "You're not making this up to get back at me for fixing you up last month?"

She shuddered with exaggerated violence, simply for effect. "Didn't we agree never to mention Six-Hands-Stan ever again?"

An angry grumble vibrated in Max's chest. "I should've broken his arm."

She chuckled. "And then I would've broken yours. Who was it taught me to take care of myself?"

A faint flush of guilt stained his cheekbones. In direct contrast, a healthy dose of smug pride curled one corner of his lips. The sharp contradiction made her grin. Most people never witnessed the mushy heart beneath the rough exterior. His stern face and tattooed fighter's body normally made people cross the street rather than risk getting too close. Unless that person was a woman, of course.

She shook her head. What was it about bad boys?

Four years her senior and living on his own for the first time after a childhood spent bouncing around in the foster care system, the self-trained cage fighter won her undying gratitude shortly after she and Sarah moved in across the hall in one of the city's toughest neighborhoods. Coming upon a frightening scene in the building's stairwell where two teenage residents had cornered her, Max had effectively appointed himself as her protector, chasing the boys off and promising swift retribution if anything should happen to her in the future.

Insisting a naïve, domestic kitten had no hope of surviving in the wilds of New York City's public housing, he began instructing her in the art of street fighting. Like a Harley-driving drill instructor, he pushed her until achieving his goal of transforming her into a wiry, jungle cat, capable of self-defense through stealth and smarts. She'd quickly developed a case of hero worship. The hero worship eventually grew into a friendship she needed more than she cared to admit, especially since Sarah's death, and as she'd come to understand, he did as well.

Unfortunately, when your best friend was a guy with a knight-in-shining-armor complex, things got a little wonky whenever the subject of relationships came up. Crying on his shoulder over her first real *boyfriend* her second year of college had been a colossal mistake. First, because she hadn't actually loved the guy and second, her blubbering turned Max into a matchmaking maniac, determined to find her a good man who would keep her safe and never break her heart.

Ha! Like such a man existed.

She'd hoped the Stan incident would finally put an end to Max's matchmaking, especially since his concern wasn't necessary. She dated. Not often, admittedly, but since relationships rarely worked out anyway, what was the point? Considering the way they'd both grown up, and his scorn for the concept of happily ever after, at least for himself, she marveled at his insistence there was a man out there who would make her dreams of a family come true, if she only remained open to the possibility.

"I'm not making this up. Jake is the twins' half brother. He moved into the farmhouse last night."

"Holy shit." He blew a sharp breath in an airy whistle.

"Hello! Tell me about it." She jammed a finger to the kill switch on her machine and slowed her pace as the belt came to a stop. "God, what am I going to do?"

Stepping off his machine to take her arm, he led her through the gym toward his office. Across the room, Vern, the retired boxer who had befriended Max years ago and acted as the gym's honorary manager, nodded when Max cocked his head back toward the busy machines in silent communication, then shut his office door behind them. She wandered over to the file cabinet in one corner of the small room and rubbed a fingertip over the laces of the ancient pair of boxing gloves hanging from one of the handles. When she couldn't stand the silence anymore, she glanced around.

He leaned against the front of his desk, arms crossed. "You okay?"

She shut her eyes. He'd been at her side throughout Sarah's illness, holding her hand when the cancer finally took her and they lowered her sister's body into the ground. He, more than anyone else, understood what custody of the girls meant to her. He'd also be the first one to tell her *the fight ain't over till it's over*. She sucked in a deep breath, turned, opened her eyes and nodded.

"Atta girl." He studied her in silence for a long moment, then his lips turned up on one side, the way they did when he was up to some kind of mischief. "As for what you're going to do? For all intents and purposes, Jake Malone is your new roommate. If you put your mind to it, I'm sure you'll come up with a few ideas."

A nervous quiver permeated her derisive smirk. Thanks to the kiss she'd shared with Jake in the foyer this morning, she'd have no trouble coming up with a few incredibly yummy ideas. Ideas better left unexplored.

"I'm serious."

"So am I. You've had a thing for the guy for years. People rarely get the opportunity to realize their darkest dream. It's a sin not to act when a chance like this comes along."

"I'll go to confession." She narrowed her eyes at his grin.

He crossed his legs at the ankles. "All I'm saying is, you've been handed the chance of a lifetime."

"What I've been handed is the housemate from hell. This is going to end in disaster."

"You don't know that."

"I don't?" She set the gloves to swinging with a flick of her finger then flopped onto the old leather couch along the wall. "Setting aside the elephant in the room for the moment, I cost the guy twenty-five grand after insulting him on my blog."

"He insulted you, remember? You both apologized, so what's the problem?"

"The problem is, our mutual apologies have only generated more interest. I had seventeen requests for dual interviews in my e-mail this morning. If they find out we're housemates...." She shuddered, this time with no exaggeration. "I don't even want to think about that possibility, but more importantly, what about the girls? I can't lose them."

He dipped his head, holding her gaze intently. "You won't. You said they'll ultimately do the choosing. Do you really think they'll pick him over you? Come on."

"A big brother?" She ripped the sliding scrunchy out of her hair and jammed her fingers through the damp strands before twisting them back up again. "Charlie's already mesmerized by the idea. Angel may be a little slower to come around, but she'll get there eventually. We're talking about Jake Malone here. He's Mr. Irresistible to females."

"Mr. Irresistible?" His sly smile and drawn-out words were declaration and question in one.

"You know what I mean." She blew out a breath. "Anyway, it's not only the custody worry, though, that's my main concern. Pro football is an elite but relatively small club. They *know* each other, Max."

He sighed. "Ah, the elephant."

"Yeah, the elephant. What if Jake makes the connection?"

"Why would he? Your mother's diary claimed she wasn't sure if your father even knew about you. Since he's never tried to make contact, odds are he doesn't."

"Odds aren't exactly my friend these days. I mean, what are the odds Jake would turn out to be Sarah's stepson, or he'd arrive at the farm three days after showing up on my blog? I swear, evil gremlins have taken control of my life."

Max's bark of laughter made her smile and eased some of her building panic.

"I see your point, but as usual, you're paranoid when it comes to this subject."

She opened her mouth to argue.

He held up a hand. "You're the only one who knows your father's dirty little secret."

"*You* know."

"Yeah, but I'm not about to blab. You're in the clear. Unless you follow my good advice by walking up to the man and saying, 'Hi, Pops. Nice to meet ya.'"

She groaned, not having to imagine how that bombshell would go over. Throughout the years, she'd spent countless hours imagining springing the truth of her paternity on the man who fathered her. In every single case, he'd worn the same horrified grimace as the one tightening Jake's features when he discovered he had not one, but two, little sisters.

She swallowed back the oily film rising in her throat. "Not going to happen."

Max's sigh was long-suffering. "I think you're making a mistake there."

"So you've said before, but nothing good would come of introducing myself. He has a family, for heaven's sake."

He shook his head. "Gracie. You're his daughter. That makes you family, too."

* * * *

Quiet conversation, accentuated by an occasional burst of male laughter, filled the crowded media conference room. The Marauders' offensive line milled about in small groups or sat in the rows of molded plastic chairs facing the large, flat screen TV where the game tapes for this week's matchup would be queued up. In his usual spot in the back corner, balanced on the back legs of his chair, Jake leaned against the wall. He tossed a football from hand to hand, enjoying the good-natured back and forth of his teammates.

At least this part of his life hadn't gone bat shit crazy.

What the hell was with the women in his life lately? First, his lady boss threatens to bench him, then V insists she'll no longer represent him if he didn't get his ass to the farm. What did it say about him that he hadn't had the balls to call either of their bluffs? *If* they were bluffing. He didn't think so in either case.

The fact was, he trusted them both to tell him the truth. They were strong women who spoke their minds and didn't need to bluff to get what they wanted. Apparently, Gracie Gable was cut from the same cloth. Damn, she was a piece of work. She'd surprised the hell out of him with her unexpected attack.

Either he was losing his touch, or she wasn't what she appeared. He'd place his money on the latter. Clearly, he'd misjudged her. It was early yet, but between her sincere anxiety over the girls' future, evident in her comments when he arrived at the farm, and observing her with them last night and again this morning, he couldn't see her bolting anytime soon. He couldn't see her bolting period. She loved the twins and it showed. The knowledge loosened the stiff knot of panic he'd been suffering since he agreed to V's demands.

Unfortunately, his faulty judgment in another area left him dealing with a different kind of stiffness. Who knew a simple kiss could be so damned erotic? When she twirled her tongue around his, the top of his head nearly blew off. Which, at least, offered him a plausible excuse for how she'd managed to dump him on his ass.

The memory brought forth a grin.

Considering her reaction to a bit of harmless flirting and that kiss, she wasn't the party girl he expected either. A woman comfortable with the idea of no-strings sex would've jumped at the sensual lures he tossed out. Gracie definitely hadn't jumped, but she hadn't been immune either. Sure, she'd attempted to disguise the feminine awareness in her stunning violet eyes with her surprising show of bravado, but the way her mouth came alive under his, and her charming blush when he suggested she join him in the gym, spoke volumes.

Her mind might insist he comply with her no trespassing demands, but her body had other ideas. The blatant struggle between those conflicting desires stroked his ego as much as his libido.

He shifted in his chair, dropping the front legs to the floor. God help him if she ever did volunteer to join him in a workout session. The thought of the princess bending over him as he sprawled out on a workbench produced some hotly erotic images, and as he'd discovered over the last hour, working out with a hard-on was damn uncomfortable.

Of course, if she had her way, he wouldn't have the opportunity to turn any of those images into reality. That would be a damn shame, but probably for the best. The situation was complicated enough without adding sex to the mix. Then again, complications were the spice of life, and he'd never been able to resist taking on a challenge, especially when the challenge came with legs a mile long.

Still, he couldn't blame her for her reluctance. He might not consider her the enemy, but she didn't feel the same. She saw his inclusion in Pete's will a threat to her custody hopes. The honorable thing to do would be to put her fears to rest. To settle V's ruffled feathers he'd agreed to go to the farm—temporarily. He'd be leaving as soon as his reputation was back in good standing. V's hope he'd end up playing permanent Daddy to two orphaned girls wasn't going to come to fruition. He'd do the big brother thing and make sure they were taken care of, but he had nothing more to offer them.

Unless Gracie turned out to be some kind of crazy nut job psychopath, a possibility he couldn't imagine since seeing her with the girls and Mary, he had no intention of fighting her for custody. She'd already won, but didn't know it yet.

As for doing the honorable thing and telling her, where would be the fun in that? He might not be spending the full three months at the farm, but he was still putting his life on hold. Why shouldn't he take advantage of a built-in diversion? Besides, a woman as unpredictable and prickly as Gracie begged to have her life shaken up a bit.

He ran his tongue over his teeth and contemplated a couple of particularly appealing diversions he'd like to share with the leggy princess. He owed her for her trickery in the foyer, and he was a "class A shaker," if he did say so himself. Anticipation thrummed through his veins, and he marveled at the difference a single day made.

He arrived at the farm last night royally pissed. At himself mostly. He'd made his mark on the field long ago, earning the respect he enjoyed from his peers, fans, and the press alike. If not for his temper, he never would've found himself in the position of having to accept Pete's demands in order to repair his reputation. He could've dealt with his newly discovered sisters on his own terms.

Discovering he'd be spending even one night in Pete Thompson's old bedroom only made matters worse. He hadn't slept a wink, but he'd never been the kind of man to make a commitment without giving the effort his all. He spent the night studying the situation from every angle and, somewhere around dawn, he'd come to a realization. Pete might have gotten his way, but he wouldn't have the last word.

He'd play Pete's game, but on his own terms. He couldn't see himself as the head of the twins' new family, and thanks to Gracie, that wasn't necessary. The value of Pete's estate guaranteed the girls would never want for anything financially, and Gracie and Mary would see to their physical and emotional needs.

He had no more experience at being a big brother than he did a father, but shit, how hard could it be? Yeah, they might be girls, but kids were kids. Gifts on their birthdays and holidays were a must, but in his experience with Tom's boys, kids were happy with the simple things. Like an occasional movie or a meal. What kid wouldn't like a trip to the zoo or maybe a day spent sledding the hill out behind the barn? He grunted in satisfaction.

Piece of cake.

Whatever Pete's true motivation for shoving the twins at him, Jake would have the last word *and* twist the situation to his advantage. He grinned.

Beginning with Gracie.

Kevin Tucker dropped into the chair in front of him, straddling it backward. Jake bit back a groan. Matching, serrated barbed wire tattoos stretched across Tuck's thickly muscled biceps when he propped his arms on the back rest. He leaned forward. Cobalt blue eyes twinkled beneath a mop of sun-bleached blond hair. He curved his lips in a sly smile.

"Who is she?"

"She who?"

The grin widened. "The she who has you sitting here grinning like an asshole."

Fighting back the groan grew more difficult. They'd been friends since the tough kid from South Boston was drafted in Jake's third season. Tuck's nose had been broken numerous times and had the prominent bump to prove it. A jagged scar bisected his right eyebrow above his crooked beak. Despite the imperfections, the ladies flocked to him. When it came to his exploits with women, Tuck was a legend. In comparison, Jake was a Boy Scout.

Which didn't mean Jake couldn't hold his own. In a game of friendly competition, they'd both stolen a lady love from the other on more than one occasion. The latest victory belonged to Jake, when he convinced Daphne, the underwear model Tuck escorted to a fundraiser last spring, to toss the veteran wide receiver over for a weekend in Bermuda. Tuck had been waiting seven months for the chance to retaliate.

Gracie's gem-toned eyes, drugged with passion as she fought against the pleasure of their shared kiss, filled Jake's mind. *Not this time, buddy. I'm keeping this one to myself.* "What makes you think I'm grinning over a woman?"

Tuck's nostrils flared on a sharp laugh. "Costa has you in his crosshairs, you've been slapped with a bullshit fine, and every sports talker in the country is gunning for you. The fact you can still smile can mean only one thing." He jabbed a finger toward Jake's nose. "You're under the influence of some damn sweet poison. Who is she?"

Jake crossed his arms and bared his teeth in a *fuck you* smile.

"Gentlemen. We have our work cut out for us this week."

The chatter in the room quieted immediately as the offensive coordinator arrived. Tuck thinned his lips in a challenging smirk. "You know I'll find out." He spun his chair around to face the screens as the lights blinked out then spoke in a low voice over one shoulder. "By the way, next week's poker game is at your place."

Shit.

Chapter 10

"Thanks for the ride." Gracie scrambled from Max's low-slung sports car, hoping to rush inside before he could follow. She wasn't quick enough. Thanks to his long-legged stride, he joined her before she reached the porch steps.

"Go away." She searched her purse for her key.

"Not a chance, kiddo. This is Jake Malone we're talking about. You don't always think clearly when your heart's in play. I'm here to help."

She rolled her eyes. "My girl parts are in play, you idiot, not my heart."

He grinned and bumped her shoulder with his. "I've known you since before your girl parts *knew* they were girl parts, and I've watched you moon over Jake Malone, despite there being no chance you'd ever meet him. Now you have...Fate has spoken. You're a one-man woman, and your heart's already made its choice. You're toast."

Dear Lord, please don't let that be true.

Eyeing Jake's big SUV parked beneath the old pines, she hoped to kill Max's matchmaking agenda, at least for tonight. She uttered the lie without an ounce of remorse. "Jake may not even be here, you know. Curfew isn't for another three hours."

He shrugged. "I've got nothing planned for tonight, and I haven't seen the twins in a while. I'll wait."

After insisting he drive her home, he'd pumped her for details on everything that happened since the reading of the will. She'd spent the entire ride doing her best to say as little as possible. Not an easy task, considering she'd never been able to keep a secret from Max, including her long-time crush on Jake Malone.

Under normal circumstances, she'd have savored describing how she dumped Jake on his ass. Max would've gotten a kick out of it, but she could imagine his reaction should he learn of the molten kiss she shared with Jake prior to the dumping. Even worse, what would his reaction be if, when they went inside, Jake picked up where he left off this morning with his blatant flirting?

The matchmaker song from *Fiddler on the Roof* echoed in her head. She ground her teeth. Why hadn't she insisted on taking the train? She glanced up with a scowl. "You're being an obnoxious jerk."

Max grinned, not bothering to refute her complaint, as the door swung open suddenly and ripped the key from her fingers. Larger than life and looking as if he'd recently come from a board meeting, Jake stood on the other side of the threshold in a stark white dress shirt and black slacks.

In contrast, Max resembled a biker gang president in his battered leather jacket, time-faded jeans, and black boots.

"I'll be damned." He shot her a wink. "You were telling the truth."

Her jaw went lax, then she sniffed. "You thought I was lying?"

He slung his arm around her shoulders, tightening his hold when she attempted to toss it off, and tapped a fingertip to her forehead. "Nah. I just like seeing this zigzag wrinkle you get between your eyes when you're pissed."

Her elbow to his rib did nothing to diminish his gleeful sneer. Facing Jake, he stuck out his hand. "Max Grayson."

"Jake Malone." Jake's intent gaze bounced between them as he shook Max's hand.

Max would never know how close he came to getting dumped on *his* ass. He was saved when she noted Jake's watchful gaze crawling over Max's arm wrapped around her shoulder. Well, well. She might be able to salvage this situation after all. If Max would only cooperate.

Why hadn't she considered playing the boyfriend card? Surely, if Jake thought she and Max were an item, he'd back off from his heavy-handed flirting. Then maybe her girl parts *and* her heart would settle down, and she could focus on the all-important task of winning the custody battle.

Tucking closer to Max's side, she blinked at him with a simpering smile as if he alone could deliver the moon and the stars. Deviltry flashed in his eyes. Not a good sign, but at least he wasn't busting a gut laughing. She pinched his waist in a silent demand he play along.

Jake stepped back to let them enter. Max proved himself as perversely contrary as usual. He dropped his arm from around her and left her high and dry. She scurried after him, hoping to salvage the ruse, and shrugged from her coat without meeting Jake's eyes.

"Where are the girls? *Uncle Max* thought he'd surprise them by coming for dinner."

Max shot her a pointed smile, but if he planned to contradict her, matching squeals from above stopped him in his tracks.

"Uncle Max!"

Two pair of tiny feet thumped on bare wood as the twins raced down the stairs. They'd reached the landing when Murphy shoved by them to launch himself to the foyer floor. Gracie choked on a laugh when Jake jerked up one knee and crossed his leg in front of his crotch. Horror flooded his features, and he called out a warning when Murphy pivoted toward Max.

Well acquainted with her dog, Max spun sideways at the last second. Murphy skidded to a stop and plopped to his butt like a perfect gentleman. His tail swished back and forth over the floor. Max bent to greet him with a rub and a grin.

Jake glared at the dog. Gracie bit her lip to keep from laughing.

"Uncle Max!" Angel plowed into Max's leg. Charlie joined her a moment later.

He dropped to a squat, pushing Murphy aside to grab the girls in a bear hug. Employing his usual ritual when greeting the twins, he purred an animal growl and rubbed his whiskered chin over Angel's jaw then repeated the tickling caress with Charlie.

Their delighted giggles made Gracie's heart swell with appreciation for her friend's demonstrable affection for her nieces. They'd had far too few reasons to laugh lately. Count on Max to understand and set aside his matchmaking agenda long enough to greet them the way he always did.

He winked at her over Charlie's shoulder. Gracie's smile stretched wide until she happened to glance up and caught Jake watching the warm welcome with tightened features. As if sensing her attention, his guarded gaze ricocheted off hers before he turned his back and closed the door.

Her smile slid away. Though unsure of exactly what he was thinking, she didn't need to read his mind to know the scene playing out left him uncomfortable. Because the girls were his sisters and yet hadn't greeted him with warm hugs, as they were Max? Was he stung by the reserved welcome he'd received last night? Could he possibly be that naïve?

He'd been here less than twenty-four hours and he'd made more headway than she'd have expected in a week. Give Charlie another day or two, to shed her residual shyness, and she'd be slobbering all over her new big brother the moment he walked through the door. Angel might be holding him at arm's length at the moment, but deep down, she dreamed of a big brother and all that entailed. This morning at breakfast, he'd proven he was willing to try to build some kind of relationship with his half sisters. Didn't he realize he'd already won over Charlie and, with the tiniest bit of effort on his part, Angel would soon fold like a bad hand of cards?

Gracie didn't want to think about where that left her.

Max lifted his nose in the air and sniffed. "What do I smell?"

"Sketty and meatballs." Angel wrapped her arm around his neck.

He twisted his head to meet her smiling gaze. "Do you think Miss Mary made enough for me?"

Charlie rubbed her fingers over Max's scruffy chin and nodded. "Miss Mary made an extra big pot 'cause Jake said sketty is his favorite." Her smile grew huge. "He's our big brother!"

"Oh, yeah?" Max grasped Angel's hand and rose to his feet. He rested a hand on Charlie's shoulder and, in true Max style, offered Jake a pained smile. "That must have come as a shock."

Jake snorted slightly, but his shoulders relaxed marginally. "You have no idea."

Max chuckled, squeezed Angel's hand, and wrapped an arm around Charlie's shoulders. "Well, I'm jealous. I've always wanted a couple of petite, black-haired twin sisters." He grinned, and the girls giggled their pleasure. Then he swung his gaze to Gracie. His grin tilted into a taunting smile, and he winked. "Instead, I had to settle for a tall blonde with a smart mouth and an attitude."

She dared a glance at Jake.

He crossed his arms and the tension on his face melted away with his challenging smile. "I didn't realize you had a brother."

So much for her boyfriend ruse. She was going to kill Max when she got him alone.

He drew her attention when he spoke to Jake. "She has no brother, but she has me. When a woman's been tagging along behind you and generally causing you grief from the time she was fourteen, she can't help becoming the next best thing." Affection softened his smile and his voice when he looked back at her. "A best friend."

The rat! Typical Max, slipping something sweet into the middle of his trash talking. *Tagging along behind him.* Ha! He'd be getting a lesson in grief, all right, and soon.

She angled her chin defiantly. "Don't you mean *ex*-best friend?"

His teeth flashed with his pleased laughter. She rolled her eyes.

Jake's eyes twinkled boyishly as his gaze bounced between them. "Remind me to tell you about my best friend sometime."

Max turned his smile on Jake. "Is she a leggy blonde?"

"Nope. She's a petite redhead, but she could give Gracie a run for her money in the attitude and smart mouth departments."

"Auntie Gracie has a *pretty* mouth!" Lips puckered in a mulish twist, Angel glared up at Jake.

On Max's far side, Charlie wrung her hands uncomfortably and bit at her bottom lip. Surprised by the vehemence of Angel's defense, Gracie opened her mouth to say…what, she wasn't sure. Clearly too young to understand the nuance of the conversation, Angel had misread Jake's comment as an insult, but neither Sarah nor Pete would have tolerated her disrespectful tone. Neither could she, not if they were going to live in peace for the next eleven and a half weeks.

Jake didn't notice, or he chose to ignore Angel's hostility. He propped his hands on his knees and leaned down until he was on her level. "Do you think so?"

He rotated his head and studied Gracie for a long moment. She refused to squirm beneath his intent regard, especially with Max paying such close attention, and was relieved when Jake returned his focus to Angel— until he spoke.

"You know, you're right. Your Auntie Gracie has a *very* pretty mouth."

Max's smile lit up keenly. For a moment, Gracie half expected him to slap Jake's hand in a high five. Humor simmered in Jake's eyes. She'd have smacked them both if she could've moved, but her toes were curled in her boots.

Angel spun away, her brow puckered with confusion, and headed down the hallway. Charlie skittered after her.

The hell with her curling toes. She fried both men an exasperated glare then ground her teeth at the deep laughter trailing her as she huffed toward the kitchen.

Chapter 11

Twenty-four hours later, Gracie's feet dragged as she climbed the stairs to prepare the girls for bed. If these first few days were any indication, she'd be a raving lunatic by the end of the three months. Hell, by the end of next week! No one could ever accuse Gracie of being weak, physically or emotionally. Losing nearly everyone you loved either broke you or made you tough. The events of her teenage years had forged a strong backbone and an ability to adapt. The problem was, her willpower had never been tested the way it had the last couple of days. Max, the jerk, was right. She was toast when it came to Jake.

If only she hadn't attempted to teach him a lesson, then they wouldn't have shared that kiss. That completely stupid, completely...*wonderful* kiss. The shared memory simmered in Jake's eyes when they met hers across the dinner table earlier this evening, and the accompanying heat in those green orbs nearly seared her soul.

Ugh! She was an idiot. Give a man like him an inch and …

Right. Like their heated clutch was all his fault. She'd been right there with him, gleefully embracing the opportunity to taste what she'd only dreamt of in numerous fantasies. One taste would never be enough, but sipping from that well again was out of the question. Lusting after her unwanted housemate was one thing, acting on the lust was another matter altogether.

Max insisted she'd already lost her heart to Jake. She disagreed, but she wasn't foolish enough to believe her heart wasn't dangerously vulnerable where he was concerned. She'd been helplessly fascinated with him from the moment she first learned of his existence. Meeting him in person only intensified the fascination. The leap from fascination to love would be a short, disastrous one.

At the end of Pete's time frame, one of them would lose. If the loser ended up being her, she'd at least like to walk away with her heart intact. She scowled and climbed to the second floor.

It simply wasn't fair. Jake Malone emitted some kind of secret pheromone, slaying females without working up a sweat. His presence threatened both her custody hopes *and* her peace of mind, but did the invisible forces knocking her well-ordered life off its axis care? Hell no. If they did, Pete's son wouldn't have been a sexy hunk and famous athlete with a killer smile and the body of a god. He'd have been a short, rotund, *toothless* accountant from Hoboken.

She reached the top of the stairs and shuffled down the hall toward the nursery, where Charlie had dragged Jake several minutes earlier. The truth was, beyond her helpless fascination with the man, watching him work to connect with the twins depressed the hell out of her. First, because his efforts were working. Charlie had already fallen under his spell. From her giddy reaction whenever he spoke to her, she was in the grips of full-blown Mr. Irresistible worship, and she wasn't the only one. Mary was a goner, too, fussing over him as if he were the crown prince of Long Island or something, and despite Angel's continued sullenness, it would only be a matter of time before she caved.

The man might not know much about little girls, but he was a frigging quick study—and clearly, he wasn't afraid to use bribery. After yesterday's minor altercation with Angel, he'd stepped up his game. Gracie had no idea how he'd discovered Angel was horse crazy, but his sources had skills. He couldn't have used a better carrot to dangle before his reluctant half sister than to mention he'd be bringing his prized horse to the farm. Though Angel tried to hide her reaction, dipping her head to poke at her dinner with her fork, there was no missing her desperate flush of pleasure at the idea.

Gracie ground her teeth. Damn it. How was she supposed to compete with a stallion named Hercules? Maybe she could find a unicorn for sale on eBay.

Jake's charm and seeming success at winning the girls over wasn't her only problem. Since reading her mother's diary and learning her father's name, she'd been beyond curious about the man who'd fathered her, becoming a football junkie in an effort to feel close. Yet she froze in terror at the thought of making contact with him. Jake, on the other hand, faced a similar scenario by waging a single-minded campaign, determined to make the best of a situation he'd neither expected nor wanted.

She tried not to envy his confidence as he did his best to befriend the twins, but his focused effort made her feel like a coward in comparison. How she wished she could simply forget about the man who fathered her. He was out of reach. End of story. But thanks to this situation with Jake, shame and envy prodded her, and Max's comment in the gym kept taunting her.

That makes you family, too.

Ha! As if sharing a person's DNA automatically made you family. Jake's unexpected arrival as the girls' family caused plenty of upheaval, but at least he'd been invited. No, springing herself on her father was a bad idea. She already had enough turmoil in her life. She'd simply have to get used to feeling like a coward.

They say a picture is worth a thousand words. The one meeting her eyes when she stopped in the nursery doorway spoke volumes.

Murphy lifted his head, his tail thumping against the mattress, where he lay sprawled beside Angel on one of the matching bedspreads. On the opposite side of the room, Jake dwarfed the oversized chair where Sarah had fed her infant daughters. His bulk left barely enough room for the slight form of Charlie to squeeze in beside him, their dark heads dipped in concentration over the book in his hands.

As though sensing Gracie's arrival, he glanced up. His gaze clashed with hers, and his widened eyes held a desperate appeal for help. Okay, his confidence wobbled here and there, but that only made his efforts more admirable. Her insides went mushy on a soft wave of sympathy, and her depression deepened. For crying out loud, going soft over his vulnerability with the twins would shoot her straight toward that disastrous leap if she wasn't careful.

She heaved a relieved sigh when Charlie flipped back a page and spoke, regaining his attention.

"You skipped a part. See?"

He looked away, down at the book.

Charlie tapped her finger to the page. "Right here. The princess smiled and her dragon scales shimmered with happiness." She twisted her neck to grin up at him. "The princess has a secret. She's a dragon lady, but the prince doesn't know it yet."

He tucked his chin to his chest, staring at her. "How do you know what it says?"

Angel looked up from her coloring book. Rolling onto her side, she sneered across the room. "She's in the first grade. She knows how to read." She flopped back to her stomach, grumbling, "Even a dummy knows that."

Charlie's eyes bugged wide. She peeked at Jake before shooting a warning frown at her sister.

"Angel!" Gracie stepped through the doorway, as concerned at the heated animosity in Angel's eyes as she was surprised to see color spread on Jake's high cheekbones. "Apologize to Jake, young lady."

"I don't need an apology."

"She needs to offer one." She stiffened and turned. Her intent gaze locked on his, silently demanding he not contradict her. After a moment, he dipped his head in a slight nod. The breath she'd been holding came out in a sigh. She turned to Angel. "Sarah and Pete taught you better than to speak to *anyone* like that."

Angel paled at the mention of her parents. Gracie flinched at the tears popping into her niece's eyes before she ducked her head once more. Wanting nothing more than to race over the wide plank floor and wipe the starkness from Angel's eyes, Gracie remained where she was. Enough was enough. They had to find a way to live together civilly.

"Angel?" She prompted softly.

"I'm sorry," Angel muttered without looking up. She pretended to color, though the crayon in her hand never touched the page.

Gracie cleared her throat. "If you don't mind, Jake, the girls need baths before they go to bed."

Beside a watchful Jake, Charlie's lips puckered in a stubborn pout. "But we didn't have our snack yet."

"Okay, you can go downstairs, but don't be too long. Fifteen minutes, tops."

"How many *Spongebobs* is fifteen minutes?"

Jake's brow wrinkled comically, and Gracie squelched a smile. He had a lot to learn, including the intricacies of a six year old's time clock. "Fifteen minutes is half of one *SpongeBob*."

Charlie nodded and bolted from the chair to race toward the door.

"Maybe Jake wants a snack," Gracie called after her.

Charlie's sneakers squeaked on the hardwood when she skidded to a stop and spun around. "Do you want a snack, Jake?"

Gracie lifted a brow at him, hoping he'd take the hint and give her some time with Angel, who pretended to ignore them all.

He closed the book and stood. "What kind of snack?"

Charlie fiddled with the hem of her sweatshirt. She shot a glance at Angel and a worried crease marred her brow. Her nose wrinkled in distaste. "Miss Mary likes us to have fruit, but Angel and I prefer ice cream."

He cleared his throat. From the way his lips twitched, he was fighting a smile. "I prefer ice cream, too. It's my favorite." He winked. "Especially when you add a few chocolate chip cookies."

Charlie beamed a smile and rushed forward to grab his hand. She blinked up at Gracie. "Can Angel have a snack, too?"

"I'll see to Angel. You go on and have yours."

"She didn't mean to be bad."

Gracie's heart squeezed at the worry in her eyes. She ruffled her hair. "I know she didn't."

Charlie nodded. Satisfied her twin would be okay, she tugged at Jake's hand.

Regret flickered in the glance he sent in Angel's direction, and butterflies fluttered in Gracie's stomach. He might claim to know nothing about little girls, but he wasn't a complete novice at understanding human nature. Or maybe *feminine* nature was what he understood. He let Charlie lead him from the room. Murphy bounded from the bed to trot after them.

Their footfalls quieted as they descended the stairs. Sighing, Gracie crossed the room and eased down to lie next to Angel. The crayon suddenly skidded across the page of her coloring book, leaving a streak of blue behind.

Gracie bumped Angel's shoulder with hers. "So, you mad at me?"

Inky curls danced when Angel shook her head.

"But you *are* mad at Jake?"

Tiny shoulders shrugged and, though she kept her face averted, there was no hiding the teardrop splashing onto the page. Gracie's eyes stung. She wrapped an arm around Angel's shoulders and tucked her tight.

Crayon abandoned, Angel turned and burrowed closer, darting her skinny arms around Gracie's neck. She held on as if her world were spinning out of control. Her small body jerked once, twice, and the dam broke. Wrenching sobs wracked her tiny frame, reminding Gracie of the days and weeks after she lost her own mother.

Sarah had been there to soothe the worst of *her* fears, all those years ago. Life had come full circle. Losing her own battle with tears, Gracie tightened her arms around her sister's daughter and held on.

Angel's storm raged for long minutes, her small body bucking in time to her pitiful sobs. When she eventually quieted to an occasional hiccup, Gracie pulled back to brush the damp curls from her cheeks.

Crystal blue orbs, still shiny with tears, met Gracie's watchful gaze. "I'm sorry I was mean to him."

"I know you are, baby."

Silence stretched out. "Miss Mary says people won't like you if you're mean."

"Miss Mary is right."

Bright white baby teeth worried at Angel's lower lip. "Do you think he'll like me now, even though I was mean?"

"Well," she pretended to consider the question. "I don't know Jake well, but he seems excited to be here."

Angel nodded in hopeful agreement.

"Maybe if you apologized again? For real, this time. If he knows you mean it…"

Angel seemed to consider the possibility and her brow furrowed on a slight frown. "He likes Charlie better."

She fought back a smile. "Because Charlie talks to him. You've been awfully quiet since he got here, don't you think? He's your brother, Angel. Give him a chance. Once he gets to know you, he'll like you as much as your sister."

Angel dropped her gaze and picked at a thread on the quilt. "My belly hurts when he talks."

"Oh, baby, why?"

"He sounds like Daddy."

Oh. Well, crap. The cadence of Jake's speech *was* similar to her brother-in-law's and, to a six-year-old's ears, Jake's Texas twang would resemble the southern accent Pete carried from childhood.

She brushed at the fringe of Angel's dark bangs. "He does sound like your daddy, doesn't he?"

Angel twirled the thread around her fingertip before glancing up. "Mommy died, and Daddy did, too. What if you die?"

"Oh, baby." She pushed up on her forearms to stare into Angel's tortured eyes. "I'm not going to die."

Fresh tears popped, magnifying Angel's crystal blue irises. Gracie hugged her close and rolled her eyes heavenward. How did one ease the fears of a child who'd already known too much loss? She rubbed a soothing hand up and down her back.

"Did you know my mother died when I was a little girl?"

Angel pulled away slightly to stare at her. "Really?"

"Really. I was fourteen. Not as young as you and Charlie, but still young. I had no daddy either. Only Sarah. We had each other. Your mommy took care of me."

Desperate curiosity flooded Angel's eyes as she blinked owlishly. "She did?"

"Yes, she did. When Momma died, Sarah made me a promise. She said she'd always be there to take care of me, and she was. She kept me safe, even though she was barely more than a girl herself, and I'll be here to make sure you and Charlie are safe."

"You promise?"

Gracie nodded.

Baby teeth flashed in Angel's trusting smile. "Pinky promise?"

Laughter bubbled up from her chest, and she held out her pinky finger. Angel scrambled to sit. Though her nose was red and her eyes puffy from crying, relief brightened her eyes as she linked fingers with Gracie. "Do you think Charlie and Jake ate all the ice cream?"

"I don't know." Gracie cocked her head. "You know how Charlie loves ice cream, and Jake is awfully big."

Angel nodded solemnly and proved she hadn't missed a detail at dinner, despite her seeming disinterest. "He ate four pieces of chicken and two piles of mashed potatoes. He can eat a lot, and he said ice cream is his favorite, too."

"Then we'd better get down there before it's gone."

Angel jackknifed off the bed, sprinting for the door. "Last one to the kitchen is a rotten egg."

Chapter 12

Gracie tapped at her keyboard. Greeting the minions, she smiled at their universal acceptance of Jake's apology. If nothing else, their blog battle was something she no longer had to worry about. That left plenty of other troubles to gnaw on, however. Like the continued interest from the press and how she was going to survive the rest of the custody stipulation time frame with Jake underfoot.

Beyond his professional football connections threatening to expose her parental secret, there was his reputation with women to consider. She shouldn't be surprised by his flirtatious behavior. After all, the man was photographed with a different woman every week, but his flirting had to stop or she was doomed. Jake Malone slaughtered her willpower.

She didn't know a lot of men. Other than Max, she couldn't think of anyone she could try and pass off as a boyfriend, except maybe Stan. Not a chance in hell. Of course, she could always claim she was gay, but considering the way she'd kissed Jake back, he wouldn't buy it. No. He was a pro. A competitor. Offense was the best defense against his kind. Some hard and fast ground rules were necessary and she'd need to make them crystal clear. Anything even remotely resembling flirting would be out of bounds, and there could be absolutely no more kissing!

Confident she had a plan, of sorts, if not of her ability to get him to follow it, she put the finishing touches on tomorrow's Gridiron Girl blog with her predictions for this week's match-ups. She jumped when the grandfather clock in the hall bonged the half hour then chuckled at her jumpiness, until the tiny hairs on her arms stood on end. Swallowing and stifling a shiver, she could swear the air actually shifted.

She looked up. Sure enough, Jake stood framed by the archway to the foyer. A tattered T-shirt hugged his broad shoulders and chest and faded jeans rode low on his hips. She dropped her gaze to her laptop, trying to slow her accelerating heartbeat as he crossed the room.

He slumped onto the couch beside her, propping his large bare feet on the coffee table then jerked his chin at her laptop. "Am I interrupting?"

"Ah, no." She backed out of several open windows. "I was…finishing up a few things."

"Feeding the football chicks?" His eyes sparkled with humor.

She lifted her chin. "Those chicks are intelligent women who happen to enjoy discussing football."

He grinned. "Among other things."

Instant heat flared on her cheeks. Discussions about certain players occasionally slid toward suggestive on her blog. Okay, raunchy, but the minions were true fans who loved the game. Figures Jake would narrow in on the ladies' more personal observations. Unable to mount a solid defense, she flattened her lips in a reproachful line.

He chuckled. "They do seem to understand the sport. For the most part, anyway. As do you."

She blinked at the unexpected compliment and the heat of her blush deepened. She cleared her throat. "Thank you."

He grunted and cast a glance toward the foyer and the stairs. "Are they asleep?"

"They were out before I reached the end of the first chapter."

He dropped his head against the back of the couch and rolled his neck to meet her gaze. "*SpongeBob?*"

Some of her tension eased with her grin. "*SpongeBob* is the oracle of six year old understanding. You'll catch on in time."

He shoved the fingers of both hands through his overlong hair, still damp from a recent shower. Uneasy with the idea of assisting at bath time, once they'd finished their snacks, Jake had wished the girls good night and escaped to the master suite, leaving the chore to her. She hadn't expected to see him again tonight, but since he was here…No time like the present to lay out those rules.

He sighed. "Thanks for earlier. I don't know what you said to Angel, but it made a difference. Though, I don't think I'm completely off the hook yet."

She couldn't help but agree. Upon arriving in the kitchen, Angel had offered him a stilted apology and, although she didn't attempt to join the conversation over bowls of ice cream and cookies, at least she quit scowling at him. That was, until he accidently dropped several spoons as he carried them to the sink. Whatever ground Gracie had gained him with Angel was lost with his colorful curse.

At Angel's insistence, a used pickle jar now sat in a prominent position on the counter, doing duty as *Jake's swear jar.*

She grinned. "I tried to warn you about your language."

"You didn't tell me the consequences would be financial. Twenty bucks!" He snorted. "Those two are miniature extortionists. Doug Costa could use them in the league's front office."

Oh, shit. Dangerous subject. She covered the tightening of her muscles with a stiff smile and shoved the conversation away from the pro football. "She's scared and confused. Despite evidence to the contrary, she's not usually such a brat."

"I figured as much." He sighed. "If she's half as nervous as I am, it's a wonder she spoke to me at all."

Surprised at the admission, she turned on the couch, tucking one leg under the other. "I wouldn't think anything could make the Outlaw nervous."

He narrowed his eyes at the nickname, but there was humor sparkling in them. "Yeah, well, you know us semi-famous *soccer* players. We're sensitive guys."

She snickered, pleased by the evidence her earlier attempt at insulting him had hit its mark.

He smiled. "If they didn't look so much alike, it'd be difficult to tell they're twins."

A sigh accompanied her nod. "In some ways they're very different. Charlie's always been easier with new people, but then, Angel is the first born. Think of her as the Alpha twin. She considers it her duty to protect them both."

"That's a heavy burden for a six year old."

"Yeah." She chewed on her lip. Personal ground rules aside, they were in this together, whether she liked it or not, at least for now. Best he know what he was dealing with. "She says her belly hurts when you talk because you sound like Pete."

"Well, damn." He stared at her in silence for a long moment. His head suddenly came away from the couch back. "Wait. Do I?"

"A little."

He scowled.

She grinned but sobered quickly. "And she's worried I might die, like her parents."

His scowl slid into a wince. "Ah, shit. She said that?"

She dipped her chin in a subtle nod. "She also thinks you don't like her."

"Great." He dropped his head back again and dragged a wide palm over his face with a heavy sigh. "I don't have a fu—" He cleared his throat. "Sorry. I don't have a clue what I'm doing here."

His insecurity over the situation struck a chord of empathy in her heart. She stiffened her spine against going all mushy but offered him an encouraging smile. "Relax, Jake. You're doing fine. You're getting to know the girls, like Pete wanted."

Air blew from his nose in a sharp snort. "Pete Thompson never did anything without an ulterior motive. I can't figure out what he was after is in this case."

There he went again, describing a man she couldn't equate with her sister's loving husband and the twins' father. From what Anthony Spinoza said about Pete wanting to make amends, she supposed there were reasons for Jake's poor opinion of his father. Still… "I'm having a hard time picturing Pete the way you describe him."

"You mean as an arrogant asshole?"

She blinked at the heat of his question. He turned this time, pulling up his closest leg until his knee was an inch away from brushing her thigh. The healthy muscles beneath his T-shirt shifted along with the arm he rested on the back of the couch. She shot a wary glance at his hand, dangling far too close to her shoulder for comfort. As casually as she could manage, she inched away from him.

Like the predator he was, he narrowed his eyes at her subtle movement. She jerked when he lifted his hand but, instead of brushing his fingers over her shoulder, he brought them to his chin and stroked at the sharp edge of his bristled jaw. Pure mischief sparkled in his eyes.

"I'm starting to believe you don't trust me, Gracie."

Well, hello! She exaggerated the batting of her lashes. "And they say jocks aren't perceptive."

The warmth of his laughter washed over her, prickling the fine hairs on her arms and beading her nipples. *Willpower, Gracie.* She hoped her smirk covered the sudden hammering of her heartbeat. "The Pete you describe doesn't sound like the man I knew."

"Then we're even. Married with a couple of kids doesn't sound like the Pete Thompson *I* knew."

"You knew him well?"

"I didn't know him at all, actually. We only met once."

Her brows flew up in surprise and her mouth dropped open. She snapped it shut. "Once?" Wow! He'd met his father exactly one time more than she'd met hers. Their family situations took a big step closer to *holy crap* similar.

"Once was one time too many as far as I'm concerned." His complaint was little more than an angry growl.

"I'm sorry. I shouldn't have asked. It's none of my business."

He shook his head. "Don't apologize. Considering we're stuck here together, thanks to Pete, you have a right to understand why I'm reluctant to comply with his demands."

"*Are* you still? Because you certainly didn't seem reluctant at dinner." The accusation flew from her mouth without her thinking. She squeezed her eyes shut. "Forget I said that. God, that was rude."

"Not rude. It's a legitimate question. You deserve an answer." He sighed and stared at the ceiling. "It pisses me off to be here in his house, but you're right. The twins are innocent in all of this. I'd be as big a bastard as Pete if I let my feelings for him spill over onto them."

She was well acquainted with the various emotions surrounding a father one had never met, but the abhorrence in his tone spoke of more than bitterness over Pete's absence. "If you don't mind my asking, why do you hate him so?"

"Because he was an arrogant prick who looked down on anyone who couldn't live up to his family's wealth. He knocked up my mother and walked away without a backward glance. When she tracked him down after I was born, he sent a team of lawyers to the ranch where she'd found work." He dropped his gaze to hers. Loathing heated his eyes. "They offered her five thousand dollars and a warning. If she contacted him again, he'd destroy her. He had the wealth and the powerful contacts to do it, and she backed down. We never heard from him again. Correction. *She* never heard from him again. Years of boozing eventually destroyed her liver. She'd drunk herself to death by the time he contacted me."

Gracie had no idea what to say. If what he said was true, she couldn't blame him for his bitterness, but how could this be? In the too-short-years Sarah had with him, her brother-in-law treated her sister like a queen, and he doted on the twins. How could the caring man she'd known have walked away from his own son?

"I don't..." She bit her lip. "Oh, Jake, if what you say is true..." She shrugged helplessly. "I don't understand."

"What's not to understand? He was the golden boy heir to the Thompson fortune and Mom was a waitress from west Texas. End of story."

She blinked. "You think he turned his back on your mother and you because of the differences in their financial situations?"

A sardonic lift of one brow was his only response.

"He didn't look down on my sister, and she certainly didn't measure up to the Thompson wealth. In fact, *she* was a waitress when he met her."

Disbelief narrowed his eyes. "Right."

"It's true. She worked the lunch counter, serving sandwiches and soup, and sloshed beer and ale at the local pub in the evenings."

He sat back. "Sorry, but that sounds like a load of bullshit."

She stiffened. "Excuse me?"

"No offense, princess, but Pete only had one use for the type of woman you're describing, and it wasn't *wife*. Besides, why would a debutante hold down two jobs?"

"Debutante? Sarah?" She laughed. "Oh, she'd have loved that. For your information, she held down two jobs to feed and clothe us because she had an aversion to our living on the street."

"*She* fed and clothed you? What about your family?"

Adrenaline rushed through her and she became slightly lightheaded. A discussion of her *family* was the last place she wanted to go, but refusing to answer would only make him curious. She spoke carefully and shrugged as if she wasn't wading her way through a verbal minefield. "My sister *was* my family. Mom died of respiratory failure after contracting viral pneumonia when Sarah was eighteen."

"How old were you?"

"Fourteen."

She held her breath, waiting for him to ask about her father.

He tugged at his earlobe and studied her face. "You're serious?"

"Of course, I'm serious."

"And Max?"

Relief flooded her. "He lived in the apartment across the hall."

"What about your father?"

Shit. Relief plunged into instant panic.

His head whipped around toward the foyer before she could formulate an answer. Murphy's tags jangled as he loped across the room toward them. She quickly controlled the giddy smile threatening to split her face as the dog leapt onto the couch between them. Jake immediately crossed his legs. Helpless, she laughed at the defensive movement.

Ignoring her, Murphy paid homage to his new best friend, forgoing Jake's face to lick his hand when Jake straight-armed him.

"He likes you." Not a hint of the hysteria squeezing her throat sounded in her voice.

"From what I've seen, he likes everyone. Almost as much as he likes ramming his head into a guy's balls."

He grunted, but silent laughter brightened his eyes. Her fascination bloomed as his already-broad chest expanded on a cleansing breath. This wasn't the first time she'd witnessed him shedding dark emotions for lighter ones. How did he pull it off with such casual ease? She wished she could figure out his secret. What a great trick to *not* be a prisoner to her moods.

He thumped Murphy's side roughly then shoved him in her direction. The dog attempted to climb onto her lap the way he had thirty-five pounds ago.

She grinned and held him off, scrubbing his head. "He's a good boy, and we're working on the head butting thing. Aren't we, Murph?"

He leaned into her hand with a doggy groan.

"Besides, he's good with the girls. They need his kind of unconditional love right now."

Jake shook his head. "No wonder you're good with the twins. You've been in their shoes."

The way he swung from complaint to compliment made her head spin, as did the dimple popping in his smile.

"I don't get it," Jake said.

"What?" She chewed her bottom lip and nudged Murphy off the couch. He trotted off, toward the kitchen, no doubt.

Jake coughed on a self-deprecating laugh. "I'm not sure what the problem is, but, for some reason, I keep jumping to the wrong conclusions about you."

She instantly relaxed, curving her lips in a taunting smile. "Too many hits to the head?"

The low timber of his laugh caressed her skin like stroking fingers.

"See, that's what I mean. You're a mass of contradictions. You come across as a cool princess until you open that smart ass mouth."

She shifted her shoulders in a casual shrug and smirked. "What conclusion did you jump to?"

"I had you pegged as a spoiled little rich girl."

"I wish!" She grinned, delighted at the image. "Wait. Why would you think that?"

He glanced purposefully at her feet. Today's supple boots were knee-length leather dreams. "Princess, the contents of your shoe closet would break the budgets of a lot of third world countries."

Was he kidding? She chortled a laugh. "You based your opinion of me on my footwear?"

The mischievous sparkle returned to his eyes. He sat forward, leaning his upper body toward her. "I'm a leg man, remember? And the way you keep chewing on your lip reminds me how much I'd like to nibble on your lips, right next to that sexy little mole at the corner of your mouth."

Warning sirens pealed. She slapped a hand against his chest and ignored his reference to her mouth for a safer subject. "They're knockoffs, and since you brought it up, we need to talk about this flirting habit of yours."

He closed the distance marginally, despite her stiff arm. "I'd rather talk about that mole, *or* your legs."

She shoved, hard. He fell back, a grin curving his lips.

"I mean it."

"Me, too. You've got incredible legs."

Her glare made him laugh. She shifted, preparing to stand. He held up both hands in surrender. "Fine. Talk away, but don't blame me if I have a hard time concentrating." His grin twisted sensually. "Because, damn, princess, you're awfully pretty when you're mad."

She scooted as far away from him as she could get. "That kind of comment is exactly what I'm talking about. You have to stop."

"Why? I'm only speaking the truth."

"Because there are two little girls upstairs whose lives are already complicated enough. They need a stable environment. Since, as you say, we're stuck here together for the next three months, we need to set some ground rules and it would be best if we could be friends."

"I agree."

She blew out a breath. "Good."

"And I don't see the problem with telling my *friend* she has great legs."

"The problem *is*, that's flirting. Friends don't flirt."

"Of course they do, if they're of the opposite sex."

"Mine don't."

"Then you need new friends."

Was he being purposefully obtuse? She pushed to her feet. "Forget it. I'm wasting my time talking to you."

He laughed and rose beside her. "Damn, you're prickly."

She pivoted to step by him.

He stopped her with a hand to her arm. "I get what you're saying. I don't happen to agree."

She tugged her arm free. "Then we're going to have to agree to disagree, because this is non-negotiable."

"If this is about that kiss…"

"Of course this is about that kiss. I was trying to make a point, and you…and then…"

If his spreading grin was an indication, he found her stilted stammer highly entertaining.

She straightened her shoulders. "It *cannot* happen again."

He crossed his arms, all cocky, sexy male, well pleased with himself. "I consider that a damn shame."

"Yeah, well. Like I said. Non-negotiable."

"You're a heartless woman." He sighed and his downturned lips resembled those of a pouting little boy. "I'm stuck in the middle of nowhere with a heartless woman, and you say no kissing? Heartless."

One by one, his flirtatious comments over the past few days echoed in her head and, like the tumblers of a lock clicking into place, his behavior suddenly made excruciating sense.

"Wow." She shook her head and coughed out a mirthless laugh. "I'm *so* glad I'm not a guy. It must suck to have your every thought driven by your penis."

Dimples popped in his unapologetic grin, and he cocked his head, dipping his knees to meet her gaze more directly. The hot deviltry in his smiling eyes threatened to melt her on the spot.

"True, but every now and then, my penis has an especially good idea. Like kissing you."

Oh, dear Lord. How was she supposed to argue with a man who used seduction as a weapon, instead of arguing back?

She lifted her chin and did her best to appear unaffected by his sneaky charm. "I'm not your personal toy, here to keep you from being bored."

Bull's-eye. His grin fizzled beneath a guilty frown.

"Cheer up, Jake. The will didn't say anything about not having people over. I'm sure you can find any number of women on your long list of *friends* who'll be willing to help keep you entertained." She flounced off toward the foyer. "Just keep your play dates away from the twins."

"Princess…."

She hated ruining a perfect exit but couldn't resist. She paused to glance over her shoulder. He stared at her boots.

"Are those really fakes?"

"Of course they're fakes. How else could I feed a high-end shoe fetish on a low-end budget? These things would be six hundred dollars if they were the real thing."

He sucked air through his teeth and tucked his hands into his front pockets. "A shoe fetish, huh? Man, that's sexy."

"Oh. My. God. You have a one-track mind."

He started toward her, and she hoped the lapels of her blouse weren't pulsing under the sudden pounding of her heart. She tucked her laptop to her chest like a shield. Maybe the radiation waves would act like some kind of weird counteract to her overheated blood.

He drew close, and she held out a hand to ward him off. "Don't get any ideas."

"Too late." His secret weapon dimples popped, but he came to a stop several feet away.

She swallowed. Turning around and running was out. Considering what he did for a living, he'd probably tackle her. *Hmmm.* A vivid picture of the two of them entwined on the throw rug bloomed in her head. She tucked the laptop closer. Un-uh, running was a bad idea. No choice but to brazen it out. She narrowed her eyes. "Why did you come downstairs, anyway? I thought you'd gone to sleep."

He dipped his brows in a dangerous tilt. "Coward."

Her blood went hot. She bared her teeth in tight a smile and refused to acknowledge the truth of his remark.

He shook his head and laughed. "Actually, I came looking for you. Funny, you mentioned having friends over. It's my turn to host our monthly poker game. Nothing special, just a couple of guys from the team."

Monthly poker game with his teammates? Here?

"Monday night. Don't worry. We'll keep it down, and they won't arrive until after the girls have gone to bed."

Shit. Shit. Shit!

"I also wanted to remind you I'll be leaving for Tampa in the morning."

"Oh." *That* bit of news cooled her blood, and her building panic over a house full of players receded behind an odd disappointment.

Gracie! Pay attention! He's leaving town. A few Jake-free days is a good *thing!*

"I'd like to drive the girls to school before I leave. I'll be gone until late Sunday night and, with things the way they are with Angel, I thought…" He jerked a shoulder in a stilted shrug.

"Oh."

"If you don't think it's a good idea…."

"No." Her heart sank. Bad enough he could sizzle her insides with a look. Did he have to be a nice guy, too?

I am so screwed. She sighed. "I think it's a sweet idea. The girls will love it."

He dipped his head. "All right, then. I'll see you in the morning?"

"I've got an early appointment."

"Need a ride?" His teasing grin touched her in places she didn't want to think of at the moment.

She rolled her eyes, recalling their one wild ride. "Not on your life. Anyway, I'll be gone before six."

"Then I'll see you when I get back."

She nodded, turned, and headed for the stairs.

"Oh, and Gracie, about that shoe fetish—"

She glanced over her shoulder. "Jake—"

He grinned. "You might want to pick up some knockoff snow boots. There's another storm moving in."

Chapter 13

As Jake predicted, a cold front moved in two hours after the Marauders' plane took off for Tampa the next morning. Howling winds and plunging temperatures made for a dreary Saturday. The fast-moving storm swirled through the northeast, leaving behind six inches of fresh snow. Anxious to break in their new snowsuits, the twins greeted Gracie bright and early Sunday morning, dragging her down to breakfast before the sun cleared the treetops.

Snow angels, tobogganing, and girlish giggles were the order of the day. Gracie wouldn't need a workout for days after schlepping the toboggan repeatedly to the top of the rise behind the barn, only to sail down again. Murphy joined them for their chilly, three-hour romp, bounding alongside the sled and nipping at hats, mittens or flapping scarves.

Pleading exhaustion, Gracie convinced the girls to take a break in time for the kickoff in Tampa. Not that she'd planned her day around watching Jake on the field. There were *numerous* teams she followed on a weekly basis, including the Marauders. Her interest in the weekly matchups was business. She had a blog to write. The minions would expect a complete report.

The rationalization poked at her as she gathered the makings of a game time snack. Ignoring the prick of guilt, she carried a tray of sandwiches into the den. Never interested in football before, the girls now had a vested interest in the game. They insisted on experiencing today's broadcast from the beginning. The pregame analysis didn't impress either of them, but the young pop star, belting out the national anthem on the large flat screen TV, perked their interest considerably. Strutting their stuff on the coffee table like miniature divas, they sang along, with the help of the remote control and a hairbrush as make-do microphones.

Charlie squealed, dancing with excitement when the camera zoomed in on Jake. Helmet tucked under one arm, he paced the sideline like a caged animal as the commentators tore apart his stats and placed odds on his breaking the touchdown record anytime soon. Angel opened her coloring book and pretended disinterest, but her gaze repeatedly returned to the set. Gracie kept her hands busy making up plates of snacks for the girls. Between sips of hot chocolate and bites of sandwich, they peppered her with questions.

Why did Jake have black stuff under his eyes? Did she think Jake would bring them to meet the cheerleaders? How far away is Tampa?

When the teams took the field, Angel proclaimed Tampa's red uniforms far prettier than the Marauders' blue and gold. During halftime, they huddled at the coffee table. Angel leaned on her elbows, making suggestions as Charlie sketched alternate uniform designs with her crayons. They planned to present their favorite, a dazzling, sparkly purple with pink stripes, to Jake upon his return.

Gracie bit her lip to stifle a laugh at the image her mind provided then jumped to her feet when Jake snatched the ball out of the air a split second before two red uniforms slammed him to the ground on the one-yard line. The girls cheered with delight and copied Jake's end zone spike celebration when he added his tenth and, later, his eleventh touchdowns of the season to his stats, bringing him within seven of the record.

Larger than life, and twice as handsome, his familiar face and form filled the screen during a brief, post-game interview. Sweaty and exuberant over the win, he repeated the usual platitudes about how it was a team game and sure, the record would be nice but a check in the win column was the ultimate goal. He winked into the camera, and Gracie's heart quivered in her chest.

Good Lord. Even from one thousand miles away, he managed to flirt effectively. She grimaced. Technically, his flirting was in her imagination in this case, but geez. His dimpled smile and gleaming eyes stared through the screen as if aimed directly at her and did a number on her system.

Not good. Not good at all.

Hours later, she crawled into bed with a heavy heart and didn't fall asleep until long after he arrived at the farm a few minutes before midnight. Neither her ground rules nor the unflattering motive for his heavy-duty flirting made a bit of difference. She pounded at her pillow. If she were going to survive the next three months without doing something stupid, like sneaking into his bedroom down the hall, she'd need to employ some tougher tactics. To prop up her flagging willpower, some good, old-fashioned avoidance was in order.

She was up and gone before he woke the next morning. After meeting with several clients, she parked her butt at the library to do some research and kill time. She wouldn't take the chance of missing curfew, but she'd shave it as close as she could. A sandwich at her favorite deli passed for dinner. Guilt at neglecting the girls for an entire day gnawed, but this was about self-preservation. She planned to spend as little time as possible with her sexy housemate. Especially tonight, with his poker buddies descending on the farm.

Darkness had long since arrived before she boarded the train to Long Island. When the cab from the station finally bumped down the driveway, she hoped to slip into the house, peek in on the girls, who should already be asleep, and then lock herself in her bedroom.

The gremlins had other ideas.

Headlights from a strange car blinded her as she climbed from the cab. At the foot of the porch steps, she shielded her eyes from the glare and bit her lip in dismay. Three large, obviously male forms slid from the big SUV.

Shit. The poker jocks have arrived.

She considered making a run for it, but this was her home, at least for the next three months. She'd be damned if she'd run.

"Looks like our evening just got a lot more interesting, boys. *Hello*, beautiful."

She lifted her chin. Geez, was Flirting 101 a required course at training camp? Snow crunched beneath large feet as two of the Marauders' offensive tackles, Mario Davis and Jamal Knight, stepped into the light of the porch lamp along with Kevin Tucker, the team's top wide receiver.

God help her, she couldn't help but gape. Like a warrior delegation to the United Nations, a third of the Marauders' offensive line stood before her, representing the African American, Latino, and Nordic factions. Talk about eye candy. These three would sell out the house in a sports version of a Chippendales Review. The female in her sighed in appreciation. The football junkie danced a silent, manic jig. How many fans got the opportunity to meet not one, but three all pros? The minions would lose their minds.

She shook her head. Though her father was long since retired from the field, he still held a prominent position in the sport. If not exactly peers, these men stood at his side in an elite brotherhood. Spending any amount of time with them was out of the question. "You're here to see Jake, I assume."

Kevin Tucker moved closer, a wide smile creasing his tough-guy face. "Jake? Jake who? I'm here to see you, sweetheart." Behind him, Mario and Jamal snickered.

"Uh-huh." She turned her back and climbed the steps. "If you're coming in, come on. I'll let Jake know you're here."

"Blocked at the line of scrimmage, Tuck." Male laughter echoed in the night.

Tuck grinned and bounded up the steps, taking them two at a time. "I've got a couple more downs."

She opened the door and glanced over her shoulder. "No, you don't."

"Sweetheart, you don't understand the rules of the game. Have dinner with me. I'll explain them to you."

She bared her teeth in a smile. "Oh, you'd be surprised what I understand. Let me put this a way *you'll* understand. Consider yourself benched."

Mario and Jamal howled and joined them on the porch.

Tuck shook his head, but confident humor made his blue eyes sparkle. "That's cold, sweetheart."

She laughed as she stepped inside—and slammed into a solid wall of chest. Strong arms came around her shoulders and a woodsy spice scent caressed her senses. She immediately shoved free, or tried to. Jake tightened his hold, keeping her where she was with her cheek and nose pressed against his throat.

"Looks like Jake already has the ball, Tuck."

Her mouth dropped open, and she turned her head to scowl at Jamal. His dark eyes twinkled with mirth as he jabbed Tuck in the ribs with an elbow. A chuckle vibrated beneath her cheek as Jake tucked her even closer.

As if he'd been in on the ridiculous conversation from the beginning, he didn't miss a beat. "Intercepted and already on the scoreboard."

Strong arms and woodsy spice cologne aside, she stiffened in his arms. Her sex-on-heels boots were as practical as they were pretty. She stomped a heel down on his instep.

"Ouch!" The cage of his arms opened immediately, and she jerked free. He sucked a pained hiss through his teeth. "Damn it. That hurt."

She shrugged her shoulder, adjusting the strap of her laptop bag. "And your point is?"

"Fumble!" A sly smile creased Tuck's face.

Mario and Jamal hooted with laughter. Jake didn't join them. His brows formed a disgruntled line as he lifted his foot to dip his fingers inside his loafer and rub. The action only increased the poker jocks' amusement.

She rolled her eyes. "I'm going to bed. Keep the noise down or you'll wake the girls."

"Girls?" Mario pinned Jake with a questioning gaze.

"Bed?" Tuck drew out the word, his eyes glittering.

Jake dropped his foot to the floor. Discomfort wrinkled his brow, but from the damage caused by her heel or because of his friends' nosey demands, she wasn't sure. Come to think of it, how *had* he explained his presence at the farm? Did his friends know about the stipulations in Pete's will? From the expectant curiosity on their faces, the answer was no. She delayed her departure, interested in hearing Jake's account of the situation.

He cleared his throat and shot her a narrow-eyed scowl.

She scowled right back. "Don't look at me like that. I didn't want you here in the first place. *You* chose to accept Pete's demands."

"Like I had any choice, thanks to you and your minions."

Me and my minions? Like a crisp winter sunrise, comprehension dawned cold and clear. He wasn't at the farm for the money *or* the twins. He was here because their blog exchange threatened his image, which in turn, would threaten his career. *Why you dirty diva!*

Determined fury bubbled. There must be a way to get him to break the custody rules, because she'd be damned if she'd lose the girls to such a self-centered…jock. She jammed her fists to her hips. "Me? I'm just a homely blogger who wouldn't know incidental contact if it bit me on the ass, remember?"

He winced, but his scowl darkened. "I apologized for that."

"Wait a minute." With raised brows and disbelieving eyes, Tuck raked her from head to feet before snapping his gaze to Jake. "*She's* the blogger bitch?"

"Hey! Watch it, buster."

A flush colored his cheeks, and he cleared his throat. "Sorry. *Lady* football blogger who got you fined?"

"In the flesh," Jake grumbled.

"Ho-ly shit." Mario's eyes went wide.

Jamal shook his head as if to clear it.

"And you're *sleeping* with her?" Tuck's disbelief disappeared behind a full-fledged grin. "Shit, buddy. That's fucked up. But I like your style."

Jake's lips curved in a wolfish smile.

She gasped. "He is *not* sleeping with me." She pointed a finger at Tuck. "And I'm not sleeping with him. I'm not sleeping with anyone."

Tuck dipped his head closer to hers and dropped his voice into a rumbling purr. "Would you *like* to be?"

She leaned away from him, even as her cheeks heated. "Oh, for heaven's sake. You're all insane."

Male laughter filled the foyer, not quite drowning out the click of nails and a jangling collar. Murphy burst from the hallway.

Jake whipped his head around. "Oh, shit."

He had no time to say anything else, and she wasn't about to sound a warning. The poker jocks were on their own.

Shooting forward like a canine bullet, Murphy's body wriggled with excitement. He avoided Jake's outstretched hand, racing by on dancing feet. Slamming on the brakes, the dog slid to a stop at Tuck's feet, dipped his head and...*pow*!

The tough guy wide receiver from the mean streets of South Boston went down like a stone to a chorus of male groans.

Chapter 14

Jake had no trouble empathizing with Tuck's pain. Bent at the waist with his hands on his knees, his normally congenial friend clutched a bag of frozen peas in one fist and scowled at the staircase where Gracie and her dog had disappeared. He groaned suddenly and hunched farther, his eyes sliding shut.

Jake winced. Gracie's dog might be a menace, but he owed the exuberant mutt a T-bone for the timely interruption.

What had he been thinking, wrapping Gracie in his arms in a blatant claim of ownership? He should've ignored the quick stab of jealousy at the smile in her eyes for his friends. No, not jealousy. He didn't *get* jealous of women. His uncomfortable reaction was a natural byproduct of his competitive nature, plain and simple, but his life was a cluster fuck at the moment. As much as he enjoyed pitting his seductive skills against Tuck's, the next round of chick tug of war would have to wait for some other time. Some other woman. He had too much on his plate to enjoy the exercise right now.

From what he'd heard of the conversation on the porch before they filed inside, Gracie was doing a fine job of slapping down his skirt-chasing friend. He should've left her to it. Though her brush-off would come as a challenge to a hound dog like Tuck, he'd never been known for his patience. Too many women didn't bother running to keep him chasing after one who did for long.

Unfortunately, thanks to Jake's blatant show of possession, he couldn't count on Tuck's interest in Gracie waning anytime soon. From the sly intensity of his smile, he'd zeroed in on the source of that sweet poison he'd mentioned. No doubt Tuck's interest in Gracie had shot straight past natural male attraction into a gleeful obsession to even the score over Daphne.

Damn bad luck Gracie would arrive home at the same time as the guys. He'd expected her home much earlier. Considering the way she was always trying to avoid his company, keeping her a secret should've been a slam dunk. Too late now. The cat was well and truly out of the bag.

He jammed his fingers through his hair. Mario was the biggest blabbermouth on the planet. By this time tomorrow, the entire world would think he was shacked up with the Gridiron Girl. Not that he'd mind, if they were shacked up in truth.

A sharp knock drew his attention. He crossed the foyer to open the door.

V swept inside, bringing the cold air with her. "We need to talk."

"It's poker night. Whatever it is can wait."

She tugged off her red leather gloves. "No, it can't." She bumped up her chin in greeting to his teammates. "Hiya, boys. Where's Gracie, and…." Her sharp brows snapped together as her gaze landed on Tuck. "What's the matter with you?"

Tuck straightened stiffly. His skin held a twinge of green.

Mario chuckled and slapped Tuck on the back, eliciting a painful groan. "The blonde blogger ran upstairs, right after her dog rearranged Tuck's balls."

Jamal's teeth flashed in a vicious smile. "Hey, at least she offered to ice his balls down before she left." He ducked when Tuck whipped the bag of frozen peas at his head.

V laughed. "Murphy got you, too?"

"Too?" Tuck sent Jake an accusing glare.

Jake rolled his shoulders in an apologetic shrug and turned to glower at V. He didn't appreciate her obvious humor any more than he had when she had a good laugh over *his* mishap with Murphy. He shut the door with a thud. "It's not funny, V. That dog is a ball busting menace."

She patted his cheek. "Poor, big football jocks. What would the rest of your teammates say if they knew you'd both been taken down by a puppy?"

"They'd say 'Damn, Jamal, why didn't you get that shit on your phone?'" Jamal laughed, dancing out of reach when Tuck took a swing at him.

"Wait! Did I hear football blogger?" She spun toward Jake. "You told them?"

"I was about to, before the canine ball crusher arrived."

Tuck winced and limped across the foyer to retrieve the package of frozen peas.

V shrugged out of her coat. "Then it's a good thing I got here when I did." With her coat hung over one arm, she pointed a finger at Mario. "Pay attention, big guy, and this goes for the rest of you, too." She glanced around, leveling each of them with a *cross me at your own peril* stare. "None of this leaves here. Not one word. No one is to know where Jake is living *or* that Gracie Gable is the Gridiron Girl. Understood?"

Mario shook his head. "I don't understand *any* of this. I mean, yeah, she's smokin' hot." Tuck's sly sneer and Jamal's nod said they agreed with his assessment. "But hot chicks are a dime a dozen. Why would you move in with one who cost you twenty-five grand?"

Something hot and primal heated Jake's blood. He forcefully relaxed his curled fists, fighting back the desire to rearrange the old bump on Tuck's nose before adding new ones to Mario's and Jamal's. He sucked in a calming breath, shook off the over-the-top reaction, and blamed nerves at having to announce the cluster fuck his life had become.

"I'll explain it all over the cards."

* * * *

The knock on her door made Gracie groan. The twins wouldn't bother knocking. They'd come right in. Apparently, Jake couldn't sleep either, but if he was here to threaten Murphy again, she was going to scream. "Go away."

"Gracie? It's V. Can I talk to you for a few minutes?"

V? The clock on the dresser read eleven fifty. What was Jake's publicist doing here, and what could she possibly have to say that couldn't wait until a decent hour?

Sliding from the bed, Gracie flipped on the lamp and scooped up her jeans. She shucked them up her over her hips as she hopped across the room. Jeans zipped and buttoned, she paused in front of the closed door. She tugged the loose collar of the oversized T-shirt up over her shoulder, plunged her fingers through her hair, fluffing the tangled strands, then grimaced at the attempted grooming.

She dropped her hands to her sides. When an unwanted visitor knocked on your door in the middle of the night, they got what they got. She pivoted her neck and shoulders to loosen the sudden knots and opened the door.

"I'm sorry to disturb you." Decked out in another of her red power suits, with a pair of genuine, to-die-for Jimmy Choo heels to match, V offered her an apologetic smile. Of course, her makeup and hair were perfect as well, despite the hour.

Gracie gritted her teeth and lifted a questioning brow, instead of hissing and slamming the door in the woman's stunning face. "Is something wrong?"

"Yes, I'm afraid there is."

She stiffened. "Look, if it's about Murphy, he's still mostly puppy. We're working on his manners." And if her dog was here where he belonged instead of snoring in bed with Angel, he'd no doubt be showing his lack of manners by pouncing on Jake's perfectly coiffed publicist. An opportunity missed. Rats!

V's laugh tinkled. A light, happy sound. "Oh, hon. Bless your heart. No, Murphy is fine, and I have to tell you, though I've yet to meet him, I'm in love with your dog."

She blinked.

V's blue eyes sparkled with gleeful mischief. "I would've given anything to see him take Jake down, and do you know how many women would pay a fortune to claim they'd rearranged Kevin Tucker's balls?"

Gracie winced.

V waived a slim-fingered hand. "Serves him right. The man is a player of the first order. He's littered the entire East Coast with broken hearts and a good portion of the south."

A reluctant smile formed. The horror on his face when she handed him the pees *had* been funny.

V stepped forward to link her arm with Gracie's. "No, I'm here because we need to talk about what we're going to tell the press."

"The press?" Gracie's gut churned. "Why would we tell them anything?"

"Jake's living here. It's only a matter of time before the story gets out. Now his friends know about you, it's even more essential we get ahead of the story. They'll keep his whereabouts secret since he asked, and he's threatened to break their necks if they say one word about you being the Gridiron Girl, but Jake is watched. They all are. How long do you think it will be until some enterprising reporter shows up at the door?"

"Oh, I don't think—"

V tugged her out into the hall and started toward the stairs. "Between the two of us, we could come up with a plan of action on our own, but you know how men are. Jake will turn positively nasty if he doesn't get to put in his two cents. He's waiting downstairs."

Gracie hesitated, but like a force of nature, V continued forward, dragging Gracie along in her wake and barely letting her get in a word edgewise.

"Jake tells me you design websites. How fascinating. I can barely open my e-mail, and you blog, too. I checked out your archives. I nearly peed my pants laughing at some of your posts. And your minions? Why, they're fabulous. How long have you been following football?"

"Well, I—"

"You certainly know your stuff. I could've slapped Jake for insulting you the way he did. He knows better, and he's usually more tempered when dealing with women. I don't know what's gotten into him."

"He's arrogant and rude, and I don't want to talk to him *or* the press."

V propelled them forward as though she hadn't heard a word. She led Gracie down the stairs, chattering like they were the best of friends. "He's been a bear since that hit on Brian last week. They're old friends, you know. Played together in college. Have you ever been to a Marauders game?"

Did the woman ever stop to take a breath? Or let a person answer? Probably about as often as she took no for an answer. They reached the foyer and Gracie dug in her bare heels, refusing to take another step. "V?"

V lifted her brow but kept their arms linked. "Yes?"

"Are you like this with everyone, or do you save the pushy agent routine for the women you see as a threat to Jake's career?"

Her smile turned wry, with a twinge of apology. "Everyone, I'm afraid. Comes from having to grow up fast. I have the feeling that's a concept with which you're familiar."

How, exactly, did she know that? Sure, one could recognize the signs of a rough childhood, if they knew where to look, but they'd only met the one time. Either V was incredibly perceptive, or she'd been digging for information. Neither option appealed.

The chattering girlfriend vanished as the publicist stepped into the breach. "Yes, Jake comes first, but I know for a fact the press has been hounding you. I also know you've been able to avoid them, so far. That won't last for long. The anonymity of the Internet is a powerful thing, but every communication leaves a fingerprint. The press will eventually find you and if you think they were in a frenzy before, you haven't seen *anything* yet."

She tugged gently on Gracie's arm until they were moving down the hall again. "This situation between you and Jake is news, Gracie. Big news. It's my job to spin the story so it shows in the best possible light. Something I can't do if my clients refuse to cooperate."

"I'm not your client."

"No, but Jake is. He's also my best friend, and I won't see him or his career hurt when I can do something to avoid it. Since the two of you are a package deal for the next three months, you're in this, whether you like it or not."

"I don't."

She pulled Gracie through the kitchen doorway and finally released her arm. "Yes, that much is obvious. I suggest we all sit down and you can explain why."

Elbows leaning on the kitchen table, Jake sat alone, a deck of cards in one hand, a beer bottle in the other. He shrugged, bumping up a shoulder as if to say, *don't blame me, this was her idea.*

Gracie paused inside the doorway and crossed her arms. Explain she was the love child of a league insider? Right. News? Hers was the kind of story that made journalism careers and destroyed lives. No way in hell. Whether her father knew of her existence or not, he didn't deserve to be blindsided. Neither did his family, and *she* had no interest in having her face splashed across every rag and cable broadcast in the country. "I'd rather not."

Jake sipped at his beer before setting the bottle aside. "You might as well talk to her. She'll wear you down eventually. She's stubborn."

V smiled serenely at her friend and client.

Gracie shook her head. "Tell me about it. What's her alma matter? Bull Dog State?"

His bark of laughter brought her a reluctant smile.

V huffed out a breath. "If you two don't mind, I suggest we get to work."

Gracie eyed the aftermath of his poker game. A dozen empty beer bottles sat on the counter behind him. A pile of multi-colored chips rested by one elbow. The stubs of several cigars lay in an otherwise clean ashtray.

"Where are the poker jocks, and I hope you didn't smoke those things in here? Mary will have a fit."

He chuckled. "Relax, princess. We stepped out back. V sent the poker jocks on their way so we could have our powwow."

"With instructions to keep their big mouths shut." V slid into the chair across from him. "But the clock is ticking. Whatever statement we come up with, we need to release it first thing tomorrow morning."

Gracie swallowed back a rush of nausea. "You don't need me for this. I don't care what statement you put out as long as the girls are protected and it doesn't include me."

V sat back, her gaze intent. "We'll protect the girls, but leaving you out of the press release is impossible."

"Why? The press has plenty to chew on with Jake and his surprise sisters. You don't need to mention me."

Jake cocked his head. "Why would a woman who runs such a popular blog shy away from free publicity? I'd think you'd jump at the opportunity."

The question hit a little too close to home. She crossed her arms. "Well, you'd be wrong."

V leaned forward, her face deadly serious. "Unfortunately, you don't have a choice. As soon as they learn Jake is here and in competition with you for the girls' guardianship, you won't have a moment's peace. They won't stop until they know everything about you."

Unease bloomed into full-blown panic. "Fine. Make something up. Tell them I'm a maid from the Bronx or a clown with the circus, I don't care, but keep my face out of the limelight and my name out of your press release."

"Lies always come out, Gracie. I won't jeopardize Jake's career that way."

True. But sometimes the truth was more dangerous than the lie. "Then tell them this. The twins' maternal aunt is in the running for guardianship. At the end of the allotted time, a determination will be made and the situation settled. In the meantime, she wishes to retain her privacy."

"They'll never accept that."

She was going to throw up. "They'll have to, because that's all they're going to get."

Chapter 15

"We've been invaded." Mary's voice shook breathlessly.

Gracie sat back in the coffee shop booth and tucked the phone closer to her ear. "Invaded? By whom?"

"I'm looking out the front window. There are three news vans outside the gate. You know, the one's with the big satellite dishes?"

"Oh, shit."

"Language, young lady."

Gracie winced. "Sorry."

"The phone hasn't stopped ringing for the past hour. Reporters are calling, asking for Jake."

Oh, God! She'd expected some type of fallout, but why hadn't she considered they'd flock to the farm once V released the story this morning? "Are the girls all right?"

"They're fine. Their bus arrived shortly before the first van showed up."

"Thank God. Have you called Jake?"

"He's on his way, as is Miss Price. He asked for your number and said he was going to call you. I wanted to warn you of what you'd be coming home to, in case he didn't reach you."

"I appreciate that." More than she'd ever know. "Do me a favor? Call him back and tell him when he speaks to the press…" What? She'd made her wishes clear, but what of the girls? She didn't want their pictures plastered all over the news any more than hers and with a crowd outside constantly, they'd become prisoners in their home. An unacceptable possibility, but would the press stay clear of the farm if he insisted?

She pulled her beeping phone from her ear to glance at the screen. Manic butterflies burst into flight in her belly. "Never mind, Mary. There he is now. I'll be there as soon as I can." She pressed the screen to switch calls and didn't bother with a greeting. Anger and dread made her tone harsh. "Damn it, Malone. Why are the press at the farm?"

He snorted, a derisive burst of air. "You can't be that naïve."

"That's not what I meant. Why are they at the *farm*? Why aren't they chasing *you* down at the sports complex?"

"My guess is they consider the farm sexier than the stadium, and since they know about the will and its ridiculous stipulations, they know I'll show up there eventually."

"Well, what are you going to do about it?"

"Where are you? I'll pick you up. We can discuss how we're going to handle things on the way home."

Home? Since when did he consider the farm home? "Not on your life. This is *your* problem. I'm not coming anywhere near the farm until those people are gone."

"How do you figure it's my problem? Last time I checked, there were two of us thrown into this custody competition."

She groaned and dropped her head into her free hand.

"Sorry, princess, but you don't have a choice. Take my word for it. The crowd at the gate won't be going anywhere until they get their story. Have you forgotten about the curfew stipulation?"

Her head snapped up. Crap. As a matter of fact, she had. She lied without qualm. "Of course not."

"Then tell me where to meet you."

She swallowed. Run the press gauntlet at the gate—with Jake at her side? No frigging way. If he couldn't get rid of them, she wouldn't be going through the gate. There was another way onto the property, but she didn't look forward to using it. She glanced at her pretty, sex-on-heels boots and wanted to cry. "Don't let them get any pictures of the girls, Malone. In fact, don't let them get near them."

"The girls are fine. Mary's with them and V's on her way over there. Where are you?"

"I'll find my own way home. You get rid of the press." She hung up before he could respond.

* * * *

Jake leaned a shoulder against the doorframe of the converted gym, crossed his arms, and settled in to see what Gracie would do next. His initial belief, when he spotted the unmistakably feminine figure dart from the woods at the back of the property, was one of the reporters gathered at the gate had decided to slip onto the property for a closer look. His promise to keep the twins out of the spotlight fresh in his mind, he left V to handle the mob and went in search of the determined press babe.

The wet snow made the effort easy. He followed the woman's clearly defined trail straight to the barn, only then realizing his mistake when he arrived in time to watch her slip inside the door. Even at a distance, there was no mistaking Gracie's fine ass in the hip hugging skirt or her long, slim legs.

Following her inside, he moved stealthily through the dimly lit hallway to stop in the open gym doorway where he nearly swallowed his tongue. Having already shed her coat and kicked off her boots, she bent over at the waist. With her back to him, she reached beneath her skirt and shimmied her hips as she peeled down the soaked netting of her panty hose.

His suddenly dry throat clicked on a helpless swallow. On closer inspection, he'd been right. Despite being red and chafed from the cold, her legs were definitely better wet.

"Holy crap, it's cold!" She shivered visibly and glanced around. "Yes!" She rushed to the far wall and snatched down one of a half dozen fluffy towels from a rack.

His gaze flicked to her waterlogged boots and panty hose, discarded in a soggy heap in the corner, and swung back to her bare feet. He frowned. She'd obviously arrived back on the farm on foot, but how? From what he understood, the only other access to the estate was a gate at the far end of a half-mile dirt track through the woods. The gate was reportedly locked, and he didn't think the track had been plowed.

Shit. Had she walked in? A desire for privacy wouldn't account for such drastic measures, would it? The question was, what did?

Hopping on one foot, she swiped blindly at the other leg and stretched her neck in an attempt to peer out one of the high windows. Her low growl echoed through the room. After an equally ineffective brush over the other leg, she tossed aside the towel and bent at the waist to shove a weight bench up against the wall.

He ran his tongue around his teeth at the visual gift of her tight, short skirt riding up breathtaking thighs. He held his breath as the dark material rose, coming tantalizingly close to displaying a view rivaling Christmas morning and a lifetime of birthday gifts, all rolled in one.

Disappointment coursed through him when she straightened but quickly gave way to baffled amusement when she climbed onto the bench and plastered her body against the wall in a furtive crouch. She dipped her head to the side, barely quick enough to peek through the window with one eye then immediately jerked back.

"Shit! They're still here." She dropped her forehead to the wall on a soft whine.

He'd seen enough. Pushing off the doorframe, he crossed the room and stopped a foot from the bench. "Gracie."

Her scream pierced the air. Only blind luck saved his nose from being broken when she whipped around. He flinched back, causing her flying elbow to glance off the side of his head. Momentum from her flailing arms threw her off balance. She started to topple sideways. He grabbed her around the waist and pulled her off the bench and into his chest.

They stared at one another, nose to nose.

"I'm wondering what makes a seemingly sane woman trek through the woods in six inches of snow, simply to avoid a few reporters."

Her breasts plumped against his chest when she drew in a ragged breath. "You scared me!"

"You nearly broke my nose. I'd say that makes us even. Now, answer my question."

She squirmed against him in an attempt to free her pinned arms. "Put me down."

He held her firm. "Answer the question first."

She flattened her lips in a mutinous line. "I told you. I don't want any part of your media circus."

He tightened his arms marginally, refusing to feel guilty for enjoying the way her chilled curves molded to his frame from chest to knees. "I'm not buying it, princess. Nobody walks a half mile in the snow to avoid questions when a simple no comment will suffice."

She shifted her wedged arms until her hands rested against his collarbone. Her eyes narrowed to dangerous slits and her thigh brushed against his as she shifted one leg.

He contracted his arms in a bone-crushing squeeze. "Don't even think about using that knee, or you'll end up over mine."

The mental image of Gracie draped ass up over his lap sent a rush of blood flooding toward his stiffening dick. Riotous color instantly flooded her cheeks, and he could swear the sensual image was reflected in her widened eyes. Her nipples, puckering beneath the silk of her blouse, stabbed his chest. She bit at her bottom lip.

Tempted to say the hell with it and drop his head the inch it would take to cover her mouth with his, the militant gleam in her eyes stopped him cold. Considering her surprising skill at laying him out in the foyer the other day, and his increasing hard-on, he was bound to sustain significant damage if she chose to call his bluff. He set her on her feet none too gently.

She skittered out of his reach, immediately heading across the room.

He sighed. "The truth, Gracie."

The hesitation in her step was slight, but he noted it.

She continued to a cabinet in the far corner and opened the door. "I told you the truth. I can't help you don't believe me."

She didn't look his way, rummaging for something at the back of a high shelf. He didn't need to see her face to know she was lying. The stiff movements of her body told the story, but with her quick temper, pushing her wasn't going to get him any answers, at least not now. "What are you looking for?"

"Something to put on my feet. They're freezing. Ah!" Her hand reappeared grasping a pair of sneakers. She dropped to a backless bench and bent over her thighs to shove a bare foot into one.

"You should've listened to me and changed your sexy boots. They're ruined."

She glared at him across the distance. "What are you doing in here? Why aren't you out front, getting rid of the rabid wolves?"

"V is handling things. For now. But she's only delaying the inevitable."

She dropped her forehead to her knees and groaned.

He crossed the room and dropped to a crouch in front of her. "What's going on, princess?"

She peeked at him from beneath thick lashes, her eyes wary. "I have no idea what you mean."

"Only someone with something to hide tromps a half mile through the snow to avoid driving through the front gate. What'd you do, rob a bank?"

"Of course not."

"Did you steal a car? Sleep with a married politician?"

She narrowed her eyes.

"I know." He snapped his fingers. "You're a computer whiz, right? You hacked into the Pentagon."

Her lips pulled tight. "Very funny."

"I'm serious. This is all about custody of the girls for you, and that's how it should be. They come first, but I also have my career to think about. I'm not sure if you've read the sports pages lately, but my reputation is in deep shit these days."

"Which is your own fault."

"Yeah, it's my fault, but I've apologized. I'm doing the best I can here. Help me out a little. I can't afford to give the press another scandal to chew on. If you're hiding something I need to know about, tell me already and we'll deal with it."

She sat up. A bright slash of red stained her cheekbones, but her violet eyes met his. "I assure you, I've done nothing I need to spill. I haven't slept with anyone's husband, politician or otherwise, and the only law I've ever come close to breaking is jaywalking."

Her eyes quickly skittered away. From her comments the other day, she was none too happy with the interest from the *rabid wolves*, but traipsing through the woods to avoid them qualified as more than an aversion to the limelight. Gracie had secrets. Secrets she wasn't willing to share. Not today, at any rate. They'd have to do something about that. In the meantime, they still had to deal with the crowd at the gate.

"Then let's sit down with V and figure out the best way to satisfy the mob out front. She's brilliant at handling this type of thing."

"If she's as brilliant as you claim, she can handle things without my help. I told you. I want no part of this."

He leaned in menacingly. "I'll find out what you're hiding, princess."

"I'm not hiding anything!"

She shoved against his chest. He straightened away from her but remained balanced on the balls of his feet. The blush deepening on her cheeks pleased him immensely, until she lowered her lashes, shuttering the flickering shadows in her amazing eyes. Guilt or alarm? He wasn't sure.

He shook his head. "Has anyone ever accused you of being stubborn?"

She bared her teeth in a daring smile. "Frequently. Has anyone ever accused you of the same?"

He grinned. "At least once a week."

Cupping her chilly calf, he slid his palm down the sleek column of her lower leg. In a slow caress, he rubbed the pad of his thumb over the firm tendons. The daring smile slid from her lips, and she blinked. He leaned in closer until her stilted breath bathed his lips. Sensual awareness glazed her eyes, and the pink tip of her tongue peeked out to wet her upper lip, right next to that sexy little mole, before disappearing again.

If she was playing him, the way she had in the foyer... Shit, who cared if she was playing him? The results would be well worth the risk. The blood drained from his head, flowing straight to his dick as, tempted beyond the edge of reason, he dipped his head and nibbled at the corner of her mouth.

She whimpered.

Adrenaline surged.

He lifted his head and stared into her unblinking eyes. Propping his free hand on the bench beside her hip, he braced the weight of his upper body and leaned in closer. She pressed her spread fingers against his chest, but not in rebuff. Her hand lay still over his pulsing heart as if unsure what to do.

If she was unsure, he wasn't. He wanted to sink into her, to absorb the darkly sweet scent of her. He lowered his head, craving the taste of her until he couldn't think straight. Her eyes slid shut. He captured her mouth beneath his. No rebuff as he nibbled and nipped then twisted his head to deepen the kiss. Her lips softened beneath his, and he sunk his tongue deep. Her fingers clenched at his sweater as she curved into his chest.

Excitement coursed through him, heating the blood in his veins. A caressing squeeze of her shapely calf demanded further investigation. His exploring fingers rode up her knee and over her skirt-covered thigh. Another squeeze to the curve of her hip, and he dropped one knee to the floor. Cupping her bottom, he slid her forward.

Like bellows in a medieval forge, his lungs labored when he broke the kiss and lifted his head. Oxygen became a more desperate need when he glanced down at where he rested in the cradle of her spread thighs. The hem of her skirt rode deliciously high and played peekaboo with the pale peach satin of her panties. Bared to his view, the firm, white columns of her thighs hugged his hips. His erection thickened, straining dangerously at the confines of his jeans.

Damn. If he ever actually got her *naked*, he wasn't sure he'd survive.

She sniffed in a sharp breath, drawing his gaze. Dazed and hungry, her eyes shimmered with a matching desire. What little control he had left slipped its tether. He took her mouth hungrily. She met his desperation, pressing closer and opening her lips to give his probing tongue entrance, and...

"Ha-choo!"

Pain exploded, shooting out from the throbbing cartilage where her forehead slammed against the ridge of his nose. He jerked back and toppled over, landing on his ass. Again.

Her eyes popped open. "Oh, God."

She immediately sat forward. He lurched to one side, attempting to dodge her reaching hand and ended up with her finger in his eye.

"Ouch! Stop!"

She snatched back her hand and slapped her fingers over her mouth.

Tears leaked from his right eye and his nose was running—or was he bleeding? He swiped his upper lip with the back of his hand. No blood, but fuck! Had she popped him one on purpose? "Damn, you're more dangerous than your dog."

Her blush went scarlet. He eyed her critically. The seductive siren from moments ago was gone. In her place was a woman who looked far too young for the lascivious fantasies she evoked in him and way too vulnerable. She caught her lower lip with her teeth. Horror etched her wrinkled brow.

Shit. Was she about to cry?

Oh, hell no. He could handle anything else, but not tears.

The best defense was a good offense. He took a stab, hoping to prod the scrapper who'd tossed him on his ass *purposefully* the other day into reappearing. *That* Gracie would never use tears as a tool. "Playing dirty again, princess?"

"No!" Her jaw dropped open. She snapped it shut. "I sneezed!"

He rose to his feet, snorting. A mistake. His nose resumed its throbbing. "How do I know you didn't do it on purpose?"

The horrified vulnerability on her face flashed out with the immediate return of the scrapper. She narrowed her eyes and stood. "You'll have to take my word for it."

He smiled inwardly. Her buttons were damned easy to press. Now, if he could find the seductive siren switch, they could get back to fanning the raging fire.

Her lips flattened in an angry slash, and he swallowed a sigh. He was on his own in putting out the blaze…this time, but if she believed he'd back off, she was mistaken. The sexy football blogger was about to be blitzed by a pro.

Her chest rose on a bracing breath. Before she got all worked up and started to spout off about ground rules and why that kiss shouldn't have happened, best he remind her of her part in the passionate encounter. "Why is it every time you kiss me, I end up on my ass?"

She crossed her arms on a strangled cough. "*You* kissed *me!*"

He mirrored her stubborn stance, crossing his arms. "Yes, I did." He made his smile slow and intimate. "And I plan to kiss you again, soon, but I distinctly recall your tongue in my mouth. Not that I'm complaining, but you kissed me back."

She angled her chin defensively. "Well, I *don't* plan to ever again."

He couldn't prevent his chuckle.

She dropped her arms, doubling down on her attempted brush off. "As for why you keep landing on your ass, maybe you're clumsy."

Leaning close, her stiffening flinch made him smile. He tapped a fingertip to her pert nose. "Be careful, princess. I never could resist a smart ass woman."

She slapped his hand away. "Try harder." Bolting past him, she disappeared out the door.

Chapter 16

Jake rapped his knuckles against wood and waited.

"Yes?" Gracie's muffled reply came from behind her closed bedroom door.

"It's Jake. Can you do me a favor?"

Silence, then, "I'm working."

Not for long.

He had yet to discover what her furtive trek through the woods yesterday was about, but he would eventually. In the meantime, other than dinnertime and getting the girls to bed, she'd spent the entire afternoon and evening hunkered down in her room. Did she plan to hide herself away like a hunted animal indefinitely? The tactic wouldn't do her a bit of good with either the press *or* with him. The crowd at the gate might have dwindled down to a couple of determined holdouts, but they'd eventually get their picture of his elusive housemate, and they'd continue hounding her until they got their answers and their story.

He meant to do the same, subtly, of course.

First, he needed to gain her trust. A tall order, but not impossible and necessary. He could hardly seduce the prickly princess if he never got her alone. From her sultry reaction to his kisses, she had no more willpower when it came to him than he did with her. Apparently, her solution was to deny the primal pull between them and run off and hide. Her strategy was fatally flawed as far as he was concerned. The gut-wrenching attraction between them was simply too strong to ignore. She'd cave. He'd make sure of it.

No way in hell was he about to "*try harder*" to resist her as she suggested. He wanted her. More importantly, she wanted him. An irresistible reality. Sure, concern over complications with the girls, should the two of them become involved intimately, made her skittish, but why did a simple fling have to be a problem? They were consenting, reasonable adults. Keeping any romantic maneuverings separate from their care of the girls was a matter of logistics. All it'd take was some conscious time management… and a bit of luck. With the girls in school and Mary out of the house for a few hours, time was his friend and luck was on his side, for the moment. The only thing left to determine was how to convince her to give in to the helpless desire burning in her eyes whenever their gazes met. He had a few ideas on how to help her along with that. Anticipation flooded him, increasing the heavy thud of his heart. He grinned and laced his tone with a healthy dose of appeal. "It'll only take a few minutes."

A soft huff. "I'm in the middle of something."

"Five minutes, Gracie."

More silence. About to knock again, a rush of satisfaction heated his blood when the door creaked open and wary violet eyes peeked through the two-inch gap. She held the door before her like a shield, her expression guarded. Murphy wedged his nose in the crack and began to whine and wiggle.

Suddenly her eyes went wide and she gasped. "Oh, God. Did I do that?"

"Do what?" The crescent moon slashes beneath both his eyes were his ace in the hole. No doubt he'd face a ration of shit from his teammates when he arrived at the sports complex later this afternoon, but their teasing would be well worth the discomfort. After all, what woman could say no to a man who wore the dual shiners she'd given him over a melting kiss they'd both wanted? Obviously, she hadn't meant to blacken his eyes. She'd sneezed. An accident, as she'd said, but the guilt on her face was one more point in his favor.

The door cracked open and Murphy muscled his way through. He danced around Jake's legs, yipping happily. Rubbing a palm over the excited dog's side, Jake kept his gaze on her. Saliva pooled on his tongue. The woman knew how to wear a pair of faded jeans and a sweater. Damn, she was an incredibly sexy package, and he was in *big* trouble.

"Do they hurt?"

The husky guilt in her voice sent a lash of fire across his midsection. His gut clenched in discomfort. Temporary discomfort, he hoped. He shrugged. "Nah. I got worse in practice last week."

"Ouch." Stepping forward tentatively, she lifted a slim hand. The fingertips she brushed over the swelling, as if to take away his pain, were cool and her touch tender. Hissing between her teeth, she dropped her arm to her side. "I really am sorry."

He wanted to dive after her hand and beg her to continue stroking him. Instead, he cleared his throat. "So you said. About that favor."

"I'm in the middle of a project, and the code for this job is intense and complicated."

"Then a break will do you good."

She sighed. "Jake—"

He didn't let her finish. "Come on. Mary ran out to do a few things, and I can't manage on my own." He'd never mastered humility, and pleading wasn't one of his strong points. He curled his lips in a hapless smile and pulled out the big guns. "Please?"

Doubt clouded her eyes. She said nothing, studying him. Beneath the soft sweater molding her breasts with mouthwatering perfection, her chest rose and fell on an annoyed huff. "Five minutes."

Despite the thrill of anticipation leaving a trail of heat behind, he kept his smile bland. "You'll need your coat."

As expected, she immediately stiffened. Her knuckles whitened with her tightening grip on the doorknob. "I'm not going anywhere with you."

"Just out to the garage. Under the hood work relaxes me." A flat-out lie, of course. As a teenager, he'd spent more hours than he cared to remember under countless hoods. The money he'd made doing tune-ups kept him fed when his mother was too drunk to notice there was no food left in the house. After signing his first pro contract, he'd vowed never again to get grease under his nails, but for a chance to get his hands on Gracie, he'd gladly dunk them in a vat of dirty motor oil. "I need someone to keep the engine running while I adjust the carburetor."

Indecision joined doubt in her eyes, and he lifted a brow. Knowledge was power, and he'd learned long ago the surest way to victory was using an opponent's weaknesses to your advantage. In less than twenty-four hours, he'd discovered Gracie Gable was as stubborn as the day was long. Lucky for him, she couldn't resist a challenge.

Casually scratching behind Murphy's ear, he pressed his advantage. "You do know how to turn a key, right?"

The gambit worked like a charm. Her lips flattened at the insult and she lifted her chin. "Ha ha."

He shrugged, though he wanted to laugh. Baiting her was damned easy and highly entertaining. "Hey, you said you never learned to drive."

She crossed her arms. "Do you want my help or not?"

Grinning, he straightened and stepped back. He swept out an arm. "After you."

Murphy scrambled after her when she disappeared back into her room then bounced back out into the hall a moment later. She reappeared shoving her arms into a sleek, winter blazer. His quick survey ran over the downy sweater beneath the jacket, down her long legs to land on today's footwear.

He arched a brow at the silver-studded, black suede shoe-boots. The princess definitely had a thing for sexy as hell shoes. He liked that about her.

She followed his gaze. Her brow puckered with annoyance. "What?"

"Nice knockoffs."

She fidgeted with the middle button on her jacket and dropped her gaze. "Not that it's any of your business, but these are the genuine article."

He let loose a wide grin when she scurried past him and hurried down the hallway with her dog at her heels. Following them downstairs and through the kitchen, Jake snagged his coat from the hook by the back door.

After the past few days of winter cold and weather, late fall had returned. Balmy temperatures in the low sixties and the bright sun had done a valiant job of melting away the heavy snow, leaving behind a sloppy mess of slush and mud, except for those spots where shade prevailed. The covered breezeway leading from the farmhouse to the six-bay garage was liberally dotted with patches of wet snow.

Murphy loped over to lift his leg on a bush. Gracie hesitated at the edge of the flagstone path. Jake moved close behind her and lowered his mouth to her ear. "Those sure are sexy boots. Maybe I should carry you. You don't want them to get ruined."

She arched her neck, putting some distance between her throat and his mouth and sniffed. Stepping gingerly, she tiptoed an erratic pattern through the mine-field of boot-destroying slush. He chuckled, his own boots crunching on the thin layer of snow as he followed her. She stopped short inside the garage doorway to stomp her feet delicately.

He chuckled as she met his gaze over her shoulder, tilting her chin defiantly. "They were on sale, okay!"

Her guilty tone made him laugh. Opening his mouth to tease her about the price of her fetish, the vision beyond her right shoulder captured his attention. Every muscle in his body went taut. Like a kid stepping into his first candy store, the breath jammed in his throat. Sexy shoes *and* his immediate plans for her seduction melted like the first snow of winter.

Mary had mentioned an old Ford pickup and a Mercedes this morning, when he asked about the contents of the large garage, but she hadn't said

Mackenzie Crowne

a word about the rest of the vehicles in Pete's collection. Jake's stunned gaze ping-ponged from one gleaming mass of machine and muscle to the next. As if caught up in an incredible dream, afraid to move, he froze for long seconds and waited for the vision to fade. When the dream vehicles remained, he rushed past Gracie toward the half dozen, rare classic muscle cars.

A low rumble of covetousness rolled through his chest. He stretched out his arms to run his fingertips along the cool metal of both the sleek GTO and the Chevelle SS parked at its side. Refurbished to showroom perfection, the beauty of a midnight blue Charger and flame embossed Firebird made him moan in appreciation. The moan slid toward something near a whimper as he bent to inspect the leather interior of the '68 Shelby Mustang and morphed into a full blown groan when he stopped in front of a candy apple red '57 Corvette Coupe Roadster.

Pete Thompson might have sucked as a human being, but Jake could say one thing about the old man. The fucker knew cars. The breath left him in a low whistle.

Gracie stopped at his side. "I guess you're a car guy, huh?"

He didn't look at her. "These aren't cars. They're metal, rubber, and horsepower dreams."

"If you say so." She flicked out a hand. "This one's pretty."

He shot her a disbelieving, sidelong glance. "A '57 Vette is sexy, not pretty. About as sexy as you can get." He tossed her a leering grin. "Gives me a hard-on just looking at it."

She rolled her eyes and kicked the closest tire. He winced, making her laugh.

"Geez, you've got it bad."

His wince softened into a helpless smile. Moving around the hood, he squatted in front of the grill, pushing Murphy aside when he pushed close, looking for attention. "When I was a kid, every spring a new crop of dudes, looking for seasonal work, showed up at the ranch where I lived. Most of them drove ranch-dented pickups, but this one year, an old cowboy rumbled up the dirt road in one of these babies." He danced his fingertips over the chromed-out grill and shook his head appreciatively. "It was in much rougher shape than this one, but I was sixteen and a car nut. I fell in love."

"Huh. Sounds sort of *Brokeback Mountain*-ish." She bared her teeth in a smile. "What did the old cowboy think of *that*?"

He straightened and snorted a laugh. "Smartass."

"Just checking." Wearing a cheeky grin, she scooted around him, opened the door and slid into the low-slung bucket seat. "You fell in love, huh? Did you ever buy one?"

Hip cocked, he propped his hands on his hips and met her easy smile. "Nope."

"Why not?" She shimmied in the molded seat, glancing around the interior before titling her head and giving him a once-over. "Too big?"

Nothing but innocent curiosity showed in her eyes, but he couldn't pass up such a sweet opening. He crossed his arms. "I'm big, princess, but I always manage to fit. Especially when the incentive is so sexy."

Her smile deflated immediately. Damn. Her pretty blush sent a hot rush of blood to thicken the semi-erection he'd been sporting since yesterday's kiss.

"You're doing it again." Her blush deepened, along with her grumbled complaint. She attempted a pissed off scowl. The fact she couldn't quite pull it off pleased him immensely.

"What's that?"

"Flirting."

He whipped out his most charming drawl. "I sure am giving it my best effort, darlin'."

"Well, stop it." She ducked her head. Popping open the glove box, she glanced at the empty pocket, shut it again and changed the subject. "This car was Pete's favorite, too."

Talk about killing the mood. His smile fizzled, along with his hard-on.

Busy fiddling with the turn signal levers, she didn't notice. "I remember the summer he bought this one. He took it out for a spin every Saturday then spent two hours cleaning it." A smile of remembrance grew. "Sarah would sit on the porch steps and watch him, her belly huge with the girls. She teased him ruthlessly about what the neighbors would say with him polishing his shiny, two hundred eighty-three horse power penis in the driveway."

Low and throaty, her laugh was a sexy, yet happy, sound. She glanced up and met his frown. Her smile dimmed but didn't fade completely. "I'm sorry. I know how you feel about Pete, but I can't help it. He made my sister happy."

He grunted a non-answer, once again unable to equate the man she described with the one he'd despised his entire life.

She looked away finally, and he sucked in a slow breath. Luck and time might be on his side this morning, but only for a few hours. The last thing he needed was a self-centered ghost fucking up his seduction plans. Focusing on Gracie's lovely face helped ease his unwanted tension. Touching her would replace what remained with another type altogether.

Several seconds passed as she dipped her head and pushed several buttons on the dash. Finally, she sat up straight. "I don't see the keys."

"What do you need the keys for? You don't drive, remember?"

She rested her forearms on the steering wheel. "Yes, I remember. Didn't you ask me to come along and help while you did some *under the hood* work?"

His remaining tension slipped away with her innocent comment. The grip of old bitterness didn't hold a candle to the dirty images his mind provided at the idea of checking under *her* hood.

Oh, princess, you're killing me. Don't stop.

He propped his hands on his hips. "I doubt this baby needs any work. From the looks of her, she purrs like a kitten. I need your help with *that*."

She followed his jerking chin to the old pickup truck in the far bay. "Oh." Eyeing the big four-wheel drive critically, she cocked her head. "If this one purrs like a kitten, why bother with an old truck? Come to think of it, do you have the time? Don't you have practice this morning?"

The buttons on the dash caught her attention. Like a child, she pressed one, then another. He rounded the hood, amused when she gripped the steering wheel and mimicked maneuvering a sharp curve. He gave an inward snort. She wasn't as averse to driving as she let on. She simply hadn't come up against the right incentive. He was about to change that.

"I have a couple of free hours before I have go to the complex." Resting an arm along the top of the doorjamb, he curled his lips in a challenging smile. "I thought we could use the time to teach you to drive."

Chapter 17

Gracie's head jerked up at his absurd suggestion. "Teach me to drive? Not on your life." She scrambled from the car and shut the door with more force than necessary. His helpless wince pleased her.

"Why not?"

"Because I've driven with you. You're suicidal. If I do ever decide to learn to drive, you're the last person I want teaching me."

He dipped his head to bring their gazes even, and his tone dripped with apologetic charm. "Ah, princess. I was showing off. I'll be on my best behavior. I promise."

Right! She opened her mouth to amend her answer to *no way in hell*.

He held up a hand. "Hear me out. You're determined not to speak to the press. I'm sure you have your reasons, and although I wish you trusted me enough to share them, I respect your request to remain anonymous. There's still a crowd at the gate. It's gotten smaller, but the diehards aren't going anywhere. Do you plan to hide out here for the next three months?"

Hide? Damn. He made her sound like a complete weenie, but he had no idea of the potential ramifications should she introduce herself to the press. She bit down on a guilty groan. How dare he point out the truth?

She notched up her chin defiantly. "If necessary."

His eyes glittered with mischief. "What if it *wasn't* necessary?"

Wasn't necessary? If only. Sighing, she crossed her arms. "Okay, I'll bite. You teach me to drive. Then what? The crowd at the gate knows the stipulations of the will, and thanks to your press release, they know I'm here. There are only three adults living on the property. An elderly woman with an Irish accent, an overgrown jock with an addiction to flirting," she growled when his lips curved smugly, "and me. Are you going to supply a disguise so I can drive past the press with a wave and a smile?"

He rocked back on his heels and grinned. "You won't *have* to drive past the press if you go out the back gate. From there, it's only a quarter mile to the train station."

His victorious smile and the boyish twinkle in his eyes combined charmingly until she was in danger of weakening. Yeah, right. In danger? Hell, she was tempted to leap across the distance and kiss him senseless.

On no. She wasn't about to fall for that glittering twinkle again. Look what happened last time? She studied the twin bruises beneath his glittering eyes. Wishing she could sink through the floor, she curled her fingers into fists against the need to dab cool fingertips to the swelling and take away his pain. Her fault! Okay, in truth, it was an accident. Which wouldn't have happened if she hadn't given in to his sultry seduction and kissed him back.

Sticking her tongue in his mouth was a bad idea, no matter how pleasant the exercise. Then again…. She shook her head. As much as she'd enjoy locking lips with him again, she couldn't count on another opportune tickle in her nose to bring her back to her senses. No, kissing Jake was dangerous business. She'd be better off slamming her head against the hood of his dream car, but damn, he was a temptation she didn't want to resist.

Logic, Gracie!

Yes. Logic was her best defense. "The back gate leads to a county road. Last time I checked, you need a driver's license to operate a vehicle on one."

He waved off her argument. "You can get your license eventually but, in the meantime, I'll teach you to drive well enough to get to the gate. You leave the truck, walk to the train, then pick the truck up again on your way home." He held up both hands as if to say, *there you go, I'm a genius*.

She stared at him in stunned disbelief. "I don't understand. You *look* like a grown man. Then you open your mouth and it's clear you're thirteen."

He grinned.

She rolled her eyes. "Make that twelve."

He bumped up one shoulder in a careless shrug. "Hey, it's a plan."

"*Hey!* It's a *ridiculous* plan."

Perhaps she shouldn't have used such a sarcastic tone. He closed the distance between them, his eyes narrowed dangerously. The charming teenager disappeared, replaced by the full-grown man who faced down behemoths for a living. He pinned her between his hard body and the car.

When her ass bumped up against the fender, he dipped his head until they were nose to nose.

"As ridiculous as trekking through snowy woods in the dark? In heels?" She winced. Okay, he had a point, but still.

"I'm serious, Gracie. What you did wasn't only foolish, it was dangerous. You could've broken an ankle, been attacked by an animal, or worse, been accosted by a human. I'll narc you out to the press before I let you do something that stupid again."

She opened her mouth on an offended gasp then thinned her lips in aggravation. This was Long Island, not the Amazon. It wasn't as if she'd been in danger of meeting up with a bear or a lion or something, and she traversed the hazardous jungle of Manhattan's sidewalks on a daily basis, in much higher heels, without breaking her ankles.

Being accosted by a human was another story. Max would have a fit were he to learn what she'd done.

The first rule of self-defense was to never willingly put yourself in a vulnerable situation. Like walking through the woods…at night…alone. Hadn't she described the press as a pack of rabid wolves on more than one occasion? Considering how determined they were to get their story, she was surprised none of those at the front gate had slipped around to the back of the property, the way she had.

She mentally rolled her eyes. Walking through the woods had been a bad idea, but she wasn't about to admit it out loud. Like he needed her admission. He certainly wasn't waiting for one. He dropped his brows menacingly.

"Your choices are to talk to the press and put this ridiculous game of hide-and-seek behind you, plant your ass on the farm for the next eleven weeks and stay put or learn to drive. With *me*." He straightened to his full height.

"I told you—"

Back came the charmer, complete with those adorable dimples creasing in his spreading grin. "I vote for the driving lessons."

She wasn't fooled by the pointed innocence in his eyes or the hand he held up like he was some kind of corn-fed Boy Scout. Jake Malone was a devil, pure and simple. A devil with a one-track mind. He had an ulterior motive for teaching her to drive, and she'd bet her shoe closet his motive had everything to do with the kiss they shared in the gym yesterday.

Damn it! She slammed her mind's door on the memory of his spice and sex scent. His hot mouth moving over hers and his wide palmed hand cupping her butt to pull her to him. The incredibly large, iron hard bulge pressing against her thigh... She swallowed a groan. Oh, hell. What was she going to do? How was she supposed to resist a man who made her girl parts demand she strip naked every time he was near?

She and Jake were locked in a multi-level tug of war and the battle would leave only one of them standing in the end. On one level were the twins and who would steer their future. Gaining guardianship would deliver her dream of a family of her own and would fulfill her promise to Sarah. The twins should be her only concern and would be, if not for her traitorous body, confused mind, and helpless heart.

All he had to do was smile and her insides began preparing for the promise of paradise in his verdant green eyes. The sad fact was her body was his for the taking. In the meantime, her mind couldn't settle on which was the better plan—get the hell away from him or rip off his clothes.

As for her heart? How long could that emotional organ hold out against its deepest wish? She'd been reluctant to accept the truth, but apparently love at first sight *was* possible. She'd been the victim of a digital whammo! Cupid's arrow had pierced her heart right through the TV screen long before Jake arrived at the farm for the reading of Pete's will.

How was she supposed to stand her ground against his attempts at seduction when she was battling herself as much as him? The answer made her want to cry. Ultimately, she wouldn't be able to hold him off because she didn't want to and, at twenty-six, she understood and accepted the cold hard truth. Men didn't stay. Sooner or later, whatever happened between them would end. Letting him go would hurt like hell, but defeat was inevitable.

When it came to the girls, defeat wasn't an option.

For her, that part of their battle could be nothing less than a game of keeps. She simply couldn't lose Angel and Charlie. For a woman with a heart full of love to give, the girls represented a lifeline to the family she craved.

As for Jake, loving him might lead to heartache, but how could she deny the feelings she had for him when, as Max said, she was a one-man women? Despite their having no future, did she want to waste the time he *was* here, fighting against the instincts screaming at her to take what he offered?

She studied him as he studied her. Strong and proud, his magnificent body called to hers. His smile teased and his eyes seduced. Heat bubbled the blood in her veins and between her thighs, her panties dampened. God, the guy did such delicious things to her insides.

Her heart was already lost to him, and she had no doubt he'd break it in the end. How could she possibly be any worse off for taking of him what she could while she had the chance? The answer was, she couldn't. The breath left her in a cleansing sigh.

Decision made, she cast aside the lingering threads of doubt. Seduction was in the air and she'd be jumping in with both feet—as soon as she came up with a plan guaranteeing the twins wouldn't be hurt in the bargain. Whatever happened, she'd be the one calling the shots.

She cocked her head as her heart rate accelerated dangerously. "Admit it. Teaching me to drive is an excuse to get me alone."

His brows arched at her blatant accusation. "Not an excuse. In this day and age, everyone should know how to drive, if for no other reason than to have the ability to jump behind the wheel in an emergency. We're out in the middle of nowhere here and cell service isn't always a guarantee. What if one of the girls or Mary got hurt and you couldn't make a call?"

Hell, that made sense. Damn it. Why did he have to go all logical at the exact moment she'd decided to toss logic out the window? Disappointment weighed on her shoulders like a leaden yoke, until the bawdy waggle of his black brows made her heart rate spike with excitement.

"Having said that, I freely admit, getting you alone is the real reason for offering to teach you to drive."

Now they were talking, but she wanted verification. "For the purpose of seduction?"

He scratched at his chin as he performed a slow survey of her face, pausing on her mouth and touching on her hair before meeting her gaze once more. "Not the way I would've put it, but yeah. I never hid the fact I find you attractive, and don't bother denying you feel the same about me. I've held your body against mine, princess. I made you quiver. Pleasures, sweet and untold, await us when we finally come together."

Speaking of quivering. Holy shit!

Her spiking heart rate shot into overdrive. She held out her hand. "Where are the keys?"

"Is that a yes?"

"I'll accept your offer of driving lessons. For the girls' sake."

He dropped a set of keys in her outstretched palm. "And the untold pleasures?"

Oh, hell yeah. The key ring dug into her clenching fist. "I'm not making any promises, but I'll think about those."

White teeth flashed in his quick, dazzling smile, then he swooped down and kissed her, hard and fast.

A flash fire raced over her nerve endings and sparked in her veins, threatening to make her bubbling blood boil over. He released her mouth far too quickly for her liking and straightened.

Several clearing breaths were necessary before she could speak. "I said I'd think about it."

Wicked intent flashed in his eyes. "Then I can't lose."

"What's that supposed to mean?"

One brow arched in sensual warning. "Shall I show you?"

She slapped a hand to his chest when he began to dip his head once more. Too many more of his kisses and her plan to have carnal knowledge of him would be out of her hands. He'd have her naked and begging in no time. "That won't be necessary."

A knowing smile tipped up the corners of his lips. The braggart.

Apparently he hadn't gotten the memo on who was calling the shots. He grabbed her wrist and immediately began dragging her toward the old pickup. She attempted to dig in her heels and failed. He tugged her along behind him. Murphy danced and bounced at her side.

Finally, she yanked her hand free and stopped. "Wait."

He turned and propped his hands on his hips. "What?"

"If I'm going to learn to drive, I want to learn in *that*." She jerked her thumb back toward the Vette.

He barked a laugh, grabbed her hand again, and continued toward the truck. "No way, princess."

She didn't bother tugging free. "Why not?"

They reached the truck. He opened the driver's door. Murphy leapt inside. Spanning her waist with his large hands, Jake lifted her as though she weighed no more than a child and deposited her on the bench seat. As he had the day before, he moved forward until his hips were cradled in the V of her spread legs.

He dipped his head, bringing his lips within a breath of hers, paused, then closed the remaining distance to kiss her as if he was a man dying of thirst and she the last drop of water. The keys tinkled as they plopped into her lap. She tangled her fingers in the soft material of his sweater. He cupped her face in his warm palms.

His lips owned hers, devouring and giving, demanding and asking at once. Her muscles liquefied and the blood in her veins turned to steam. She was surprised she didn't disburse into a vaporous cloud when he finally broke the heated connection.

He continued to nibble at her lips. "Because, although most of the snow has melted, there's still some on the ground, and I want you until I can't see straight." His mouth traveled in a sensual journey from her lips to her jawline. The damp heat of his breath bathed the sensitive shell of her ear, and she shivered. "Unless you agree to save the lesson for some other time, I'm going to need all my concentration to teach you to drive instead of stripping you naked."

He paused as if awaiting her answer. She held her breath, ignoring the X girls when they began to screech in disbelief at her hesitation.

His chest shuddered on a ragged breath beneath her fists, and his voice was a low rumble. "Having to worry about that car at the same time...." He lifted his head. His eyes burned with need. "Cut me some slack, princess. I'm not that strong."

Neither was she. Everything in her cried with the need to throw caution to the wind. To grab hold of Jake's incredibly tempting body and dive into paradise. She might have given in to temptation if the bulky buckle of the truck's seat belt digging into her hip didn't remind her of their location. Instead, she uncurled her fists and pushed gently at his chest. He stepped back from between her thighs.

She immediately mourned the loss. Weakening, she tore her gaze from his and looked around. As garages went, this place wasn't so bad. Why shouldn't she grab a little garage paradise?

Oh, for heaven's sake. Have some self-respect, Gracie.

Before she could give in to her craven side, she pivoted on the seat to grip the steering wheel. "Teach me to drive, Malone."

He said nothing, and she shot him a sidelong glance from beneath her lashes.

"I'll let you know when I'm done thinking about the other."

Chapter 18

"Give it more gas."

The truck shot forward. Gracie's head snapped back to bounce against the headrest. She squeaked in surprise and immediately slammed on the brakes. Next to her, Murphy scrambled for purchase on the worn vinyl of the bench seat. Jake flung out an arm to keep the dog from sliding to the floor, bracing himself against the dashboard with the other. The vehicle bucked and rocked. The motor coughed and died.

She cringed. "Sorry. My fault. I forgot to use the clutch, damn it." Grumbling beneath her breath, she pushed in the clutch, pumped the gas pedal, and twisted the key. The motor roared to life once again. With her tongue tucked between her teeth, she feathered the pedals in a delicate balance. The truck rolled forward as smoothly as if she'd been driving for years.

According to his earlier instruction, she built speed then performed a seamless shift into second gear. She gripped the steering wheel, maneuvering the truck over the large area of open ground behind the house, and rounded the barn. Rutted and muddy with the melting snow, the barnyard's uneven surface required complete concentration, but soon the bouncing truck smoothed out as they approached the entrance to the narrow track leading toward the gate at the back of the property.

"Now?"

"If you think you're ready."

Her craven side was *definitely* ready, but what woman could simply go on with life as if nothing had changed once she decided to let the sexiest man she'd ever met seduce her? A much better woman than her, that was for sure. Without waiting for further consent, she turned the truck onto the single lane trail.

"I was *ready* half an hour ago."

He chuckled but made no comment. The house and other farm dwellings soon disappeared from her rearview mirror. She slowed to round a curve then sped up once more along a straightaway. Winter sunlight filtered easily through the leafless trees and she smiled wryly. What a difference twelve hours made. Another thing she'd never admit was how spooked she'd been hurrying through the dark and cold last night. This morning, the spooky shadows had been erased by bright sunlight and sweet imaginings of what would happen between her and the man at her side, as soon as she said the word.

The guest cottage left to Mary in Pete's will came into view—the fully furnished, including a queen-sized bed, empty of guests at the moment, guest cottage.

She shook her head, attempting to refocus on her driving. The helpless lust simmering aside, she was having a ball. Why hadn't she learned to drive years ago? He was right. Slipping behind the wheel was pure joy.

"Watch your speed. Trees are a lot less forgiving than a wooden fence."

She shot him a toothy grin. "Relax, Malone. It's a simple matter of picking your route and showing no fear."

The deep rumble of his male laughter filled the cab and set her girl parts to tingling. Oh, God. She wished he wouldn't do that. Smashing into one of those unforgiving trees wasn't how she wanted their time alone to end this morning. The question was, how *did* she want this morning to end?

A slightly naughty and extremely delicious picture formed, and she bit back a groan. She'd told Jake she'd let him know once she'd given *the other* some thought, but the truth was, she couldn't *stop* thinking of the pleasures awaiting them. If she acted too fast, he'd think her easy. Hell, who was she kidding? She was more than easy, she was a sure thing. Knowing Jake in the biblical sense was a matter of when, not if, and the knowing sparkle in his eyes said he was fully aware of his pending victory.

Sheer stubbornness and a need to prove *she* still held the reins of her willpower were the *only* reasons they were bumping along a dirt road and not curled together on a makeshift bed, resting up for another round of garage paradise.

Her heartbeat increased as they approached the turnoff to the cottage. She bit her bottom lip. Controlling the willpower reins was difficult with sweaty palms. Her gaze roamed over the charming, two-bedroom bungalow. Mary had yet to move in, now the old foreman's quarters were hers. Remodeled by Sarah after she and Pete married, the cottage had housed his out of town associates when they visited. To Gracie's knowledge, no guests had visited since Sarah's death, but Mary continued the practice of keeping the cottage in readiness.

The reins slipped dangerously close to being ripped from her fingers.

Maybe she was rationalizing, grasping at a convenient opportunity to take a step she desperately wanted to take, but who knew when she and Jake would find themselves truly alone again, without the girls or Mary around? The air shuddered in her lungs when she dragged in a desperate gulp of oxygen. If she was going to do this crazy thing, now was the time.

She glanced over at his strong profile, slammed on the brakes, and twisted the key.

The truck skidded to a halt at the entrance to the cabin. Murphy tumbled to the baseboard at Jake's feet.

Jake met her nervous gaze with a questioning lift of his brow. "What are we doing?"

She blew out a shuddering breath and embraced crazy. "I'm done thinking."

* * * *

Jake eyed the guesthouse for a long moment then slowly turned his head. Gracie lifted her chin defiantly, as if she expected an argument. Right. He needed no explanation or qualification for why she stopped the truck at the steps of the small cabin. She'd said she needed time to think. Apparently, she was done.

Hell, yeah. A quick-thinking woman was a beautiful thing.

Gripping her shoulders, he dragged her across the bench seat and onto his lap. Her eyes went wide, but she didn't protest when he lowered his head to capture her mouth with his. She wrapped her arms around his shoulders and gave as good as she got.

Blindly searching for the latch at his back, he swung open the door. He held her to his chest as he stumbled into the cool morning air. Beneath the canopy of leafless trees, patches of icy snow spotted the shadowed ground. Unwilling to take the chance she'd change her mind, he gave her no opportunity to speak. He peppered her mouth with greedy kisses as he slipped and slid toward the steps leading to the cottage.

Murphy darted back and forth around his legs, making the crossing more treacherous. Jake lurched to one side on the uneven ground and almost went down. He caught himself at the last moment. To his surprise, instead of demanding he put her down before he dropped her, Gracie wrapped her long legs around his waist. Feminine desire flashed in her eyes. She palmed his cheeks with both hands, pulling his head down until she could kiss him back. He staggered to a stop. The hot pleasure of her tongue tangling with his nearly made his head blow off.

Murphy barked, reminding him where they were. He climbed the two steps to the porch and released her mouth. "Is there a key?"

On a breathless shudder, she jerked her head toward the top of the door. "Right top corner of the doorframe."

He ran his fingers along the top of the door. Shoving the key into the lock, he twisted. The door swung open without a sound and he carried her inside. With his mouth fused to hers, he kicked out blindly. The crash of the cottage door slamming shut behind them pierced the quiet like a gunshot. Murphy slammed up against one knee in his mad scramble to squeeze past.

Thrown off balance, Jake's shoulder collided with the corner of a cabinet beside the door. The glassware on the shelves tinkled. He tightened his arms around her, planting his feet to keep from toppling over. Crashing to his ass and bringing her with him wouldn't surprise him, considering where he'd landed every other time he kissed her.

Fuck that. Not this time.

He crushed her close, from mouth to knees, and thrilled when she pressed closer, as if trying to sink into his skin. Every ligament and muscle contracted in fevered anticipation. He answered her unspoken demand by doing some sinking of his own. He plunged his tongue deep. Her mint and musk scent wafted through his nostrils and her tangy sweetness exploded on his taste buds.

Heartbeat thundering, he struggled against the surprisingly potent urge to bypass the usual foreplay, shooting straight to the mind-blowing moment when he'd press inside her and make her his. He battled against the unprecedented need to forego the scintillating touches and caresses and the mouthwatering tastes he'd anticipated in each and every hot fantasy over the last few days. As if ancient instincts drove him, his body sizzled with molten fire, demanding he claim immediate victory by dragging her to the floor for a hard and fast, no frills mating.

The way his cock throbbed, resisting those instincts was downright painful, but the fantasy images running through his mind since first laying eyes on the prickly princess were impossible to forget, or ignore. He wanted to whisper his sensual intentions in her ear before playing out each and every imagining, then he wanted to try a few more.

Ego demanded this first time together last more than the time it took to roll on a condom, but unless he got control of himself, he wouldn't last even that long. He needed to slow things down. They *both* needed to slow down.

Her lips chased his when he broke the kiss and lifted his head. She squirmed in his arms. Her body rubbing against his was nearly his undoing. He shut his eyes, savoring the incredible friction of her soft curves sliding along his hard plains. Teasing fingers of pleasure walked their way up his spine.

Lord have mercy.

"Gracie."

Lush lashes fluttered open to reveal fathomless pools of passion. She blinked and a wrinkle suddenly puckered the skin between her delicate brows. "*Please*, tell me you have a condom in your pocket."

The huskiness of her voice caressed his ego and the band of urgent tension squeezing his chest eased. He threw back his head and laughed. An embarrassed flush deepened the blush on her cheeks, but a wry smile grew.

He shook his head and grinned. "I'm covered."

Horror bloomed in her eyes. She arched back in his arms, enough to shoot a quick glance down at his crotch, then her amazing eyes lifted to his, narrowing in an accusing frown.

He chuckled, tucking her up against his chest when she unwrapped her legs from his waist and attempted to shove out of his arms. "I'm not *wearing* one, if that's what you're thinking. That was a figure of speech. I've got several in my pocket."

"Oh." Her body softened against his and her frown evaporated, replaced by telling relief. She blew out a sigh. "Well, then. Okay. Wait!" The frown returned. "Then why did you stop?"

"Because I'd rather lay you down in a warm, comfortable bed than on a cold tile floor."

She fidgeted within his embrace. In embarrassment or excitement? From the way she'd been wrapped around him, his money was on the latter. He didn't have to worry about the princess changing her mind. Not now anyway. She was as caught up in the urgency as he. As for later….

She shot him a teasing smile from beneath lowered lashes. "That tile does look cold."

He smiled.

"And hard."

His smile slid toward a pained grimace. "Speaking of hard."

Her teeth flashed in a grin. "Poor baby. There's a bed in the next room. Right behind you."

She laughed when he immediately spun around and headed for the open door of the bedroom. Murphy bumped his knee in his race to get there first.

"I don't think so, mutt."

Using one booted foot, he blocked the dog and quickly shut the door in his face. Gracie's low laugh made his balls contract painfully. He crossed the room in three long strides, which only increased her humor, but if he was in a hurry, she was too. She slid one hand under the hem of his sweatshirt and open jacket. His stomach muscles quivered beneath her questing fingers. Cool and searching, they roamed over his stomach to his chest, pressing, kneading, caressing.

Her palm skimmed upward until she cupped the ball of his shoulder. His sweater rode her wrist, baring his chest to her view. She dipped her head and pressed her open mouth to a tightened nipple.

On an anguished moan of pleasure, he tumbled them onto the queen-sized bed.

Chapter 19

The world tilted wildly. Gracie clung to Jake, tightening her arm around his neck and wrapping her other around his waist. Her surprised squeak joined his growled moan and ended on a breathy *oof*. Arms and legs tangled, they bounced once before settling on the patchwork quilt. Sprawled over him on the antique brass bed, she had no opportunity to enjoy her perch. He immediately rolled, reversing their positions to lean over her.

Behind him, soft rays of sunlight fell through the window. Cast in semi-shadow, the fiery red halo framing his broad shoulders and wild mane of black hair reminded her of the demonic qualities she'd assigned him earlier. A devil with sensual intent sparkling in his emerald eyes.

He brushed his thumb over her cheekbone, watching her intently. "Your eyes are incredible, princess. Damn. I could drown in them."

Flustered, she wasn't sure how to respond. The unusual eye color she inherited from her mother had always drawn its share of attention, from the taunts of the kids in school, to the time she was harassed outside a west side gallery by a pushy photographer insisting she model for him. That wasn't to say the soft violet hue hadn't received its share of praises, especially from men, but never in a lazy Texas drawl capable of stroking her soul.

Hot excitement flashed through her as he slid his muscled thigh between hers, and *whoa!* He wasn't kidding about hard. A large, rigid length pressed against her hip. Her girl parts immediately puddled with anticipation, and she thrilled when he bent to kiss her long and hard.

As his mouth performed an exhilarating, carnal mating of hers, employing lips, teeth and tongue, his hands roamed in a sensory exploration, rubbing, plucking, caressing, and squeezing. Layers of clothing were magically swept aside. Off came her jacket. He flicked an arm over his head, and her black and white check wool blazer flew through the air to land on the floor in the corner. Several long moments later, he released her mouth long enough to tug the sweater over her head. It joined the blazer on a high-arching toss.

Rising on one elbow, he hung over her. Hot passion glazed his eyes and his chest rose and fell on ragged breaths. Elation skittered up her spine as her ego twirled in a mental happy dance. *She'd* done that to him. How lovely knowing she wasn't the only one about to go up in flames.

She blinked when he continued to watch her in silence. Suddenly jittery at the interruption, doubt crept in. Why had he stopped? She frowned. "What?"

He brushed a curl back from her temple. "I was just thinking."

"About?"

Dimples made an appearance in his slow smile. "This is the first time I've kissed you and didn't end up with a bruise."

A helpless laugh gurgled in her throat. And he called *her* a smart ass? Relief made her giddy. A man who could make a woman laugh was impossible to resist, but how the hell could he make jokes when she was about to *combust*? She grinned. "The morning's still early, funny guy." She shoved at his shoulders.

Laughing, he let her push him until he lay sprawled on his back. She happily crawled on top and swung her leg over to cradle his hips with her knees. He gripped her waist with both hands. Lowering herself to sit, she met his laughing gaze with a smirk—a difficult task considering her eyes wanted to cross.

His groan nearly drowned out hers. Instant bolts of electric heat shot out from the point of delicious contact, sizzling in her lower torso and turning the muscles in all four of her limbs to lead. Warm and rough, his wide palms caressed as they travelled her sides and up over her ribcage to cup her breasts.

At a healthy C cup, she filled his hands. Goose bumps popped with a running shiver as he brushed the pads of his thumbs over her stiffened nipples and they beaded further beneath the silk of her bra.

"You like that? It feels good?" His harshly spoken question was another form of caress.

She nodded.

"I can tell. Your nipples are incredibly sensitive, baby. I can't wait to taste them."

He plucked at one beaded tip with index finger and thumb, and she helplessly swiveled her hips, rubbing herself against the hard ridge of his erection. Relief and frustration battled. Between her jeans and his, they were wearing far too many clothes.

"Do they like to be sucked?"

She whimpered.

"The idea makes me so hard I could explode."

The paradox of his languid attentions and suggestive comments left her teetering on the edge of a precipice with nothing to hold onto.

Oh, God. He's a sex whisperer.

She'd heard of men like him before but had never slept with one. The concept pierced the core of her femininity. Her inner muscles clenched on the verge of climax. She gasped in dismay. If he didn't get on with it, she wouldn't be sleeping with one now. She'd be reaching paradise, half-dressed and on her own. She dove for his belt buckle.

He laughed. "I guess they do."

His rippling stomach muscles frustrated her attempt to slip his belt from the loops. She sat up straight. "If you're going to be all talk and no action, I'm outta here."

He had her on her back before she could blink. Wicked laughter shone in his eyes. "How did I know you'd be greedy in bed?"

She blasted him with a disappointed glare. "I'm not a greedy lover. I know how to give back. It's just that—"

"Good to know."

Oh, for heaven's sake. This was a huge mistake. She tried to sit up then froze in midair when his mouth latched onto a nipple. Heat scorched her, shooting arrows of white, hot pleasure straight to her groin. He tongued her through the silk of her bra and guided her back down until she lay prone beneath him.

Her back arched at the scrape of his teeth, scoring the sensitive bud. A low purr gurgled in her throat, and her eyes slid shut. He tore the damp material of her bra away to capture her flesh in his open mouth as if he meant to swallow her whole. Bright shards of excitement flashed like a kaleidoscope of color on the backs of her eyelids.

She slid dangerously close to orgasm. Clenching her thighs together, she tried desperately to hold on. Not yet. Not yet.

The button on her jeans popped free and the zipper rasped open under his experienced fingers. Burrowing his hand under both denim and the lace panties beneath, he peeled the garments down over one hip. She shifted, lifting her hips to aid him in their removal. He shoved the materials to her knees and she scissor kicked them free.

Leaving languid behind, he wasted no time. His open mouth left a hot trail behind as he found her other breast. Pleasure shards sliced at her as he gently bit her turgid nipple at the exact moment the rough pads of his talented fingers unerringly found that for which they searched. He cupped her damp heat in his large palm and with a tweak of her tightly budded clit, she erupted on a scream.

Need, as hot as lava, rolled through her and seared every molecule of her being. Wave after wave tossed her higher. Her legs fell open and her hips arched, grinding against his kneading palm and chasing a pleasure so keen she was left panting until she didn't think she could stand any more. When his mouth replaced his hand, she learned the folly in her thinking.

With tongue and teeth, he drove her to a place she didn't know existed, where pleasure danced with joy and fire burned hotter than the sun. She rocked against his murmurs of encouragement, whimpering and clenching her fingers in his hair until the harsh sucking of his mouth sent her tumbling over the edge once more in a shower of heat and light.

Boneless and replete, she struggled to open her eyes several long moments later. Head resting in one palm on a bent elbow, Jake lay on his side next to her. He wore a satisfied smile, but the elevated color on his cheekbones and his burning eyes told a different story. To say nothing of the rigid length pressing at her hip beneath the jeans he still wore.

Her lips twisted in a guilty grimace. "What was it you said about me being greedy?"

He grinned. "And I was right, but I wasn't complaining."

She groaned and slapped a hand over her eyes. He chuckled, and the soft cotton of his sweatshirt brushed her side and breast when he leaned forward and kissed her briefly. Musk and spice teased her nostrils. She slid her hand to the side of her face. He continued to lean over her. Humor sparkled in his watchful eyes.

"That was a compliment. To both of us."

"How do you figure? So far, all I've done is take."

He stroked a hand over her hip. One winged brow arched. "Are you saying we're done here?"

"God, I hope not!" The greedy admission slipped out before she could stop herself.

He grinned and used his wide palm to yank her up against him. He dipped a knee between hers thighs once again and lowered his mouth. "Then I'll soon get my turn, won't I? Watching your beautiful body take flight on an orgasm *I've* given you is more than an incredible turn-on.

It's a gift. There's nothing sexier to a man than a passionate woman who wants him so badly she can't wait."

Delivered in a seductive croon, his whispered words reignited the delicious heat in the folds still swollen from his earlier ministrations. God, the man had a magical tongue. In more ways than one. Who knew a little dirty talk could make her this frigging hot? If he kept that up, she'd be leaving him behind again.

Well, as the old saying went. Two could play that game. Ripping a page out of his sex whisperer book, she lowered her voice to a purr. "Nothing sexier, huh? Then, I must be the sexiest woman alive."

His deep laugh vibrated through his chest to hers, and he dipped his head to kiss her. She twisted away out of his arms and scooted to the far side of the bed. "I mean it. I'm this close." She held finger and thumb a fraction of an inch apart and made her expression as stern as possible, which wasn't very, considering how badly her body throbbed. "Unless you want me *taking off* without you again, I suggest you get naked. Like, right now."

He immediately rolled off the bed to his feet. Giggling, she scrambled to sit. Shoving the pillow behind her back, she made herself comfortable propped against the brass headboard to watch the show. She'd forgotten how quickly he could move, or how effectively. Arms and legs flailing, the famous dexterity he displayed on the field was nothing compared to the moves he employed as he shed himself of sweatshirt, boots, jeans, and briefs.

When he was down to bare skin, he tossed several foil packets on the table beside the bed and turned to face her. Seemingly at ease, he stood still under her inspection with his hands fisted on his lean hips.

In casual street clothes he was the picture of a *superbly* healthy, modern male. Dressed in uniform and pads he was larger than life, a fantasy hero of the gridiron. Naked? Oh, Lord. Naked he was an X-rated *superhero*.

A six-foot-five impossibly *healthy*, muscular man of steel.

Incredibly wide shoulders narrowed over impressive pecs down to a trim waist. She didn't know if there was a technical name for the sharply cut lines of muscle where his washboard stomach met his lean hips, but the well-cut ridge made her mouth water. As for the imposing evidence of his desire…his cock stood strong and proud between thick thighs. She gulped. Forget eye candy, the man was a freaking candy factory.

"Wow." She breathed the word like a benediction.

His wicked smile should've warned her. As if released from invisible chains, he dropped a bent knee to the bed, wrapped long fingers around one of her ankles…and yanked.

She squealed with laughter as he dragged her forward and didn't complain when he lowered himself until he lay cradled between her thighs. Propped on his elbows, he locked his gaze with hers.

"Better?"

She nodded. "Much."

"Then come fly with me, princess."

Considering how he'd ruthlessly pushed her toward a quick and explosive release earlier, and how aroused he appeared during her inspection, she was surprised by the pace he set, an easy lover completely content to take his time. For her, sex had always been a pleasant passage of time. Not so with Jake. To her joy, she discovered laughing with a lover was more than pleasant. It was *fun*.

By nature or design, she wasn't sure which and didn't care, he kept her pleasantly off balance with his playful brand of foreplay. The tools in his seduction bag were varied and irresistible. Teasing smiles and murmured praises accompanied trailing touches and penetrating gazes that reached down to tempt the soul. He seemed to sense whenever she ventured close to the abyss, courtesy of a hot, bone-melting kiss or spine-tingling caress, then he'd yank her back from the precipice with nipping teeth and naughty whispers, or a frisky tickle of the ribs.

He wasn't the only one with a sensual bag of tricks. He'd teased her about being greedy. He was right. She greedily savored the opportunity to touch him at her leisure. A laughing and naked Jake in her bed was a dream come true. She took full advantage.

Tucked partially beneath his big body, she turned her head to break his mind-stealing kiss. Sliding her hand down over his stomach, she curled her fingers around the hot length of him and whispered in his ear. "Your turn."

He rolled to his back, giving her complete access. She rose on one elbow and shimmied closer to his side. Loosening her grip on his engorged cock, she dragged her fingers up the swollen length to trace circles around the sensitive tip with a fingernail. He shifted his legs, restlessly.

"Ah, you like that." She leaned closer, causing her breasts to plump against his chest, and held his gaze. "You're so hard, baby."

His eyes flared with emerald heat and his erection jerked slightly within the cage of her fingers. She laughed, low and quiet. He narrowed his eyes, but a smile tugged at his lips.

"Witch."

Teeth bared in a pleased smile, she rose to her knees. With her free hand resting on the clenched ridges of his stomach muscles, she held his gaze as she bent at the waist. His breath hissed in sharply when her curls floated over his sensitive flesh. She paused there, suspended over him, her lips a scant inch from the swollen tip. Heated promises glittered in his eyes. Excitement shimmered in wet waves between her legs.

"Tell me. Do *you* like to be sucked?"

She didn't give him the opportunity to answer, surrounding him with her mouth. His low moan thrilled. Hot and hard, the salty taste of him registered on her tongue as she explored his varying textures, silk and steel. Too soon, his fingers slid into her hair and when he tugged slightly, she released him to look up.

Tension stretched the skin on his cheekbones tight as he reached for her shoulders and dragged her up his body. His arm swung out in search of a condom as he rolled her to her back at his side. White teeth flashed, foil tore, and he fisted the latex over himself before she could offer her help.

For the moment, her sex whisperer was silent. He mounted her without a word. Gripping her left calf, he guided her leg up and around his waist then flexed his hips. He pushed inside her and her inner muscles stretched deliciously around his invading length. She arched into him, spiraling close to the edge and needing to take him completely. He slid home and immediately began to move heavily.

Like well-lubed pistons, his hips pumped. She clung to him and matched his pace. His biceps bulged, propping his wide chest above hers, and his shaggy hair curtained his face. Emerald fire burned in the gaze locked with hers. With a grunt, he shifted onto one arm and reached between them, pressing a thumb to her tightened clit.

"Fly with me, baby."

With a keening cry, she answered his irresistible demand.

Chapter 20

Saturday morning was spent on the phone, directing a nervous client on the launch of her new website. Once the call ended, deliciously sweet scents drew Gracie to the empty kitchen. The third double batch of cookies in less than a week cooled on the counter. She rolled her eyes and snagged a water bottle from the fridge. Propping her hips against the counter, she selected a cookie and nibbled on the evidence she wasn't the only one to fall victim to the sexy bruiser in their midst.

With the exception of Angel, who showed signs of weakening but had yet to surrender completely to Jake's irresistible charms, the rest of them had melted like Mary's chocolate chips. The housekeeper had it bad, clucking around Jake like a mother hen, whipping up his favorite recipes and feeding his sweet tooth. As for Charlie, she'd been toast from the beginning, following him around like a doe-eyed groupie.

Shaking her head, Gracie's lips curved in a secret smile. She, by far, had been the easiest of his conquests, succumbing to his seduction in record time. Still, she couldn't be sorry, despite the wispy shadows of doubt and guilt occasionally blurring the sultry waves of contented pleasure at where things stood between them.

A lovely tingle tiptoed up her spine and she easily shoved aside her misgivings. Whatever the future held, she meant to enjoy this time they'd been given. Besides, how could she regret the hours they spent together in the cottage yesterday?

Remembered pleasure made her smile. The guy knew what he was about. His talented fingers strummed her body like a Stradivarius in a master's hand. As bold and brazen as he could be, she'd anticipated sex with him would be earthy and audacious and hadn't been disappointed. What she hadn't expected was his underlying gentleness and generosity.

Hardly a player in the sex department, she couldn't be considered a blushing virgin either, and yet with Jake she might as well have been. Did the newly accepted love in her heart account for the unexpected intensity of the experience? Perhaps the difference lay in the way he telegraphed his every sensual move, vocalizing his desires and whipping her body into a frenzy of anticipation before delivering all he promised and more. Then again, she'd never been with a man who could make her laugh while in the throes of passion. His bawdy teasing invited her quirky sense of humor and somehow kept her off balance *and* simultaneously put her at ease.

Whatever the underlying reason, the thrilling trace of his fingertips over her skin, teasing whispers in her ear, and hot brush of his body against hers delivered her to a place she'd never visited before. A place where inhibitions didn't tread. A newly discovered sense of feminine power grew stronger with every low moan, sultry smile, and shudder of his big body until she'd teetered on the edge of euphoria.

And if she was reading him right, she wasn't alone on her blissful journey to uncharted ground. His intent gaze, boring into hers when she wandered into the kitchen for breakfast this morning smoldered with heat and remembrance. The possibility he'd been as bowled over as she by their encounter kept her body humming throughout the rest of the morning. Even now, when he was nowhere in sight, her nipples puckered in anticipation of a repeat performance.

He'd named her greedy, with good reason, but her need for him was so much more. Jake Malone was a craving in her soul. She was in danger of becoming addicted.

Murphy scratched at the back door and she shoved off the counter. Addicted to Jake Malone? A grin pulled at her lips. She could think of worse things.

At Murphy's whine, she held his collar as she opened the door. Though the words were unclear, the unmistakable, low rumble of Jake's deep voice floated across the distance from the barn to her ears. A pleasant shiver rippled over her. Girlish laughter followed whatever he'd said, and her lips stretched in a helpless grin at the happy sound.

Several muffled thumps made her brow wrinkle with curiosity. What were he and the girls up to? Grabbing a stray jacket from the hook beside the door, she let the dog out and set off to investigate. The noises coming from inside the barn made sense when she rounded the building. Her steps slowed as she eyed the strange pickup truck. The open ramp of the attached horse trailer could mean only one thing and the giddy joy thrumming through her system cooled by several degrees.

Hercules had arrived at the farm.

Talk about a reality check. While she'd been floating on a haze of pleasure, Jake had been busy making arrangements. No real surprise, considering how determined he was to win the twins over. He'd said he planned to have the animal brought to the farm, hadn't he? Before he touched her and made her forget the true reason they were both here.

Well, she remembered now. If she were a more cynical type, she might think he'd distracted her on purpose, but her heart denied the possibility he'd slept with her simply to throw her off guard. Would a man playing a role experience four orgasms in two hours if he wasn't truly attracted? She didn't think so.

Who was she kidding? With men, her middle name was skeptical, but she couldn't blame cynicism and couldn't, in good conscience, blame Jake for her loss of focus, not when she'd willingly fall back into his bed in a heartbeat if given the chance. The sad fact was, the man scrambled her brain and she wanted this...*temporary fling* with him almost as badly as she wanted to make a family with the girls.

The trouble was, no matter what her heart might feel, or how exciting sleeping with him might be, when it came to the custody of the girls, she and Jake were at war. No escaping that fact. She'd known going in, sleeping with him would have drawbacks.

A scrambled brain was apparently one of them and something she'd need to guard against in the future.

Squinting, she studied the empty horse trailer and cleared her throat against the completely unacceptable fist of disappointment clenching in her belly. His sleeping with her might not be a ploy to win custody, not consciously anyway, but the pleasure they shared certainly hadn't kept *him* from keeping his eye on the prize. She'd do well to follow his example.

She patted a hand to her thigh. "Come here, Murph." The dog trotted to her side obediently. She gripped his collar tight. Though he got along fine with other dogs, she wasn't sure what his reaction would be to a horse. She briefly considered returning him to the house but decided against it. This was his home, too—at least for the next few months.

Heart heavy and steps dragging, she pasted on a smile and led Murphy through the open barn door. Moist warmth and the pungent scent of hay and horse enveloped her. After the bright sunlight, her eyes were slow to adjust to the low light of the large building. When they did, she headed down the long center aisle.

On sneakered feet, Angel climbed the metal rails of the last stall and tossed one leg over the top rung. Mary hovered behind her with Charlie clinging to her hand. "Here now. You be careful. That's a mighty big animal."

Angel didn't spare the housekeeper a glance. Balancing her bottom on the rail, she leaned forward and peered into the stall where Jake raked a rough-bristled brush over the flank of a huge black horse. "Look how pretty he is."

Unnoticed, Gracie came to a stop beside Mary and couldn't disagree. Like his owner, the proud animal was larger than life and gloriously appealing. Tall and muscular, he exuded strength and power. His glossy, ebony coat gleamed with good health as did his matching mane and long, flowing tail.

The metal clip on his harness jangled when he jerked his regal head in a lurching nod as if agreeing with Angel's assessment.

Warmth bubbled in Gracie's belly at Jake's soft chuckle. He straightened, and her gaze followed his wide palmed hand sliding over the horse's back to his neck. He thumped the strong column twice in a rough caress. The warmth in her belly intensified to a smolder when he glanced up from his grooming and his laughing gaze clashed with hers.

Pinned in place by the mesmerizing beam of his sparkling green gaze, she bit back a groan. What did it say about her that moisture pooled between her thighs, despite the presence of a grandmotherly housekeeper and two six year-olds? But, damn it, guarding against a scrambled brain was severely problematic with her insides performing a bump and grind shimmy dance to the strippers' beat echoing through her head.

It made perfect sense she'd fallen in love with a devil like Jake, since she was obviously going to hell.

Her breath escaped in a relieved shudder when he glanced away to wink at Angel.

"I think he agrees with you, Angel face."

Pleased color bloomed on Angel's cheeks.

The stripper beat screeched to a halt on a sour note. Gracie resisted the urge to rub a palm over the pang squeezing her heart as right before her eyes, her lone ally slipped an inch closer to surrender. Over the idea of sharing an accord with his horse or from Jake's use of the nickname? Gracie wasn't sure, but either way, the arrival of Hercules had already altered the dynamics of Angel's and Jake's relationship and further threatened Gracie's hopes for a family.

The sting of impending tears registered, but they didn't have the chance to form before Hercules swished his thick tail in a whipping arc. He stomped a back hoof to the floor with a resounding thud. She'd forgotten about Murphy until he jolted at the unexpected sounds. He jumped back from the stall and tore the collar from her fingers after nearly wrenching her arm from the socket.

Startled by the dog's sudden thrashing, Hercules skittered to the side on clomping hooves. Jake scrambled to grab the dangling reins and missed. The horse's momentum carried him to the other side of the stall where his large rump crashed against the rails and knocked Angel off balance.

Jake shot out his free arm. With a cry, Gracie leapt forward, as did Mary. None of them were quick enough to prevent the six year old from tumbling over the bars to land between the horse's stomping front hooves. The clear snap of a bone sent a jagged blade of terror slicing down Gracie's spine, even as she bent to squeeze between the rails to get to her niece.

Jake grunted gutturally. Gracie jerked a quick glance his way. He struggled to control the nervous animal and prevent him from trampling the tiny body at his feet. The horse balked, high stepping and dancing sideways. Finally, Jake jammed a shoulder into the horse's solid chest. Using brute force, he shoved the animal back toward the far corner of the stall.

"Shh. It's okay, boy. Settle. Settle." He crooned to the fractious animal. Holding the reins in a firm grip, he ran his free hand back and forth over the horse's quivering shoulder. "Did he step on her?" he called over his shoulder in a deceptively soothing tone.

"Oh, my sweet Lord." Mary's brogue thickened with her concern. Tears dripped down Charlie's scrunched face as she pressed against the railing and ineffectively reached her hand out to her twin.

Gracie dropped to her knees beside Angel's crumpled body. Busy scrambling into the stall, she hadn't seen. *Had* Angel been stepped on? The sound of a breaking bone had been unmistakable, but from what cause? The fall, or the horse's hooves? Terror threatened as she ran gentle hands over Angels back, and she almost fainted with relief when the little girl rolled over on her own. No paralysis, thank God.

Angel moaned and opened her eyes. They immediately flooded with tears. Gracie carefully wrapped one arm under her shoulders when she struggled to sit up, cradling her left arm. Beneath the bulky sleeve of her winter coat, the arm was clearly broken. Angel began to cry in earnest. Charlie joined her, sobbing into Mary's side.

"Gracie!" Soft and quiet, Jake's voice held a definite demand.

The lump in her throat made speaking difficult. "No. No, he didn't, thank God, but I think her arm is broken."

The heavy rush of his expelled breath registered over the twins' whimpering sobs. Gracie glanced over Angel's shoulder. He turned his head and ran his gaze over his half sister. A rolling shudder rippled over his body and searing relief darkened his eyes before they slid shut. Gracie could sympathize with the flash of vulnerability in those green orbs. She'd never been so scared in her life.

His shoulders slumped and his chest expanded on a rough breath. When he opened his eyes a moment later, all sign of vulnerability was gone. Unmistakable anger glittered there.

"Get her out of here." His gaze sliced briefly to Charlie. His lip curled on a soft snarl when he cast a glance at Murphy. "Get them all out of here. Now." Though he kept his voice soft, there was no missing the fury in his tone.

Angel winced at his growled demand and ducked her head to burrow her face tighter against Gracie. She wrapped the child tighter to her chest and scalded him with a heated glare. Neither she nor her dog were in any way at fault for what happened with his stupid horse. No skin off her nose if he decided to lay the blame at her feet, but for a guy normally a pro when it came to the female mind, he was acting like a rookie in this case. Couldn't he see Angel considered his anger aimed at her?

Fine. He was upset, with good reason, but Angel was already distressed enough. Did he have to make matters worse?

Furious with herself as much as with him, she shook her head and turned away. How could she have fallen for a man whose *horse* had a deeper understanding of a little girl's gentle heart than he did? She rose to her feet with Angel tucked close in her arms. Mary unlatched the stall door and pushed the rail wide so they could exit. Charlie immediately raced forward and curled her fingers around her sister's ankle.

"Wait."

Gracie paused at his guttural demand and turned to arch a bitter brow.

His chest expanded with his sigh. "Please, Gracie." Silently, he stared at his half sister, weeping quietly against Gracie's shoulder. His Adams apple convulsed on a ragged swallow and his fury seemed to deflate in time with his drooping shoulders. His gaze skittered back to Gracie and the anger hardening her heart was no match for the shadowed uncertainty in his eyes.

Helpless against the silent plea in the darkened, green orbs, the sting of tears scratched at the back of her throat. Time froze as he held her gaze and the confident predator who took on the world and emerged victorious faded into the shadows. In his place stood a handsome, if imperfect, man.

A man unsure of his footing as he struggled with a reality he had no experience handling.

Her heart quivered in her chest, freefalling in a crazy tumble and slid dangerously close to full out, undeniable love.

Finally, he dipped his chin in a nod, and turned away. Gracie squeezed her eyes shut briefly and shoved aside the dizzying fear. Nothing had changed. No matter her feelings for Jake, the twins were what mattered. She rubbed a soothing hand over Angel's back.

Oblivious to her inner turmoil, Jake unclipped the harness from Hercules and looped the strap over a hook on the wall. After a last pat to the horse's neck, he strode out of the stall and closed and secured the latch. Pivoting, he stepped forward until he stood less than a foot away. The pained smile he offered Gracie caused a shimmering throb beneath her heart.

The smile slid away as he wrapped his long fingers around her upper arm and squeezed gently. "Sorry. I guess I don't react well when I'm rattled, either."

He dropped his gaze to Angel and, after hesitating slightly, rubbed a hand down her back. "Angel?" He waited until she shifted her head to peek up at him and proved he was indeed aware of the consequences of his anger. "You didn't do anything wrong, sweetheart. This was my fault. No one else's."

Angel sniffled and swiped at her nose with the back of her uninjured hand. Mary promptly dug through her pocket and pulled out a handkerchief. Gracie's jaw nearly dropped when he took the folded cloth, held it to Angel's nose, and insisted she blow.

He nodded at the arm she held tucked to her side. "Does it hurt?"

Angel nodded and fresh tears leaked down her cheeks.

"Then we'd better take care of it. How far is the nearest hospital, Mary?"

"About three miles."

He winked down at Charlie then curled his fingers around Gracie's elbow to lead her toward the door. "What do you say, Charlie? Can you help Miss Mary with the next batch of cookies while Gracie and I take Angel to get her arm fixed up?"

Charlie sniffed and nodded.

Gracie's steps faltered. Hospital? How could she leave the farm with them when the mob still waited at the gate?

Oh, God. She'd need to do some quick thinking because Jake wasn't taking Angel anywhere without her. As they exited the barn, her gaze was drawn to the old pickup parked near the track leading to the back gate. Maybe she could convince him to let her drive.

Chapter 21

Gracie stopped short in the kitchen doorway, blinking her eyes at what surely must be a mirage. Littered with the evidence of a baking disaster, Mary's pristine and organized kitchen was in shambles. The uncharacteristically cluttered counters held several open canisters, their lids discarded haphazardly in the midst of a half dozen dirty bowls of various sizes. Mary's prized industrial mixer sat with its blades upended. A dark, oozing matter dripped from them to form a brown puddle. The same substance coated the tile backsplash in a splatter design. A fine layer of flour, or possibly sugar, dusted the counters and floor.

Murphy's footprints told the tale of his prancing attempts to snag a treat. They crisscrossed the large room, concentrating mostly in a circular track around the table by which he stood. The tags on his collar jangled against the metal of the bowl he was doing his best to lick clean.

At the center of the disaster, with their backs to her, the twins each perched on the edge of a chair. Leaning over the table and swirling pink icing over a lopsided brown block Gracie assumed was a cake, each held a…*Dear God. Were those steak knives?* Between them sat Jake, his broad back dwarfing their tiny frames in contrast.

"What in the world?"

Three pairs of innocent eyes met her gaze when they turned their heads.

"Jake has to crush Atlanta tomorrow. He's gonna miss Thanksgiving," Charlie chirped happily. "Miss Mary said we could have another Thanksgiving when he gets home, but Jake said that's a lot of work for her, so we made her a cake. It's a surprise."

Considering the mess they'd made, on Thanksgiving eve, no less, Mary was in for a surprise all right. Gracie opened her mouth to start barking orders for an immediate cleanup when her gaze landed on Angel. The slash of pink icing marring the cast on her left forearm wasn't responsible for Gracie's hesitation, nor was the chocolate ring around her tiny mouth.

What made Gracie's heart quiver off balance was the wide smile tilting her lips. Genuine and easy, her smile softened the shadows darkening the little girl's eyes for the past month.

She waved her broken arm. "I cracked a egg with one hand and didn't lose any shells in the batter!" Her jubilant smile didn't dim when she spun her head to grin up at her half brother. "Right, Jake?"

He tapped a finger to her nose. "Right, Angel face." He grinned at the icing left behind and popped the finger into his mouth.

Angel wiped the smear from her nose and following his example, sucked the icing from her fingers. Her happy giggles wrapped around Gracie's thudding heart and squeezed painfully. Tears of equal parts relief and fear stung at the back of her throat.

"That's terrific, baby." She ducked her head, passing by the table to make her way to the ransacked counter, and blinked furiously. The sponge at the edge of the sink provided a purpose for her shaking hands. Running the sponge under the water, she squeezed it out and attacked the counter.

As she had numerous times since the incident in the barn several weeks ago, she cursed Pete for thrusting her into a situation destined to tear her apart. Building a family with the girls was a dream she harbored in the depths of her soul but, despite what her helpless feelings for Jake meant to her custody chances, she loved Angel too much not to find joy in her happiness. The same went for Charlie. How could she resent the girls' growing affection for Jake when the innocent love he inspired in them eased the sting of their grief over the loss of their parents?

As for Jake? She loved him as well. How could she not celebrate his surprised pleasure as he opened his heart to his sisters? Not thrill *for* him as he slowly cast aside a lifetime of bitter memories to discover the delights of being part of a caring family?

And how ironic his apparent acceptance of her dream might well be the vehicle by which it was stolen?

The scrape of chair legs reached her. She dipped her head to the side to wipe away an escaped tear on her shoulder. Damn it. Tears never achieved a thing except to make her eyes puffy and her nose red. They certainly didn't change anything. She jumped when Charlie appeared at her elbow.

"You wanna lick?"

Gracie blinked to clear her watery vision and stared at the chocolate-covered serrated knife Charlie held up. "Oh, baby. Let me have that." Fingers clenched around the sponge, she carefully plucked the lethal looking cutlery from her niece's icing-smeared fingers.

Charlie glanced from Gracie's face to the messy counters and back. She scrunched her nose in a quizzical frown. "Don't cry, Auntie Gracie. I'll help you clean up."

"Gracie?"

She refused to acknowledge Jake's quiet inquiry. Hugging Charlie to her side, she bent to press her cheek to the top of her head. "Thanks, baby. Miss Mary won't like it if she comes home to find her kitchen messed up."

"I can help, too." Angel tugged on her sleeve.

Straightening, she swiped a finger under her eyes before smiling at Angel. "Then we'll have it cleaned in a snap."

Without meeting Jake's gaze, she directed Angel to begin sweeping up the flour-coated floor, then she rinsed the sponge and helped Charlie onto the counter where she could take care of the splatters on the backsplash. Next, she turned on the tap, added soap, and set the mixing bowl and blades to soak. Murphy raced to lick up the last of the batter, his nose following the bowl she picked up from the floor.

Jake appeared at her side, carrying tubs of icing and other cake decorating paraphernalia. She stared at the lethal-looking knife in his hand and arched a brow. "Steak knives?"

He offered a guilty smile. "They wanted to make squiggles in the icing. Charlie insisted the sharp knives have the perfect ridges they needed to pull it off." He popped one shoulder in a negligent shrug. "It worked."

She shook her head and handed him a roll of paper towels, jerking her chin at the chocolate mess coating most of the table. "You're lucky neither of them cut off a finger."

He screwed up his mouth in a grimace. "Finger, hell. I was more worried about their tongues. They kept licking the icing off the blades."

Despite the heaviness weighing on her shoulders, she laughed. He tucked the paper roll under one arm and cupped her chin in his palm, lifting her face for his study. She stood silent, drawn in by the intensity of his gaze skimming over her cheeks and down over her mouth before lifting back to her eyes. He spoke softly in the voice she'd come to love over the weeks since they first made love. The one he used whenever they managed to find some time alone. The voice only she heard. "What is it, princess? What's made you sad?"

Her eyes stung with renewed tears. She shut them briefly. Did he know how much she wanted to step into his arms and never leave? If she gave in to the overwhelming need to cling to what she wished could be, would he welcome her there for longer than the next eight weeks? Forcing a smile, she opened her eyes, wrapped her fingers around his wrist, and squeezed.

"Not sad." She searched for an excuse he'd accept without further questions. "Tired, I guess."

He didn't buy it. His doubt was there in his eyes, but he didn't push her either. Dropping a kiss to her nose, he stepped back. "Then relax and have a seat. I'll get you a glass of wine." He raised his voice to include the twins in the conversation. "The girls and I caused this disaster. We'll clean it up. Right, ladies?"

"Right!"

"Right!"

Gracie shook her head. Like Cinderella's mice, the twins dove into their tasks with happy smiles. Charlie brushed the broom across the floor, creating a fine cloud of billowing flour. Angel dipped the sponge into the sink, dripping soaping water down her arm and onto the floor before dropping it on the counter to scrub industriously.

Gracie jumped when Jake cupped her shoulders in his hands. He spun her around and urged her toward the table with a palm to her ass. A familiar tingle rippled up her spine when he ended the touch with a caressing pat. She glanced over her shoulder, squinting her eyes when he winked.

The devil. He knew full well that kind of touch wouldn't help her relax. She flopped onto a chair, and he had the gall to laugh. True to his word, he delivered a chilled glass of wine, returning her to her seat several minutes later when she attempted to help Charlie locate the dustpan and brush. Finally, she gave in gracefully and sat back to watch.

For a bachelor, he didn't shy away from cleaning. Rolling up his sleeves, he tackled the bowls and dishes, scraping away the worst of the drying batter, then handed each piece off to the waiting girls, who loaded everything into the dishwasher.

All three of them were sidetracked by a rogue bubble formed when he dunked a glass into the soapy water. Of course, he then had to show the girls how he managed it. They each took a turn, shrieking with laughter when one of the resulting bubbles popped on the tip of Angel's nose.

The bittersweet sight scraped at Gracie's heart, even as it made her smile. As crazy as Pete's stipulations were, they'd also been a gift, allowing her a sweet glimpse of the family she craved. For that, she'd be forever grateful, but with the crumbling of each stone in Angel's wall of distrust, Gracie's dreams disappeared more and more beneath the rubble.

Jake didn't realize it yet, but he was falling in love with his sisters, as they were with him. He might have arrived at the farm against his will, but she could no longer imagine him walking away when Pete's terms had been met.

In slightly less than two months' time, no matter what decision was made, someone would be hurt. Several someones. The girls would suffer, too, forced to choose between two people they loved.

Jake was right. That particular stipulation of Pete's was asinine. It was also cruel.

The decision to enjoy her time with Jake and the girls while she could burned with a new urgency. Was it only a month ago she despaired of losing custody? Now she understood she stood to lose much more. If not for her secret parental connections, she'd be free to fight for her dreams *and* Jake with everything she had. Instead, a shadow hovered over the time they shared.

He suspected she was hiding something, but then, how could he not after her foolish trek through the woods and her furtive behavior the night Angel broke her arm. In the end, she hadn't bothered suggesting they sneak out the back gate, but ducking onto the floorboards of his SUV as they passed through the front gate and insisting they slip out the back door when they were done at the hospital, only made him more suspicious. Like a dog on a scent, he continued to press her for answers. Answers she didn't dare give.

On second thought, if Pete were here, she'd strangle him for serving up her dream, temporarily, in such a way that left her furtive and guarded with the man she loved.

* * * *

"It's going to piss me off if I have to spend the day disposing of a body."

Gracie glanced up from her laptop. Max filled her doorway. One broad, muscled shoulder propped against the frame, he'd tucked his battered leather jacket under one arm. The conservative, pale blue dress shirt collar peaking from beneath the coal gray sweater contrasted with the scarred black biker boots covering his big feet below disreputable jeans—he looked like a GQ thug.

Her reluctant smile faded quickly. There were times when having a best friend who knew you better than you knew yourself was comforting. This wasn't one of them. Hiding any kind of upset from Max had always been difficult. Doing so when she was raw and confused over what the future held would be even more difficult, and pulling it off while sharing the girls' repeat Thanksgiving with Jake *and* V? Ugh. The idea left her jittery with nerves.

Though she'd never measured up to Max in the sarcasm department, she tried anyway. "Dispose of a body? Have you been into the eggnog already? What are you thinking, spiking it? What if the girls get into it?"

His steady gray gaze studied her. "You're upset and bets are one of the jocks downstairs is to blame."

Geez. First Jake, now Max. What was it with the men in her life? "Wait. Jocks? As in plural?"

"Kevin Tucker arrived right before me."

"Oh, no." She slapped a hand over her eyes. After Murphy's painful greeting the night of the poker game, the last thing she'd have expected from Tuck was a declaration of love, but that's exactly what he'd given her when he showed up at the farm unexpectedly early the following day. And every Tuesday since.

"Mary invited him to stay for dinner." Max grinned manically. "Despite moving two catches closer to breaking the record in yesterday's game, Jake is not a happy man." He pushed off the doorjamb and crossed the room. "I've got to hand it to you, kiddo. Using Tuck to make Jake jealous might be evil, but it's also ingenious. I would've suggested it myself if I'd known Tuck was interested."

A scowl twisted her lips. "I'm not using Tuck to make Jake jealous, and Tuck isn't interested. He's delusional."

Max laughed. "Well, that explains it."

"Explains what?"

"He told Jake you and he would be spending Christmas together—in the Bahamas."

Her mouth dropped open. "What?"

"What I want to know is why you've been holding out on me?"

She shook her head. "Holy crap. He didn't!"

He held up two fingers. "Scout's honor."

"You were never a scout." She scoffed.

He shrugged and slipped a pack of gum from his pocket. "You're a slave to details. Which one of them am I going to have to kill?"

"Shut up. You're not going to kill anyone. Not today anyway."

He peeled off the wrapper and folded the stick of gum into his mouth. "Typical woman, getting pissy with a man when the situation is her fault."

"How are your homicidal tendencies my fault?"

Tossing his coat to the bed, he dropped to stretch out on his side with his ankles crossed and a palm supporting his head. "It's those violet eyes. They go all murky and bruised looking when you're upset. You know I can't resist them."

She batted her lashes. "Maybe I should get some colored contacts."

Rolling his shoulders in an easy shrug, he grinned. "Won't matter what color they are. It's what they reveal that matters." He laughed when she looked away. "Just doing my job as bodyguard and protector."

Her gaze snapped back to accuse. "A job for which you were never hired. I'd rather you butt out."

"Oh, I plan to."

"When? When I discover my first gray hair?"

"When you find the right guy, settle down, and have a houseful of babies."

She snorted, sharp and concisely. "There's no such thing as the right guy."

"Tell that to Jake and Tuck. From what I saw downstairs, you have two candidates vying to prove you wrong. I'm rooting for Tuck, by the way. He drives a Ferrari. Once you've got him all fired up and flustered, you can talk him into letting me borrow it."

She laughed as he'd surely intended with the remark. "You're so easy."

A sly grin grew. "Easy, but not cheap."

"Well, you're shit out of luck on the Ferrari. I'm not sure what he's up to, but Tuck doesn't even know me."

"And Jake? What's he done to make you sad?"

Typical Max. Toss out a question, add a little verbal dance to throw her off balance, then circle back and slam her with his true agenda. He never believed for a second there was anything going on between her and Tuck.

She lifted her chin. "I have no idea what you're talking about."

"Uh-huh. Save it. You look like your favorite mother board blew up."

She crossed her legs. Feigning casualness, she forced a smile. "How do you know my motherboard *didn't* blow up?"

He pushed off his elbow and sat up. "Maybe I should go ask Jake?"

"No!" She held out a hand to stop him then dropped it quickly when he pinned her with a sly smile. Her lips thinned in a scowl. "Quit being a jerk."

"Then tell me what's wrong. What'd he do?"

"He didn't do anything."

Okay, that wasn't strictly true, but she could hardly tell Max she'd discovered sex was much more intense when love was involved. Not without having to put up with a double dose of smugness and a great big, honking *I told you so* anyway. How could she admit Jake had guided her on her first real trip to paradise? Fine. First *dozen* trips. How could she explain having finally admitted her heart *was* engaged, she couldn't imagine hurting the man she loved by keeping him from the girls if he decided he wanted custody.

"Talk to me, Gracie. I can't help if I don't know what's wrong." He spoke in the gentle tone he used to prop her up in the days following Sarah's death.

The tears simmering below the surface welled up to spill over. Embarrassed and heartsick, she dropped forward to rest her forehead on her knees.

The bedding whispered and his boots appeared in her vision as he squatted in front of her. He brushed a gentle palm over the back of her head. "Hey, what's this? You're scaring me, babe."

She shook her head beneath his hand. "I'm going to lose everything, Max."

"By everything, you mean the girls? You don't know that and hey. Hey." His hand slid from her head to cup her chin, forcing her to sit up. His concerned face wavered in front of her. "It's not like you to throw in the towel if there's still a chance."

"I'm not throwing in the towel. I'm facing reality." She swiped at her running nose with the back of her hand. "The girls are falling for him and what's more, he's falling for them."

"He's their brother. It's only natural."

"I know, but..." She rubbed a knuckle under one eye then the other. "Even if they choose me at the end of this"—she sliced a hand through the air—"this *stupid* custody battle, how can I claim victory? Don't you see? How can I make a family with them when by doing so, I'll be denying Jake *his* family?"

He sat back on his heels, his gaze keen. "You said he didn't want custody."

She shook her head. "I don't think he did. Not at first."

"But he does now? Did he tell you that?"

"No." She sniffled.

"Then all you're doing is borrowing trouble and that's not like you. What's changed?"

What could she say without admitting she'd already taken his advice and found the guy with whom she'd love to settle down and raise a houseful of babies? God, a home and kids with the man she loved. With Jake. How could she admit to craving a future she didn't believe was possible? Turned out she didn't have to say anything.

Surprise lit Max's eyes and a sly smile lifted one corner of his mouth. "Oh, babe. You slept with him, didn't you?"

She sniffed and frowned. "I love you, Max, but that's none of your business."

He tilted his head and leaned closer. "It's my business if he hurt you."

"Well, he didn't, so back off." She shoved at his shoulders, but he had eighty pounds on her. He held steady.

Grinning, he dropped a kiss to her nose and rose to his feet. He propped his hands on his hips. "Admit it. After sleeping with him, you've realized I was right. When it comes to Jake Malone, you're toast. Now you're struggling with the idea of doing battle with the guy. Am I right?"

She shot to her feet. "Not exactly."

Exactly, damn it. How the hell did he *do* that? She shoved by him and walked to her closet. Selecting a pair of knee-high leather boots with a crisscross strap pattern at the ankle, she returned to the bed, sat, and yanked on the first boot.

"Damn. I was looking forward to taking him apart."

She peered at him from beneath lowered lashes. "I thought you liked him."

He sat beside her. "I do."

She shook her head. Would she ever understand the male mind?

Murphy trotted into the room. Spotting Max, he loped over, jumped onto the bed, and rolled onto his back. Max scrubbed his belly as the dog's tongue lolled out in ecstasy. "So? How was it?"

She coughed and dragged on the other boot. "How was *what*?"

He waggled his brows. "Realizing your darkest dream."

"I am *not* talking to you about this."

"Why not? You've talked to me about every other guy you've slept with."

He had a point, but Jake was different. "I'm just not."

"Come on. What's wrong with him? His size is false advertising, right?" Deviltry flashed in his eyes. "Shit, don't tell me he suffers from erectile dysfunction. Man. That sucks." An exaggerated shudder shook his frame.

"You're such an ass."

"But, hey, there are medications he can take."

She crossed her arms and stared at him blandly. "You're a funny guy."

He grinned unapologetically. "You said he didn't hurt you, but something's wrong. I figured he failed to get it up."

Memories simmered in her mind, leaving behind a familiar heat. She couldn't prevent a smug smile. "Believe me, he has no problems in either the size or performance departments."

He chuckled but sobered quickly. "Then, as usual, you're overanalyzing the situation and thinking the worst."

She shook her head. "Not in this case. Wait until you see him and the twins together. Then you'll understand." She sighed. "It's magic."

"That sounds like a good thing."

"It's a *great* thing—for the girls. They've found a big brother who shines in their eyes, and the thing is, the magic is in his eyes when he looks at them, too."

"And?"

"That leaves me out of the picture."

His eyes darkened with disappointment. "Then you're not seeing what I am."

"Max." She clenched her fingers together in her lap.

"Gracie." He lifted her hands and linked his fingers with hers. "I've seen the two of you together, remember? You want to see magic? Look in his eyes when he looks at *you*."

She shook her head.

He squeezed her fingers. "Hear me out, kiddo."

She loved him for trying and knew him well enough to know he'd keep at her until he'd had his say. She nodded.

"I don't like to say anything disparaging about your mother. She lived a difficult life and circumstances weren't kind to her, but she did you a disservice when it came to men. By her own words, she never attempted to discover what happened with your father, and yet she allowed her bitterness to seep into your perception of love and loyalty. You have an opportunity to claim everything you've ever dreamed of and, because of your distrust of men, you're afraid to take the chance."

"That's not true. As you so gleefully pointed out, I slept with Jake. I'd say that qualifies as taking a chance."

"Some chance." His laugh was little more than a scoffing cough. "You've had the hots for him for years and he's a guy. There are always exceptions, but unless a woman is married or psychotic, most men have a hard time turning down available sex."

"You forgot to add if the woman isn't attractive."

He cocked his head. "No. Sex is sex. In bed, every woman is beautiful."

"Eww. Men are such dogs."

He shrugged. "We can be, but it's not our fault. We're hardwired to screw at every opportunity, but that's not what I'm talking about. I'm talking about the down and dirty stuff, about your dream of a family. I'm talking about your heart and how you're afraid to chance it."

Considering her feelings for Jake, she'd already done that and no matter how she looked at the situation, her heart was headed for a fatal hit. "Look who's talking, Mr. A-New-Woman-Every-Week-So-None-Can-Ever-Get-Too-Close."

He sighed. "We're not talking about me. We're talking about you, the twins, and Jake. Nothing worth having is easy, kiddo. If you want him as part of the family you plan to make with the girls, you'll have to fight for him. That'll require a leap of faith. How else will you ever learn if he's the right man for the girls and you? Do you love him?"

She blinked at the sudden question and, because he'd thrown her off balance again, she nodded without thinking.

The shadow of a smile lit his eyes. He tugged at a lock of her hair. "Not all men leave. Give Jake the chance to prove it."

Chapter 22

"I'm heading out to do some grocery shopping. Will you be here for dinner, Jake?" Stopping in the doorway of Tom's spacious home office, Sharon Walden slipped the strap of her purse over one shoulder.

Tom spoke before Jake could answer. "Tomorrow's Sunday."

She smiled sweetly. "Which is why I was planning to make meatloaf."

Jake laughed. He'd taken a lot of ribbing from Sharon, and others, over the years for his quirky superstition, but he held firm. Eating meatloaf and mashed potatoes the night before a game didn't always guarantee a win, but skipping the ritual had proven a surefire precursor to a loss. He hadn't varied his pre-game diet in years and wasn't about to now.

"I'll have to pass this time." He grinned. "The twins are cooking tonight. It's a surprise. Apparently, they've pestered Mary, the housekeeper, into teaching them how to make my pre-game meal. They're expecting me back at the farm in less than an hour."

"Then I'll wish you good luck tomorrow. Back in a bit." She blew Tom a kiss.

He winked at his red-haired wife. She disappeared down the hall, and he turned back to Jake. Tossing a football from hand to hand, he wore a smug smile.

Jake shifted in his seat. "Go ahead and say I told you so. I know you're dying to."

Tom laughed but didn't say a word because, well, there was no need. Jake was the first to admit the twins had grown on him, as Tom predicted. With sticky fingers, they'd wrapped their tiny hands around his heart, but he wasn't here because of the girls. He was here because a mouthy blonde with killer legs and a ton of attitude was driving him nuts.

Tom slouched back. "What's so important you decided to come by in person instead of calling?"

"I need the name of a good private detective."

Tom immediately straightened. His brows beetled with concern. "Why? What's going on? Are you in some kind of trouble?"

Major trouble, but until he figured out what to do about the *big* girl working her magic on his previously impervious heart, he'd keep that problem to himself. "No, but Gracie is. She's hiding something."

Tom's shoulders slumped when he relaxed visibly. "Why do you think that?"

"A bunch of things. Most of the time she's as ballsy as they come." Her smug smile as he lay sprawled at her feet on the foyer floor his first morning scrolled past his mind's eye, followed by others. Like the evasive fear in her eyes the night she tromped through the woods or the sadness the day he and the girls trashed Mary's kitchen. "Other times she's like a scared rabbit, jumping at every sound." He sighed. "Whatever is bothering her is at the heart of her refusal to speak to the press."

"She still hasn't spoken to them? It's been two months."

He shook his head. "She believes if she ignores them, they'll eventually go away."

"That's a naïve attitude."

He shrugged. "So I've tried to tell her."

Tom cocked his head and rubbed a thumb over his chin. "You can't blame her. They came down hard on the two of you after the blog thing. If they found out the Gridiron Girl is on the other side of your custody battle…."

"They'd have a field day. Yeah, I know."

Tom chuckled. "According to V, Gracie is as stubborn as the cook's mule back on the ranch where the two of you grew up."

Jake winced at the unflattering comparison, but couldn't disagree completely. There wasn't a lot of give in Gracie when it came to the idea of facing the press.

Tom spun the ball until the laces lined up with his grip. "How do you think she'll react if she learns you've hired a private detective to snoop into her past?"

Jake scraped a palm over his jaw to hide his scowl. He could just imagine, but what choice did he have? He hated the flash of panic in her mesmerizing eyes whenever a strange vehicle rolled to a stop at the end of the driveway. Worse, they'd been sleeping together for nearly six weeks. He hated that she trusted him with her body but not her secrets.

"I think she'll be pissed, but I'm willing to take my chances. I get the distinct impression my presence at the farm has made the situation worse somehow. I owe it to her to help if I can."

Tom arched a brow. "It wasn't your idea to spend time at the farm, remember?"

He shook his head. "Doesn't change the facts. Something's scaring her, Tom. She needs help, even if she's too stubborn to ask."

"If I recall correctly, you have your own problems. Like the upcoming playoffs and finishing the season healthy. Not to mention breaking the touchdown record."

What the hell? He scowled, tightening his fingers along the brim of his hat. "What's with you all of a sudden? From the time we met, you've lectured me about not making my life all about football. You've been hounding me for years to find myself a good woman. I figured you'd offer to plan the bachelor party, not suggest I hang Gracie out to dry."

Tom chuckled and deviltry glittered his eyes. "And for years, you've been telling me a woman's baggage belongs at the bedroom door—along with her clothes."

"Fuck you." He couldn't help returning the grin splitting Tom's face.

The humor slowly faded from Tom's eyes as he studied Jake intently. "With the exception of V, and maybe Sharon, you've never cared enough about a woman to be dragged into her problems. What's different about this female? Is she *the* one? Are you in love with her?"

The question hit Jake hard, as if he'd been stopped cold at the line of scrimmage. Was she the one? Was he in love? Hell, was he even capable of loving a woman? Was he capable of loving Gracie?

His palms broke out in a sweat. Jesus, she scared him shitless. What had started out as a pleasant diversion had built into something he wasn't willing to name. Not yet, anyway. Tom was quick with the snap, tossing out the L word, but what did real love look like? Was the gut-wrenching tangle of lust, laughter, and alarm charging his system whenever he was with Gracie the real thing?

She was something else. Beautiful and quirky. He'd never met a woman who could make him laugh the way she did, even when he was hard. Hell, especially when he was hard, which, it turned out, was most of the time lately. He hadn't laughed so much in bed in…ever.

Baiting her was a pleasure he couldn't resist. He loved the way her eyes flashed violet steel daggers at his teasing, and the memory of their smoky purple hue when he had her beneath him never failed to give him a woody. However, it wasn't just the sex, though damn, coming deep within her slick and sultry depths left him breathless, satisfied, and impatient for the next time. He also loved her bold spirit and adored her smart-ass mouth. But most of all, he loved the way she loved the twins.

Truth be told, the idea of Angel and Charlie claiming a permanent place in his life no longer scared the crap out of him. He still couldn't see himself taking full custody—he couldn't do that to Gracie—but the girls *would* be part of his life after he left the farm.

As for Gracie…he loved many things about her, but was he *in love* with her? He honestly couldn't say.

"Maybe. No!" He jammed his fingers through his hair. "Hell, I don't know."

Tom's smile widened. "I wouldn't hire a private detective until you do. Take my word for it. Having a woman you're in love with pissed off at you sucks."

"Speaking from experience?"

"I married a redhead, remember?"

Tom's grumbled response loosened the knot of tension in Jake's gut a bit, but not completely. "I didn't say I was in love with Gracie."

"You didn't say you weren't, either." Tom flipped the football at him. "Before you resort to hiring a professional, does she have any family you can talk to?"

He caught the ball clean.

Well, shit. Why hadn't *he* thought of that? "No, but she has a friend."

Chapter 23

Jake swept the Stetson from his head and glanced around the busy gym. Rock music pumped in the background, competing with the clang of weights and humming treadmills. At least two dozen men sweated through their workouts and half as many women. Max Grayson's place wasn't what Jake had expected.

Though the equipment was top notch, the machines were utilitarian, with none of the sparkle and chrome one would expect in a gym located on the pricey, upper west side. Unlike many of the sports clubs in the area, whose floor-to-ceiling windows were designed specifically to allow their clientele to show off their physiques and be seen by the foot traffic passing by on Manhattan's busy sidewalks, Max's storefront windows were blacked out. From what Jake could see, his clientele were serious about their exercise regimens.

Respect bumped up against the kernel of jealousy he couldn't quite dismiss. Not that he considered the cage fighting champ and gym owner a rival for Gracie's sensual affections, despite her attempt to make him believe they were a couple at first. He chuckled recalling the way Max derailed her ploy before she ever gained any traction convincing Jake they were an item. After watching the teasing and jarring between them over the past two months, there was no way in hell he'd mistake what they shared for an intimate relationship, and the way she consistently came alive in Jake's arms denied the possibility of Max and her being lovers. They shared a history and, clearly Max held her heart, but she wasn't sharing her bed with any other man. Not even Tuck—the bastard— despite his having stepped up his game to include offerings of expensive jewelry after his Bahamas Christmas plans failed to sway her.

Jake curved his lips in a feral smile. Tuck's diamond baubles hadn't gotten him any further than his claim of love at first sight.

Several feet away, a bulky young black man, no more than a kid, with a gold bar piercing one eyebrow and more tattoos than he'd have had birthdays, lowered the weight bar into the cradles and sat up. He bumped his chin in Jake's direction. "Hey, ain't you the Outlaw?"

He slid the brim of his hat through his fingers. "That's what some call me."

"Cool, dude. Gonna take the record?"

With three weeks left to the regular season, he was three touchdowns away. If he kept up his current pace, the record was in the bag. "I'm doing my damndest. Any idea where I can find the owner?"

"Max?"

Jake nodded.

"He's back in his office." The kid jerked his head toward an open door on the far wall.

"Thanks." Jake made his way across the crowded gym, greeting several patrons who called out to him by name and shaking a few hands. He paused in the office doorway. Max looked up and springs squeaked when he sprawled back in the ancient desk chair.

Along the far wall, a familiar figure slumped on a worn leather couch. He wore a shit-eating grin. "Hey, buddy."

Jake swore beneath his breath. "Tuck."

Max's steely gray eyes glittered with humor. "Well, I'll be damned. Interested in a gym membership, Jake?"

He ground his teeth. No, but that wasn't a bad idea. "The thought crossed my mind."

The chair groaned when Max rocked back even farther. His smile went sly. "Huh. It's the oddest thing. I've been in business several years and, with the exception of a Wall Street mogul and an actor with a reoccurring role on a soap opera, I haven't signed a single famous client. All of a sudden, I've got two in one month."

"What are the odds?" Jake slid his gaze to Tuck and bared his teeth in a patently false smile. "You don't mind if I have a word with Max, do you?"

Tuck crossed one leg over the other, brushing nonexistent lint from his sweatpants, but didn't move otherwise. "Nope."

"A *private* word."

Wicked laughter danced in Tuck's eyes. "Hey, buddy, if you've got a problem, maybe I can help."

"The only problem I have is with you."

Tuck slapped spread fingers to his chest. "Shit, and here I thought we were friends. You're breaking my heart."

He crossed his arms. "Better your heart than your neck. Get lost."

Tuck grinned but rose to his feet. Max stood as well.

Tuck stretched an arm over the desk to shake his hand. "I'll take you up on your offer to let me in early for workouts starting next week." He paused beside Jake on his way out the door. "I was on my way out to the farm, anyway. Max says Gracie's an art lover." He waggled his brows. "I'll be taking her to the gala fund-raiser at The Met at the end of the month. See you on the practice field, buddy."

She'd attend the fund-raiser with him over Jake's dead body! He glared at Tuck's retreating back until Max chuckled behind him.

"I wondered how long it would be before you dropped by."

He shook off the desire to rearrange his friend's nose and turned to face Max. "Did you? Why is that?"

Max slid back into his chair and tucked his hands behind his head. His thickly muscled, tattooed arms, bared by his sleeveless shirt, winged out. The league was full of huge, supremely developed men capable of striking fear in strangers with a simple glance. Max would fit right in, but the humor in his eyes belied his hoodlum looks.

"Same reason Tuck showed up. You're looking for answers."

"What questions did Tuck have?"

"Not quite the same as yours, I'll bet, but then, you're sleeping with her. He's not."

Surprised by the candor of the comment, he automatically braced himself for an attack. "You have a problem with that?"

"With you coming to me with your questions? No. I happen to like you."

"I was talking about Gracie and me sleeping together."

Max dropped his arms and sat forward to lean on his elbows. "She's a big girl. She makes her own choices on who she invites into her bed and doesn't appreciate my interference there." A slicing smile beamed. "But, if you hurt her, I'll kill you."

Humor jerked at the corner of Jake's mouth. He couldn't take offense. He'd do the same for V. "I thought you liked me."

The gym owner picked up a pen and ran it through his fingers. A small smile danced at the corner of his lips. "I do, but not *that* much."

Jake chuckled. "And Tuck? How do you feel about him?"

Mischief glittered in Max's eyes. "I like him, too."

"He's only interested in her because of me."

Max cocked his head. "I'm sure she'd be interested in hearing that."

Jake scowled. "That wasn't an insult. She's a beautiful woman. Any man would be interested, but Tuck and I…." He slapped his hat against his leg. "Well, the truth is, we've had this friendly competition going for a couple of years."

"Daphne, the underwear model."

He arched a brow in surprise.

Max laughed. "It's no big secret. Not if one reads between the lines in the papers. Gracie may not have put two and two together, but then, she's got other things on her mind. Your friendly competition with Tuck isn't exactly a secret."

He grunted.

Max grinned. "Even if Tuck was truly attracted to her, she isn't interested in him. Amused maybe. Flattered, definitely, but not interested."

Something suspiciously like relief weakened his knees. He sank onto the couch Tuck had vacated. Jesus, he was pitiful.

White teeth flashed in Max's smile. "Honestly, I expected a visit from you weeks ago. What is it you want to know? I won't betray her trust, but I'll answer what I can."

"I want to know what she's hiding."

The smile remained on Max's face, but as Gracie's did whenever Jake brought up the subject, his eyes shuttered. "What makes you think she's hiding something?"

"Because she'd rather put herself in danger than make a statement to the press."

All signs of humor vanished and he sat up straight. "Shit. What'd she do?"

Jake explained about her nighttime walk through the woods. Max grumbled beneath his breath about stubborn women, obviously no happier hearing about what she'd done after the fact than Jake had been at the time.

Jamming his fingers through his hair, Jake sighed. "She's barely left the farm in two months and when she does, she sneaks out through the back gate. She thinks she'll be able to outlast the interest of the press, but she's wrong. The girls will still be my sisters at the end of the month. Nosey reporters are an unfortunate side effect of my career choice. They may leave her alone once I'm gone, but every time I show up at the farm, she'll have to worry about their renewed interest. Does she plan to continue sneaking around indefinitely?"

Max tapped the pen against the blotter on his desk. "Sounds like you don't plan on winning the custody battle. From what Gracie says, the girls are completely dazzled by their big brother. You don't think they'll choose you?"

"She said that?" Dazzled by him? Inordinately pleased by the idea, a surprising warmth coursed through him. He tugged at the denim covering one leg and crossed his booted foot over the opposite knee.

The pen stilled in Max's fingers. "On more than one occasion."

Jake chuckled. "Huh. I hadn't ever considered the idea. They belong with Gracie. I never planned on taking custody."

"Does *she* know that?"

Guilt burned in his belly. He cleared his throat. "Not yet. You going to tell her?"

Max sat back. "I should. I don't think you realize how important winning custody of the girls is to her."

"I know she loves them."

Max waved a hand. "Goes without saying, but beyond fulfilling her promise to her sister, Sarah, she's always dreamed of having a family of her own. She believes the girls are her last chance at achieving her dream."

"Last chance?" His brows slammed together with his scoffing snort. "What is she, twenty-five? That doesn't make sense."

"Twenty-six, and she obviously hasn't told you about her childhood."

"She's told me some. I know her mom died when she was fourteen and her sister raised her from then on. Until she died, too."

Max nodded. "Gracie shut down after that, stopped going out, except with me, and only when I forced the issue. She also quit dating. She's never had a lot of trust where men are concerned. Her mother's warped view on the subject did a job on her when Gracie was too young to understand the concept of bitterness." He sighed and shook his head. "Anyway, the girls and I are one thing. We're already in her life and her heart, but she no longer lets anyone new in because losing anyone else is unacceptable. Hence, no romantic relationships. Custody of the girls will allow her to have the family she desperately wants without risking her heart to further loss or rejection."

"And yet she's entered into a romantic relationship with me."

"Yes, she has. Interesting, isn't it?"

Max tossed up a brow, but Jake wasn't touching that one with a ten-foot pole. "She didn't mention her father."

Max grinned briefly then sobered. "Nor will she."

"Why not?"

"If I told you, I'd be betraying her trust." Max studied him silently for a long moment. "Let's just say, she has daddy issues."

Jake arched a brow. "And these daddy issues are at the root of her secret?"

"I didn't say that. Not outright, anyway."

No, he hadn't, but his smile said Jake's conclusion was dead-on. "You didn't have to. If her father isn't the problem, why bring him up? I know when I'm being led."

Max shrugged, and his smile slid into smug.

"So, what's the deal? Who's her father and what does he have to do with her fear of the press?"

Max slowly stroked his fingers and thumb over his chin. "That, I definitely can't say."

"Can't, or won't?"

"Both. I love Gracie. I may not always agree with her thought processes, but she's *my* family."

"And?"

"And, if you want more details on her *daddy issues*, you're going to have to ask her."

He slapped his hat against his knee. "Right. She snaps shut like a clam whenever I ask her what's wrong."

"Then look somewhere else."

"Why do you think I'm here?"

Max arched a brow and didn't say another word.

Jake sighed. "You're as bad as Gracie. Any suggestions on where I should start?"

Max grinned. "Why don't you start by asking how and more importantly, why, a female computer geek becomes a rabid football fan?"

Chapter 24

Gracie peeked through the curtain with a scowl. God, would they never give up? Over two months had passed since the reading of Pete's will and, if not for the sporadic reappearance of the stubborn vultures at the gate, she'd be happier than she could ever remember being.

Sure, doubt occasionally crept in to steal her contentment, but her leap of faith was one of the sweetest decisions she'd ever made. The pure bliss of being Jake's lover aside, those lingering moments of reservation couldn't compete with the sheer joy of living like a family with him and the girls. Her temporary family even included extended members, thanks to Max's frequent visits and the poker jocks' staggered drop-ins—which always seemed to occur right around dinnertime. A leaf had been added to the kitchen table, along with several chairs. But for those days when Jake and the jocks were out of town for a game, one or more of the extra chairs were filled more often than not.

The image of her dream family hadn't included an overprotective best friend and bodyguard, half the Marauders' offensive line, or a bossy publicist, but Gracie couldn't complain. Laughter and happiness echoed off the walls of the old farmhouse and contentment swelled in her heart.

V had made no mention of the change in her and Jake's relationship, but as observant as his agent was, she must have noticed. Jake wasn't exactly circumspect, flirting mercilessly and never passing up the opportunity to touch her. Unless the twins were present. Whenever they were around, he behaved like a perfect gentleman. She couldn't decide if that was a good thing or bad.

Then there was Tuck's apparent inability to take no for an answer. His declaration of love at first sight was flattering, and his bold invitations to slip away with him for a weekend of debauchery made her laugh, especially since he was full of crap. And, she had to admit, Jake's dark scowl, every time he learned his friend had been by the farm to see her, was thrilling, until Max explained the truth behind Tuck's claims of undying love.

Max found the whole thing hilarious. She, not so much. Imagine, a friendly competition to steal a woman away from someone you called a friend, simply to prove you could. Men were pigs. She should've accepted Tuck's diamond tennis bracelet then dumped him on his ass.

She should be furious to find herself an unwitting player in their sexist game and was, partly, but in those moments she and Jake managed to steal away, Tuck and the faceless women he and Jake had fought over through the years vanished. That suited her fine, considering the temporary nature of their romance. She'd taken the leap of faith Max insisted on, with thrilling results, but he was delusional if he thought what she and Jake had would last beyond the twelve weeks they'd been given.

Pete's custody stipulations set up a scenario allowing them to play house for a time, but Jake didn't believe in forever any more than she did. The time was fast approaching when play time would end.

She dropped the curtain and stomped from the window. She should be on top of the world. Instead, she was ready to rip her hair out. Sneaking around like a criminal when she hadn't done a thing wrong rankled, and she was sick of it. No matter how the custody situation turned out, she and Jake would always have a connection through the girls. V was right, one way or another, either now or later, she'd have to face the press. Until she did, she'd be a prisoner of her own cowardice.

To hell with that. Sharing her story without revealing her secrets would be a challenge, but not impossible. Looking at the situation logically, there were things she could do to lessen, if not eliminate, the possibility of anyone connecting her to her father. The idea of standing before the press made her stomach revolt. She'd do it, however, to reclaim her freedom, but not today. The only thing she'd be claiming today was a certain, hunky tight end.

Thanks to the Marauders' road schedule, and a Thursday night game, Jake had been gone for close to a week. When they spoke last night, he sounded tired but exuberant over the team's latest victory. His single end zone dance of the night hadn't clenched the record, but his thrilling one-handed touchdown catch brought him within two of the stat he so badly desired. They needed to celebrate, and she planned to make good use of the empty house.

The rumble of his SUV coming up the drive sent her heart skittering. A quick click to save the data on her computer screen and she flew out into the hallway and down the stairs. Murphy raced at her heels, yipping with excitement. She skidded to a halt at the front door. Shifting her shoulders, a side-to-side toss of her head cracked her neck and settled her jumping nerves. Three deep breaths settled them further. Her hands shook but she didn't care. She threw open the door.

Jake wore a huge grin as he strode up the walkway and vaulted up the steps. His duffle bag hit the planks of the porch with a thud. She squeaked in surprise when he grabbed her waist. He lifted her off her feet and tucked her close. She moaned as his mouth claimed hers and her toes curled in her boots. Hot damn! Every woman should be greeted with an utterly ravenous kiss at least once in her life.

She'd told herself she hadn't fallen for him completely, and maybe she'd been right, but in the end it didn't matter. The dizzying roll of her heart signaled its disastrous fall. Her world shifted seamlessly into a new dimension, and though she'd surely regret this moment later, she plunged her fingers into his hair, wrapped her legs around his waist, and embraced the inevitable—and the madness.

Dappled sunlight skittered across her closed eyelids. Her head spun as his mouth devoured hers. Greedy, she met and returned his urgency, nipping and sucking, her tongue doing sensual battle with his. She clung to him, pressing her breasts to his chest in an attempt to assuage the pleasure/pain of her violently peaked nipples. He growled into her mouth and ran his hand along the back of her thigh, bare beneath her skirt, until his fingers closed around one silk-covered cheek and squeezed.

Moist heat pooled between her thighs and she arched against him. He grunted, stepped inside the house, and slammed the door shut with the aid of a well-placed kick. She absorbed the shock of her back and ass slamming up against the hard wooden surface of the door and mourned the loss when his mouth left hers. Opening her eyes, she met the emerald fire burning in his.

The shadow of a single dimple appeared with his lopsided smile. "Hi."

"Hi, yourself." Was that her voice, all breathy and low? Geez. She could do voiceovers for old Marilyn Monroe movies.

"Are the girls here?" He shoved Murphy's head aside when the dog attempted to squeeze between them.

"It's Friday morning. They're in school."

His nostrils flared with his deep inhale. He dipped his head to rest his forehead against hers. "Mary?"

She had to take a bracing breath. "She went to visit her sister in Connecticut and do some last minute Christmas shopping. She'll be back by six."

He straightened immediately and surprise lit his eyes. "The house is empty?"

She nodded. "Empty except for you and me." The dog whined happily at their feet. She grinned. "And Murphy."

Jake groaned and his eyes slid shut.

Huh? Considering his heated greeting and the solid steel erection prodding her through his jeans, why was he groaning? And why had he stopped?

Unease slithered down her spine. "Jake?"

"Give me a moment, will you?"

To do what? They had the house to themselves, an opportunity that came along rarely. Why wasn't he kissing her senseless and carrying her upstairs at a run? "What's wrong?"

"Nothing." His chest expanded on a rumbling sigh. "I'm trying to slow things down."

"Why?"

He opened his eyes and his lips twisted in a guilty grimace. "I barely said hello before I stuck my tongue down your throat. You've already accused me of having a one-track mind. I don't want you adding horny bastard to the complaint."

Relief loosened her muscles, and she relaxed in his arms. He tightened his hold.

She cocked her head and studied him. "*Aren't* you a horny bastard with a one-track mind?"

His grimace slid into a wide smile. "Pretty much."

"Thought so."

"Oh, really?"

She giggled and shimmied her hips, pleased when his pupils dilated. "Is that a goalpost in your pocket, Malone, or are you happy to see me?" She yelped when he swatted her ass and headed for the stairs. "Ouch. That hurt."

"Serves you right, smart ass. I was trying to be a gentleman." His long legs took the steps two at a time.

"Well, don't strain yourself. I happen to have changed my opinion on your one-track mind."

"You have, have you?" He grinned, passing by the door to her bedroom to enter the master suite.

"I've decided horny bastards have their uses." She laughed and twisted a finger in his silky hair. "By the way, you forgot your bag on the porch."

"Shit." He stopped short beside the bed.

She fluttered her lashes and grinned.

"Fuck it. I'll get it later. His teeth flashed in a wicked smile. Mischief danced in his sparkling eyes, warning her of what was coming. She let herself fall when he opened his arms at the edge of his bed and wasn't surprised when he landed on top of her a moment later. The blood rushed from her head, thanks to his single-minded attention to her mouth, and raced to the apex of her thighs when he switched the focus of his talented mouth to her straining breasts.

He played her like an expert. She thrilled at the results. He drove her upward, stripping her of her clothes and taking his time in paying sweet homage to the bare skin he exposed with each sweep of his wide palmed hands. His mouth followed, whipping her into a frenzy of heated excitement. By the time he had them both naked, she was in danger of combusting.

When he slipped inside her, his fevered gaze locked with hers, the world exploded on a bright and beautiful shower of color and sound.

Chapter 25

Gracie must have dozed off, waking to the thrill of Jake's naked body spooned against her back. A muscled forearm draped over her hip to rest against her belly. His big hand cupped one breast. Content to while away the time surrounded by Jake on a lazy winter morning, she let her gaze wander around the suite her sister had lovingly decorated, and she sighed.

He hummed quietly and tucked her closer. "You okay?"

"Better than okay." She rolled over and trailed her fingertips through the downy treasure trail bisecting his ridged abs. "I was thinking of how much my sister loved this room."

He raised his head from the pillow and shifted his body until she lay on her back with her head settled in the crook of his elbow. "Shit. I never once considered how painful spending time in your sister's old space would be for you."

"Surprisingly, it isn't. Maybe because Sarah was happy here." She smiled gently at the realization then bit her lip. "What about you? Considering how you felt about him, I'm surprised you agreed to stay in Pete's old room for one night, never mind twelve weeks. Does being in here make you uncomfortable?"

She ducked her head to hide her cringe the moment the words left her mouth. Mentioning his father was like waving a red flag, inviting him to inquire about hers. Since they'd become intimate, he'd stepped up his attempts to discover her secrets. Oh, sure, he was charming in his quest, teasing her into talking about herself, but he was also sneaky, waiting until she was boneless and lightheaded from an orgasm he'd given her to hit her up with his probing questions.

She couldn't help being impressed by the tactic. If the ramifications weren't dire, she might actually enjoy watching the way his mind worked, but the way he kept systematically introducing potential reasons for her avoidance of the press, he'd eventually arrive at the right subject.

His smile turned lecherous, and he slid a thick thigh between hers. "Do I look uncomfortable?"

Relief danced giddily up her spine, and she smiled. He dipped his mouth to hers, and her greedy body dampened despite its recent release. Flames of renewed excitement licked over her. She ran her fingertips over the naked expanse of his muscled chest and sighed when his lips left hers.

The soft scrape of his stubbled chin, as he dropped nibbling kisses across her cheekbone, sent tingles of pleasure rippling over her skin. His breath bathed her ear in moist heat. "Speaking of fathers. You never did say what happened to yours."

The fire sparking its way through her blood stream fizzled, leaving her dizzy and chilled. Apparently eventually was now. The rat! Restarting her engine only to leave her idling. Ha! If he thought he had her so far gone she'd spill her guts, he had another think coming.

Stick as close to the truth as possible, Gracie, and if he keeps pushing? Lie your ass off!

"No, I didn't." She shifted enough to extricate herself from his arms. To her surprise, he let her sit up. Covering her breasts, she tucked the sheet under her armpits and settled her back against the headboard.

He rolled on his side and propped his head up with one palm. "You aren't close?"

"How can someone be close to a person they've never met?"

He blinked in surprise. "Ever?"

She shrugged. "I didn't have a clue who he was until after mom died and Sarah found her diary. Mom rarely talked about him and then mostly in generalities."

She fought the urge to squirm under the intensity of his stare.

Finally, he grunted. "Who is he?"

Overreacting would only alert him to the fact he'd finally hit pay dirt, but fielding his questions with a practiced aloofness would be dangerous as well. He knew her father personally. One wrong word and she could accidently tip him off. Then again, she'd been reticent to answer his questions up to this point. He'd be suspect of any change in her behavior.

She tilted her chin in challenge and stabbed him with an accusing stare. "Why do you want to know?"

Humor glittered in his eyes. "Calm down, tiger. I'm curious."

She elevated a brow. "No, you're nosey."

He grinned. "Guilty as charged. I told you once I'd find out what you were hiding eventually. Why do I have the feeling we've finally stumbled on the reason behind your fears?"

Shit!

"Who is he?"

Shit. Shit. Shit! How to answer? There was no way in hell she'd be giving him a name. She jerked up her chin. "He *was* a client of my mother's boss."

"Was? Is he dead?"

"No. Yes!" She growled low in her throat and her lips compressed into a self-disgusted frown. Damn it! He handed her the perfect solution and she'd spoken too quickly to take advantage. She wanted to smack her head back against the headboard.

"I'll take that as a no." White teeth flashed in his smile. "A client, huh? What type of client?" Tiny wrinkles appeared at the corners of his watchful eyes. "Where did she work?"

He thinks he can trick me into dropping clues to my father's identity, does he? The sneaky rat.... Two could play that game.

"For a guy. In an office."

He chuckled and some of her tension eased. "Damn, you're suspicious."

Look who's talking. She bared her teeth in a tight smile.

He shook his head. "Lots of people are the product of a fling. Including me. You have nothing to be ashamed of."

"I'm not ashamed." She stiffened and jerked up her chin. "And their relationship wasn't a fling. Not according to my mother's diary, anyway."

Geez, she sounded defensive. Was she ashamed? The possibility was one she'd never considered. She'd have to give it some thought. Later. When Mr. Twenty Questions wasn't around.

"Then what happened? Why'd they break up?"

She frowned. "They didn't. Break up, I mean. He disappeared one day and from what Mom wrote, her boss may have had something to do with it."

"How so?"

He might be a sneaky rat, using charm and sex appeal in his determination to discover her secrets, but there was no calculation in his eyes at the moment. Simple curiosity glimmered there.

She tucked a lock of hair behind an ear. "Mom wasn't a party girl. That's what I meant about their relationship not being a fling. After Sarah's father left Mom for another woman, she didn't sleep around. Her boss knew that. He also knew she and my father had a summer romance, something he wasn't happy about. One day everything was fine. The next, my father was gone, returning to college several weeks early without a word to my mother. When Mom turned up pregnant a month later, her boss fired her."

Disapproval wrinkled his brow. "Asshole."

She nodded. "With a capital A. Anyway, it was a long time ago."

He grunted. "Did she ever try to contact him? Your father?"

"I don't think so."

"Why not?"

She chose her words with care. "Who knows? Maybe she didn't know how to reach him, or maybe she was afraid she'd receive the same kind of reaction as your mother. Either way, she got another job and moved on. We weren't rich by any standard, but we made do. She took care of us."

"Until she died." His eyes full of sympathy, he trailed the fingertips of his free hand down her exposed arm.

Goose bumps popped. "Yeah, well, viral pneumonia can be a real bitch."

He winced softly and curled his fingers around hers. "I'm sorry, princess."

As diversions went, discussing her mother's death was a painful one, but she'd embrace the change of topic happily. Still, her heart fluttered at the empathy in his eyes. She squeezed his fingers and sighed. "Me, too."

He brushed his thumb back and forth over the back of her hand. "My mom died when I was eighteen. As self-centered and as big a mess as she was, I'd basically been raising myself for years, but losing her was still a blow. Thankfully, she never had any more kids, because I don't have what it takes to do what your sister did. She must have been a special woman."

Yes, her sister was special, but she disagreed with his assessment of what he would have done in Sarah's place. Despite his upbringing, deep down, he had a caring heart. He could no more have walked away from his sisters at the age of eighteen than he could now. He'd have done what needed doing to keep them safe, exactly as Sarah did for her.

She smiled and nodded. "I was pretty young, but old enough to understand how difficult things were for Sarah. She worked her ass off to take care of me, holding down two jobs, sometimes three, when she should've been off at college getting an education and falling in love."

He brushed a thumb over the back of her hand. "She loved you."

The tiny hairs on her arms stood on end. "And I loved her. I promised myself someday I'd pay her back. I never got the chance."

Sudden understanding darkened his eyes. "Until now."

She nodded. "Until now."

Whether the glint of emotion flashing in his eyes was guilt, determination or something else altogether, she couldn't say with certainty.

He glanced away too quickly, looking at their entwined fingers. "Did *you* ever try to contact your father?"

Oh, for heaven's sake. He was like a dog with a bone. "No."

"Why not? Aren't you curious about him?"

So curious she'd become a football junkie in a pitiful attempt to share something of his life. She shrugged. "I'm a computer geek, remember? With a couple of keystrokes, I learned everything there is to know about him."

He cocked his head in question. "Does he know about you?"

Ughhh! "I have no idea." She shifted to leave the bed.

He tightened his hold on her fingers to prevent her from going.

His intent gaze tangled with hers and stayed. "With your computer skills, you'd be able to find out about anyone, but with most people the data available is limited. Unless he's a public figure." He left the unspoken question dangling.

Her heart lodged in her throat. The less said the better, but if she was going to avoid being steamrolled into confessing all, she'd have to rely on his compassion. If he had any.

She sighed. "A public figure with a family I'm not willing to destroy. You, of all people, know how vicious the press can be. Please, Jake, drop it."

Chapter 26

"Good morning, lovebirds." V breezed into the kitchen the next morning, shortly after the girls and Mary left for the day, and crossed to the coffeepot.

Gracie choked on her coffee. Jake whipped his head around to follow V. "Do you want to explain that comment?"

V carried her mug back to the table and slid into an open chair. Tugging the folded newspaper from under one arm, she tossed the morning edition on the table between Gracie and Jake. Gracie almost knocked over her mug as she snatched the paper toward her. He immediately rose and rounded the table to stand at her side.

"Shit." He bent at the waist, slapping a big hand on the table beside the paper and began reading.

Dismay cut off Gracie's air supply like strangling fingers. She scanned the front page, but there was no need to read the article. The large photo and accompanying headline were bad enough.

"'Custody Battle Or Hideaway For Country Lovers?'"

She slid her hand over her mouth. "Oh, no!"

"Oh, yes." V locked her unhappy gaze on Jake. "I'm not even going to ask what you were thinking."

An instant blush heated Gracie's cheeks.

Jake straightened at her side. "Good. My personal life is none of your business. Nor is it theirs." He jerked his chin toward the paper.

V snorted delicately. "You know better than that. What the hell is wrong with you? Don't we have enough to deal with already without you letting your Johnson do your thinking?"

He propped his hands on his hips. "Leave my *Johnson* out of this."

"I wish I could."

"Meaning?"

"Meaning, the reason I'm here at this ungodly hour is because I've been on the phone since six doing spin control. Tom called and woke me." Gracie went cold and couldn't control her gasp. *Oh, dear Lord.* She glanced away from Jake's concerned gaze.

"Doug Costa is on the warpath." V pointed a finger at his face. "He wants to see you in his office at one today."

Gracie moaned. Holy hell. What had she done? Jake rested a hand on her shoulder and squeezed, obviously reading her anxiety as concern over what this new uproar would mean to his career. Which was true—partly, but not completely.

"Relax, princess. He doesn't have a leg to stand on, and he knows it." V laughed harshly. "Tell *him* that."

"I'd rather tell him to go fuck himself."

Unhappy color bloomed on V's cheekbones. "Oh, that's lovely." She slipped her phone from her pocket. "Let me get him on the line. I'm sure he'd appreciate hearing your response personally."

"I mean it, V. I didn't fight him on the fine, but this isn't business. This is my private life and has nothing to do with him or the league."

Gracie slapped her fingers to her forehead. *Oh, if you only knew.* Neither of them paid her any attention. He swept up his empty coffee mug and stalked to the pot.

V arched a perfectly shaped brow at his back. "He obviously disagrees."

Jake spun around. "Tough shit. Call Tom back. It's his job as player liaison to run interference in cases like this. He can use whatever language he wants as long as he lets Costa know I'm not taking his shit on this one."

V rolled her eyes, all but snarling her disapproval, and shifted her angry stare to Gracie.

She blinked. Silly her. In her haze of pleasure at playing family with Jake and the others who visited the farm, she'd forgotten first and foremost, V was his publicist. The realization hurt, but the truth was, what Gracie saw as a potential for friendship was nothing more than V's single-minded attention to Jake's career.

She flinched when V tapped a red-lacquered fingernail to the photo filling the front top fold of the paper. The photographer captured the moment she'd thrown herself into Jake's arms yesterday. Though her face was obscured, thanks to Jake's voracious kiss, the image clearly showed her wrapped around his body like a clinging vine.

V's Texas twang sharpened with her anger. "If you're going to insist on remaining out of the spotlight, this is *not* the way to achieve your goal."

"V!"

His barked warning wasn't necessary. Gracie fought her own battles. As he approached the table with his mug, she lifted her chin and met and held V's angry blue glare. "Do I need to point out that picture was taken while I was on the porch of my home? My private, *secluded* home. Your sarcasm isn't appreciated."

V's flinty blue gaze flashed with frustration before she slumped back with a long sigh. Her eyes slid shut momentarily, and she forked her fingers into the curls at her temples. They held an apology when she opened her eyes once more. She dropped her hands to the tabletop. "I'm sorry. Truly. I don't mean to take this out on you. On either of you, but I've had a bitch of a morning." She jerked her chin toward the mug in front of her. "And that's my first cup of coffee."

Gracie nodded her acceptance of the apology and swallowed against the guilt gnawing at the lining of her belly. V had good reason to be pissed. She'd warned Gracie the press wouldn't give up. They both had, but had she listened? Of course not.

She shifted her gaze between V's dismayed frown and Jake's angry scowl. Her stubbornness had accomplished exactly what she'd been trying to avoid. In her blind attempt to protect her secret, she'd drawn the attention of the league's front office. Worse, she'd dragged Jake into this mess with her. The fact she'd already decided to give the press a statement only made her feel like a bigger heel.

Jake claimed V was brilliant at handling spin. Gracie hoped he was right. "I'm the one who should be apologizing. Would it help if I agreed to speak with the press or has the time passed already?"

Jake dropped into his chair, surprise wrinkling his brow.

V sat forward. "That depends."

"On?"

"On whatever it is you're hiding."

She stiffened and sliced Jake with an accusing glare. *Frigging blabbermouth.*

He cocked his head and met her gaze steadily. "Really? When you've been sneaking around the farm like a guilty wraith for weeks. Don't look at me like that. I didn't have to say a word."

She'd love to argue his point. Unfortunately, she couldn't.

V cleared her throat. "Your secrets are your business. The last thing we want to do is pry."

"Speak for yourself." He slumped back in his chair.

V rolled her eyes. "I'm serious, Jake."

"So am I."

Narrowing her eyes, Gracie met his smug smirk with a scowl.

"My point is," V continued, "if what you're hiding will hurt Jake's image, I'd prefer you keep your distance from the microphones."

"Fuck the microphones."

Gracie's gaze snapped back to his. The smug smile was gone, and the pleading intensity in his eyes set her girl parts to quivering and her heart to pounding.

He sat forward to cover her hand with his. "Talk to me, baby. Tell me his name."

Not fair. How was she supposed to keep a clear head when he dropped his voice to a crooning purr? He didn't clarify who he meant and didn't need to. He'd asked directly after the man's identity yesterday and clearly concluded her father was the source of her fears. Tough luck for her, he was right.

Ignoring him seemed the best bet. She met V's concerned gaze. "I'd as soon keep my distance from the microphones period, but that's not an option any longer, is it?"

"It never was, sweetie, and you didn't answer my question."

"I promise you, nothing in my past can harm Jake's image."

V nodded, apparently satisfied.

Jake wasn't. He shoved back from the table and pushed to his feet. Grumbling beneath his breath about stubborn women, he stalked from the room without sparing her another glance. She wanted to call him back and plead with him to understand. She remained silent and started slightly when V squeezed her hand on the tabletop.

"You've tweaked his ego. He's not used to women who don't jump to do his every bidding. Well, except for me." She smiled softly.

A smile tugged at Gracie's mouth then dimmed quickly. "He wants me to talk to him about things I don't discuss."

"He wants your trust."

She knew that and wished she could give it. She couldn't. Not in this case. She shrugged helplessly.

V spoke hesitantly, and what she said proved Jake wasn't the blabbermouth Gracie accused him of being in her mind. "Gracie, it's none of my business but, if some man hurt you, you *should* talk to someone about it."

"Oh, no!" She shook her head. "Oh, God, no. It's nothing like that. It's…complicated." She shrugged. "Believe me, there are a whole lot of people who would be better off if I kept my mouth shut. Including Jake."

V considered her in silence for a moment then nodded. "All right, but if you change your mind and need someone to talk to, I hope you'll come to me. I'm a great listener and spin control is my specialty."

"You don't say?"

V grinned. "And don't worry about Jake. He'll get over it. Now, speaking of spin control."

* * * *

This is a bad idea. A very bad idea.

Only sheer force of will, and Jake's arm, kept Gracie in place. Despite the oversized sunglasses covering her eyes, she blinked at the flashing cameras and dug her fingernails into her palms in an effort to ignore the urge to flee.

Tweaked ego or not, Jake seemed to sense her faltering courage or maybe her shaking in her calf-skin and goat hair, furry white knockoffs clued him in. He gave her shoulders a squeeze and dipped his head to whisper in her ear. "Picture them naked. It's what I do."

She snapped her head around and up to meet his gaze.

He jerked back and barely avoided her head butting him in the nose. He grinned at yet another near miss and dipped his head once more to rest his cheek against hers. "Relax, princess. V knows what she's doing. Watch."

She wasn't sure whether to punch him or kiss him when he nipped at her earlobe before straightening. Either way, she couldn't suppress the shiver. When he chuckled, the scale tipped toward the punch, but clobbering him would have to wait.

Cool and serene, V addressed the vultures, laying out the story they'd agreed on for the statement. Denying the two of them were involved in a hot and heavy affair was out of the question, considering the picture on the front page of the paper, but everyone loved a love story, V had insisted. Why not use that to their advantage?

Like a bard of old, she wove a dreamy tale of boy meets girl, where the handsome, famous boy and lovely, talented girl overcome their public difference of opinion to care for orphan twin girls and find romance in the process. If she wasn't so nervous, Gracie would've laughed at the predicted response of the vultures.

With the exception of a particularly cynical press babe named Dina Sutton, who made her doubt clear with a constant smirk, the vultures bought V's story like romance readers at a paperback convention. They latched onto the romantic element of the story with single-minded intensity and went wild when V played their ace in the hole. After V announced

Gracie's online identity, all interest in her true identity evaporated beneath a voyeuristic desire for juicy details.

Jake wore his most charming smile, skirting the more pointed questions. He worked Dina and the crowd like the pro he was. Innuendo and charm were his weapons, and he wielded them expertly. As previously agreed, he also fielded the questions directed at Gracie. Except for Dina, whose narrowed eyes gave Gracie the willies, the press didn't seem to notice. That suited her fine. Her energy was focused on not throwing up. If she'd been forced to speak, there was a good chance a scandal of a different kind would be documented on the front pages of tomorrow's morning editions.

When, at last, V pronounced the press conference ended, relief made Gracie's legs weak. She wasn't stupid. The vultures' dangerous attentions wouldn't simply fade away, but she'd accomplished what she set out to do. The mob had their story and, thanks to her subtle disguise, her resemblance to her mother wouldn't be evident in any of the pictures they snapped.

Jake kept tight hold of her arm and turned her toward the farmhouse. She shuffled alongside him on wobbly legs and shoved the sunglasses higher on her nose. Those colored contacts she'd teased Max about were beginning to sound like a good idea. The moment they got back inside the house, she was going online to order a half dozen pair.

* * * *

Ten minutes later, Jake disconnected the call with a satisfied grunt. Tom was right. Hiring a private detective was a bad idea and unnecessary when almost everything could be found online these days. He might not have Gracie's skills at accessing information on the web, but he had connections who did. She'd asked him to drop the subject of her father, claiming the man's family would be hurt should his identity become known. In the meantime, keeping the man's secret was tearing her apart. Recalling the fine tremors wracking her sleek body as she faced the press at last, he refused to feel guilty about utilizing his connections.

If loving a woman meant suffering an irresistible need to shield her from harm, the question of what he felt for Gracie had been answered. His gut clenched with panic, but he'd never been a man to deny the truth. Like the girls, Gracie had found a way into his heart. What he should do about that was a question he'd have to answer soon, in the meantime, he was through watching her live like a scared rabbit.

Chapter 27

Something prodded Gracie from her drowse.

She stretched languidly and purred as Jake tightened his arm around her waist and tucked his naked body closer to hers. Contentment simmered. The day had been long and busy, but she couldn't remember a sweeter Christmas than the one she'd shared with Jake and the girls. Not since Sarah's death anyway.

A peek from under her lashes showed the glowing numbers of the clock on the nightstand. Midnight. She yawned and considered going back to her room. It was what she should do but, for the life of her, she couldn't bring herself to move out of his warm embrace.

From that first afternoon in the cottage, they'd agreed to keep their intimate meetings a secret from the girls. The clandestine nature of their relationship hadn't changed, but since Mary moved out of her bedroom in the farm house almost two months ago, to take up residence in her cottage, the temptation to sneak into Jake's room after the girls were asleep became increasingly difficult to resist.

Perhaps she could've held out if he hadn't been single-mindedly persistent in his sensual invitations. Then again, maybe not. She was a complete sucker for his *love me, baby* drawl. All he had to do was whisper his naughty invitation in her ear, and her eventual caving became a matter of when, not if.

She arrived at his door, several nights later, hot with embarrassment. The heat quickly exploded into flames of excited pleasure when he snagged her wrist and dragged her, laughing, into his big, four-poster bed. She hadn't looked back.

Silent laughter shook her shoulders. If she'd proven bold and insatiable, she certainly hadn't been alone.

"Jake?" The muffled call, spoken in a childish voice, was followed by a soft knock on the bedroom door.

Panic exploded in her chest. Oh, dear Lord! Why was Charlie knocking at the door?

Gracie bolted from his arms, her terrified gaze on the closed door. What had she been thinking not flipping the lock when she slipped inside earlier? Oh, God. What was she thinking sneaking in here in the first place? What kind of guardian gleefully participated in wild monkey sex with two small girls sleeping down the hall? An irresponsible, slutty one, that's what.

Jake sat up beside her, slapping a hand over her mouth and cutting off her groan. She scowled at the laughter glittering in his eyes as he held a finger to his lips.

Was he serious? After ten weeks, he should know the girls well enough to realize a closed door wouldn't stop either of them, especially not Charlie. Shoving his hand away, she scrambled over his chest and tumbled off the far side of the bed. She landed on her shoulder with a breath-stealing thud.

"Gracie?" Concern thickened his rumbling whisper.

Gulping for breath, answering was impossible. She rolled to her back on the thick carpet and lifted her arm high enough to flap a hand in response.

The bedding rustled and his worried face appeared over the side of the mattress. "You okay?"

She would be as soon as she could breathe again. Nodding, she sat up then found the air to yelp when Charlie called his name again from the hallway.

He pushed to his knees and glanced over his shoulder toward the door. Legs spread, he kneeled on the bed with his hands on his hips. In spite of her justifiable anxiety, Gracie's attention was momentarily snagged by the sight of him. Dear Lord, the man was magnificently built. She'd never seen anything as beautiful as Jake Malone naked.

He was naked. *They* were naked—with Charlie banging on the door!

"Put something on!" Breathlessness made her frantic whisper barely audible. Her fingers closed around the edge of the quilt, and she yanked. The potential covering didn't budge from under his knee. She glared at his crooked grin and yanked harder. "Hurry, you idiot. Before she bursts in."

Completely freaked out, she couldn't enjoy the natural male confidence evident in his casual knee walk across the mattress. He stepped off the edge and bent to scoop his jeans and T-shirt from the quilted bench at the foot of the bed. "Relax, princess. The door's locked."

She stilled in the process of wrapping herself in the quilt. "It is?"

Stepping into his jeans, he shucked them up over his hips as he sauntered toward the door. He glanced over his shoulder, speaking softly. "I locked it when I went to get the new box of condoms from the bathroom." He waggled his brows.

She'd have blushed if she had the time. "Wait!"

He paused with his hand on the knob. She scurried around the bed and ripped her dangling panties from the arm of his desk chair then gathered her silk nightshirt from the floor. Tiptoeing on bare feet, she slid past him to press her back to the wall beside the door.

Soft laughter drew her gaze. He pointed at his bare feet. Her flirty, fuzzy pink, high heel slippers lay haphazardly where she'd kicked them off at the foot of the door. She scurried around him, snatched them up, and returned to her hiding spot.

Dimples popped in his maddening grin. She swung out an arm, waving her hand toward the door in a silent demand he get on with it.

Chuckling, he did as she suggested and gave Charlie his attention. "What are you doing up, sweetheart?"

"I can't find Auntie Gracie." The whine in her statement immediately pricked at Gracie's guilt, doubling it. What was wrong?

"Auntie Gracie had to, ah, run out for a bit." Jake gripped the door high enough to flash Gracie a grin from beneath his forearm. "She said something about a midnight shoe sale."

She rolled her eyes, not sharing his humor. In all the weeks they'd been at the farm, the girls hadn't come looking for either of them in the middle of the night. Charlie was here, after not finding Gracie where she *should* have been, which said something was definitely wrong. She jerked her chin toward the door.

He winked and ignored her answering glare. He turned to Charlie. "What's wrong? Why aren't you asleep?"

"Angel woke me up. She's crying."

Gracie started to push off the wall and make her presence known. He released the door, straight-arming her with a hand to her chest.

"Is she sick?"

"I don't know."

Though Gracie couldn't see her, Charlie's tears were evident in her voice. Gracie pushed against his hand. He held her firm and met her gaze with a stern shake of his head as if to say, *let me handle this*.

Squeezing her shoulder, he looked away and smiled at Charlie. "Let's go see."

Gracie yanked on her nightshirt and slipped into her panties the moment he pulled the door closed behind them. She appreciated what he was doing, but guilt gnawed at her insides. If she hadn't been selfishly enjoying a sexy romp in his bed, she'd have been where she belonged when the girls needed her.

Barefoot with her slippers in one hand, she dashed down the hall and slowed to a stop outside the nursery door.

Jake's voice rumbled in a soothing purr. "What's wrong, Angel face?"

Gracie dipped her head to peek around the door. Jake's hip rested on the edge of the bed beside Angel's tiny body, curled in a tight ball. His hand ran over the bumps of her spine beneath her pink, princess pajamas.

Angel's shoulders jerked on a sob. "I had a bad dream."

"Aw, sweetheart. Can you tell me about it?"

She shook her head.

"I guess you're used to talking to Charlie when you have a nightmare, huh?"

Angel sniffed, and Charlie stepped closer to rest a hand on his shoulder. He turned his head to smile at her.

In the shadows of the door, Gracie's chest tightened.

He turned back to Angel. "You're pretty lucky, you know. When I was a kid and had a nightmare, I woke up and wished I had a brother to talk to, or a sister."

Angel peeked at him from beneath dark lashes spiked with tears. "What about Miss V? She said you grew up together."

He nodded solemnly. "We did, and she was the next best thing, but she wasn't a *real* sister."

Charlie bent at the waist and cocked her head to look him in the eye. "Like Angel and me?"

He tapped a fingertip to her nose. "That's right."

Angel slowly rolled her head to meet his gaze. "Did you ever dream you were lost, all by yourself?"

He titled his head as though searching his memory. "Not that I can recall. Is that what you dreamt about?"

She nodded, and he cupped her tiny cheek in his large hand. Gracie bit her lip. Burning tears stung her eyes and nose at the tenderness of the touch.

He brushed a thumb over Angel's cheek. "That sounds like a scary dream, but look around. You're not alone. You've got Charlie, your auntie Gracie, Miss Mary, and me."

She sniffled. "I was lost."

A growl of sympathy rumbled in his throat. "That sounds *very* scary, but you know what?"

She blinked and uncurled to roll to her back. "What?"

"You'll never be lost." He glanced between both girls. "Either of you. Because I won't let that happen. Not e*ver*."

"You promise?"

He held up a pinky, and Gracie's heart shuddered in her chest. Where had the reluctant warrior who'd shown up at the farmhouse door claiming to know nothing about little girls gone? The Outlaw playboy had been completely vanquished by a pair of miniature heartbreakers. While the development warmed her heart, her watery smile was more sad than joyful.

Angel sat up and linked her pinky with his. He grinned then bumped his shoulder to Charlie's in a teasing invitation for her to join them. She giggled and curled her pinky around both of theirs.

"You have to say it," Angel instructed solemnly.

He dipped his head and spoke as if his promise was the most important of his life. "I pinky swear."

Angel nodded. Releasing his hand, she rose to her knees. She dropped her head shyly. "I love you, Jake." She lifted her gaze to his.

His lips tilted upward in a surprised smile, and she threw herself into his arms.

Charlie giggled and squeezed in beside her sister to smile up into his face. "Me, too!"

As though sensing Gracie's presence, he lifted his head, his eyes full of wary wonder. He glanced down at the top of their dark heads and his Adam's apple skittered on a swallow. His suspiciously bright gaze climbed back to Gracie's. He blinked, shook his head, and smiled at her, unaware of how the razor sharp pieces of her shattering heart sliced at her soul. For sure he had no clue he and his sisters were instrumental in the death of her most cherished dream.

Heartbreaking, it seemed, was a Thompson family trait.

Chapter 28

"Ho-ly *shit*!"

Twin gasps reminded Jake of where he was and who was listening. With his heart slamming against the wall of his chest, he lifted his gaze from the screen on his phone and met dueling sets of identical, condemning blue eyes.

"Language!" Mary pinned him with narrowed eyes.

Using charm to get around her disapproving frown would require a clearer head than he possessed at the moment. Talk about taking a blind hit! He wiped a sweaty palm across the front of his sweatshirt. "Sorry."

Across the table, Charlie paused with a crayon held over her open coloring book. Her mouth puckered with accusation and she spoke in a stage whisper. "You said the S word."

"Yeah." His palms were sweating, but his throat was bone dry. He swallowed with an audible click. "Sorry about that."

Angel's attitude might have done a complete one-eighty from the distrust she'd shown him when he first arrived at the farm, however, her thinned lips proclaimed her newfound hero worship wouldn't help him in this case. She pointed a crayon at the jar on the counter without saying a word.

Too rattled to plead his case down to a lesser charge, he rose to his feet, pulled out his wallet and dug out a twenty. After what Max said about asking why a female computer geek would become a rabid football fan, he'd expected her father was someone in the world of football. He'd even been prepared to recognize the man's name, but… Suddenly, her furtiveness, as well as her fear, made perfect sense, but…holy shit!

His guilty gaze sliced back to the twins. Maybe he should stuff a C note in the jar. He'd no doubt be dropping plenty more verbal bombs before coming to terms with Gracie's father's identity.

Holy! Fucking! Shit!

He peeled off a couple more twenties and tossed them in. "Where's Gracie?"

Mary eyed the jar, and his face, before turning back to her dinner preparations. "In the city. She had a business meeting and a hair appointment. She said she'd be home by four."

Oh, hell. She was primping for tonight's date. He glanced at his phone, squeezed his eyes shut, and bit back a groan. What the hell did he do now?

He forked the fingers of his free hand through his hair. He'd only scanned the first paragraph of the report his computer friend sent, but that was enough. What were the odds Gracie's mother's boss had been a sports agent with a client named Doug Costa? A second Doug Costa who *wasn't* the man who lived to make Jake's professional life miserable?

From her initial horror at learning he was Pete's son to her fear of facing the press, Gracie's unreasonable behavior these past three months suddenly made perfect sense. His princess was none other than the illegitimate daughter of the league's new commissioner.

Son of a bitch!

The mother fucker had dogged him for years in his quest for revenge for Jake's having slept with his niece, despite the fact Bridgette had gone on to screw her way through half the starting lineups in the league before bagging herself a Brazilian soccer star husband.

For years, Costa had worn his squeaky clean reputation like a cape, looking down his nose at Jake and making things difficult whenever possible. What a crock of shit. Jake would be the first one to admit he wasn't perfect, but at least he hadn't knocked anyone up and walked away.

At the table, Angel giggled at something Charlie said, drawing his attention as she chose another crayon from the box between them. He drew in a slow breath, recalling the afternoon he'd attempted to get Gracie to give him her father's name. She'd shot him down, arguing the man had a family she wasn't willing to destroy.

He didn't understand her logic. Like Pete, Costa had walked away from her to build a family with his other children and yet, she'd been turning herself inside out to protect him. The irony of the situation didn't escape him. He, who never expected nor particularly wanted a family, had one dropped in his lap. She, on the other hand, spent her life yearning for what would've been hers, but for Costa's abandonment. The asshole didn't deserve her.

He scrubbed a hand over his face. As commissioner, Costa would play a prominent role at tonight's fund-raiser. Did Gracie realize he'd be there?

With a little effort, arrangements could be made to publicly take the sanctimonious fucker down a few pegs and prove to Gracie her concern for the man was misplaced. V would pitch a fit if she knew he'd even considered exposing Costa for the fraud he was, but damn, he was tempted.

* * * *

"Well, how do I look?"

Gracie spun in a slow pirouette. Ending at mid-thigh, the wispy silk sheath dress shifted and shimmied, floating around her curves with every move. The silvery hue captured the soft glow of her bedside lamp in shades of magenta, pink and purple, a vision of pearlescent magic, as the sale's clerk had suggested. The dress was beautiful and should be for what she'd paid, but she needed the extra boost in confidence tonight.

Like runway judges, the twins huddled on her bed and eyed her critically. In her position as diva in training, Angel offered the twins' consensual opinion on anything fashion.

Breathless, she clasped her hands together beneath her chin and sighed wistfully. "Like a princess."

Gracie grinned and made them laugh by performing a deep, flowing curtsey. She ended the move by displaying the toe of one high, Armadillo boot. Considering *his* shoe/leg fetish, she couldn't wait to see Jake's reaction to the silver, peek-a-boo sexy ribbons hugging her ankles.

"Are you nervous?"

More than I've ever been in my life! She cocked her head at Charlie's guileless question. "A little, but what would make you ask such a thing? Do I look nervous?"

Charlie smiled. "No, but Jake is. We thought you might be, too."

Angel nodded in agreement.

Jake, nervous? "Why do you say that?"

"He said a bad word."

"The S word," Angel added. "Miss Mary said it's cuz men hate to wear tuxeebos."

She grinned. "Tuxedos."

Angel nodded. "But I don't know why he's mad. I think he looks pretty in his," she spoke the word slowly, "tuxedo."

A laugh gurgled up from her belly. "Did you tell him that?"

"Oh, no. He was *really* mad." Angel's brow puckered. "Should I? Do you think it would make him feel better?"

"I think you definitely should. Everyone likes hearing they look pretty, right?"

They bobbed their heads in agreement. "Right!"

She smiled mischievously as she stepped in front of her long, oval mirror to attach her earrings. The dangling silver baubles danced and sparkled in the artificial light. Wispy tendrils framed her face and softened the sophisticated up-do her hairdresser had created. Coffee brown eyes blinked back at her, courtesy of her new colored contacts.

She spun away. What would Jake think of the change in her eye color? As suspicious as he was, she doubted he'd buy her claim the contacts were simply for fun. Too bad. That was the story she'd be pitching. If he didn't like it, well, this wouldn't be the first time he'd been unhappy with her over her secretiveness.

She sighed. The truth was, the secretiveness between them was probably no longer necessary. Even if she was to do as Jake asked and give him her father's name, she couldn't see him blabbing the information to the press. The resulting firestorm would be something he and V would want to avoid at all costs.

Nor were the contacts necessary, other than to assuage her *better safe than sorry* philosophy. Facing the press three weeks ago had proven Max right. There was no reason for anyone to make the connection between her and her father. Other than their shared hair color, she looked nothing like the man who sired her, and after twenty-six years, who would be looking?

The freedom her epiphany represented left her giddy with relief. Sure, she hadn't shed the press completely. Though they were no longer camped at the gate, they remained interested in fleshing out her and Jake's romantic tale. The phone rang incessantly with requests for interviews, and much to Gracie's horror, Dina Sutton had actually ambushed her outside the door to Max's gym last week. Max, the hound dog, managed to sidetrack the redheaded reporter by convincing her an interview with Gracie's best friend would be the next best thing. Ha! Beneficial to him, maybe. No doubt the subject of carnal knowledge came up at some point during their *interview* last night.

In any case, no longer fearing discovery, the continued interest of the press wasn't nearly as menacing. Unfortunately, she had a much more alarming issue to deal with, specifically, deciding what to do with her life now she'd lost the custody battle to the man she loved. Watching him with the girls on Christmas night, witnessing Angel's ultimate surrender to his insurmountable charms, had been like taking a sledgehammer to the chest. Envy burned, yet, there was a certain relief in having the uncertainty behind her. Maybe she was rationalizing, but that was better than curling into the fetal position and howling out her despair.

The silver lining, because she believed in looking for one in every bitter loss, was the peace in her heart, knowing the girls would be settled and safe with Jake. They loved him and he loved them. They were family. She above most people understood the magic of that kind of miracle.

It wasn't as if she'd be left out completely. The girls would always be a part of her life. As for Jake? When he moved on with *his* life, she'd have her memories. Including those she planned to make tonight.

She loved seeing the surprise on his face when she accepted his invitation to tonight's gala fund-raiser—the very same fund-raiser Tuck requested she attend with *him*. She stomped a spiked heel down on a niggling kernel of doubt. Whether Jake truly wanted to spend an entire evening away from the farm with her as he claimed, or tonight was simply another salvo in his friendly competition with Tuck, in the end, it didn't matter.

She loved Jake and their time together was running short. Less than forty-eight hours remained. She meant to make the most of them. Tonight she'd have her one and only date with him. The idea made her smile. Dressed in black tie and dancing the evening away in a ballroom packed full of muscled warriors didn't exactly qualify as a normal first date, but in her case, the over-the-top scenario made sense. When a woman loved a larger-than-life man, the word normal rarely came up.

She suspected tonight would be no exception. Any night that required making arrangements with a lawyer to extend curfew was anything but normal.

Amazing as it seemed, tonight she'd be walking out the front door of the farm without worrying her life was about to explode before her eyes. For the first time in months, she could finally relax and be herself without the specter of discovery hovering over her like a ghost from her past. She'd be spending a rare evening in the arms of the man she loved, building memories to last a lifetime, and if that weren't enough, she was also looking at one hell of an added bonus. Though he'd never know it, tonight Jake would give her a gift she could never repay.

The league was the official sponsor of tonight's event, which meant her father would be in attendance. She sucked in a bracing breath to ward off the sudden lightheadedness. Quite a trade-off. The loss of one dream for the realization of another.

Butterfly wings battered against the lining of her belly as she swept up her purse and turned to the girls. She tapped a fingertip to her puckered lips. "Am I missing anything?"

"Lipstick!" Angel bounced on the bed.

She laughed and her spiraling nerves settled some. A few moments later, they descended the stairs. All three of their smiles sported a slick application of dusky rose. Both the nerves and the lightheadedness came galloping back the moment she reached the landing and spotted Jake speaking with Mary in the foyer.

Oh, Angel, you're wrong, baby.

Jake Malone in black tie wasn't pretty, he was drop dead gorgeous. Tall and lithe, yet impossibly broad through the shoulders, he was the quintessential modern day warrior. Straight and proud, his muscled body exuded good health and power. Undeniably attractive, he was James Bond handsome and Chippendale sexy. And tonight, he was all hers.

He turned his head and his emerald eyes widened. His focused gaze slid down her body like a heated caress. Goose bumps popped and her girl parts puckered helplessly. When his gaze stalled at the silky straps crisscrossing her ankles and lower calves, and he swallowed convulsively, her lips tipped up in a smug smile.

Oh, yeah. A man's healthy fetish did wonders for a woman's ego.

Her smile skittered away when he lifted his head at last and his gaze locked with hers. None of the usual teasing humor she'd become accustomed to seeing lingered in his eyes. The twins were right. Something was off. Subtle tension rode his shoulders, stiffening them beneath his black suit coat. Intent and sober, his concentrated study held her pinned in place.

"What's wrong?"

He shook his head. "How could anything possibly be wrong when I'm looking at you in that dress?" As he'd done several times before, he instantly shed whatever nerves hung over him. Dimples winked on with his smile. He folded his fingers around hers and held out her arm to give her another once over. He whistled through his teeth. "Wow. You're beautiful."

She shook off the subtle fingers of unease trailing down her spine and returned his smile. "You're pretty *wow* yourself."

He winked and leaned close to stare into her eyes. "Something's different."

She forced a smile. "Must be the contacts. Aren't they fun?"

He nodded then lowered his head to brush his cheek against hers. "Nice, but I hope you don't mean to wear them all the time. Your violet eyes drive me crazy, baby."

He straightened and, as if noting the blush heating her cheeks, winked. She sucked in a ragged breath in lieu of fanning herself. He laughed and turned, crouching down in from of the twins.

His gaze bounced between them. "I don't believe I've had the pleasure of meeting either of you lovely ladies."

Charlie immediately collapsed against his shoulder in a fit of giggles. Angel propped her hands on his hips and cocked her head. "We're Angel and Charlie, silly."

He jerked back and made a production of studying them. "No way! Angel and Charlie are only six. They don't wear lipstick." He shook his head. "You're both *way* too grown up to be my sisters."

Gracie's heart squeezed. Did he realized this was the first time he'd formally recognized them as sisters? With no hyphens? No qualifications?

Angel giggled hard enough she could barely speak. "It's us. Auntie Gracie let us try her lipstick, but we have to wash it off before we go to bed."

"Which I'll make sure they do." Mary appeared at Gracie's side. "Go on with you now. Have a good time."

Jake straightened to his feet, accepting Gracie's long dress coat from Mary. He shot Gracie a smile as he helped her into her coat, but the humor didn't translate to his eyes. Unease chilled her. No matter what he said, something was definitely wrong.

Chapter 29

One would think after spending the last three months in Jake's presence, and experiencing the frequent visits of his famous teammate friends, Gracie would be immune to the spectacle of pro football's most recognizable athletes mixing with famous faces from the entertainment industry, finance, politics, and the press. Not so. Busy searching the crowd milling about the atrium in the Metropolitan Museum's Sackler wing for one particular famous face, she couldn't stop herself from gawking.

It was difficult to tell who schmoozed whom as the players worked the crowd. They laughed, chatted, posed for pictures, and in the process, secured jaw-dropping pledges from star-struck, deep-pocketed patrons. Having witnessed Jake's charm first-hand, she shouldn't have been surprised at how good he was at this sort of thing but, holy cow. She'd nearly spewed champagne over the matronly wife of a retired Wall Street mogul when the diamond-adorned woman puckered her time-wrinkled lips to blow dry the ink before handing Jake her check for a cool half million.

After an hour of smiling at strangers as Jake worked his wiles, she left him to wring a bundle of cash from a senior congressman as famous for his watchdog interest in the spending of the people's money as for his family name and fortune. Wandering around the edges of the crowd, she scanned the room for a familiar head of blond hair and a broad set of shoulders, but though her heart lodged in her throat several times, none of the big blond men she spied were the one for which she searched.

Disappointment settled between her shoulder blades like an overstuffed backpack. What if her father didn't plan to show after all?

Spotting Dina Sutton scanning the room as well, she plucked a glass from a passing waiter and pushed through the crowd to pause at the foot of the Temple of Dendur. Considering the staggering amount of money changing hands, the grandeur of the ancient stone edifice was the perfect backdrop for tonight's party. She stared up at the ornately carved columns framing the entrance to the temple porch. Sipping at her glass, she sensed someone at her side and turned her head. Expecting Jake, she smiled at Tuck.

He dropped his arm around her shoulders. "I've been looking everywhere for you."

"You have? I thought you'd be angry with me."

He cocked his head. "For turning me down tonight in favor of Malone?"

She nodded.

"Nah." He sipped from his glass. "I forgive you for that. You're living in the same house with him. I know how whiney he can be when he doesn't get his way."

She laughed. "Whiney?"

He bared his teeth in a leering smile. "What can I say? He's a diva."

"As opposed to you."

He looked down his nose. "I don't whine. I get even."

"So I've heard."

He chuckled. "Hey, there're a lot of jealous people out there willing to spread lies. You can't believe everything you hear."

She turned away to study the hieroglyphics on the right column. "Then I shouldn't believe Jake stole Daphne out from under your nose, or that you've stolen countless women from him over the years?"

His smile morphed into a wide grin. "Oh, you can believe the part about the countless women I've stolen, but the Daphne thing is patently untrue. Jake only *thinks* he won that round. I'd already dumped her for a curvy redhead."

She shook her head and he dipped his head to peer into her eyes.

"Does the idea of me with countless women bother you?"

She smirked. "Get real."

"Because, for the right woman, I'd be willing to change my wicked ways."

"Why, Tuck?" She batted her lashes. "Are you saying *I'm* the right woman?"

He cocked his head and considered her face. "Maybe. Maybe not. But I'm willing to spend a few nights with you to find out."

He grunted when her elbow landed solidly in his side, and she couldn't help but join him when he chuckled.

He indicated the temple with his beer glass. "Cool, huh?"

"Very cool."

"Ever seen this kind of stuff in person?"

She glanced at him. "You mean, have I been to the Middle East?"

He nodded.

"No. Have you?"

"Nope. The Marauders' front office is filled with a bunch of tight asses. They insisted on including a safety clause in my contract. No base-jumping ski trips. No mountain climbing. Not even hang gliding, and no traveling anywhere I might say something that could get my head chopped off."

They shared a grin and he tightened his arm around her shoulders. "However, the world is full of wicked old shit, uh…stuff like this. Say the word and we can be in the air in less than an hour."

She grinned. "You do know how to sweep a girl off her feet, don't you?"

He ran his fingertips down her arm and dropped his voice to a distinctively seductive murmur. "Your wish is my command, baby."

Please. Did he think she was buying his crap? She heaved an exaggerated sigh. "Tempting, but my get out of jail free card from the farm expires at midnight."

"Then we'd better get going. We can be at my place in ten minutes."

"Be careful, Tuck. She may look like a princess, but she's more skilled at bringing a man to his knees than her dog."

She twisted her head around. Jake stood behind them.

Tuck spoke over her head. "I'm willing to take my chances."

Jake bared his teeth in a taunting smile. "I'm not willing to *let* you."

"Oh, for heaven's sake." She stepped clear of Tuck's arm. "You sound like a couple of Neanderthals. Personally, I'm not interested in being the prize for either of you. No matter *who*," she spun toward Jake, "wins this rooouuu…nd."

Like lightning bugs on crack, pinpoints of light scrambled haphazardly across her field of vision. She swallowed convulsively as she stared at the two big blond men and the tall redhead who came to a stop behind Jake.

Doug Costa spoke with a distinctive sneer. "Sounds as if the two of you have finally set your sights on a woman smart enough to see through your games."

Jake's head whipped around. When he turned back, his eyes slid shut briefly. Beneath his tuxedo jacket, his shoulders went stiff and a muscle quivered in his jaw. Tuck's indignant snort registered behind her, but their antagonistic reactions to the league commissioner's statement weren't her problem.

None of her daydreams throughout the years could've truly prepared her for this moment. This wasn't how their first meeting was supposed to happen. Her father was supposed to pass by her at a distance. She'd look her fill, perhaps move close enough to hear him speak. Then he'd move on without them ever making eye contact, and her life would go on as it had before. Normal. Boring. Safe.

Unfortunately, normal had disappeared from her vocabulary the moment Jake arrived at the farm and this situation was neither boring nor safe. She struggled to control her erratic breathing and calm her roiling stomach. Jake wasn't stupid. He was bound to put two and two together if she threw up on his shoes—a distinct possibility considering the churning in her belly. She glanced away, frantically searching the room for a possible escape route. None presented itself.

Jake closed his fingers around her elbow as Doug stuck out his hand. "Hell of a catch last week, Jake. We'll be adding your name to the record books before the regular season is over."

After Jake's blatant refusal to meet with him when that damning photo hit the stands last week, the compliment made her blink.

Jake shook his hand. "Not if New England has anything to say about it. We've got our work cut out for us this week."

Tuck's sharp snort made clear what he thought of *that* nonsense.

Silent until now, Tom Walden laughed. "Pride goeth before the fall, Tuck."

Tuck bared his teeth in a wicked smile. "Skill. Pure, superior skill."

As stealthy as she could manage, Gracie leaned her head to the side and spotted an exit sign on the far wall. Would this crowd of oversized warriors buy her claim of not feeling well? It was the truth after all. She never got the chance.

"Where are your manners, gentlemen?" The redhead smiled and extended her hand. "I swear. Men can be completely rude. I'm Sharon Walden. You must be Gracie Gable."

All eyes turned Gracie's way, and she couldn't help her flinch. She placed her hand in Sharon's briefly and murmured something. Her lips were numb and bees buzzed in her ears. She had no idea if what she said made a lick of sense. She suspected *not* when she turned her head and her gaze locked with the watchful, denim blue eyes her mother's diary had described in minute detail.

Sharp creases bracketed her father's mouth in a strained smile far different than the carefree grin she'd come to recognize from the covers of all those magazines and newspapers she'd pored over throughout the years.

"I've heard a lot about you, Miss Gable."

And I've devoured everything I could find about you.

She sucked air through her teeth as quietly as she could manage. Ripples of joy battled with crippling fear. The competing sentiments rioted through her system and left her weak. She had to lock her knees to keep them from giving way beneath her as she placed her hand in Tom Walden's. "Likewise."

Beside her father, the commissioner dipped his chin and offered her a smile. "I knew an Angela Gable once. You remember her, Tom. She was Simon White's secretary. As I recall, the two of you were an item for a time. Ah, that is—" He offered Sharon a sheepish smile.

Sharon waved him off with a laugh, but Gracie's eyes sliced back to Tom.

He stared at her mouth, or more precisely the mole at the corner. He looked up and his intent gaze held her spellbound. "I remember. Any relation?"

This couldn't be happening. She swallowed. Utterly aware of Jake's fingers flinching convulsively on her elbow, she couldn't look away from the question in her father's eyes.

Was it possible for a pounding heart to break through the chest wall? *Oh, God.* "She was my mother."

Tom's face paled. A painful lump formed in her throat and clawing talons clenched her manically beating heart. Her gaze dropped to the hand Sharon silently slid onto his arm.

"Well, I'll be." Oblivious to the melodrama taking place around him, Doug chuckled. "She was a lovely young thing. How is she?"

Jake's fingertips dug into her elbow painfully. The lump in her throat expanded, threatening to cut off her supply of air. "She passed away."

"I'm sorry."

"When?" Sadness competed with the dawning shock in Tom's eyes.

"A long time ago," Jake answered sharply before she could. His gaze locked onto Tom's. "*You* dated Gracie's mother?"

Tom squeezed Sharon's hand, but his gaze never left Gracie's face. "She worked for Simon White, my first agent. A lifetime ago."

Biting her bottom lip, Gracie chanced a sidelong glance toward Jake and flinched. Horrified fury crackled like emerald fire in his eyes. Suddenly his gaze jerked to something or someone over her right shoulder, and he cursed under his breath. She followed his gaze and mumbled a curse of her own. Dina Sutton had set a direct course and was headed straight for them.

Jake glanced around and tugged her close to his side. He directed his comment to no one in particular. "If you'll excuse us, Gracie and I need to talk."

"Oh, I don't think—"

He overruled her. "Now."

Clearly not recognizing the gravity of the situation, Tuck stepped in front of them. "Sounds like the lady isn't interested, buddy."

"Shut up, Tuck."

At Jake's growled demand, Tuck held out both hands spread wide. Disapproval beetled Doug's brow, and Tom opened his mouth as if to object. Jake didn't give him the chance. He dragged her toward the exit.

Chapter 30

Jake stalked down the hallway, ignoring curious glances in his search for a private corner in the busy museum. Other than her grumbling commentary on what she was going to do to him once he finally let go of her arm, Gracie didn't put up much of fight at being dragged about like a naughty child. Perhaps she'd spotted Dina, perhaps not. Either way, her cooperation was a good thing. Tossing her over his shoulder and carrying her through The Met might contribute to the tale of their romance, but the way his luck was running, he'd end up getting hauled to jail on abuse charges instead.

The sign above a door twenty feet away caught his attention. He grunted and changed direction. Shoving open the door, he tugged Gracie inside. Startled by his sudden appearance in the feminine enclave, a pair of blondes stared at him wide-eyed from their place in front of the vanity mirrors.

"If you don't mind, ladies, we need a bit of privacy."

"I mind." Gracie tugged at her arm.

He held tight.

The taller of the two women laughed. "You do realize this is the ladies' room?"

Ignoring them for the moment, he dipped his knees and bent at the waist to scan the floor beneath the stalls. All were empty. He turned to Gracie, dropping his head until they were nose to nose. "Stay put if you know what's good for you." Releasing her arm, he stalked to the blondes. He offered them a smile, took each by the arm, and escorted them to the door. "I do indeed, and since the two of you are the only ones here, we'll have plenty of privacy once you leave. Thanks for understanding."

"Wait—"

He shoved the door closed behind them and turned. Dropping his shoulders back against the metal of the door effectively locked him and Gracie in, and anyone else out.

She stood before him with her hands on her hips. "You've got a lot of nerve—"

"*I've* got a lot of nerve? You've been lying your ass off from the moment we met, lady."

She winced but then crossed her arms. "You asked if anything in my past could hurt you, and I said no. When did I lie?"

"Nothing in your past can hurt me, huh?" He jerked his chin over his shoulder. "He may have been semi-cordial out there, but don't fool yourself. Doug Costa hates me. He's a powerful man. Powerful enough to ruin my career. He wouldn't blink an eye at using his power to grind me into the ground if he thinks I can hurt *him*." His chest expanded on a painful breath. Fear clenched in his gut. "But as bad as discovering the league commissioner is your long lost daddy would be, I'm afraid the truth of this situation is even worse."

She jutted up her chin in an obstinate angle, but her gaze skittered away.

Bile rose in his throat. "Jesus, Gracie. Please tell me *Tom* isn't your father."

"If I do, will you drop the subject?"

Unshed tears shimmered in the angry brown gaze she shifted to clash with his. Brown, not violet. He hadn't questioned the change when she'd come downstairs looking like a magical creature in glimmering silk. He should have. Was nothing about her real?

"Only if it's the truth."

She said nothing and her eyes slid shut. Her mouth quivered before she bit her lower lip. A single tear cut a shiny path down her cheek to catch on the mole at the corner of her mouth.

Oh, shit. His stomach did a rolling twist then crashed in a freefall. Locking his knees when they threatened to buckle, he slumped against the door.

Fuck!

His chest heaved as he gasped for breath. He swallowed the bile burning its way up his throat. He'd never been as furious or scared in his life. "You're a piece of work, you know that?"

"*I'm* a piece of work? You're the one—"

He spoke over her, his voice rising to a shout. "Because of you, one of the best men I know is about to see his life destroyed, right before his eyes! Do you know what this is going to do to his wife? Sharon doesn't deserve being dragged through the mud of the coming press storm."

"I never meant for anyone—"

He snorted, narrowing his eyes. "For months, you've been harping at me to do what's best for the girls. I'm thinking that's all a smokescreen."

"Excuse me? A smokescreen for what?"

"You're true agenda."

"What would that be?"

"How the fuck should I know? You clam up whenever I ask a question, but anyone who cares for kids as much as you claim to would realize what this is going to do to Tom's kids. He has two teenage boys. Do you care? Do you *fucking care* what this is going to do to their lives?"

"Not fair!" Fury flashed in her shimmering eyes, and she dropped her arms. Her hands curled into fists. "I *told* you my father had a family. I asked you to let it go. Did you listen? No! *You're* the one who kept pushing. Why couldn't you just let it go?"

"I wish I had." He flung out an arm and pointed back toward the door. "You saw his face. He looked like he'd seen a ghost. He's been my friend for a long time. I know him. Tom Walden doesn't *let things go*. He'll go all honorable and dig in until he has his answers. When he has them, a lot of people I care about will be hurt!"

Pain flashed in her eyes, but she didn't back down. Her chin bumped up a notch and she spaced out her words. "This. Isn't. My. Fault."

Beyond furious, he saw red. If she'd only trusted him, he could've handled this in a way where Sharon and the boys weren't dragged into any fallout. "You should've told me!"

She shouted back. "I did tell you. I told you to drop it!"

Someone pounded on the door at his back. He jammed a hand through his hair. "What a complete cluster fuck." He sighed and glanced around the room. Maybe he could still salvage the situation. If he could get her out of here before the shit hit the fan. Tom would have questions. They'd figure out how to handle this fucking mess together. "Let's go."

She didn't move, except to cross her arms. "I don't happen to like you much at the moment. I'd rather not go anywhere with you, thank you very much."

The pugnacious twist of her lips only added fuel to the fire of his anger.

He couldn't help the sneer in his voice. "Yeah, well, ditto to that, lady. Unfortunately, neither of us has a choice in the matter. Not for the next forty-eight hours anyway."

He refused to feel guilty when she flinched. Damn it, she should've trusted him. What did she think he'd do if he found out Tom was her father, narc his best friend out to the press?

Disgusted, he straightened away from the door, turned, and yanked it open. The simultaneous flash of numerous cameras made him blink. Dina Sutton fronted a half dozen members of the press. Her snapping green eyes broadcast her almost manic glee at snagging such a juicy story. She held out a tape recorder and tossed out the first question. "Is it true you're Tom Walden's daughter, Ms. Gable?"

The excited gasps and murmurs of several of her colleagues filled the hallway. Unlike Dina, the others had obviously come late to the party and hadn't yet realized the blockbuster story they'd accidently tripped on to. Jake whipped his head around. Dark eyes wide and full of dread, Gracie's face was as pale as the white tile walls behind her.

"No comment." Jake spoke before turning around. When he did, he strung together several lurid curses as more than one reporter peeled off from the group to race down the hall. He didn't have to guess where they were headed. Pulling his phone from his pocket, he hit speed dial and held up his hand to block his face when the remaining cameras continued to flash. Tom answered on the third ring. "Get Sharon out of there. Now! I'll explain later."

Wearing a triumphant smile, Dina Sutton snapped one last picture over Jake's shoulder, spun around and, along with the remaining reporters, broke into a run.

* * * *

Too numb to put up a fight, Gracie nearly broke an ankle staggering on her heels behind Jake as he raced after the fleeing press. He gave her no time to examine the wide fissure splitting her heart in two. She had no opportunity to mourn the fact he didn't include her amongst those he cared about who would be hurt by the revealing of Tom Walden's secret.

The lack of reflection was a blessing. Her heart had taken enough damaging blows tonight.

Dragging her along at a swift clip, he rounded a corner. The breath left her in a whoosh when he stopped short and she slammed into his broad back. Breathing became even more difficult when she peeked around his shoulder. A band of horror squeezed her lungs. Geez, did members of the press have some kind of telepathic intercom system allowing them to shoot one another silent messages whenever a juicy story reared its head?

She sucked air through her teeth in a wheezing gasp. Menacing. Frightening. The quietly serene, sophisticated atmosphere of the elite fund-raiser had degenerated into the harsh din of a frenzied lynch mob. Several yards away, nearly two dozen reporters competed for answers, surrounding Tom and Sharon Walden like a human noose.

Sober and tense, deep grooves bracketed her father's tightened lips as he pushed forward toward the front entrance of the building, one arm raised to shield his pale wife from the cameras and tape recorders thrust at them. Scanning the crowd, his gaze sliced past Gracie and immediately whipped back. For several long seconds, their gazes fused. The glittering recognition in his eyes left no doubt he'd discerned her secret.

The world stopped, along with her heart. The crowd disappeared. There was no Jake. No angry accusations. No light or sound. No lingering sense of menace. Only she and her father existed in that moment. Like an old eight millimeter movie scrolling through her mind, the lonely moments of her life flashed through her head. Her mother's sudden death. The countless nights Sarah left Gracie alone in their small apartment because she had no choice. Receiving the news of Sarah's diagnosis and standing in the chill wind as Sarah's body was lowered into the ground.

Time stood still as the memories washed over her soul, as if to remind her how different things would've been had a pair of denim blue eyes been there to share those moments. A piercing sadness jumpstarted her heart, *and* the world, when an overeager reporter jostled Tom and he looked away, breaking the connection.

Tightening his arm around his wife's shoulders, he pushed forward. Minus his typical carefree grin, Tuck stuck close to Sharon's other side, using his body to keep the pressing throng from getting too close. Doug Costa had disappeared.

Like a mobile interrogation unit, the press tossed out their demands. The questions grew more and more personal, and rude, in Gracie's opinion. Neither Tom nor Sharon answered. Not even to say no comment.

"Rumor has it, Gracie Gable is your daughter, Mr. Walden. Can you confirm that?"

"Why have you kept her existence a secret?"

"Are there any other secret children out there you haven't mentioned?"

Dina shouted over the others. "Do you approve of your daughter having an affair with Manhattan's most notorious womanizer, Mr. Walden?"

Gracie winced at the woman's scornful tone until Tuck took exception to her premise. "Excuse me, but that title belongs to me." Tuck caught Gracie's eye and winked. For some reason, tears burned at the backs of her eyes.

Twitters of laughter rippled through the crowd. Dina's lips screwed up as if she'd swallowed something foul. "Yes, I noticed you've been spending a lot of time at the Thompson farm. I wouldn't have taken you, or Jake, as they type of men to share." She turned and ran a dismissive glance over Gracie. "But when a woman is willing…." She shrugged.

Gracie stiffened, and a low growl rumbled in Jake's chest. A shiver raced down Gracie's spine when the snarky reporter met her gaze. A smirk stretched her thin lips. Both Tom and Tuck held up a hand when she shoved her small black tape recorder under Sharon Walden's nose.

"Mrs. Walden, as the mother of Tom Walden's sons, how do you feel about your husband having a love child with another woman?"

Sharon gasped, as did Gracie, and amazingly, several members of the press. Jake immediately released her arm and stalked forward. She scrambled after him and blinked when the crowd parted, effectively giving them access to the Waldens and Dina.

To her credit, Dina backed down…sort of. The snarky smirk slid from her lips and she pulled back her tape recorder. She even spun to the side as Jake approached, which brought her directly in Gracie's path. Unfortunately, Dina flung out her elbow at the same time. With her eyes on her father, Gracie never saw it coming. Dina's elbow slammed into her cheekbone with a sickening thud.

Stars burst before her eyes. She blinked and teetered on her high heels but remained on her feet. Strong fingers wrapped around her upper arm, steadying her.

A chorus of groans echoed off the tall ceiling and, though she couldn't see him, she recognized Tuck's laughing admonition. "Oh, shit."

"Don't do anything stupid," Tom warned.

She turned her head and squinted in an attempt to bring her father into focus. When she did, he wasn't looking at her. She glanced back at Jake and understood. Like a storm cloud about to unload its fury, he glared at Dina. *Oh, shit was right.* His inability to control his mouth when in a temper was the reason he was in this mess with her in the first place. As mad as she was at him, as hurtful as his words had been, she couldn't stand by and watch him undo everything he'd done to repair his reputation over the past three months.

His fingers dropped away from her arm when she turned her back on Dina to look into his angry face. "Whatever you're about to say, don't. It's not worth it. Think of the girls."

Dina spoke behind her in a taunting command. "Listen to your girlfriend, Malone. She's not worth it."

Gracie might care about Jake's reputation, especially since everything he did would now affect the girls, but she didn't give a shit about her own. Her secret was out. She no longer had anything to lose, and Jake wasn't the only one with a temper. She welcomed the hot splash of anger coursing through her. Dina was about to learn the first rule in self-defense. Don't ever let your enemy get too close. Having delivered her sneaky hit, the reporter should've moved away. She'd lost her chance and would pay the price.

"Wait—" As if he'd read the intent in Gracie's eyes, Jake reached out.

She didn't bother moving stealthily. She stepped clear of Jake's reaching hand, spun around, and had the satisfaction of seeing the reporter's eyes go wide as she drew back her fist and let it fly. Dina crumpled to the floor like a broken doll.

Behind her, Jake's groan registered. Tuck's laughter mixed with gasps and exclamations of shock as Gracie danced from foot to foot and shook her hand.

Ouch! She'd forgotten how badly a bare knuckle punch hurt.

"Are you fucking crazy?" Jake's furious whisper sounded in her ear as his fingers closed around her arm once more. "This situation isn't bad enough already? You have to make things worse?"

Her gaze flew to Tom. No emotion showed on his blank face, but his eyes were wide with shock.

Well, shit.

Jake gave her no time to defend herself. She didn't even have the opportunity to tell him to go to hell. He shoved her at Tuck. "Get her the hell out of here."

Chapter 31

"It's true. She's my daughter, isn't she?"

Jake raked his fingers through his hair. "She believes so, yes."

Tux jacket cast aside and his tie removed, Tom sat with his head resting against the high back of his desk chair. He raised his glass to his lips and swallowed a healthy gulp of amber liquid. "How long have you known?"

Legs spread and forearms propped on his thighs, Jake sat across from the desk on the couch. He held his drink in one hand, dangling between his knees. "I didn't know anything until earlier today. I had a friend check her out." He winced at Tom's disapproving stare. "Not a private detective, a friend who's at home on the Internet. He finally sent me the links for a few articles about Simon White. I didn't have time to read them. I only glanced at the first one, listing Doug Costa as one of his clients. Until he commented on *your* having dated Angela Gable, I thought Doug was her father."

Tom grunted. "The pictures from the press conference don't do her justice. She's a beautiful woman."

He stared into his glass. "You'll get no argument from me on that point."

"And an amazing one. Damn, she throws a mean punch."

The laughter in Tom's voice made him look up. He dragged a palm over his face. "She's a piece of work, all right."

Tom smiled softly. "Her mother was beautiful as well, though Gracie doesn't resemble Angela, except for the shape of her eyes." He met Jake's gaze. "Angela had the most amazing eyes. A stunning, violet blue."

"So does Gracie."

Confusion wrinkled Tom's brow. "I don't understand. Her eyes are brown, aren't they?"

"She was wearing contacts." When Tom's brow shot up, Jake shrugged. "Long story, but I think she was trying to disguise their distinctive color."

Tom nodded. "If they're anything like her mother's, that would be some trick. Her eyes were what attracted me to Angela in the first place. It wasn't long before I'd fallen in love."

Jake shot a wary glance at the empty doorway. Sharon was in the house somewhere.

Tom followed his glance, staring at the empty doorway for a long moment before turning back. "It's okay. She's in bed."

Jake nodded and wished her good luck. He wasn't sure sleep would be possible for any of them after what they'd faced tonight. There would be headlines in the morning they'd have to deal with, but Sharon was his concern for the moment. "How is she?"

Tom smiled sadly. "You know Sharon. She cried for a while, then she kissed me and told me to get to work gathering facts because she doesn't plan to face the press again until we have them all. She also demanded I invite Gracie to dinner tomorrow."

Jake smiled, somewhat relieved. "I'm sorry about all of this. I fucked up. I should've gotten Gracie out of there the moment I realized what was happening."

"Don't do that. If anyone is to blame, I am. Sharon is the love of my life and I wouldn't change our life together for anything, but none of this would be happening if I had listened to my inner voice all those years ago and tracked Angela down."

"What happened, if you don't mind my asking? If you loved her, why did you walk away?"

Tom rubbed a palm over his chin. "If you're wondering if I'm like Pete, that's not the case."

He shook his head. "I'd never think that of you, Tom. If you'd known about Gracie, you would've made her a part of your life."

Tom nodded. "Yes, I would."

"Then what happened?"

A deep breath heaved Tom's chest. "I was young, ambitious, and stupid. The pros were calling, and although I loved Angela, a wife would be a complication. I thought Simon's warnings, when he discovered Angela and I were seeing one another, were a case of him looking out for me. In hindsight, I see he was protecting his investment. He stood to lose quite a bit of money should I wander off the career track he'd set for me."

He lifted his drink again then set the glass aside without drinking. "One day, shortly before I was due back at school my senior year, he met me for lunch instead of calling me to his office where she worked. He was sorry, he said. Hated to be the one to tell me, but he'd discovered I wasn't the only boy Angela was seeing that summer.

"I'd never been in love before. I was hurt and angry. My uncle had a horse farm in Tennessee. He'd been after me to come down that summer. Said he'd put me to work for a few weeks. I packed my stuff and took off. I kicked myself a million times over the next couple of months for not going to Angela and giving her a chance to refute Simon's charge, but by then it was too late. I'd left without a word and, according to Simon, she moved away less than a month later."

"From what Gracie says, he fired her."

Tom's eyes slid shut.

Jake cleared his throat. "Are you positive she wasn't?"

Tom's eyes opened, and he arched a brow in question.

"Seeing someone else?"

One of Tom's shoulders lifted in an abbreviated shrug. "I have no idea, and with Angela dead, I'll never know."

Jake's heartbeat tripped into triple-time. Considering the way he'd yelled at her earlier, questioning Gracie's paternity stunk of one more betrayal on a day where she'd already seen too many, but was there a chance this entire mess was a bullshit misunderstanding? Could her father be some faceless man her mother spent time with in addition to Tom? Had he screwed up royally, lashing out at her over a fucking mistake?

He'd been angry enough, panicked enough, to say some shitty things to her. Shitty? He'd been a complete prick, accusing her of not caring about Tom and his family when the complete opposite was true. He knew first-hand how much she yearned for a family and yet she'd denied her chance to know her father because she wasn't willing to see him hurt.

What kind of asshole starts a shouting match in a public bathroom, anyway, then expects the conversation to remain private? He *was* an asshole, plain and simple. Instead of growling at her for dumping Dina on her ass, he should've kissed her and thanked her for doing what he wanted to do but couldn't. He grimaced inwardly, remembering the way she refused to look at him as she walked away with Tuck. Pale and silent, her righteous anger couldn't hide the hurt in her eyes, as if her heart had been scraped raw.

If he could reach his own ass, he'd kick it. Twice. Then again, the self-abuse probably wasn't necessary. Knowing Gracie, he'd most likely end up with a bruise or two before she forgave him.

If she forgave him.

He shook his head. She'd forgive him. She had to. The alternative was unacceptable.

He set his drink on the coffee table. "Gracie believes you're her father, but what if Simon was telling the truth? What if Angela was seeing someone else?"

Tom shook his head.

"A DNA test would give you the answers you need."

"She's my daughter. Of that I have no doubt."

Jake sighed. "That's nostalgia speaking. With negative DNA evidence, this story will fizzle in less than a week. Think of Sharon. Think of your kids."

Tom sat up and rested his elbows on his desk. "I *am* thinking of my kids, particularly the one I left behind to race after my career." He pushed to his feet and crossed to the oak credenza along the far wall. Shifting several framed photos, he selected one, returned to the desk, and sat. He passed the photo over the desk.

Jake held the frame up to catch the light. The breath caught in his throat. A young blonde woman smiled at him in full color. Her eyes were the exact shade of Gracie's in her chocolate brown disguise contacts. Jake swallowed. The woman in the photo could've been Gracie's twin, right down to the sexy mole at the left corner of her mouth.

He slowly dragged his gaze up to lock on Tom's.

Tom nodded. "My mother the year she turned twenty-one."

"Holy shit." His breath escaped on a rush.

"Exactly. I don't need a DNA test, my friend. Gracie Gable is mine."

* * * *

"Would you mind doing me one more favor?"

"For you, babe, anything." Fingers wrapped around the steering wheel of his ridiculously expensive sports car, Tuck turned his head and smiled at Gracie. "Although, I think we should go somewhere besides the farm to get naked. Jake may whine like a baby when he loses, but he *hits* like a sledge hammer." He glanced at her bruised knuckles where her hands were clenched in her lap. "Come to think of it, you two have that in common."

He grinned and winked. She attempted a smile and failed. Trading quips with him wasn't possible when her world was falling apart, but she appreciated his effort to charm her out of the sober funk threatening to tug her under like a riptide.

"I don't want to go to the farm." She followed his gaze when it slid to the clock on the dash. Ten forty-five.

"What about curfew, Cinderella?"

She shrugged. Pete's stipulations were no longer her concern.

Scratching his fingertips over his clean-shaven jaw, his grin slid away. "You know I was teasing, right? He may be a pain in my ass most days, but ultimately, Jake's a friend."

"Tell that to Daphne and the girls."

His nostrils flared on a scoffing snort. "Daphne and her ilk are nothing more than fun and games. Groupies who know the score."

"You think I don't know the score?"

"Oh, sweetheart. You're not even playing in the same game."

"I didn't realize I was playing at all."

He nodded. "Exactly my point."

"What's that supposed to mean?"

"That means I don't have a chance in hell of seeing you naked because you aren't like Daphne and the girls. You're not the type of woman to sleep with one man while you're in love with another. Besides, the playoffs start next week. Jake won't do the team a lot of good if he's serving time for attempted murder."

She smiled slightly but didn't bother denying his charge of her being in love with Jake because, well, what difference did it make? Her temporary glimpse at happily ever after was over.

Keep it light, Gracie. Get through tonight and tomorrow will sort itself out.

"Some friend you are. Hanging around the farm and putting the moves on me when you clearly knew Jake and I were sleeping together."

He grinned and shrugged.

She made her smile sickly sweet. "With friends like you, who needs enemies?"

He laughed. "Hey, it's not every day a man gets to make his friend nuts because he's going down in flames over a woman."

Surprise made her blink. Going down in flames? Her heart shivered with pleasure even as she dismissed the possibility. She liked to think Jake cared more for her than all those other women he'd stolen from Tuck, but going down in flames was a complete stretch. Besides, relationships never lasted longer than the heat that sparked them. Both she and Jake understood that, even if no one else seemed to. Bottom line, he was Jake Malone. By next month, she'd be nothing more than the twins' aunt and hopefully, a sweet memory to the Outlaw tight end. Playtime was over and after tonight, he'd no doubt be relieved to see her go.

She sighed. What she'd feared would happen had, and Jake was right. Because of her stubbornness, the fallout would be much worse and people would be hurt. The least she could do was minimize the wreckage.

There was nothing she could do to stop the firestorm her father and his family faced because of her, but with her out of the picture, the damage to the Waldens *and* the girls and Jake would be lessened. The press loved a heartwarming story and what better than a famous bachelor doing the right thing by taking on the care of his orphaned sisters?

No matter where she lived, the girls were still her family. Once the furor died down, she'd quietly demand they work out an agreeable arrangement for visitation. Jake owed her that much and, ultimately, he wasn't cruel, even if the broken pieces of her heart laid at his feet.

"You can relax. You, Jake, *and* the Marauders are safe. I wasn't asking to run off with you. I simply need a ride to my apartment. We're not far. I live at Twenty-third between Fifth and Sixth."

"You *live* at Thompson farm."

She shuddered. "Not anymore."

His brows clashed together in confusion. "I don't understand. Jake has feelings for you. He won't be happy learning you cut out without a word."

"It's complicated."

"It's bullshit." Tuck cut her a challenging glance. "Anyone with eyes can see how you feel about Jake, and what about the twins? You belong with them. I never would've taken you for a quitter."

The charge stung, but she was too heartsick to explain in detail. "I'm not a quitter. I'm pragmatic."

Anger flashed in his eyes when they cut her way. "And Jake? Doesn't he have a say in this?"

She thought of the accusations he'd thrown at her less than an hour ago and fought back tears. "Believe me, he had plenty to say when he was screaming at me in the ladies' room. None of what he said was good."

"Women. When will your kind realize it's a mistake to take a man's words to heart when he's on a tear?" He shook his head. "How much has he told you about his childhood?"

She blinked, wondering where he was going with the out-of-the-blue question. "What does his childhood have to do with any of this?"

"Plenty. What has he told you?"

She shrugged. "Some. I know he grew up on a ranch in Texas with his mother."

"His mother." His sharp laugh held no humor. "It's ironic, since he rarely has more than one or two drinks, but he got smashed one night and told me some shit that would curl your hair. Let's say his mother was a useless drunk and leave it at that. But for V, he grew up virtually alone. She, Tom, and Sharon are the closest thing he has to family. Is it any wonder he's upset?"

"No." She sighed. "Believe it or not, I don't blame him. I'm simply trying to do the right thing. For everyone involved. Are you going to take me to my place, or do I need to take the train from the farm?"

His jaw tightened, but other than mumbling about stubborn women, he remained silent and spun the car in a tight U-turn. Neither of them spoke another word. She battled the pity party threatening to engulf her until he pulled the car to the curb. She glanced up and turned to him with a frown. "Why are we here?"

He opened his door without a word, rounding the hood to open hers. She joined him on the sidewalk in front of Max's gym.

"If you think I'm facing Jake after dumping you off alone at your apartment, you're nuts." He wrapped strong fingers around her arm and jerked his chin at the illuminated windows of the second floor apartment. "Maybe Max can talk some sense into you."

Chapter 32

Though Max tried, Gracie held her ground. "This has nothing to do with my feelings for Jake."

Slouched on the other end of the couch in Max's upstairs apartment, Tuck snorted and flipped through the TV channels with the remote. She shot him a glare.

Max handed her a bag of frozen peas and dropped onto an oversized chair across from her. "If I thought you truly believed that, I'd be laughing my ass off."

She pressed the bag to her cheekbone and hissed softly. "Weren't you paying attention? My father and his wife were virtually attacked because of me."

"I caught every word and nuance, and from what I heard, they weren't the only ones attacked." His frown grew as he studied the already bruising skin around her eye. "I can't believe Dina did that to you."

"I can't believe you went out with her. Please tell me you didn't sleep with her." She wasn't the least bit surprised when his forehead creased in a guilty grimace. "Ick!"

"I'm sorry, kiddo. I didn't realize she was such a vindictive bitch."

Surprised by the anger in his voice, she waived his guilt aside. "She's not important. Well, unless she decides to sue me for assault."

"She threw the first punch, or elbow." Tuck spoke without taking his eyes from the TV. "With as many witnesses as there were, she has no case."

Gracie patted the cold bag against the swollen bruise Dina's elbow left behind. "I hope so, because I already have enough on my plate and, come tomorrow morning, I'll have yet another catastrophic scandal to worry about."

"I don't think you'll have to wait that long."

Both she and Max turned at Tuck's bland announcement and she groaned. A clip of Tom and Sharon Walden filled the TV screen, with Jake at Sharon's side, surrounded by a throng of frenzied reporters as they descended the famous steps of The Met. As the film rolled, the commentator reported on the breaking story. Gracie couldn't focus enough to comprehend what was said. Only a few words pierced her misery.

Allegedly, shocking, family man, love child, blah, blah, blah. She dropped her head to her knees.

"Hey now, there's a handsome guy."

She peeked from beneath her lashes then bolted up straight. The camera passed over Tuck, in the background of the museum's grand hall, before zooming in on Dina Sutton's face. Like a nightmare caught on film, the screen documented the moments leading up to Gracie's altercation with the vicious reporter. Gracie stared, silently begging the TV gods to provide an alternate ending to the one she knew was coming. Of course, they ignored her pleas. She cringed when Dina's elbow landed and winced audibly when her fist returned the favor a moment later.

Finally, the picture cut back to the talking head. Tuck turned to her and grinned. "Remind me never to piss you off."

Max chuckled and she shot him a glare. "Now do you see why I have to leave? I've made a complete mess of things."

"And you think running away will stop the carnage?"

She scowled at his choice of words. "I think taking myself out of the equation will diminish the interest, yes."

He rolled his eyes. "Yeah, good luck with that. Correct me if I'm wrong, but aren't you the one who hid out at the farm for almost two months while the press staked out the gate?" He arched a brow. "Face it, kiddo. When the press decides you're a story, you're a story. Nothing you do or don't do is going to change that."

She moaned and dropped her head again.

"Max is right, and you're going to have to grow some thicker skin if you're going to be a football wife."

She sat up to gawk at Tuck. "Are you insane?"

He ignored her and spoke to Max. "Funniest thing I've ever seen is Jake trying to pretend he doesn't want to rip my head off every time *his* princess smiles at me."

She rolled her eyes when the two of them shared a grin. "I appreciate the ride, but don't you have somewhere to be?"

"Nope."

She bared her teeth. "Maybe you could call Daphne."

He tugged at the knee of his slacks, crossing his leg over the opposite knee. "I never thought I'd see the day the Outlaw hung up his spurs, but damn, the idea of Malone trading in his jet set lifestyle and *Playboy* magazines for a white picket fence and children's books is enough to make me piss my pants laughing."

Max laughed despite the silent plea she shot him. "He has a point. You and Jake have unfinished business."

Frustration made her retort sharp. "What we *had* was a temporary affair after causing an inopportune scandal, followed by *another* scandal. This is number three. We won't be having any more. We're done."

"Does Jake know that?"

Tuck chuckled. "I guarantee you, he doesn't."

She bristled at his lighthearted tone. "Weren't you paying attention when he shoved me at you and demanded you get me out of there? You didn't hear him in the ladies' room. *I* guarantee, he was mad enough to wring my neck."

"Big deal. He was pissed off. You should know him well enough by now to realize he has a temper."

"He wasn't in a temper, he was justifiably furious."

"You're mistaking shock for fury." He spoke over her when she growled her frustration. "I was there, Gracie. I saw his face. He about shit his pants when he found out Tom dated your mother. Hell, I about shit *mine* when the press came running up and announced you were Tom's daughter. When Jake has time to think things through, he'll calm down." He waggled his brows suggestively. "Hell, he probably already has. A thousand bucks says he's already looking forward to the make-up sex."

Max nodded, clearly agreeing with Tuck's assessment of the situation.

She growled low in her throat. "Do you ever take anything serious? This isn't about sex."

Tuck shrugged a shoulder. "Take my word for it. For guys, everything is about sex."

She rolled her eyes. They were veering way off track. She sucked in a calming breath and attempted to regain control. "Neither of you get it. I'd already decided to leave the farm. Tonight's disastrous ending only makes my immediate departure more essential."

"I'm betting Jake would disagree."

"Then you'd lose. He blames me for putting Tom and Sharon in this position. With good reason."

"You're blaming *yourself* for that?" Tuck tossed a thumb toward the TV.

"Why wouldn't I when it's my fault?"

"What a crock." Anger sparkled in Max's eyes. "Tom Walden may have been young when he knocked up your mother, but that doesn't mean the consequences aren't his to bear."

She jutted out her chin. "You're missing my point."

"What *is* your point? Because blaming yourself for your father's behavior is bullshit as well as stupid."

She shook her head. "I'm not blaming myself for his behavior, but I can't blame *him* either. How could he handle a situation he obviously knew nothing about?" She shoved to her feet and paced the room. "How many times have we talked about this, Max? I knew. I *knew* having any kind of contact with him would lead to disaster, but I let my curiosity get the better of me. None of this would've happened if I had stuck to the plan and stayed away from him."

Max sighed. "Gracie, you know I love you, but none of what you said explains why you would leave the farm with forty-eight hours to go. It's done. The world knows you're Tom Walden's daughter. How will giving up on your dream possibly repair whatever perceived wrongs your female brain has decided are your responsibility?"

She ignored the insult to her femininity and searched for the words to make him understand. Even if tonight's disaster hadn't taken place, the outcome of the custody battle had been sealed in her heart the moment she witnessed the glittering emotion in Jake's eyes as his sisters curled in his lap.

Forcing them to choose between Jake and her was cruel. She wouldn't do that to the girls and couldn't do it to Jake. They might not have a future together. He might not love her, but she loved him. She couldn't do something so hurtful.

"Don't you see? I love the girls, but they've been through enough." She pointed at the TV. "This story isn't going away anytime soon, and I refuse to subject them to any more upheaval. What good is achieving my dream if the people I love are harmed in the process?"

Max crossed his arms. "What about Jake? If you try to deny you're in love with him, I'll call you a liar."

She shook her head and sighed. "No. I can't deny I love him. I've loved him since long before I finally met him, but this isn't about me. This is about the twins and Jake. They love him, and he loves them. They belong together." She glanced briefly at Tuck and smiled sadly. "The little boy who grew up dirt poor and alone on a Texas ranch deserves the family he was denied."

"What about what *you* deserve?"

She turned back to Max, and the frustrated love in his eyes eased the sting of her broken heart. "No matter what, the twins will always be in my life in some way, but don't you see? I couldn't live with myself if I claimed my happiness at the expense of his."

Chapter 33

Jake pushed by Max the moment the door opened. Gracie's friend didn't object. Jake wished he would. Spoiling for a fight, his temper simmered close to boiling. He spun on him. "Where is she?"

Max shut the door. His normally congenial smile held a sharp edge. "Good morning to you, too." Wearing only a pair of black silk drawstring slacks, he padded barefoot into the galley kitchen.

"I spoke to Tuck. He said he left her here."

Max slid a mug onto the tray of a large black coffeemaker, punched a button, and turned to lean against the edge of the counter. "Did he?"

Frustration flared in Jake's gut. "Is she here or isn't she?"

"Do you see her?"

"Answer the fucking question."

A dark eyebrow arched above the searing gleam in Max's eyes. "Be careful, my friend. I may like you, but after the way you treated her last night, I wouldn't turn down the chance to rearrange your face."

The warning did nothing to lessen his frustration, but his shoulders stiffened with guilt. "I'll hold still and let you, if you'll tell me where she is."

Max propped his hands beside his hips on the countertop. "I'd take you up on that, if I knew. She took off during the night and isn't answering my texts."

Jake dragged the Stetson from his head. "She forfeited custody."

"I know." Max nodded, his tone calm.

Panic hit Jake low in the gut. He jammed stiff fingers through his hair. "Why the hell would she do that? She had less than forty-eight hours to go."

Max twisted his upper body to retrieve his full coffee mug. He shrugged and sipped. "Women. Who knows how their minds work?"

True, but Jake didn't need the mischievous gleam in Max's eyes to know he was being played. He and Gracie shared everything, the exact reason Jake was here at six a.m. instead of resting up for this afternoon's practice. He cocked his head and met Max's waiting gaze with an intent stare. "I have the feeling you do in this case."

One corner of Max's mouth hitched up in a taunting smile. "Yeah. I do."

He ground his teeth, too jacked up to play games. "Are you going to tell me or stand there grinning like an asshole?"

Max laughed. "Grinning like an asshole works for me."

"*Please.*" The desperate plea, bursting from his lips, shocked the hell out of Jake and knocked the grin from Max's face. Jake shook his head. "Please. Tom's like a father to me. You're right. I freaked out when I learned he's her father and took my panic out on her, but damn it. She's the ballsiest women I've ever met. Why isn't she at the farm, fighting mad and making me pay for every cruel word I tossed at her? What the hell is she thinking, walking away from the girls? Walking away from her dream?"

"She's thinking with her heart."

Jake sighed heavily. "I'm too fucking tired and too short of time for riddles. Are you going to help me, or not?"

Max stroked his chin thoughtfully. "That depends."

"On?"

"You." Max pushed away from the counter. "Coffee?"

Hell, yes. He nodded.

Max turned his back to set another mug in the single brew machine. "Do you love her?"

Though Jake bristled at the question, the blatant demand didn't surprise him. If not exactly pushing them together, Gracie's brash and bold friend made clear from the beginning the idea of Jake and Gracie together was fine by him.

Saying the words aloud, with only Max present, rankled. Since Gracie was solely responsible for the momentous step Jake was about to take, she should at least be a witness but, what the hell? He'd come this far. Might as well go all the way. "Not that it's any of your business, but yes, I do."

He expected smug laughter. Max surprised him by spreading his hands wide to lean on the countertop. He briefly dropped his chin to his chest with a drawn out sigh. He straightened again and pulled the filled mug from the coffeemaker. When he turned around, he wore a relieved smile. Jake took the offered mug.

"She loves you, too." Max dropped his hips against the edge of the counter and crossed his feet.

Jake sucked in a gasping breath. To have his hopes confirmed.... Pure, unadulterated joy pulsed in his chest and made breathing difficult. Confusion left him floundering. "Then, why? I don't understand."

Max reached behind him for his mug. "Not long ago, she described watching the twins and you together. She said it was magical."

He swallowed as his chest expanded on a warm glow. Her description pleased and humbled him. Magic perfectly described what he'd found with Gracie and the girls.

Max studied him over the rim of his coffee. He lowered the mug and dipped his head in a knowing nod. "She left the farm because she couldn't live with the idea of claiming her happiness at the expense of yours."

Without moving a muscle, Jake staggered under the blow. She'd given up her lifelong dream to give him a chance at building a life he'd never thought to have. Didn't she understand, without her in his life, any dream he might desire would soon turn to ashes?

The need to find her and set her straight, on a number of things, became a raging fire. Unfortunately, Max didn't know where she was. Over the next six hours, Jake grew increasingly desperate until Max called to say he'd received a text from her saying she was all right but needed some time to herself. As one day passed, then the next, desperation became fury. Where the hell was she?

Other than for practice, he refused to leave the farm. She had to return sometime. Her things were there and she wouldn't leave Murphy behind, not permanently. As the time approached to head to the stadium Sunday morning, frustration left him prowling the farmhouse like a caged animal.

Max had suggested game time would be the logical opportunity for her to return to the farm and move out her stuff—if she didn't want to run into anyone in particular. Instinct raged at Jake to remain where he was and pounce on her the moment she arrived. Reality made different claims on his time.

He punched a button on the dash as he drove his SUV to the end of the drive.

Tom picked up on the third ring. "Have you found her?"

"No."

"Damn. What are we going to do?"

"I'm going to the sports complex. How soon can you get to the farm?"

Chapter 34

Gracie shut the door behind her with a gentle snick. The soft gong of the grandfather clock at the far end of the hall broke the absolute quiet. Only three days had passed since she'd left the farm, but it might as well have been three years. Everything had changed.

She'd begun to think of the farmhouse as home in the nearly three months she lived there with the girls and Jake. This morning, she felt like a stranger. A *sneaky* stranger. Guilt ducked its head, doing a perp walk down her spine.

Stealing into Jake's home while he was safely away at the stadium rubbed her the wrong way on several levels. First, because the move could backfire. With her departure from the farm, he became the girls' guardian. From here on in, he called the shots with them. If he wanted, he could make things difficult for her. He could stand in the way of her seeing the girls and the many voicemails in her inbox proved he was already majorly pissed. Second, slipping into the house behind his back smacked of cowardice, and she was already guilty of too much of *that*.

Still, considering his threat to introduce her butt to the flat of his hand when he finally found her, avoiding a face-to-face confrontation seemed the wisest choice at the moment. The time would come for a confrontation later because, whether he liked it or not, she *would* be in the girls' lives, but she preferred waiting to have that conversation until he'd calm down a bit.

"Mary? Murphy?" She headed toward the back of the house and the kitchen.

Max wasn't exactly happy with her either. She shrugged mentally. Nothing she could do about that. She'd made the right call by sneaking out of his place the night of the fund-raiser not long after Tuck left and Max fell asleep. Sure enough, Max's apartment was the first place Jake checked the next morning when he discovered she hadn't come back to the farm.

Jake left at least a dozen messages the first day. They'd started out pleasantly enough. In his first, he calmly apologized for acting like a prick in the ladies' room. In his second, laughter thickened his voice as he complimented her right hook and asked if she'd seen the picture of Dina and her shiner in the morning paper.

The sight of Dina's swollen and bruised eye, when Gracie picked up a copy of the paper in the hotel lobby where she was hiding out, made her wince—after grunting in satisfaction, of course.

Next, he'd dropped his voice to the crooning, love me, baby, Texas drawl that melted her circuits, and urged her to tell him where she was. Things deteriorated from there. Several hours later he regressed to calling her a stubborn fool and claiming it didn't matter she'd broken the custody rules, since he wouldn't be notifying Anthony Spinoza of her absence.

She'd called Pete's lawyer immediately.

Jake blew a gasket when Anthony called to congratulate him on winning custody of the girls. Another half dozen nasty voicemails joined the previous ones before she finally shut off her phone. She spent the next day and a half feeling sorry for herself and wishing she'd booked a quick flight to somewhere warm with sand and palm trees, instead of checking into the tiny hotel room around the corner from Times Square.

By the time she turned her phone back on this morning, there were thirty-six messages waiting for her. The bulk were from Jake. Max had left two and there was one from Tom Walden.

Her heart repeated the slow roll it performed this morning upon hearing his message. The last three days had been completely shitty. On the one hand, coming to terms with the knowledge she wasn't ever going to have her dream family sucked. On the other, her father called. Her! Talk about a silver lining.

After the fiasco at The Met and the nasty headlines in the papers the last couple of days, she wouldn't blame her father for wanting nothing to do with her, yet he called. That had to mean something and, though it was impossible to gauge his mood via the brief voicemail, he hadn't sounded angry.

A subtle gush of hope pulsed in her heart and soothed some of the pain of giving up the girls. The first smile in days tugged at her lips as she pushed open the kitchen door—and screamed.

Tom Walden jumped from one of the kitchen chairs. He held up both hands and spread them wide. "I'm sorry. I didn't mean to scare you. Mary let me in."

"Oh. Mary." She blinked and looked around. The kitchen was empty but for him. "Where is she? And the girls? You didn't, by the way. Scare me, I mean. Okay, maybe you did a little, but…." Her shoulders stiffened in embarrassment when his lips jerked up on one side as if he was fighting a smile. "Okay, I'm going to shut up."

He quit fighting. His eyes twinkled with humor and perfect, white teeth flashed within the frame of cleanly cut lips. The slightest hint of matching dimples bracketed the wide smile splitting his face. A painful pressure expanded in her chest. She held her breath, recalling a rare comment of her mother's about the man who fathered her then disappeared. *Your father had the most beautiful smile.*

Gracie couldn't agree more, but as his smile dissolved into a sober study of her face, a ball of nerves expanded in her belly. Time slowed and the moment stretched out until her skin crawled with jittery nerves. What did he see when he looked at her? What was he thinking? Was the idea of a surprise daughter an intriguing one or did he see her as a nasty burden to be handled? Did his unexpected presence represent a desire to learn more about her, or was he here simply to do spin control?

Raw yearning, painful and intense, slithered through her, wrapping around her heart and lungs, and threatened to smother her. She sucked in a ragged breath. Like every other relationship in her life, the path this one would take was out of her hands. He'd either care or he wouldn't, but the story was out. She had nothing left to hide. The only way to find out what he was thinking was to ask.

With a false show of bravado, she lifted her chin—and yelped when Murphy burst through the door. On scrambling feet, he headed straight for Tom.

"Look out!" She dove for his collar, missed and blinked upon discovering her warning wasn't necessary.

Tom twisted sideways and stepped back. He held out a hand palm forward. "Murphy, sit!"

To her utter surprise, her head butting dog dropped his ass to the floor. His tail swished the wooden planks as he offered Tom a doggy grin. She shifted her stunned gaze to her father.

He grinned. "Jake, V, *and* Tuck warned me about your dog." Bending at the waist, he scrubbed a big hand over Murphy's back.

She stiffened. Jake and his friends had spoken to Tom about her dog, but in what context? Had they discussed her in particular or simply in passing about Murphy's penchant for head butting? The suspense was killing her.

Ask already! The worst he can say is he doesn't want anything to do with you. He's had nothing to do with you your whole life and you've survived. You'll continue to survive. Stop being a weenie and ask!

She had to clear her throat against the lump lodged there. "Why are you here?"

He straightened and met her challenge. The penetrating focus of his blue eyes made her heart skip. An interest that intense had to mean something, but the haunting sadness, dimming the smile her mother had thought beautiful, shattered Gracie's fleeting hope his interest was a positive development.

What had she been thinking? That he'd jeopardize his perfect family over a stranger who happened to share his DNA? When would she learn? Happily ever after was a myth, a foolish piece of fiction perpetuated by dreamers who spun tales into books and movies. In real life, parents walked away or they died. Cancer and disease decimated lives and true love didn't exist.

She turned away, freezing when strong fingers gripped her arm in a gentle hold. She lifted her gaze to his.

"I'm here because to my utter surprise and joy I have a daughter."

She blinked against the sudden sting of tears, afraid to believe what his simple statement inferred.

He lifted the palm of his free hand to cup her cheek. "I'm sorry, Gracie. I let your mother down twenty-six years ago by not facing her with questions I had at the time. I won't do the same now, with you."

A sob fought to escape. She choked it back. "What do you want to know?"

His smile softened and determination replaced the sadness in his eyes. "Everything. I want to know everything. I want to know about your first steps and the first tooth you lost. I want to hear about the first time you rode a bike. I want to know about how your mother died and how and why you became knowledgeable about the game I love. But those questions have waited this long. They can wait a bit longer."

Unsure why he didn't consider now a good time for the answers they *both* wanted, she didn't know how to respond.

He dropped his hand from her face. "I know I haven't earned your trust, and you have no reason to believe I ever will, but will you trust me now?"

Trust him? With what? "I don't understand."

He dipped his head to meet her gaze more directly. "I know you don't, but you will. Come with me? No questions asked." When she didn't immediately agree, he squeezed her arm. "Please? It's important."

Curiosity at what could possibly be so important she go with him at such a momentous moment tangled with an all-consuming hope for a future that would include him in her life. Almost giddy at the possibilities, she nodded and couldn't help the smile when he didn't waste a moment rushing her through the house and out the door.

Chapter 35

"This is *such* a bad idea."

Tom squeezed Gracie's fingers at the complaint she'd repeated several times since he swung his SUV into the entrance to The Marauders' Sports Complex. He lifted her hand to link her arm with his. Ignoring her dragging feet, he tugged her along when she would've remained outside the unmarked gray metal door leading to the bowels of the sold-out stadium.

The roar of fifty thousand cheering fans swelled up and made him raise his voice to a near shout. "You agreed to trust me."

She bristled at his side as he led her down a long, empty hallway. "That was before I knew you were insane." She attempted to pull free of his grip.

He held her firm.

"Haven't you seen the papers the last few days? The stories have hardly been flattering to you, which is exactly the reason I never contacted you in first place. The members of the press are hateful in their never-ending quest for a juicy story. If they catch us together, they're going to go berserk!"

She ground her teeth together when he chuckled and punched his way through a set of double doors. Another long hallway awaited them.

He twisted his wrist to check his watch then hurried his steps. "Don't worry about the press. By the end of the day, they'll be singing a different tune entirely."

Unease tickled her spine. "Why? What have you done?"

"I haven't done anything." He veered sharply to the right, through another door. "Yet."

She didn't like the sound of that. Hadn't the free-for-all at The Met been enough? She opened her mouth to demand he tell her what was going on and blinked instead. Her head swiveled back and forth as he dragged her through what was clearly the Marauders' empty locker room. She gawked at the benches and equipment bins, the enormous water cooler in one corner and the rows of lockers. Her gaze snagged and her head swiveled back over her shoulder as they passed a locker with MALONE marked in big, block letters.

The metal bar of a door clanked and the locker room disappeared as Tom swept her out of the Marauders' inner sanctum and toward an elevator on the other side of yet another hallway.

She dug in her high-heeled boots, refusing to take another step. "What's going on, Mr. Walden?"

His name on her lips stopped him cold and he turned back. His mouth formed a guilty grimace. "I guess asking you to call me Dad would be pushing things, wouldn't it?"

Her heart staggered under the direct hit. *Call him Dad?* The many happy fantasies she imagined concerning him throughout the years shimmered through her mind like radiant jewels. God, did he realize how many times she'd called him Dad in her dreams? Did she suspect he was the reason she'd learned all there was to know about football? Was that why he made the comment?

She squinted suspiciously. Like Jake, Tom Walden was a professional competitor. Until she knew what he was up to, she couldn't afford to let him manipulate her. If manipulation was his game.

Please, don't let manipulation be your game.

Not sure how to respond, she said nothing.

He sighed and, though she studied him for signs of deceit, she simply couldn't find any. In fact, his eyes darkened with insecurity when he reached for her other hand.

His voice deepened with hesitation. "Mr. Walden sounds too formal. You don't know me yet, and that's my fault, but I hope, in time, to build a relationship with my daughter. A relationship much warmer than that of polite strangers." He squeezed her hand before clearing his throat of the hint of moisture shimmering in his eyes. "How about you call me Tom?"

Speaking around the lump in her throat proved difficult. Her eyes flooded with unshed tears. "I think I'd like that. All of that."

He smiled and surprised her by bending to brush her cheek with a quick kiss. Dizzy with pleasure, she staggered along beside him into the elevator. Bright lights and noise greeted them when the doors opened again and they stepped into a private skybox overlooking the field. Max, Mary and the twins turned where they were seated on a long couch before the wall of glass.

"Auntie Gracie!" The girls squealed their dual greeting.

Angel's brow puckered in grievance. "Where have you been?"

Max arched a brow. "Yeah. Where have you been?"

Charlie scrambled around on her knees to face her. "Jake didn't know where you were. He was really mad."

Angel nodded. "He said bad words. Then he said he'd need to take out a loan because of all the money he had to put in the swear jar."

Max laughed and guilt tugged at Gracie's gut. Tom came to her rescue even as he released her hand and picked up a house phone. "Gracie had some things she had to attend to." He punched in several numbers. As he waited for someone to answer his call, he met Max's gaze and bumped his chin toward the glass overlooking the field. "How's he doing?"

Assuming Tom meant Jake, Gracie's gaze swung to the scoreboard. The score was tied.

Max grunted. "He's not himself today." He shot Gracie a raised brow.

Gracie crossed her arms and notched up her chin. She already carried enough guilt and refused to take the blame for Jake's off day.

"He only needs one more catch to get the record," Charlie announced.

"But he didn't eat his meatloaf last night." Angel spoke matter-of-factly, as if there was no doubt in her mind where the blame lay if he failed in his quest today.

Mary's lips thinned and she tsked. "He claimed he wasn't hungry. Imagine, a man of his size not eating his meatloaf when he has such an important game ahead of him the following day." She shook her head and the pointed stare aimed at Gracie said clearly where she laid the blame.

"Tell Jake she's here." Tom spoke the words into the phone and hung up.

She narrowed her eyes, but he turned away to study the field below. She followed his gaze and searched the Marauders' side of the field, but spotting Jake among the many uniformed men was impossible until he left the sideline several moments later and sprinted toward the line of scrimmage at the fifty-yard line. "Wait a minute. What's going on, Tom?"

"He'll do better now. I guarantee it." He spoke without taking his eyes from the action below.

Gracie's questioning gaze flicked to Max. He shrugged. His smile resembled that of the Cheshire Cat, but he didn't say a word.

She looked down at the field. No matter what else had happened, she loved Jake. She knew how much the record meant to him and prayed with every fiber of her being he achieved his goal. Like a runner waiting for the gun, he set his feet, one in front of the other, dipped his knees, and leaned forward. He turned his head, and a quiet gasp hissed through her teeth as, for a brief moment, he looked straight up at the skybox.

Her nerves stretched taught as he looked away and resettled into his crouch, still and ready on the far side of the field.

On the quarterback's count, Jake shot from the line. His big body raced downfield before making a quick pivot toward the Marauders bench. In a perfect spiral, the ball sailed high and long over the heads of both Jake and the defensive player shadowing him like a second skin. Gracie held her breath. Impossibly, as if his legs were part sinew and muscle, part spring, Jake leapt high with his long arms extended. Soft as a feather, the ball dropped to settle in his gloved hands. The crowd roared when he landed with both feet tight-roping the out of bounds line.

Max and Tom charged the skybox's glass, shouting encouragement as the twins scrambled from the couch to press their noses to the pane with Mary right behind them. Gracie's nails dug into her palms and she held her breath, willing Jake to remain on his feet.

Though a half dozen defensive players pursued him, momentum dispensed with the one obstacle between Jake and the goal line. He stutter-stepped and spun in complete circle and the lone defensive player stumbled out of bounds. The crowd cringed along with Gracie, Tom, and Max, as Jake tiptoed one yard, then two, and a third until he finally found his balance again.

"Way to go, Tuck!" Tom shouted as Tuck appeared out of nowhere to take down a potential tackle, but his extra effort wouldn't have changed the outcome. Like a perfect athletic machine, Jake charged down the sideline to the frenzied cheering of the crowd. The Marauders' loyal fans nearly broke the sound barrier as his long legs ate up the remaining fifteen yards.

Elation pulsed in her heart as Jake claimed his place in the record book, violently spiking the ball in the end zone. Tears of joy flooded her eyes and helpless laughter gurgled in her throat when he turned to face the crowd with his arms raised and a victorious roar. He was quickly swallowed him up in a circle of his teammates, helmets crashing and bodies thumping in celebration.

The twins' wild squeals competed with Max's triumphant shout as he scooped them up and spun them in a dizzying circle. Tugged into their victory dance, a beaming grin lit up Mary's face. Tom turned from the glass. Sheer pride and joy radiated from his sparkling blue eyes. He stepped forward and swept Gracie into his arms. "He did it. The son of a bitch did it!"

"Language." Wrapped in Max's group hug, Mary, Angel, and Charlie spoke the laughing warning simultaneously. Max shot Gracie a grin and threw back his head on a hardy laugh.

She grinned at her father. "Be careful. You'll end up with a swear jar."

His smile softened and he winked. "I'm counting on having one sitting right next to Jake's." He turned away to glance at the scoreboard.

She followed his gaze. Three seconds until halftime. Her elation over Jake's accomplishment dampened under the subtle sadness permeating her heart. Tom was Jake's best friend. With Jake living there permanently, of course he'd be spending time at the farm. Life was one irony after another, but the joke was on her. Jake would not only be living her dream, he'd be sharing it with her father.

The horn sounded, bringing the first half of the game to a close. Gracie glanced at the Jumbotron mounted high on the far wall of the stadium as the teams jogged from the field. The screen filled with the replay of Jake's catch and touchdown as the announcers sung his praises. Tom slid his arm over her shoulders.

She turned her head to study him. "Is that what you meant earlier about the press singing a different tune? That they'd be blinded by his breaking the record and forget about the other stuff?"

"Nope." He grinned and bumped his chin toward the opposite side of the field. "Watch."

Confused, she slid her gaze to Max. He grinned and shrugged. Frustrated at being left out of the joke, she turned back as Jake's image filled the screen. Sweaty and gorgeous, he held his helmet tucked beneath one arm. The joy she expected to see on his face was absent, however. She dismayed at the solemnness in his eyes. Tom gave her shoulder a squeeze as the on-field reporter stuck the microphone in Jake's face.

"Congratulations on breaking the record. Though you've had a terrific season on the field, you've had to deal with some bad press personally, including your involvement in that mess at The Met on Thursday. How important was breaking a sixty-year touchdown record to your image and your career?"

The smile curving Jake's lips didn't reach his eyes. "Well, Bob, since everyone is more interested in my personal life than in hearing how lucky I am to play with such an incredible group of players, I'm going to help you out with that."

"How so?"

"You mentioned the mess at The Met, but the only mess I witnessed on Thursday night, besides a certain member of the press crossing a line she shouldn't, was my not standing firmly behind a woman who has spent her life protecting the father who didn't know she existed. I'm talking about Gracie Gable. The woman I love."

Gracie gasped and slapped her fingers over her mouth as Jake dropped his head back to look upward. She blinked when her image, twenty feet tall and slightly obscured through the suite's glass, flashed on the screen. She dropped her gaze to the field and found him along the sideline. Though the distance was far, it seemed as if he stared straight at her.

"Did you hear that, Gracie?"

She shivered as she read his lips, even as his voice came through the speakers.

"I love you. I *love* you," he repeated with heavy emphasis.

A ragged sob leaked through the fingers jammed to her lips.

"I'm sorry, baby. I was an ass."

Fifty thousand fans broke into laughter mixed with applause. Tom winced at her side, but she grinned, despite the tears welling in her eyes. There went another twenty in the jar.

"Until I met a ballsy blonde and a couple of black-haired rugrats, I didn't have a clue what family meant."

Family. His family. Her heart slammed against her rib cage in a dizzying rhythm as the girls giggled behind her.

"Hell, I never even *believed* in the concept of family. You changed my heart and my mind and there's no going back."

Lightheaded, she dropped her hand to press her fingers to the glass. Mr. Irresistible smiled up at her and worked the crowd with his legendary charm. He lowered his voice to a sexy, Texas purr. "I need to ask you a question, Gracie. Right here, in front of hundreds of thousands of witnesses."

Her heart lodged in her throat. Angel and Charlie scrambled from Max's arms to rush to her side. Max and Mary joined them.

"You ready, princess?" Not a hint of humor showed on his face.

Was she *ready*? She slapped her free hand to the top of her head. Surprise, wonder, and fear competed for top billing in her galloping heart. Holy crap, if his question was the one she hoped for…. She nodded frantically. The stadium simmered with expectant murmuring.

His face split on a wide grin. "Okay." He glanced around as if he wasn't sure where he was then choked on a startled laugh. His gaze returned to caress hers. "Okay, but you have to come down here as soon as I'm finished. I have a feeling I'm going to need to kiss you." He shifted the helmet to his other arm. "And bring the twins with you. I want my whole family present when you say, yes, Jake. I'll marry you."

His whole family. A sob escaped and she covered her quivering mouth with the back of her hand. *Marry him?* A tear plopped onto her wrist.

Tom squeezed her closer. "Do you love him, Gracie?"

Max barked a scoffing laugh.

She flicked him a watery glare before turning back to Tom. "More than I ever thought possible."

Her father grinned. "Since the day I met him, Jake's been like a son to me. If you say yes, he'll be my son in truth. What do you say?"

Speaking was impossible with her throat closed. She nodded instead.

"It's about damn time!" Max grouched, but his lips curved up in a smug smile.

"Language!" Mary and the twins spoke together then laughed.

Tom grinned, hugged her close, and leaned toward the glass to give Jake a thumbs-up. Jake whooped on the sideline and the crowd in the stands went wild. The stadium pulsed beneath the thunderous celebration.

"Then what are you waiting for? Get on down here, darlin'!" Jake's laughing command echoed through the stadium. The girls shrieked and danced from foot to foot. Gracie broke into a weepy grin and gathered them close. Hand in hand, they raced out of the skybox. Tom, Max, and Mary squeezed into the elevator with them.

Security awaited them when the doors opened a minute later. Laughing and crying, Gracie raced through the tunnel and into the cavernous stadium. Bigger than life, sweaty and jubilant, Jake awaited her several yards away.

"Yes!" She skidded to a stop before him, the girls on each side.

He grinned and opened his arms.

"Yes, yes, yes."

The girls let go to latch onto his legs and Gracie leapt into his arms and into her future with her family surrounding her.

THE END

Meet the author

Wife, mother and *really young* grandmother, **Mackenzie Crowne** shares her home with her high school sweetheart husband, a neurotic Pomeranian, and a blind cat. She calls Arizona home because the southwest feeds her soul. Her love of the romance genre has been a lifelong affair, both as a reader and a writer. A bout with breast cancer sharpened her resolve to see her stories shared with others. Today, she's a seven-year survivor, living the dream. Her friends call her Mac. She hopes you will too. Visit her website at mackenziecrowne.com, find her on Facebook, or follow her on Twitter at https://twitter.com/MacCrowne

http://www.kensingtonbooks.com/author.aspx/31681

Keep reading for a sneak peek of Book One in
Kristina Mathews' More Than A Game series.

Better Than Perfect

Life beyond the game…

Johnny "The Monk" Scottsdale has won it all on the baseball
diamond. He's even pitched a perfect game. Known for his
legendary control both on and off the field, his pristine public
image makes him the ideal person to work with young players
in a preseason minicamp. Except the camp is run by the one
woman he can't forget…the woman who made him a "monk."

Alice Harrison once traded her dreams so that Johnny
Scottsdale could make it to the Majors—and then her dreams
fell apart. Now here comes Johnny back into her life, just when
she's ready to finally go after her dreams. This time she's not
letting up. Even if she has to reveal what she kept secret for too
long from her son and Johnny. She can't be sure how things will
turn out, but she's not leaving until she swings for the fences…

A Lyrical e-book on sale now!
Learn more about Kristina at http://www.
kensingtonbooks.com/author.aspx/30540
Visit us at www.kensingtonbooks.com

Chapter 1

"Pitchers and catchers report to spring training in thirteen days, twenty-one hours and seventeen minutes," Hall of Fame broadcaster Kip Michaels announced, and the crowd went wild. "Kicking off today's Fan Fest, I'd like to introduce one of our newest players. Two-time Cy Young Award winner, perennial All-Star, and the last man to pitch a perfect game. Give a warm San Francisco welcome to Johnny 'The Monk' Scottsdale."

Thirty thousand people were expected at the ballpark today. A great crowd—for a baseball game. But instead of working the count, Johnny would be working the crowd. Answering questions. Signing autographs. Putting himself out there in a way he wasn't entirely comfortable with. He was as nervous as the day he'd made his professional debut fourteen years ago. Butterflies? Try every seagull on the West Coast taking roost in his stomach.

Focus. Breathe. Let it go.

"Thank you. I'm thrilled to be here." He'd much rather face the 1927 Yankees than sit in front of a camera and a microphone talking about his game instead of playing it. "I hope I can help the team bring home a World Series Championship."

He tried to relax his shoulders. Tried to hide his nerves. The Goliaths could be his last team. His last shot at a ring. His final chance to prove himself and leave a legacy that went beyond the diamond.

After fielding a few questions about what he could bring to the team, and deflecting some praise about his success so far, Johnny was released to another part of the park to sign autographs. Little Leaguers approached with wide eyes and big league dreams. Tiny tots with painted faces squirmed with excitement about getting cotton candy while their parents shoved them forward to collect an autograph. A shy boy with a broken arm asked him to sign his cast. The look on his face was more than worth the discomfort of being in the spotlight for something other than his on-field performance.

Johnny had signed the big contract. The team paid him a lot of money to pitch every five games. They also paid him to interact with the fans, to be an ambassador for the game he'd loved for so long. The game that had saved him from a completely different kind of life.

He shared a table with another new player, shortstop Bryce Baxter. They were set up near the home bullpen along the third base line. Several other stations were set up around the park, giving fans a chance to get up close and personal with the players. Some tried to get a little too personal.

"So you're the hot new pitcher." A busty brunette leaned over the autograph table, wearing what appeared to be a toddler-sized tank top. The team logo sparkled in rhinestones and she was obviously well aware of the attention she drew. "I'd be more than happy to show you around."

"No thanks. I'm pretty familiar with the city." He held his pen ready, although she didn't seem to have anything to autograph. Nothing he was willing to sign, anyway.

"I could take you places you've never been." She leaned over even more.

Johnny kept his head down, trying to avoid gazing at what she had to offer. He reached for a stock photo, scrawled his signature across the bottom, and slid the picture forward, hoping she'd take the hint and leave.

"You forgot your number." She pouted.

"Sorry. I don't give that out." Johnny wished he could retreat to the locker room. Get away from her and the crowd that seemed to be growing. He never understood why people would wait in line to make small talk and take his picture. He gripped the black marker, needing something to do with his hands. If he only had a baseball, he could roll it around in his palm. Feel the smoothness of the leather, the rough contrast of the raised stitches. Find comfort in the weight and the symmetry of the one thing he could always control.

His teammate inserted himself into the conversation. "Do you know who this is? The one and only Johnny 'The Monk' Scottsdale."

"The Monk?" She drew her gaze over Bryce, then glanced at Johnny before settling on Bryce once more.

"He's a god." He flashed a grin indicating he was more than willing to play her game. "Me? I'm a mere mortal." Bryce leaned toward her, clearly enjoying the interaction.

www.ingramcontent.com/pod-product-compliance
Lightning Source LLC
Chambersburg PA
CBHW020800250626
47155CB00003B/1159